ALL RISE

ROSEMARIE AQUILINA

ALL RISE

ROSEMARIE AQUILINA

Sabicha
PRESS

All Rise

Published by: Sabieha Press

This book is a work of fiction. Names characters, places, and all incidents are either the product of the author's imagination or are used fictitiously. Any resemblance to actual events, dates, locales, organizations, or persons, living or dead, is entirely coincidental and beyond the intent of either the author or the publisher.

Cover Design and Interior Layout by Melissa Williams Design
woman ©2020 Utkamandarinka, Adobe Stock; court house ©2020 bluraz, Adobe Stock

Editing by Teresa Crumpton, AuthorSpark.org

Author Photograph by Josefina Hunter, Josefina © Photography 2018

Ordering Information:
IngramSpark at: www.ingramspark.com or
Amazon Books at: www.amazon.com
Or through your local bookstore

Author Aquilina Website: rosemarieaquilina.com

Printed in the United States of America, International by permission

ISBN: 978-1-7336964-6-3 (paperback)
ISBN: 978-1-7336964-7-0 (Large Print paperback)
ISBN: 978-1-7336964-8-7 (eBook)

This book is dedicated to all those who have been
bullied, harassed and/or demeaned.
I'm hopeful it serves as a reminder
that you didn't do anything wrong.
And, that you know it is never too late to
walk away, start over, and take your power back.
Always know that you are magnificent
and that you matter!

CHAPTER ONE

As soon as I took the bench that morning, I knew it was going to be a long Wednesday.

Defense counsel was looking up in my general direction, but unable to maintain eye contact with me. "Judge Kikkra, my client—" Counsel looked embarrassed. "—he would like you to amend his terms of probation, that is, lift the restriction against consuming alcohol, that is, since breaking-and-entering is not an alcohol-related crime." He mumbled that last bit as if somebody had set his playback speed to 2X. But he straightened and added brightly, "There is absolutely no history of alcohol abuse."

I gave him the slow-blink to acknowledge his effort and turned to the defendant. He was twenty-two and needed to grow up and make some new friends.

Leaning toward defendant and his counsel, I asked, "Do you smell flame-broiled burgers?" I waited.

Defendant's eyes widened, and his attorney frowned.

"When the courthouse offers you a side of fries, and I put on a snazzy paper crown, you may have it your way. Until then, you'll abide by the law like everyone else. No alcohol on probation." I kept my face perfectly still. I could do a fair Snow-White-in-a-coma.

Defendant didn't blink, but his attorney tugged at his sleeve. "Understood, Judge." He sideways glanced at his befuddled client. "Thank you, Your Honor."

"Next matter," I said.

The assistant prosecutor grabbed a file from the top of his stack and called the case.

A young defendant and her navy-blue-suited I'm-all-business attorney stepped up to the podium.

After the prosecutor and defense attorney gave me very different opinions of how I should sentence the young woman, I turned to defendant. "What would you like me to know?" I asked.

Without blinking, she asked for time served. Then she bowed her head the tiniest bit and promised never to steal again—if only she could return to her mother and baby, finish high school, and find a job.

The only real hope she had was to turn her life around now before the system swallowed her and spat her out—forever damaged. I had one shot to sell this. So I craned forward for effect, placed my gavel where she could see it, and folded my hands just below the handle. "You had a mother when you chose to steal. You had an infant when you chose to steal. And you had the ability to complete your education, but you chose to steal."

She lowered her chin so far she left me addressing her crown of spiky pink-and-purple hair. I noticed little green and orange tufts center crown. "You're right. Judge Kikkra, I've learned my lesson." She paused just long enough to look up. "That week in jail—I can't go back; please don't send me back." She seemed to be fighting an urge to back up and run out of the courtroom. "Please."

For a second, I thought about one of my boys coming home with Crayola-colored hair and a pierced face. My own face relaxed. This girl needed a wake-up call and help understanding the gravity of her actions. I paused long enough for her to feel the depth of my best judicial stink eye. "With your Easter-egg chain-gang look, you can't be taken seriously. No respectable employer will hire you."

Then she did inch back. But her trusty Public Defender steadied her. And the courtroom deputy stepped closer.

"God put two letters together in the alphabet: N and O," I said and raised two fingers—one at a time. "Use those letters as He intended. No jelly-bean hair color, no nose rings, no blue lipstick. Follow my Orders while on probation, or you will go to prison."

Several seconds passed before the legal light bulb glowed for my young defendant. But the second she did understand, her entire body softened.

Seated in the audience behind her, a woman silently cheered me on with a steady head-nod. She was two sizes larger and two decades older than the girl. Had to be the girl's mom.

I kept my voice stern, my eyes on defendant. "I'm thinking you've heard all this from your mother, yet you chose to steal."

The older woman nodded in long swipes as if her longtime prayers had just been answered, and she was about to jump up and testify.

"Yes, Ma'am." Purple Girl wiped tears from her face. "I should've listened to my mother."

"I am now your other mother, the one you don't want." I recited a long list of probation Orders and her rights and said, “Go thank your mother and apologize. Come back and show me the magnificent things you’ve done. I know you are capable of greatness.”

She nodded, and then streaked toward her mom so fast, I swore her purple faded two shades.

On the outside, I kept my head still and my chin high, but behind the bench, I slipped out of my Ariat cowboy boots, crossed my Levi-clad legs, and propped them on my padded footstool. What went on under my robe was between me and my Maker.

CHAPTER TWO

Almost two hours and several Pleas-and-Sentencings later, I was sorely overdue for a caffeine break and a few blood-moving stretches. The ice storm plinking on the courthouse roof—only one of the perks of a Michigan January—made me want to retreat into my chambers for hot coffee and mental yoga.

I'd take a break after the next case. Right now, I was intrigued by the approaching attorney in the banana-yellow suit.

When he reached the podium, I half expected to see a mischievous monkey holding the esteemed counselor's big yellow hat. He waited while the deputy brought out a man from lockup in an orange jumpsuit and green crocs. My courtroom now glowed a few colors short of a rainbow.

"Judge Kikkra, I seek release of my client on bond," the attorney said with more apparent confidence than I'd thought a banana could muster.

I turned to the prosecutor's table. "On behalf of the people?"

The prosecutor looked disgusted. "This defendant owes almost forty-thousand dollars in back child support with an ongoing obligation."

"Judge *Keeekraaa*," yellow counsel interjected.

I wondered if he'd gotten a mini banana stuck in his throat.

"Counsel?" I turned from the prosecutor, raised a brow, didn't blink, and waited.

"That's exactly why my client needs bond—to find employment," Banana Man said. "He can't pay in lockup."

"I didn't interrupt, counsel," said the prosecutor. "Surely, I'm due the same courtesy."

I reached for my gavel, raised it a bit, and then set it down. Both counsel understood the silent warning that I wasn't afraid to pound Orders holding them in contempt. I turned to the prosecutor. "You may proceed without interruption."

"The children have a constitutionally protected right to be supported by both parents," he said, over-enunciating each syllable. "They're receiving public assistance, and one of them is in and out of the hospital. The mother has paid. The public has paid. In over four years, defendant has paid—not one dollar in support."

"Again, Your Honor—" Banana paused for effect and slow-grinned. "My client can't pay if he's incarcerated." He spread his hands, palms up, lawyerly body language for *if I didn't agree with him, I was an idiot.*

I didn't, and I wasn't. I pictured the banana suit ripening in jail.

Defendant smirked. He seemed proud his attorney was a hell of an advocate and smarter than the Judge he'd just enlightened.

I ignored the bananorama and addressed the defendant. "Sir, you are here for felony nonsupport."

No response from him. It was truth time, so I asked him, "How do you support yourself?"

"My girlfriend. Until I find a job." Defendant half turned toward a well-dressed woman with a too-low-cut blouse. Evidently, he was proud of his survival skills. The barely clad woman returned a lopsided grin to defendant.

"Defendant can be released," I said, "on a Personal Recognizance Bond." The prosecutor opened his mouth to interrupt, but I finger-signaled him to wait. "Only upon payment of twenty-five thousand dollars toward his child-support arrearage, and he must remain current on his ongoing obligation, or he will again be bench warranted, immediately followed by a chauffeured ride courtesy of the Sheriff and an extended sleepover at our County hotel."

Defense counsel looked embarrassed for me and my obvious lack of mental capacity. "Your Honor, he can't—"

"If he's inclined to stay in jail, I understand. Although it's several months away, Thanksgiving *is* the best meal and Christmas is the second best meal of the year." I grasped my gavel. "This mother deserves respite. Condoms are free; babies are not. The public will not pay for his seven-and-a-half minutes of fun."

Gavel-bang.

Defendant was escorted back through the jail exit, and the mother of his children mouthed a 'thank you' to me.

I tossed her a quick smile of acknowledgment. "That's all for the record," I called out. Experience taught me the bastard would be bailed out by tomorrow morning. "Next matter."

A court-appointed attorney in a pinstriped, gray suit stood next to a pineapple blonde in red stilettos. "Your Honor, this is a motion to modify bond conditions."

I acknowledged the prosecutor, and the people took no position.

I couldn't figure out what she could possibly want, so I spoke to the young woman's attorney. "Counselor, your client has a personal recognizance bond. All she has to do is to stay out of trouble. Get up. Go to work."

"That's it, Your Honor. She needs to work."

"I want her to work," I said. I really wanted to know how she walked through the snow in those cute, skyscraping heels.

The attorney de-frogged his throat. "She makes a good living—dancing. However, she needs you to reconsider the tether you ordered because it interferes with her pole dancing."

I tried to imagine a pole dance that would be hampered by a smooth, hard-plastic bracelet monitor, a third the size of a smartphone.

The dainty dancer leaned toward me with a sister-like pout, apparently certain that woman to woman, I would understand. "Your Honor, my costume and this tether clash. I can't go nowhere mismatched like that. And then there are the other pole dancers. We all have to match, ma'am."

I appreciate a pulled-together look as much as the next person, but let's be real. "Ma'am, bedazzle the tether to match your costume. Invite the other dancers to craft night and create matching faux-tethers. Motion denied." I slammed my gavel. "Next matter."

CHAPTER THREE

My criminal-motion morning ended just before noon, which gave me time to freshen up and toss back a handful of cashews and another of chocolate-covered coffee beans.

My early morning updo was still updone, so I combed my bangs and recharged my hair with a cloud of energizing hairspray, re-glossed my lips to berry red, and hustled into the breakroom across from the judges' suites.

Semi-patiently, I waited for the microwave to ding. Chocolate-espresso oatmeal and a mug of coffee would energize me while I reviewed my afternoon.

Pulling the oatmeal from the microwave, I inhaled the aroma, but before I could turn, some pervert smacked my backside. I whirled and sloshed chocolate-coffee oatmeal.

"Nicoletta!" Chief Judge Warren Donnettelli jumped back from the oatmeal and raised his hands. He leered down at me.

Must not throw steaming gooey cereal at the obnoxious Chief Judge.

"Nic-o-lett-a."

"It's Judge Kikkra to you." I steadied the hot cup in my hand, but the oatmeal wanted to leap out at the clod.

He jabbed a meaty finger at my nose, forcing me to jerk my head back.

A volcano in my chest flared heat up my face, and my pulse erupted in my temples.

Donnettelli raised a substantial fist to my eye level. His pointer finger bulleted against my sternum. "I told you what I expected in that Manville case." Poke. "My domain. My Orders." Poke. Poke.

He tapped my updo just above my temple. "Get that through your pea brain."

I giant stepped around him, but his robed enormousness blocked me. "You have no authority over my decisions." I kept my voice strong and steady. "We were both elected by the people. I answer to them, not you."

Grabbing my oatmeal, he snickered, then made a big show of tossing it into the trash bin. "Get in my way on this verdict, and you join the oatmeal."

His threats were getting nastier. He had to be insane to think I'd decide a case based on anything but the law. I'd lost my appetite and my lunch, but not my pride. I stepped around His Giantness, squeezed between two law clerks from other courts, and pointed my boots toward my chambers.

With his nastiest voice, Donnettelli assaulted his next prey. "Wade Mazour, why aren't you at the Hall of Justice taking care of our business?"

His palpable bullying made me shudder, and I glanced back.

Donnettelli shoved Wade into the breakroom and slammed the door. The young woman with him was Zena Royale, Laurel Briggs' Law Clerk, and Zena had turned various shades of plum from her pointed collar up to the tips of her ears. For a second, I thought she was going to go after Donnettelli, and I didn't want to see that, so I called out to her, shot her the be-careful look, and—as soon as she walked away—I hurried on to the peace of my chambers.

But I only made it as far as my door when Margo, my judicial assistant, appeared with news from the jail. Mr. Felony Nonsupport had paid the twenty-five thousand dollars on his arrearage and was being released. He must have had cash in a mattress or a girlfriend in the same vicinity. Good. That young mom would get caught up. Despite the Curse of Donnettelli, we did important work here.

Margo and I chatted for a few minutes before I escaped into my chambers to be briefed by my Law Clerk Violet about the rest of the day.

By the time I was reseated at my bench in the courtroom, my stomach grumbled. I never got to eat.

It was going to be a long Wednesday.

CHAPTER FOUR

Just after five thirty that afternoon, we finished up the day's work.

Tired of Donnettelli's threats over the past eight years, and still feeling him tapping my temple, I thought about reporting him to Judicial Tenure again, but so far, they hadn't done anything—no matter how often I reported him. I loved fighting for justice, but Donnettelli had been making threats and throwing tantrums at judges meetings for years, and he aimed his venom at the three female judges he couldn't control: Palene, Laurel, and me. Assaulting me in the breakroom—where staff and passersby could hear—was taking bullying to new and extreme heights.

It signposted *time for a change*. In neon. In giant blinking letters. But I had no desire to reopen my law office. Helping people had always been important to me, but there had to be other ways to do it.

I was tired of all the drama and ready to relax at home. I'd left my winter coat in the car, so I dragged myself to the elevator, which was—happily—empty. Once inside, I pressed G to the underground parking, and when the elevator began to drop, I started to relax. But when it bumped to a stop at the second floor, and the door slid open, every nerve I had complained.

Judge Donnettelli lumbered in. "You," he said with all the personality of freshly deposited cow excrement.

Fear zinged up the bones at the base of my skull then ricocheted to every aggravated nerve. I glanced around. No cameras in the elevators. Damn. My confidence crawled under my armpits. My scare stare would have to work. "Back at you, bub." I crinkled my eyes with enough force to repel the creep for two floors.

I was grateful to hear his phone ring. Only he would have a turbo-boost range that could ring inside the elevator.

"Sweetums," he purred. (I swear, he'd mastered a friendly tom-cat voice for his wife.) "I'm seven minutes away."

Just two floors. Just two floors. My new mantra.

But the maniac pulled the red STOP knob, the elevator shuddered to an abrupt standstill between floors, I backed into the corner of the elevator, and my arm hairs stood on end like danger-detecting antennae.

"Hold on, doll-baby, I've got another call," he said. He pressed something on his phone and barked, "What?"

Mr. Charm. I stepped into fighting stance and held my corner terrain while I figured out an exit strategy and a distraction. At first I could only hear his end of the conversation—using the term loosely.

"Not yet, but she will," he said.

Within seconds, I distinctly heard the shrill shriek of Judge Jurisa Haddes—who I was convinced was Donnettelli's private groupie. She was demanding he *take care of it* and *don't make her tell him again*. Yikes.

He clicked her off and reengaged with his wife, but he looked like last summer's dollar-store beachball.

"Wear the short blue dress," he told the missus.

My kingdom for a set of earplugs. I didn't need to know anything about his doings with Mrs. Donnettelli Number Five.

When he'd finished dressing his wife, he clicked off, gripped his phone tightly, and pointed it close to my skull. "Nicoletta, you need to understand something about the asbestos cases I assigned you."

Assigned me illegally. "Slid right off your docket, did they?" I cocked my head sideways to avoid his knuckles.

He dropped the phone into his pocket then balled both fists so close to my face I could see part of his bulging lifeline. "Listen good, and hear it this time," Donnettelli said in deep, low tones through clenched teeth. "Like I said before, the ruling you're going to make and artfully articulate in the final Order on the Manville case, is—"

I interrupted. "—is my decision to make. I filed it this morning before I took the bench." I grinned even larger and watched the red in his neck turn into burgundy.

"I'm so much smarter than you. Don't ever try to go around me. Your downstairs file clerk pulled your Order for me," Donnettelli said. "She respects my title." He tapped his chest. "Me, Chief Judge."

"Manipulating the legal system is beneath even you." I felt a sudden urge to punch something judicial and obnoxious. Instead, I gave him my deadly *you're-going-to-prison-for-life* pointing finger. But afraid he'd grab it and break it, I made a fist, which I'll admit wasn't all that impressive. I felt a little silly and shoved it into my pocket.

"I've got the sealed mail room copies of your decision, too." He waggled ridiculous jazz hands in my face. "I've got them all."

For a moment, I was dumbstruck. With nothing officially recorded, it was as if my judgment never happened. Donnettelli could do whatever he wanted with my decision. "You might want to reconsider." I spoke quietly. "When I realized you dumped all those asbestos cases on me, I asked the court administrator for a computer count to verify that all the judges in our division were assigned the same number of cases. Even as Chief Judge, you can't just decide to overload my docket. Cases are divided equally and randomly among us, something even you can't change."

He just stood there and grinned at me.

The Judge and lawyer in me wanted to report him. The common sense in me wanted to ignore him. And the woman in me wanted to deck him.

"Your incompetent ruling would have bankrupted Manville Corporation." He sounded so superior, I almost believed him.

What did the damn brute have to gain? "I'm a wild woman. I base my decisions on the law. The people they have killed and injured deserve restitution, and if that means Manville closes or files bankruptcy that is not my concern. I ruled on the evidence, evidence and a record you can't undo or manipulate."

"But the law is subject to interpretation," he said. And there was a tone. "Yours is an unjust, wrong, incompetent interpretation." He evil laughed.

I shivered. I heard the unspoken *change your decision or else,* loud and stupid. "If you wanted to rule on asbestos cases, you should have kept them. If you wanted to rule on them, why did you push them onto my docket?"

He looked off into the distance (which was a feat in a closed elevator). "You know what? Don't comply," he said. "And we'll see what happens—" He shot me a cockroach glare, "—to you."

"Don't threaten me." I wished I had bug-spray: slower than punching his gut; more fun to watch. "Don't swear at me. Don't talk to me." My voice stayed quiet for a second, but my brain shouted *if you don't get away from me this instant, you're going to meet the business end of my cowboy boot.* "Don't come near me ever again, for any reason."

"It would be a shame," he said, "if the public learned about Judge Briggs's dalliance with securities fraud." He wore his inner altar boy so well, I thought I saw a halo appear.

"Laurel Briggs has done nothing wrong." My voice remained firm, but my insides refused to back me up. Judge Laurel Briggs, Judge Palene Field, and I were close personally and professionally. We were also bound together by being long-term Donnettelli targets. But if anyone could wield liar's blackmail, it was Chief Judge Donnettelli, and I had to be careful. Hell, *we* had to be careful.

He wore a grin he'd swiped from Jack Nicholson. "When Laurel was chief judge *pro tem*, in my absence, she signed my *Opinions and Orders* on several big asbestos cases."

Donnettelli always sounded as if he were orating before the nation.

"That was her job." Sweat dripped down my spine. "She had to sign them for *you*."

"She didn't have to sign a thing. She *chose* to sign," Donnettelli whispered.

It was apparent to me he'd timed things so that Laurel would sign documents he wanted to be arm's length from. Would it be evident to others? Had Laurel realized what he'd done? "And then you shifted the rest of those open cases—and any new asbestos cases—to me," I said.

He'd been playing with our dockets, getting Laurel to sign her name on Orders that would make him look bad. When questioned, he could say he'd left her in charge, and she'd abused it, maybe used it for personal gain or to place him in a false light. Damn. He had it all covered, and now he wanted to manipulate me.

He said, "It's not my fault Laurel Briggs shared the information with her husband before the public was aware of the final decision. I believe there's a nasty term associated with that sleazy behavior."

The lack of oxygen in the suspended cubicle suddenly got serious.

He exuded evilness and leaned forward with a grimace, his nose almost touching mine.

I fought to keep my voice from quivering. "I change my ruling in favor of Manville Corporation, or you'll accuse my best friend and her husband of insider trading?"

He tapped one finger on his red-veined nose. "I knew you weren't totally stupid. Think of the bedtime stories. His and hers. All over Lansing. Hell, all over the country."

Laurel would never, and if she did, Michael would never. But I couldn't let Donnettelli castrate the justice system. "Manville Corporation recklessly ruined thousands of lives. They forced people to work with asbestos long after they knew it would kill them. They have to pay. My ruling stands. You and your threats can take a nosedive to hell."

Giant-toddler shrug. "Tell Laurel to ask Martha Stewart what to pack."

He released the emergency hold, the elevator dropped to the next floor, and the doors slid open. "Your decision will be made by eight o'clock tonight."

"My decision is already made." Chin high, I pushed in front of him to head out fast.

But something snagged a strand of hair right out of my updo, jerked my head back, and the quick jab of what felt like a metal cylinder connected with my ribcage. Donnettelli was pulling a gun on me in the courthouse? He was two hundred pounds of crazy. But I knew crazy. I'd seen enough of it in the courtroom. This was dumb, desperate, and despicable.

I half turned and slapped the gun away, and damn if he didn't scratch me again with his freaking long fingernails. As I lunged at the open elevator doorway, he jabbed the gun harder into my spine.

Enough. I shot a hard back-kick to his shin and exited into the eerily empty hall.

"Nicoletta, wait!" he called to my retreating back. But my boots clicked like silver lightning to the nearest stairwell. "Have you got a problem, dear?" he yelled.

"Damn straight!" I shouted and wheeled around, forefinger pointed straight at him, thumb hitching an invisible trigger. "Pack your bags to meet the devil. I'll be seeing to your final arrangements personally."

Donnettelli held up both hands as if posing for news cameras, no gun in sight except the imaginary one I trained on him. Then I noticed Peter Dune, Donnettelli's Law Clerk, at the other end of the hallway. Peter handed something to Judge Jurisa Haddes; she hurried away, and Peter mumbled into his phone, hand over mouth. Out of the elevator into a Grisham conspiracy scene.

I opened the stairwell door, unzipped my robe, and fled downstairs to the judges' underground parking garage. At the bottom, I punched my keycard, ran to Elvis (my classic Lincoln Continental named for Elvis the good years), slid inside, and locked the doors.

From the passenger seat, I grabbed my coat and placed it over me like a comforting blanket. Shaking all over, I realized my finger was bleeding again. Damn goon. And I was still wearing my robe. After a few minutes of calm breathing, I shimmied out of it, flung it into the backseat, and inserted the key.

Now what? Where to go, who to call? I didn't want to go home to a big empty house with only my cat for company. All three of my sons were in Colorado thanks to Dex my ex. He thought a semester off would be good for them to apprentice at his ridiculously upscale resort in Aspen. I was still mad at him for that. My career had always kept me busy, but I'd tried to do my best for my boys. Now in their early twenties, this could be my last chance to be there for them. No, I wasn't calling Dex. His brawny self and his exaggerated ego could stay on the slope, where he'd transplanted himself.

Sebastian? I could definitely use a hug from my lawyer boyfriend. Unfortunately, the hunk with a killer accent was visiting his family in Australia. Fortunately, he was due back in a week. Even if it was worth the ticket to see him, I wasn't going anywhere with this Donnettelli mess on my hands.

My fingers weren't shaking quite as bad when I hit the auto-dial on my phone.

"Meet me at Victoria's Secret. Six thirty," I told Laurel. I needed a quick talk with my best friend. I dug around in my purse for the one thing that would put the world right, and I sprayed.

"Something wrong?" she asked. She must have heard me spritzing myself with the other best friend a girl could have: Hairspray. It had been a damn long Wednesday.

CHAPTER FIVE

Promptly at six thirty, Laurel caught up with me in the silky teddy section near the dressing rooms. She was bearing an armful of Victoria's Secret lingerie in designs reflective of our rebelliousness—various shades of burgundy, pink, gray, and white—her type of wild. I was anxious to warn Laurel that our long-predicted disaster wasn't only headed our way, but he'd rounded the bend and zeroed in with loaded weaponry. Being feisty all under wasn't going to resolve this problem. But talking with her would help me decide what to do. We had to talk privately, and we had to talk fast.

"I love Victoria's Secret," Laurel said. "Pink champagne will pair nicely with these goodies."

"Jumbo sized, wedding-day hairspray pairs with everything." I needed a few more spritzes and a clear head to tell Laurel that Donnettelli had put a red laser dot on her forehead.

Laurel cocked her head sideways; she could always sense when I had a problem. "Out with it."

I gestured her into the largest dressing room and checked the other rooms. We were alone. While we undressed, I reported Donnettelli's threats.

"Michael and I did no such thing." She foot-flicked her heels off.

"I'm not accusing either of you." I shimmied into pink-and-gray sweats with matching lacey undergarments. "I wanted you to know: he's an arrogant, pompous blowhard on the attack."

"So 'on the attack' is the news?" Laurel slipped into her high heels.

I laughed. Laurel always did that for me.

She admired her reflection in a fuchsia underwire teddy. "If we weren't here being underwear-distracted, I might cry."

"Exactly why I couldn't discuss this with you in the courthouse. But, I have to ask," I paused, and she gazed back at me in the mirror. We needed to find a way to protect her. "Did you sign Orders for Donnettelli? Orders that maybe you didn't read very closely?"

Laurel's eyes held a tinge of hurt, her voice an undertone of surprise. "Same as all the trial judges. Signing piles of my own Orders, along with signing Orders for vacationing judges, including those Donnettelli gave me when I was chief judge *pro tem* when he wasn't immediately available, how can I recall specific Orders? I bet you don't recall everything you sign weeks later." Laurel's voice grew more hushed in tone with each syllable.

She sounded a little upset but more thoughtful. And she was right; I didn't recall everything I signed. I doubted any Judge did until it was handed to them again.

I gave her my *I'm on your side* look. "Donnettelli could've switched out pages, pulled pages or attachments he didn't want you to see, or set you up some other way for a criminal fall."

"He's capable of anything." Laurel sat on the dressing-room bench and tried to hide her shaking. "His ego barely fits in the courthouse."

I wanted to see the fire in her blaze. I wanted her to say she'd fight. I wanted Donnettelli to take a flying leap into the middle of I-96 at rush hour. "Donnettelli gave me an eight o'clock deadline. I'm almost out of time."

"The only one who has run out of time is Donnettelli." Laurel solemnly hung her selection on the hook and dressed.

I checked my watch. I didn't have time to return to the courthouse by eight. My return wouldn't change anything anyway. "Agreed." I hugged her, slipped on my cowboy boots, grabbed my pile of clothing, and we headed for the register. I'd somehow make sure Laurel was all right, but I still felt like I had one foot in a rusty bear trap. Maybe both feet.

We paid and left. I climbed into Elvis and leaned back on the headrest while I watched Laurel pull out of the lot in the direction of home. I had less than half an hour before Donnettelli would—what would he do? Hunt me down. Expose non-crimes to humiliate Laurel. Mess with my docket, my friends, my life. The list of heinous things he could get away with was endless. I was thoroughly tired of all things Donnettelli.

I revved Elvis and whipped into traffic. I aimed straight for the courthouse. I drove okay, but it felt like my toes were plugged into an electric outlet.

I tensed with every traffic sign, every tree, every chocolate truffle I unwrapped and popped into my mouth. When I finally turned into the courthouse and down the underground driveway, I paused long enough to swipe my keycard. I held my breath while the garage door slowly lifted. I commanded my foot to push the gas and enter the dark garage, but it balked. I ordered my hands to steer, but evidently, I was no longer in charge. I hated that more than anything.

With some fancy self-talk and a white-knuckles grip on the steering wheel, I planned to dial 911 if Donnettelli approached me in any way, for anything. I pulled into my assigned parking spot and rested my forehead on the steering wheel. Eyes closed, I counted backward and outlined my options.

"Ten: Act as if nothing has happened." Breathe. *That's a chicken-shit option. Negative.*

"Nine: Find out what Orders Laurel signed for Donnettelli." Breathe. *Better.*

"Eight: Figure out if stocks were sold because of her decision." Breathe. But once I know a crime has been committed I'm obligated to report it. Hmm. *Chicken shit* may be underrated.

"Seven: Figure out if the SEC would be interested, and if they are, how to protect Laurel and Michael—maybe a deal that hangs Donnettelli and saves them?" Breathe. Investigate before I know for sure they need protection and have something credible I can point at Donnettelli.

"Six: Figure out how to stay safe and not abandon my integrity by reverting it to my original Order." At the thought of the grieving families of asbestos victims, a cold chill skittered over me. I shook it off. Breathe.

"Five: Follow my oath to uphold the law no matter what."

"Four: Find Donnettelli's gun." Breathe. Damn. *Find his gun before his gun finds me. Or Laurel. Or some other innocent person.*

"Three: Consider if there's enough evidence against Donnettelli to bring him down. Will it look like sour courthouse grapes and not evidence?" Breathe.

"Two: Can we wait the years an investigation will take after we report him?" Breathe.

"One: Damn, damn, damn. Changing my asbestos-case Order like Donnettelli wants means a life-wrecking corporation gets away with stealing stuff, killing people, destroying families. And, if I don't change it, he sets up Laurel for something he did. That makes me the reason Laurel and Michael go to prison." No way in hell do I play with the devil, no matter the threat. Breathe.

"Zero: Decision made." I lifted my head from the steering wheel and grabbed my cell. Breathe. Swiftly I texted Judges Laurel and Palene: *I'm off to a new adventure. I leave the courthouse in your capable hands. I'm hanging up my robe for good.*

I hit send.

I revved the engine, reversed, and headed toward the door, ready to scan my keycard one last time.

But José, the head of the cleaning crew, stood in the storage closet near the keycard scanner.

I pretended to have an ounce of self-control left and slowed.

"Hello, Judge," he called out. He dumped the recycling into a pick-up bin and waved to me.

I leaned out the window and returned the wave.

"You are leaving late as always." He stuffed some papers in his pocket and waved again. "You work too hard. Relax. Enjoy what is left of your evening."

"Damn great night," I shouted. "I'm leaving forever."

He looked concerned.

José had always been good to me. For him, I ratcheted up my smile to fifteen thousand lumens. "I'd rather be a hairdresser."

And just like that, the weight of the blackmail-infested world was off my shoulders. I'd open my own high-end salon. Hair had gotten me through law school. Hair could be controlled. Hair, I understood. You just needed to know how to make the scissors sing and never, ever run out of hairspray.

CHAPTER SIX

The second I got home, I wasted no time calling my Court Reporter, Trisha. I told her I'd quit and asked her to tell the staff and explain I'd call them later. Donnettelli wasn't above going after them just to get back at me.

I offered to help them find new positions away from the blackmailing maniac. They said they understood, agreed with the danger-and-leaving aspect, and offered to pack my things and deliver them.

Another issue was getting my Order on the Manville case put back. Sebastian was still in Australia, but we found a way to mesh time zones enough for a face-to-face internet chat.

I told him about Donnettelli holding me elevator-hostage and hijacking my Order. It hit him hard. My tough-as-railroad-spikes lawyer felt deeply about anything that hurt me and was equally empathetic about plaintiffs, who were injured in any way at the hands of unscrupulous corporations.

So, when I asked him to write a cease-and-desist letter to Donnettelli to let him know he would not get away with changing Orders or messing with victims I tried to protect, Sebastian agreed, and also demanded a reversion of the Manville Order to my original. He made it clear that Donnettelli would follow the law, or we would call in every law enforcement agency possible, including legislators and the media. Coming from a position of strength is the only thing Donnettelli understood. So Sebastian sent a copy to everyone we could think of: the State Bar Association, the Attorney Grievance Commission, the Judicial Tenure Commission, and the State Court Administrator's Office. I felt relieved to have taken action and exposed Donnettelli.

But—ever the realist—Sebastian couldn't keep from predicting it would lead to endless disasters. Once I'd left the bench, I couldn't change the Order myself, but I could get my lawyer to send a damned letter. I vowed I wouldn't let Donnettelli get away with short-shrifting those already suffering from mesothelioma.

I was off to a start on a new life. Donnettelli's treachery was being addressed, my lifelong dream for my own luxury salon had been upgraded to reachable goal status, and—by week's end—my once-courthouse-staff had taken team spirit to a whole new level.

My staff kept in contact with me, triple-checking I was okay and offering to help me with anything I needed. They spent the week organizing my files and the few things I'd left behind.

Trisha could have immediately retired, but on Friday, all three delivered my possessions with a giant salad with all the fixings, including a choice of chicken and beef. Seated at my kitchen table for coffee and lunch, Trisha, Margo, and Violet took turns brandishing their impressive qualifications with each swearing their life-long dream was to work in a luxury hair salon—with me. I hired Trisha and Margo, and I had a better idea for Violet.

Margo offered to take any stylist training I'd pay for. She would be my "woman Friday." She wouldn't only cut hair but would maintain all stations and supplies. She'd even shampoo customers who were waiting. An idea I appreciated.

She didn't want to do the heavy cleaning, so we hired José and Wanda, the same couple who did my house, to clean the salon and café. I'd known them for a long time from the courthouse and was happy with the arrangement. Margo was fine with sweeping up for stylists and washing towels and other daily chores. I had to smile.

Trisha, my very Irish Court Reporter, would now be my receptionist, scheduler, and business manager for the salon, the eventual head to toe services spa my salon would morph into if successful, and my adjoining café. My new career plan had lifted off.

Trisha would make my life and businesses coordinate and run smoothly, much as she had done in the courthouse. I couldn't say *no* to such planning by people I not only respected but trusted. My former staff was taken care of, and that was a big relief. Reorganizing my life felt like a whirlwind and before I knew it, a week had passed since I'd left the courthouse.

My staff and I had turned my kitchen into our war room, and my new business was conceived, constructed, incorporated, and licensed in every sense of the word. I hand-selected café staff from among my best legal students, who'd still be available for a year or two until they were licensed. We were on schedule to open in a little over six months, July fifteenth.

I reinvented my life. I kept the essentials—my freedom, my integrity, my lawyer boyfriend Sebastian, and my friends. I was even okay that my ex had our boys with him in Colorado—for a short time—so I could focus on this new, exciting, chance-taking business venture. The legal documents, business contracts, and any other distracting paperwork were left in Sebastian's capable hands. He'd returned from his jaunt in Australia and jumped at the chance to hire Violet for his law office.

Still, I had a bazillion tasks to complete. I had to rummage through the filing cabinet in the hidden closet off the hallway near my bedroom. It was behind a set of sliding bookcases and held our family history, important papers, my sons' childhood treasures, anything I didn't want to lose.

I clambered over a trunk of Halloween costumes, crates of boys' toys, and boxes of law books until I found my ancient-history hairdresser's license. And that was nothing compared to the hunt for just the right building.

I knew I didn't want to be too far from home, but there was still a lot of territory to cover. It had to be a primo location with plenty of parking.

After several weeks of concerted looking, I feared I'd fallen into a bad Goldilocks remake. Every building we looked at—Trisha, Margo, Sebastian, and I—was too big or too narrow or too expensive, needed too much work, or was just plain ugly.

By the end of January, after seeing just about every available space in the county, I was frustrated. I thought we'd never find a building.

CHAPTER SEVEN

February fifteenth at breakfast time, Trisha texted me, then called me, and then tooted her distinctive car horn outside my front door. Within minutes, I'd grabbed a parka and climbed into the front passenger seat. She had a building to show me.

We were off. Clinging to the strap with one hand while the other braced against the dashboard, I vowed this was my last Trisha-carnival-ride.

In the back seat, Margo remained remarkably silent—my clue something was amiss. She had undergone a major life makeover after she'd bailed out of the courthouse. Classic, JC Penney, nine-to-five Margo had morphed into *Victoria's Secret meets Nike high tops, dressed at the Barbie Sparkle Studio*. When I turned back to meet her eyes, I realized she was petrified into silence. I kept waiting for her to blink.

We jerked to a stop in the parking lot on the corner of Michigan and Homer. "What do you say?" Trisha cried, the Irish equivalent of voilà.

"Is this for sale?" I ogled the exquisite building that ran the length of a city block. I hoped the roof was intact under the weight of hanging icicles and layers of snow. The long building had formerly housed a luxury jewelry store and a high-end surf and turf.

Carved oak double doors, a covered entrance, and elegant awnings said this was the place to be. We walked around the back and found ample parking and side drives on both ends. It looked as if the property was a square block. Ideal. But there was no for-sale sign or any other reason to think the building was available.

Trisha dangled the key, and we hastened toward the oh-so-elegant double doors. "My neighbor just inherited it. Told me he's placing it on the market as soon as Probate is approved." She turned the lock. "Let's take a look." Trisha pushed the door open and then motioned me to be the first inside.

Flabbergasted, I could hardly wait to get inside, and giant-stepped through the threshold. The building looked like a warehouse for the rich and famous. Margo pulled a notepad from her purse and sketched as we called out where the reception area would be and how it could lead into the work area with room for offices and a kitchen and storage in back with space left to grow into.

The rear exit led to the parking lot, and I was sure it was wide enough to stream drive-thru vehicles to the other side of the building. Perfect for the café I'd always dreamed of owning. "Let's investigate the other end," I said, and my team trooped behind me.

I explained what I was thinking: a salon, eventually a spa area in the back, and a café where the restaurant had been with an added drive-thru window. Everybody agreed. Margo's busy hands continued to make notes while I spoke. I noticed she'd drawn rough drawings in the margins. She pulled up the calculator on her phone and pressed in numbers.

"This could cost a bundle." She held out her calculator with six hefty digits spread across it. She showed Trisha the numbers, and four eyes rubbernecked me.

I thought out loud. "I love the open ceiling. I'll save some money there and keep that aesthetic. There's plenty of room. For now, we'll develop all the rooms we need, use the second floor for storage, maybe put in lockers, and work our way up as we need space. There's enough room in the back third for office space, a laundry, a color-mixing room, and a kitchen area."

Margo set her pad down and did a cartwheel down the center of the long room.

I hooted and clapped. "I'm all in, even if I have to offer my services in night court." That thought sent shivers through me, but I wasn't worried. My gavel days were over.

"We just need a few measurements, then we can begin to color coordinate," pink-glow Margo said.

I giggled. "Not so fast. We need construction permits, and Sebastian has to negotiate the right price."

"Doesn't your mother have good connections for decorators and all that?" Margo pointed her pen at me.

"I'll be color-coordinating on my own. My parents and sister are traveling in Europe *with* my aunt and *without* a date of return. They don't even know I've left the bench." I didn't want to explain it was my aunt's dying request.

Hands on hips, Trisha faced me. I felt like we were in the Old West, but I wasn't sure why. "This is crackers," Trisha began. "You only need us and that brain of yours, gal." She drew a deep breath and her question.

"Can you bake, or are you serving chocolate-covered coffee beans with espresso?"

Could I bake? Did Vidal Sassoon cut hair?

CHAPTER EIGHT

It was three weeks into February, and Donnettelli still hadn't changed my Order back to read as I'd written it, nor had he responded to Sebastian's letter, which was to be expected. Time to plot next steps to undermine him, now that he was no longer a threat to me or my staff.

Turning the tables and making him worry enough to do the right thing would be a feat, but with the help of Sebastian, the lawyer and Judge in me would prevail. I intended to bully the bully for the good of all.

The big day finally arrived, and with my hunky lawyer Sebastian by my side, I signed the real-estate papers and became the proud owner of a luxury warehouse and a stack of bills taller than a healthy kindergartener. At closing, I asked so many questions, Sebastian accused me of doing his job.

"You know I'm not one to shove issues out of sight. My style has always been *immediate* and *unvarnished*."

Sebastian laughed, placed a hand on each of my shoulders, and kissed me. In sync, we left the closing office. "The Frandor shopping area is blue-ribbon real estate," Sebastian announced in his delicious Aussie accent. "East Lansing is a smashing spot. Growing and stable."

"My law students will be able to take the bus or walk." I slid into the passenger seat of Sebastian's car and rubbed my hands together to spark heat in my fingers. "I can't wait for Laurel and Palene to see it."

"You've taken on a lot of work," Sebastian said. "I know you have lists to make and chores to assign. Let's go over there."

"I was going to go for a long walk." I needed a workout but didn't have time. "You know I've been picking Laurel up from the courthouse on her lunch hour for girl time, and if I don't get some steps and sit-ups in, I'll gain weight, have to buy new clothes, and need counseling."

"Doll, you can't get any firmer or sane. This is priority important." His mouth formed a soft smile. "We can work out later, together."

I smiled at him, touched by his ability to care for me in ways I never asked for. I texted Laurel and grabbed Sebastian's hand.

Once inside my new building, we sat on the floor, and I grabbed a notepad from my oversized bag. I drew a rough sketch and included the front lawn, side driveways, and back parking lot.

"I want the salon to be relaxing from the first step inside. Look at the product showroom I sketched in." I pointed as I spoke. "When patrons walk in, products and seating will be to the left. The receptionist can sit near the center, and there will be a coffee bar to the right. Somewhere in between the reception desk and the coffee bar will be the entrance to the workroom."

Sebastian pointed at the sketch. "It's big enough to build out rooms to grow."

"Love that. Expansion when we're ready." I added Sebastian's vision to the drawing, and he rubbed between my shoulders.

Sebastian peeked at my sketches. "You've got at least a dozen stations and what, three hair-rinsing basins?"

For a second, I wondered how he knew so much about hair salons but didn't inquire and pressed on. "There's space for extra storage and an extra-large mixing area." I drew in a large room and a wall for the private back area. "And, I want granite counters everywhere."

"Add a few plants, and it will have a grand Parisian feel," Sebastian said. "What are those areas?" He pointed to rectangles I'd drawn.

"Two, maybe three, stackable washer and dryer sets—we can save money washing our own towels. And a mani-pedi area, facial and body massage, and whatever else I can think of for services. Maybe even a henna-body-art room, mud bathroom, lash and hair-extension room and—"

"And, whoa already. I love the way your mind works." Sebastian kissed me.

I ran fingers through his hair and rested my shoulder against his. I liked sitting on the floor. "What do you think about leaving the ceiling open?"

"Makes it architectural forward and classy." Sebastian stood and walked around. "I can see some dark metallic paint on the walls—"

"Maybe on the ceiling with lighter shades going down to the floor." I couldn't keep from grinning. "And chandeliers will make exquisite reflections, maybe even rainbows." I scribbled down a list. We were on a roll.

"Staff-meeting room?" Sebastian asked.

"Full kitchen and meeting room in the back, so staff can bond and take respite from ungrateful clients—every profession has those." I laughed.

Sebastian laughed, too. "Hiding is mandatory at least once a week."

"I'll disappear into my office. And there's plenty of space left for adding a permanent makeup room, tattooing and piercing, a private coloring room, and nail services."

Near the center of the room, Sebastian rapped his knuckles against a wall. "Listen."

"Hollow," I said.

"Moveable wall," he said. "Perfect secret passage for easy movement between the salon and café for you and the staff." Sebastian grinned. "Or you and whoever you want to be secret with." The clown waggled his eyebrows at me.

"You think you are soooo smart." I returned the grin. Secret passageway was in my DNA.

Sebastian gently took my hands and helped me stand. "This is going to cost you a bundle. Can I help?"

"You've already helped immensely with the business. Now how about a little help for my pleasure."

"Abso-bloody-lutely."

I was a wild woman.

CHAPTER NINE

From winter into spring and on into summer, I finalized the design, chose furniture, equipment, cabinets, sinks, granite countertops, metallic paints from midnight blue to silver for the ceiling and walls, with special reminders to all workers to be extra careful to cover the spectacular sealed-glass floor—thousands of shards of stained glass suspended in, and coated by, polyurethane. It had depth and richness and color.

I tasted coffee from every espresso machine I could find and chose two for the café. I immersed myself in all things made to enhance and embody luxury service. I wanted *Ratification Hair Salon, Spa & Café*—a name that affirmed my new life—to be (as Sebastian had described) architectural forward, but I made certain it was also fashion-forward, classy, and comfortable.

Margo and I attended every available stylist training class, including weekend training in Chicago, while Trisha managed the work crew. I just had to brush up on my skills. Margo was behind me by fifteen hundred stylist hours.

With all the work and training, my life blurred. Most importantly, with each passing day that flowed into weeks and months, my pain from the courthouse dissipated. The more hairspray, peroxide, and lacquer I used, smelled, and purchased, the better I felt—except when I tried to work on protection for the mesothelioma victims. I complained and whined and name-called and begged. Everybody in the place was afraid of Donnettelli, and nobody wanted to poke the curmudgeon.

But I wasn't going to give up. Those people deserved justice.

Friday, July fifteenth, the official birthday of Ratification Hair Salon, Spa & Café—a slice of upscale pampering in East Lansing—had to emerge with the perfection of an Emeril Lagasse Celebrity Restaurant opening.

I needed a test run. Who better than my best judicial pals, who would bring their honesty, critical eyes, and forthrightness?

On the fourteenth, after my final walkthrough, I brewed a pot of coffee, plated my best café pastries, and swung by the courthouse to pick up Laurel and Palene.

Staff who knew me swiftly buzzed me through into the judicial corridors, I found Palene in Laurel's office, and we hugged. I announced the surprise visit to my new digs, and we hiked down to my Elvis.

I parked in front of the building, so we could enter through the front double doors. My blood pressure in the gutter, my confidence on the ledge, I unlocked the front door. "Welcome to my new life," I said.

We stepped in.

"Look at this place, glitzy but not overdone," Laurel said. "I adore the eclectic chandelier collection. Don't be surprised if one ends up missing." She turned around like a child deciding on which candy to pick.

"The chandelier crystals make the silver lines in the countertops dance."

Palene turned toward the work area and investigated the space. "You were right not to hire a designer. I see your sense of style and class. It's more than a space; it's a feeling you've created, a place I'd enjoy spending time and money in."

"So much fun," Laurel said.

Palene walked the length of the reception area reading labels on the products for sale. She finally landed at the opposite end, where the pastries were laid out. "Just like you to have a hostess area stocked with coffee and glorious pastries." She slipped one into her mouth and spoke as she chewed. "Is this just for us, or will you fortify your customers while you beautify them?"

I handed Palene an antique Aynsley fine bone-china cup and filled it with coffee. "It'll be stocked every day. Stop in and partake anytime."

Laurel grabbed a coffee cup and watched me fill it. "This is going to be my regular route to work."

Palene grinned. "I'll join you." She chose a cherry tart. "We'll have to work out on our way home." She bit into the tart and groaned with satisfaction.

We went into the workroom.

"Love this," Palene said. But she stopped short and snorted coffee, and Laurel and I almost bumped into her.

"What's wrong?" I leaned around Palene to see what she was gawking at.

A man's behind and two small feet stuck out from a bottom cupboard. "Not a worry here, missus Judge."

It was José on his knees, doing something inside a lower cabinet. He scooted back and stood and greeted us with a full-face grin. "My three favorite Judges!"

"I thought you were done cleaning, José." I didn't want to hear about a new problem at this late date.

"Si, missus Judge. My wife tells me to line the cupboards with paper to make it nice for your staff—and easier for us to clean. Thank you again for the extra work."

"I'm delighted you were willing to take on the salon," I said. "With the courthouse and my home, is it too much for you?"

"Not a worry, missus Judge. José has much family."

It was really good for me have José and his wife doing the major cleaning. I'd known them a long time, they were good and reliable, and I got to keep some of the friends I'd made at the courthouse. While José finished up, I escorted Laurel and Palene through the rest of the place.

"This workroom is as much a gallery as it is a salon. Artwork in every possible nook," Laurel said. "Reminds me of your chambers." She stopped in front of a painting of a woman at her dressing table.

"How did you find all this?" Palene, in her true style, walked around, touching everything she could reach. I smiled but didn't answer. It would take too long to tell the story behind finding each item. Someday, maybe.

Laurel stood and pointed at one of the doors that led to my back office and staff kitchen. "Is there a massage room? Maybe a his-and-hers—"

"Someday. You and that husband of yours. Is there anything you don't share?" I giggled and showed them the secret passageway between the café and the salon. "Follow me."

A minute later, we were standing in the center of the café.

"This is marvelous," Laurel said. She sat on a couch, and then a chair, and noticed the microphone. "Live music?"

"Thinking about it."

Palene ran her fingers around the glass food case. "The way my family eats, I'll be by for a box of goodies every weekend."

With her phone, Laurel snapped a few pictures. "I can't wait to show these off."

"I need you two here for the opening tomorrow. If everyone has your positive vibe, I won't have to worry about earning enough to pay back the bank."

I'd pulled the money from my retirement account, and a big payment was due in a few days. This had to work.

"You could always get into Donnettelli's poker game. You'd clean up against those men and pay the building off." Laurel chortled. Palene snorted again. But I shuddered. Damn, any mention of that oaf poisoned my soul.

"Just kidding. Anyway, I don't think they allow women. They'd lose everything, including their undies, and that would be disastrous on so many levels."

Damn, that was a disgusting picture. We giggled in a way that only good friends could.

Palene stepped into a lavatory to check out the facilities, and Laurel got suddenly serious. She whispered, "I've heard Donnettelli bad-mouthing you around—talking about you *leaving in dismay*.

"Dismay? Pfff."

"Don't ever fret about running in the red. If you ever need anything, I have enough pocket change to pay your bills and keep you afloat. I mean it, Nicoletta. I'm here for you."

Laurel's intensity and generosity took my breath away. I knew Laurel had money, and I knew it was well invested. The couple's plan was luxury retirement, so they never dipped into their stash. Where would she get pocket change, as she called it? Surely not from her judicial salary. I bit my bottom lip.

CHAPTER TEN

Friday, July fifteenth—opening day—had arrived. I stood with my new team in the lobby of my new salon. "Everyone, gather 'round. I predict we're going to have an awesome opening day without a single catastrophe."

"Getting this salon up and running has been a stormy ride, but because of you great people, I didn't know the meaning of the word 'dismay.' I couldn't have weathered the disasters without your help." I gestured toward Trisha. "After the pipes burst, Trisha washed 172 towels."

"Highly unusual." Trisha high-pitch-cackled with her face so flushed red her scalp beamed right through her white hair.

"When the painters turned some walls hot pink instead of midnight-madness plum, Margo single-handedly repainted the room."

"Would've been perfect for a brothel." Margo bowed, and the group laughed.

"And Violet, I'm grateful that Sebastian let me steal you away for hours at a time. And, thank you also for working with him to put together all the paperwork."

Violet curtseyed. "Sebastian, I mean Attorney Pearce, is wonderful. Thank you for recommending me. I love practicing law with him."

"You earned and deserve that opportunity." I patted her hands.

Trisha stepped in. "'Tis almost eight. Let's do a countdown. The second the ribbon is cut, we're in business."

All I wanted was to get through our first day without catastrophe. My stomach did a flutter-flop, and I passed an imaginary baton to my ever-vigilant, other mother and Irish confidant, Trisha.

"Before we cut that starter ribbon, I need a serious minute with all of you." I locked in a connective silent gaze with each face to ensure they understood how much they independently and collectively meant to me. "I need you to know that I appreciate you all so very much. I mean it."

They surrounded me, hugged me, released me, and clapped. We counted. "Ten, nine, eight . . ."

"Stand back," Margo announced. Her purple-sparkled nails flicked with each number. " . . . two, one. I'm unlocking the front door."

In conga-line fashion, we formed a greeting line outside. Hands together, Trisha, Margo, and I cut the ribbon. Camera lights flashed. I made a small welcome speech, and Trisha went inside and flipped on the *OPEN* sign. She released a few helium balloons out the front door and welcomed onlookers.

Half the courthouse and their friends appeared: amid the reporters and my girlfriends and I think every Ingham County woman with hair, the Governor's secretary, clerks, and court reporters from all levels of courts stood shoulder to shoulder with a gaggle of lawyers who swore they were ready for new styles from hair to heels.

"Judge Kikkra—" the *Lansing State Journal* reporter began.

I interrupted. It would take a while to train everyone. "Nicoletta, please."

"Nicoletta, before we all move inside, can we get some pictures out front?" the reporter said. His cameraman stood by his side.

I smiled and made sure to stand in sight of the salon sign as bulbs flashed and film rolled.

"Judge Nicoletta, for months Judge Donnettelli has been saying that you left the courthouse in a fog of dismay over your chaotic life—his words." The reporter began. "Would you care to address that?"

"I don't know the meaning of the word *dismay*." I pointed at the Ratification Salon sign and then held up touchdown arms.

Everybody cheered and clapped.

WILX Radio held up a microphone and asked, "But what specifically prompted such a career change?"

"Timing." I smiled. "I'll continue to help people, just in a different way."

"You're wearing your signature jeans and designer cowboy boots. Can we count on that same fashion-forward decadence in your hairstyling?" a young female reporter asked.

I grinned. "We'll be keeping it kicky, classy, and a little bit sassy."

CHAPTER ELEVEN

An hour and many questions later, photos and interviews continued inside. Clients appeared. Appointment slots filled fast. Fog of dismay, indeed.

I headed through the long reception area, past the coffee station, and through the doorway into the spacious workroom. It had a dozen workstations, three on each wall—one double station and one single. Each had a large mirror, so clients could admire themselves.

Three new hires were already busy styling hair. With them, plus myself and Margo, even though she was still new at styling, I'd filled fewer than half of the dozen stations, so I was still understaffed. After my courthouse experience, I wanted to work with the right kind of people; I had to take my time hiring.

The salon was in full chatter. Curly hair, short hair, colored hair, highlighted hair, shaves, waxes—the phone rang nonstop all through the morning and into the afternoon. We relaxed into a regimen of driers, clippers, and giggles. By late afternoon, my stylists, even ever-energetic Margo, drooped a little, but they looked delighted with their opening-day's work.

When the last freshly coiffed client finally left, Trisha flipped off the *OPEN* sign, and the whole team cheered for a terrific first day—sans catastrophe. We'd done it.

But before Trisha could lock the front door, a pair of serious-looking men and two uniformed police officers strode in.

I recognized the first two from the courthouse: Detectives Grayson and Fredericks. Geez. Prickly bumps were suddenly joyriding down my spine.

"May I help you?" I showed them my teeth. A pretend smile was better than no smile.

Stony glares all around.

Or not. I swallowed, my nose flared, and I felt the elastic in my underwear unravel. Damn. Chief Judge Donnettelli must have sent them. "Let me guess: when my chambers were boxed up, a stapler was accidentally packed?"

"Nicoletta Kikkra?" Grayson asked.

The nut knew damn well who I was.

He maintained focus as if daring me to deny my own name.

Grayson (pastel-blue sports coat over soft-blue cashmere) and his partner Detective Fredericks (white tee under a black suit. Vintage Chicago White Sox cap). Homicide. I'd heard the Miami Vice wannabes testify many times.

"Haircut, detectives?" I held out my showroom hand.

Grayson stepped to my right, and Fredericks went left. Before I could say claustrophobia, they'd each grabbed a forearm, wrenched my arms behind me, and slapped handcuffs onto my wrists. And one of them shoved an arrest warrant under my nose.

Grayson enunciated as if I were a less-than-bright toddler: "You are under arrest for the murder of Warren Donnettelli."

"The bastard's dead?" Every red blood cell in my body had been shocked prison-gray.

"Apparently," Fredericks said, "the Chief Judge was shot between three and four this morning."

"Look Mr. Baseball, there's a whole field of players who wanted Donnettelli dead. You've got the wrong slugger."

"Tell it to the Judge," he said.

The two uniformed officers looked embarrassed for them.

"Even his Judge-friends don't like him," I said. "Try them."

Fredericks snorted. "We checked everyone close to him."

Grayson jumped in. "They all have alibis. They all knew you hated him. They all have been cleared."

"You've done all that this early in the investigation?" I didn't believe it.

"Judges, law clerks, a few legislators were playing poker in another neighborhood when you were murdering Judge Donnettelli," Fredericks said. "Even his enemies can prove they were with their spouses. One was and is still in the Bahamas."

I shook my head. Unbelievable.

Grayson plowed ahead. "You have the right to remain silent . . ."

Now I knew the meaning of *dismay*.

CHAPTER TWELVE

Monday, July eighteen, at seven o'clock in the morning, in the solitude of my salon office, I kicked off my boots. Since the last time I'd sat here, I'd been handcuffed, read my rights, slammed behind bars, arraigned, and finally released on bond Saturday afternoon.

Sebastian stayed with me all day Sunday and filled me in on everything he'd learned. He said the detectives had already viewed several key security videos and had search warrants for more. Some good citizen thought it necessary to deliver footage to the detectives' squad room—and the gumps still didn't smell a setup.

The video showed that the night Donnettelli breathed his last, a whole parade of people were in or near his chambers throughout the evening, but no one in the early hours of the morning. The shooter had to be someone who knew the security cameras' dead spots.

They had another video showing last Thursday when I'd stopped in to pick up Laurel and Palene. Damn. Once I retired from the courthouse, I should have never entered it again.

From the list of people known to be in the courthouse the evening before Donnettelli died, Sebastian and I made a suspect list: Judge Laurel Briggs and her Law Clerk Zena Royale, Judge Jurisa Haddes and her Law Clerk Keldon McKean, of course Team Donnettelli: his Law Clerk Peter Dune, his Court Reporter Noel Lemmon, and his Judicial Assistant Renée Reed, Supreme Court Law Clerk Wade Mazour, José the custodian and one of his staff, and the Security Officer. Basically, because there weren't any cameras in Donnettelli's chambers or at the ends of hallways, no courthouse employee could be eliminated.

For my money, Team Donnettelli in its entirety was suspect. If I'd worked for him, he'd have been dead long ago. But none of his staff looked sinister. Law Clerk Peter Dune looked like a long, lean Howdy Doody, and where Peter was concerned, life was a mission to make people laugh. Court Reporter Noel Lemmon was tall, too. But he was strongly built, athletic, and dark. Well-cut brown hair, attentive brown eyes. And little Renée Reed posed an enormous threat to stray ladybugs and spiders on the small side. She was always neat and clean but gave the impression she'd never seen a fashion magazine.

Sebastian opened the newspaper and handed me Sunday's *Lansing State Journal*—with an above-the-fold photo of a couple of state senators, three judges, some law clerks, a court reporter—the list went on and on.

On the front lawn of Law Clerk Peter Dune's house, police were cuffing the two senators. The men, having been inside Howdy Doodyville at an all-night poker-party-turned-brawl, all tried to hide their faces from the camera.

But there was no mistake who they were.

The senators were taken into custody at 4:07 before the sun was up and were back in their own homes before lunch was served, so we scratched that party off our list.

The newspaper also reported that—from his chambers—Donnettelli had phoned Peter Dune at two in the morning. Nobody had a guess about what he was doing in his chambers at that hour.

And for the kicker, the detectives had the security video of Donnettelli and me in the hallway—that day he'd blackmailed me. With me finger-shooting him and promising to send him to hell without a handbasket.

Those recordings were overwritten every eight days, which meant somebody had gone out of his or her way to save it—just to make me look guilty. Some tech savvy person was working a long-term plan to frame me. When I left that day, Peter Dune had been standing there with Jurisa.

But Sebastian wasn't done with his report. He looked altogether too serious when he told me preliminary tests showed my DNA from some old blood found on the barrel of the gun. That would be the gun that had fatally shot Donnettelli early Friday morning—just hours before my opening.

When I reminded Sebastian I hadn't been near Donnettelli since that day in the elevator, my loyal lawyer offhandedly reported some recent news: "fifty-year-old DNA just provided a break in the Boston Strangler murder case." *Subtle, Sebastian. Very subtle.*

It was clear the detectives weren't interested in looking for the real shooter. Years of hearing expert testimony, had taught me the chance of finding a usable print on a gun was less than five percent. I knew with a DNA tie to me and a shortage of law enforcement, the likelihood of them seriously looking for the real killer was also less than five percent. I needed to find the killer myself, I was certain—one hundred percent.

I'd told everybody that I was pushing the gun Donnettelli had pointed at me, away, back toward him. Sebastian believed me.

Damn, just recalling it made me sweat. In that instant, I had wished Donnettelli dead, wished him shot, wished him away from me.

So, who wished me behind bars?

CHAPTER THIRTEEN

I bet more than one person was colluding to frame me, but—in that scenario—how does Donnettelli end up dead? I'd have put him as the lead colluder.

I needed answers and evidence. I was certain both were locked inside the courthouse, in Donnettelli's chambers or his bench desk. Fortunately, I had friends in that courthouse.

I dialed Laurel. On the second ring, she picked up, but was breathing hard. "This had better be good." She sounded as serious as Laurel ever got.

I felt my face blush. "Oh," I said. "Tell Michael I'm sorry for interrupting." I started to hang up.

But Laurel burst into laughter. "Michael left an hour ago. I'm on the treadmill listening to GMA and de-spreading the parts of me that sit on the bench."

Fewer bonbons might be the answer, but since I routinely camped out in a glass house eating my weight in coffee ice cream, I squashed that suggestion. I giggled. "I'm hoping you can help me sleuth through Donnettelli's office. Maybe spy on Jurisa. I suspect they've been bird hunting, and I was their targeted pigeon."

There was a longish pause, and then Laurel was back. "Count me in," she said.

Another pause.

Then Laurel gasped.

What on earth? "Are you okay?"

"Charley horse," she croaked. "Let's talk later. Call Palene; she's always up for undercover missions." Before I could say *goodbye*, Laurel moaned and clicked off.

I dialed Palene.

"What's up?" she said. "Need bail money?" Her warm voice was full of laughter.

"Ha. Ha. Better than bail money," I said. "I need your help. Donnettelli and Jurisa were up to something before he . . . expired. And I need—"

"Those two were always trouble, and since his murder, Jurisa seems more canine than human. Possibly rabid."

"I just need you to—"

"Sorry friend, I'm on my way to a week-long judicial-evidence-update class. I'll help you after I return. In the meantime, I know Laurel will tell you everything."

I wished her well and clicked off. Damn. Some things a girl just had to do herself. I'd have to get inside the courthouse without violating bond conditions.

Damn GPS tether locked in my location at all times. But there were ways around the GPS, and I was not above using them. I recalled testimony about tether violations—it was true that tampering with the gizmo would set off an alarm, but I could at least confuse the signal and ruin the recording for a short time.

My gut told me that once I got in, I'd figure out what the hell had happened since I'd escaped that hole of injustice for judges.

As often as Laurel and Palene and I had reported Donnettelli, the Judicial Tenure Commission never investigated or provided any assistance, and it was their job to monitor judicial behavior on and off the bench. They weren't going to help me now.

Someone hated me enough to croak Donnettelli and blame it on me, but who? What if killing him could have been a perk for someone who wanted to hurt me? That thought seemed a little ego-centric, but if I wanted to stay free, I had to consider all options, likely and unlikely.

I tugged up the right leg of my jeans and scratched my ankle. Damn tether. Damn uncomfortable. And damn ugly.

CHAPTER FOURTEEN

The salon's back door, which opened into the rear parking lot, slammed, and I twisted in my chair to see who was about to pass by.

Margo stuck her head into my office. "Nice boot bracelet, and interesting choice camouflaging that hideous tether in your leg grass."

"Haven't you got bottles of shampoo to count?" I tried not to scrunch my nose at her. Fear of early wrinkles. I could give her sixty seconds; then, I had to press forward with my murderer hunt.

She sported a new row of vibrant-blue braids intertwined with purple atop her dark roots, another step toward inventing her new look to go with her new life. "If you don't mow that nasty leg hair, people might get the wrong idea about how we beautify our clients."

I shot her my judicial eyebrow-chin combo. "I've been contemplating how to get inside the courthouse with this damn tether on."

"We can't run this place with you directing us from jail," Margo said, hands on hips.

"Someone in the courthouse knows something. Donnettelli's gun from his desk killed him. And you know I haven't been near him or the courthouse." I admit I got a little louder than I'd intended.

"I'll testify to that." Margo reached into her shoulder bag and tossed a pink, furry, beaded *thing* at my head.

I snagged it. Eek. With a finger and thumb, I held it at arm's length. "Why'd you scalp a Teletubby?"

"Just giving you a dose of your own advice." She grinned like she was up to no good. "Remember the naughty pole dancer in your courtroom?"

I did remember the pole dancer, who'd needed her costume to match. I'd been more creative than sympathetic. The irony didn't escape me.

"No one will ever know you're wearing it." Margo cracked her Juicy Fruit.

I rolled my foot right then left and looked from the tether to the fluff. "Kind of cute."

"This is just for you. And if it works as well as I expect, I'll be opening a little side business." She cruised her French manicure over her miniskirt, opened her bag, and whipped out a mini hot-glue gun.

"Thank you for thinking of me in my hour of need."

"It's pink, it's cute, it fits over your tether, and it looks better than the grasslands. Totally you." She latched onto the tether and aimed the hot-glue gun. She fired, smacked on the pink furry bling, and fingered it in place.

And there was the answer, plain as the Teletubby attached to my ankle. Disguises. I'd find my way into the courthouse.

"You know I'm here for you, Judge," Margo said with real sincerity.

"And if I get violated for tether obstruction, you're bailing me out." Pink fluff was certain to be high on their wicked-behavior radar. I expected some uniformed, over-achieving monitor to crash in any second.

I nose-pointed toward my empty coffee mug. "Bedazzle my cup?" I slipped on my boots, and the blinged-out tether fit. I couldn't stop myself from smiling.

Margo twirled to the coffee station. "You can't fool me. You love the bling." She whistled. "Need a new pink teddy, yeah, baby."

Yeah, baby. Now I had to get in and look at the public records for those asbestos cases Donnettelli cared so much about. No more interruptions.

But in less than a minute, the backdoor buzzer announced Trisha, and three seconds later she peeked into my office. I stood and greeted her with a hug.

She pulled back and fired me a look of maternal concern. "You look shattered."

"No right way to wear lack of sleep."

Trisha placed a red can of extra-strength hairspray in my palm and headed toward the reception desk. "You've no scheduled clients for two hours. Why are you here so early?" she called at me while still moving forward.

Clutching the comforting hairspray, I followed her across the long room. "I can't read your chicken-warrior scrolls. No shorthand in the appointment book, please."

At the reception desk up front, I looked at the schedule book. "I wanted to manage the café deliveries."

"The law students you hired arrived timely and are trained to please." Trisha beamed pleasure. "They're savage."

"Not *my* law students anymore. The Dean politely swooped in to teach my classes until I'm no longer starring in murder headlines." I couldn't hide my sadness about losing the ability to teach law students I loved. "It also means we can't fail, because I won't have that extra income to repay the loan I took against my retirement."

"Judge, you don't have a thing to worry about." Trisha wide-tooth grinned. She patted my hand, but then like a magic trick, her face turned to total disapproval. "But that interview you did last night on WILX—"

The tips of my ears burned. "Oh, you heard that, did you?"

"You've always been straight-to-the-point, Judge." Trisha fanned her own face. "A bold move to offer free haircuts to anyone in the courthouse."

"I'm hoping they'll come, and they'll chat."

"Frankly," Trisha said, "I'm surprised Attorney Pearce approved it."

"He didn't." And damn him, he had no right to make me feel guilty for trying to keep myself out of prison.

Trisha made a silent Oh. After a second, she gave me a knowing look. "He had a lawyerly tantrum?"

"For hours." I hated to remember it. "But in the radio spot, I urged anyone with information to turn it over to me, Sebastian, and the detectives."

"So they couldn't accuse you of interfering with the investigation."

Trisha was a smart lady. Patting my hand again, she used her strongest voice and said, "Not to worry, Judge. Somebody knows, and somebody will talk.

And Attorney Pearce adores you. He'll be around with nothing but sweet talk. You'll see."

I loved Sebastian's sweet talk, to be sure. But I need his best legal strategy to get me out of this mess.

CHAPTER FIFTEEN

Trisha and I went into the workroom, and I tightened the gap between us. "I need you to keep on top of the courthouse gossip."

At that moment, Carlye Brewer sashayed in.

"What's alla this?" All of Carlye headed toward me like a swanky, female freight train. "You bein' in the headlines is what's brung me here."

What a surprise. "Gorgeous Gal, you could have just called," I said. "But I'm so happy to see you." And I was. I'd never seen Carlye outside of a courtroom. And she wasn't on the county payroll.

She tossed her bag down between the second-and-third-chair combined station and sat. A parrot rested on her shoulder—a real parrot.

I mulled over the politically correct way to ask a patron to perch her pet on the porch. Carlye was a grateful rehabilitated prostitute I'd kept off the streets and away from a killer pimp. She extended her hand toward me, and a tiny paper bag dangled from her thumb and forefinger.

Trisha punctuated her silent giggle with a giant question mark. It was apparent she recognized Carlye.

I accepted the brown bag and opened it. It could hold anything from a candy bar to a gilded bra to a lighted belly-button ring. I felt paper. And relief. I pulled out three sticky pads letter-shaped: I-O-U. "What's this?"

"I've decided to work for you," Carlye said.

Squawk.

"I mean we—me and my Shazam—to thank you for all you done for me." Carlye handed me a pile of documents. "I am legit. I been to more hairdresser classes than anyone else you gonna get. And, you might forget alla those classes you sent me to. It's all in here. Check it out."

I flipped through, and she was right. She had been busy since I'd sentenced her and successfully released her from probation. "Impressive," I said and returned the papers to her. I needed another stylist, but a felon?

Carlye gave me a big head-bob and planted her tools on the second-station granite, gazed into the mirror, and teased her bangs and her crown. "I seen alla your ads. Been figuring you'd need help, and I got lotsa clients who love my stylin'."

"I've held off hiring spa staff and filling stylist stations—"

Carlye pulled out a black appointment book from her bag and gave it to me.

"Clients and appointments. Mostly men. They is all legit. Salon-johns." She swirled her hips and returned to Station Two and kept arranging her things while she spoke. "They say I got the best hands for all their needs: cuts, shaves, massages, manicures—the works."

"You mean here? You're bringing your clients here?" I asked her.

But she wasn't listening. After she smoothed her hair, she sprayed and clamped the long, black strands up with a green, red, and yellow feather that fluttered in front of her right ear. "I'm just loving this crimson hair color against my creamy toffee. I look de-lish."

I hadn't considered stylists as appetizers. I didn't want to consider it now. "Enticing," I said.

"My scheduled first day is full." She grabbed a hand-held mirror and positioned it high over her head and looked up. "This lighting is good on my complexion. I'm gonna like it here."

"Space hog." *Squawk*. "Sunday Astronaut." *Squawk*. Shazam was Carlye's Amazon parrot—part inheritance, part payment from a client, who'd died on her—literally, she explained, and we watched Shazam fly up into the rafters.

I was happy he didn't tip over a hanging plant or knock crystals off the chandeliers. I acted as if flocks of raucous, feathered creatures swarmed me every day. But I discreetly slid out from under Shazam—no need to be his new favorite windshield. In some respects, all birds were alike.

"I do need to hire more stylists, and a manicurist."

Carlye jumped and hugged me. I would have toppled over had we not backed into the countertop. "I knows I can help you like you helped me."

Carlye released me, and it took a second to catch up on my breathing.

She was preparing her station for her first client. I had somehow agreed to hire her—but not her parrot. "I'm not licensed for pets," I said.

I walked up front and handed Carlye's appointment book to Trisha. "These need to be entered into the computer."

"Shazam fends off bad karma," Carlye said behind me.

Squawk. "Pic-a-nic baskets." Shazam bumped a hanging spider plant, and crumbles of dirt floated down into the hair-washing sink.

"Listen, bird lady, keep your bird crap in the street where it belongs." Margo's voice reached an impressive volume. "We got a lot to manage here, and there's no time to scrape up after your bird."

Carlye squinched her eyes, upturned her nose, and turned her back to Margo. "Judge, my baby Shazam will you help relax, so you can stop that nose-flaring thing you do when you're upset." Carlye placed her hands on her hips. "When you were on the bench your tiny nose was flaring like Fourth of July on the river-front." Carlye clipped on another feather above her ear. She held up painted nails of all designs. "I do it all."

"So we've heard." Margo paused for dramatic effect. Her power was in her pause. "And leave Judge's nose alone—it's cute, flaring and all."

"Enough commentary on my nasal cavities." I advised Margo that Carlye would be presiding over station two.

"You gonna bring in gross men or handsome men—I mean considering your old line of work, I'm inquiring." Margo's re-styled life didn't include improved tact.

From one of her thigh-high boots, Carlye slid out a pair of Kamisori Emerald shears and dangled them at Margo. "Careful Schnozeratchi, I'm picky about my men. I'm just not a braggart." Her leopard-print bangles clanked together, and she smoothed her rainbow sweater over her black leopard-print shirt. Her lowered shoulder curve exposed healthy cleavage until she sat upright in her stylist chair and crossed her legs. She aimed the shears like a gun barrel. "I am a private person. I—"

"Private as red neon." Margo interrupted and cracked her gum with a teasing smile.

I double-checked my nostrils and shot Margo a raised eyebrow signaling her to behave.

"Let's see what supplies you need." Margo opened Carlye's cupboard.

"Them's enough supplies. They expensive." Carlye closed the cupboard. "There's no magical money, dream-girl, not in real-women's working world. I'll make my way without wasting valuable hair product." Carlye stopped to face Margo and pointed a head-bob with such force her chest quaked.

"Better pump up your work, like those platform, high-heeled boots you're wearing," Margo said before shuffling on to her station.

Carlye huffed. "I never been talked to like that."

"We know that's a lie." Margo bounced with a hip-hop style twirl—a clever distraction from the building tension.

Trisha's hyena laugh came from behind me, and I turned back toward her. A line had formed at her desk, and while she attended to the in-house customers, she seemed to have abandoned all callers on hold. Only one of four lines was free. Maybe it was a good thing Carlye had hired herself.

I motioned to Margo to greet an incoming customer and headed up to assist Trisha. "I've got to get into the courthouse before I do anything. I've got to find the real killer," I mumbled.

Trisha patted my shoulder.

Margo's bright-orange high tops approached and slid past me to meet a curly-headed client, and the telephone rang again.

"Judge." Trisha extended the telephone receiver toward me. "For you."

"Too early. I need to be caffeine-infused. I have too much to do. Make an appointment."

Trisha chortled at my robot voice. "It's you-know-him."

"Sebastian?" We were meeting later to discuss my case. Had something happened?

"No, it's H-I-M," Trisha spelled and emphasized each letter.

Oh, God. I'd married that him, gave three kids and eighteen years to him, and divorced him. You'd think that would be enough. At the mention of my ex, my top lip pushed up to my nose. Surviving thirty-eight years on the planet gave me license not to care that I looked fish-lipped. I edged back toward the reception desk.

"Him misses you and wants to make sure you're all right," she whispered.

"Him wants to make sure his million-dollar-bond money hasn't skipped."

Trisha giggled and stepped away.

I aimed my pained face at her and spoke into the receiver: "Tether here."

"Hey, lover." His voice, soft and deep, bed-cozy. Memory Armani fumes emanated from his flesh and soft into the sheets . . .

"Not anymore." A sniff of my own scented wrist grounded me. "Divorce. Remember?"

"It's just a piece of paper." He said it as if pronouncing it made it so.

Some days I felt the same way, but I'd never tell him that. "Money's just paper, too," I said. "But you spent all your time counting it."

"Guilty. But I've changed. And I've posted a million reasons for exoneration."

"And I owe you a million thank-yous." A tether was way better than remand. "Other than that, I'll sort this out on my own. I'll take help where I can get it, but I am in total control of the investigation. That's the deal."

"I've got news." His intentional I'm-too-sexy-for-my-jet voice struck deep inner chords. Parts of me wanted to run to him, to be safe with him, to wake up from this nightmare with him. "Open your front door," he said.

"Good news?" I stepped toward the bay window. Was it possible Dex was standing outside? Damn. I pictured Dexter Breckenridge's six-foot, muscle-firm body in the thong bathing suit he'd once bought as a joke. He'd paraded through the bedroom and carried me into a bubble-filled hot tub. Okay, hot flash, pulse increased.

Dexter's voice flipped from bedroom to boardroom. "I hired protection."

"Hairnet, panty-liner, or Sumo wrestler?"

"Lover—"

"It's not some playground fight." I swallowed. "I'm charged with murder because I refused to play an illegal, self-serving game with an unconstitutional rule book and a bully. And I have a plan." Okay, my plan was raw, but it was brewing.

Then I spotted a dark muscle truck with tinted windows—parked directly across from the salon entrance, subtle as an Uzi on fortified cereal with nine vitamins.

"Lover, this is—"

"Call me that one more time and your lips get shellacked with the deep-freeze hairspray."

"Toss back a double espresso and listen. My CEO-sense tells me you don't kill somebody for colleague bullying."

"So, you hired a Michigan Terminator to guard your investment?"

"Face facts," he said. "You're a bad shot. That alone proves you're innocent."

"You just earned a double shot of deep-freeze hairspray."

Dex chuckled. "Every clay pigeon that's ever been in your sights has lived a long and happy life and retired in Vegas. It's improbable that you killed that bastard with a single shot. The newspaper said one shot killed him."

"Quit calling me a bad shot." But I chuckled. It was true. I'd always had fun with the guys on the range, but air, dirt, and anthills were the primary victims of my questionable aim.

Dex got serious. "Reality: You. Are. Being. Set. Up. Our sons have ordered me to protect you."

"They're supposed to be learning your business, not holding spy conventions."

"I'm protecting them from the three-ring fiasco called your life," Dex said. "Their learning to run a ski resort is merely a perk."

I knew all about the intimate perks of marriage to Dex. Damn him. His voice still made me lose airspace.

"I trust you'll keep the boys entertained until I'm cleared."

"Gotta go, Lover."

I was dismissed, reminiscent of our marriage. I ripped the receiver from my ear and straight-arm slammed it, but I didn't let go, and it rang again. Overruled by my ex, like he was the Supreme Court, and I had lost my final appeal. Well, he'd forgotten one crucial thing: I was here. I had possession of my life. I had the final word. Okay. That's three things.

"Now, Judge." One finger at a time, Trisha pried the receiver from my grip. "I need to answer the phone."

I was calm.

I was going to solve this murder.

Whether anyone liked it or not, I was in control.

CHAPTER SIXTEEN

I crossed the salon to the front door and stepped outside. My immediate mission was to make it clear to the hired gun across the street that I'd take help where I could get it, but I was in total control of the investigation.

Dex might be able to long-distance steamroll me, but I could handle any other man. There wasn't anything that couldn't be resolved in a hair salon. Even murder.

With the strength of the July morning sun, I marched across the street toward the immense black truck. If there's one thing I'd learned as a Judge, everyone had a back-story. I knuckle-rapped the tinted windshield, then the driver's window.

It slid down.

I saw him. My mouth sagged open. I may have gasped.

That was the thing about ex-anyone you've slept with: they knew you. And Dex knew that Hunter Greene, who'd had the worst reputation in high school, who I'd met the first day of high school—where we'd all met—would protect me with his life.

"Toots." Hunter flashed a slow, easy grin. His teeth were as white and straight as I remembered, his forever-tan skin. Where other men wished they had muscles, Hunter had brute force. He'd filled in enough to put me in unbridled heat. His eyes and hair were dark, and he had curls like waves my fingers could ride for days. English. I had to find some. Hormones. I had to lose some.

"Toots." The word suddenly had two sexy syllables.

"That name went away with—" What was I saying? "—with my anklets and acne."

"You'll always be my Toots." His eyes meandered from my eyes to my feet. "Did you ever learn to dance?" He spoke in Michael Bublé tones.

I gave him my practiced judicial evil-eye and prayed my hormones didn't mix it up with my bedroom eye. Damn.

His reply: a closed-mouth puckery grin. The soft lips I remembered.

Covered in instant memory fog, I recalled the freshman homecoming dance. Hunter had never ridiculed my awkward slow dance, but tossed my shoes, planted me on top of his size fifteens, steadied me in his arms like a china doll, and floated me around the dance floor.

Back to reality in the light morning breeze, I found my words, but my grasp on realty remained tentative. "I learned to dance for my wedding." It came out a whisper.

"Then danced your way to divorce, while I was still enlisted." Hunter first looked sincerely sorry, then let that pass and twitched his dimple.

I ordered myself not to melt. Only one task here: make sure this ginormous hunk of irritating gorgeous knew I oversaw every aspect of my life, my protection, and my exoneration. "I'll take help where I can get it, but I remain in total control of the investigation. For the record, once with you was enough." I pushed my shoulders back to punctuate my strength, sincerity, and control—and realized I'd just pushed my breasts forward.

"I'm intrigued you still think about me like that." He winked.

Against my will, I blushed. I neither recalled nor liked this macho-winking thing. I wanted to be swallowed up in a large can of hairspray and blown out in a million particles of strength.

I stomped my right boot onto my left to shift my control into gear. I'd silently stalked Hunter's career. "During those twenty years working in military intelligence, didn't you learn to be inconspicuous?" I used all my arm power on an inclusive gesture toward his huge truck. "For my customers, this shiny black behemoth is nerve-wracking."

He shot me a wink/half-grin combo.

I felt stripped right down to my panties. Man, it was a hot July.

"In law school, you clearly snoozed through *how to avoid being charged with murder.*" Hunter inserted an exclamation point by cracking his knuckles with an enormous smirk that caused his eyes to crinkle.

He was fun and warm. Adorable in an irritating way. Just like I remembered.

Then he leaned over and opened the passenger door for me. "Get in."

Generally speaking, I don't take orders from individuals with an overload of testosterone. But Hunter Greene was an exceptional individual. I climbed in.

Suddenly he was all business and showed me last Friday's *Lansing State Journal*—the writeup on Donnettelli's death. "Toots, we've done a lot of things," he said. "But we've always told each other the truth. Did you kill him?"

I slammed my fist into his shoulder and damn near broke my hand. "No."

"Then I can help you."

You'd think his smugness would be a turn off. But no. My cheeks burned.

Hunter hit the high points of Donnettelli's demise: fifty-seven-years-old, blah, blah, in his chambers, blah, the medical examiner (ME) put the time of death by GSW between three thirty and five thirty in the morning, body found by cleaning crew at six. Witness on W. Kalamazoo heard a single shot at four. No sign of struggle. No unusual prints. No other physical evidence except the cleaning personnel said the room smelled like lemon Pledge. Hunter looked disgusted. "Not a hell of a lot to go on, Toots." He made it sound like an accusation.

"If I'd custom-ordered the hit, I'd have planted somebody else's fingerprints and DNA, and then sent an encrypted thank-you note to the shooter."

Hunter threw back his head and let out his whole-body laugh. He'd always lived easy in his skin, and now I thought about crawling right in there with him.

I returned to my teenage years bundled in confused feelings, hormones, and missteps. Why did Dex hire *him*? My insides whirled. And Hunter knew he had that effect on me. Whoa. Time to find the Ejector Button. I patted where I'd punched him, opened the door, and slid out. "I've got a business to run." Toward the front door, I double-timed it.

But the truck's door opened. "Toots."

Oooh. I stopped. But I wouldn't look back.

"Send out coffee, strong and black." He lowered his voice. "Or I'll be in to get what I want."

I felt it in soft places. Damn him, he knew that about me, too. He and Dex must believe I'm in really big trouble.

"With pastry," he called out.

I didn't look back. At least I was in control of the investigation.

CHAPTER SEVENTEEN

Back inside, I delegated every task I could, including intrusions like schlepping coffee and tarts to Hunter, and then I focused on getting files from inside the courthouse.

As soon as could, I got some time alone with Trisha. "I'm going into the courthouse—undercover—"

Trisha uncharacteristically cut me off. "You'd best take Sebastian in with you."

If Sebastian found out—Yikes! "I don't think that's necessary."

She showed me her understanding, silent face.

The day was slipping away and my freedom with it. I needed to reinvent myself in the privacy of my closet. "Trisha, hold down the garrison for a few hours. Not a word to anyone. I've got to see a closet about a hairpiece."

* * *

Forty-five minutes later, I inspected my reflection in my closet mirror. No one in the courthouse would suspect a pregnant, hippie-professor gathering statistics for a doctoral dissertation.

I'd swapped my cowboy boots for espadrilles, pinned my hair under a long blonde-highlighted wig, tossed on a worn, blue-jean jacket (which I'd rescued from Dexter before our divorce) over a padded floral sundress, and added dangling earrings. I slicked on a dark lipstick and covered half my face with sunglasses. My wrists, ankles, and neck were clad in mystical, magnetic necklaces and bracelets.

Twenty-seven minutes later, I'd made it through courthouse security, just barely. I had to convince two guards, who repeatedly scanned me with wands, that I'd set off the security warning bells with my healing magnets, which couldn't be removed because of evil health spirits.

I stood in the clerk's office gripping a stack of files the court clerk had placed in front of me. She refused to meet my eyes. I wasn't sure if she was irritated, bored, or trying not to laugh at me. Neither did I care; my getup had got up and gotten me in. I wanted to know how many corporations Donnettelli had messed with.

"Need some help?" a deep, subdued voice asked from behind me.

Startled, I stepped back, pinched someone's shoe and teetered, but big hands caught me.

"Ouch. Did you learn how to dance and forget how to walk?" He leaned down, so he could whisper in my ear. "When are you due, Toots?"

"Damn you." I headed for one of the seats lining the wall in the oblong office. "Don't you have other clients to stalk?"

Hunter followed me. "With employees in five states, I choose whom to follow."

"I don't need a homing pigeon." I planted myself in a chair next to a small table where I stacked the files. "How the hell did you find me?"

"I get bonus bucks for penetrating your disguises." He towered over me. "Tell me what you're looking for—or are you here to plug another Judge?"

"Ass." But he was doing his job, and it was unlikely anyone would recognize him or connect him to me. With every female in the room sneaking peaks at him, no one noticed me. "Sit."

Hunter sat on the other side of the table, and I placed my palm on the stack of files. "These are from my former docket. Suits against large asbestos companies that caused injury, illness, or wrongful death. They've been reassigned to Judge Jurisa Haddes—"

"And why are we looking at them?"

"Crap."

Hunter followed my line of vision. "What's wrong?"

"It's Noel Lemmon and Peter Dune—they worked for Donnettelli. They're likely on the hunt for files—maybe even the ones we've got."

Peter glanced in my direction, but I was sure he hadn't recognized me. I turned so my protruding belly couldn't be missed, focused on the files, and in a whisper, explained Donnettelli's blackmail plan to Hunter. "His ultimatum: let Manville Corporation off the hook, or he'd make a phony charge of insider trading against Laurel and Michael Briggs."

"And rather than cave, you quit." Hunter beamed with pride.

It was kind of touching. "I always wanted my own luxury salon."

"You got the salon," Hunter said, "and Laurel got a motive to kill."

"I ought to stomp on the rest of your toes." Even if I thought Laurel had killed Donnettelli, I wouldn't admit it to myself or anyone else, even Hunter.

She never did tell me what she really knew or didn't know. In any conversation, Laurel always liked to pretend to know something, but that was just her ploy to get the scoop. But what if she were withholding something? Would she do that?

I pulled the Manville file and found my last Order. "This is the one Donnettelli changed that started all the trouble. My signature is on the back page, but the critical pages before that have been swapped."

"But last winter I heard him on the news talking trash about anyone in the legal community—that's how he put it—who was heartless to workers suffering from asbestos-related illness," Hunter said.

"More liars' tactics," I said. "He was slinging mud at me for something he did himself."

"He wants to be reelected—"

"So, he makes me look bad to make himself look better," I said.

"And the nasty corporate bully goes free." Hunter's color heightened. "Unscathed except for a few legal bills." His eyes were grenades of contempt.

"Worse. The people who are sick can't afford the medical bills, and the cleanup won't happen in time to save others. And what will happen to their families?"

He'd reached for files like a hound on a scent. "What exactly are we looking for?"

"Names of anyone who touched these files the day Donnettelli was murdered or near then," I said. "Anything that reads: a reason to kill."

Noel wasn't looking for the files I had. "We're okay with the files. Noel and Peter are just loading boxes for transport to the Court of Appeals."

"Noel was Donnettelli's hired help?" Hunter said.

"His court reporter." I cocked my head. A chill enveloped me. I surveyed the room. At the long end of the counter, two more law clerks—were nodding over an open file.

"Pluto to Nic."

I turned toward Hunter. "Pluto?"

"The way you're dressed, Earth was out of the question. I asked if we're going to go through all of these." Hunter said. "There must be a couple hundred."

There were a lot of them. I showed him how to flip through and identify the final disposition. Ten-to-one Manville wasn't the only big-bucks corporation that had gotten away with slow, painful murder. "The cases that defendant corporations won, pile those to your right. The cases that the Plaintiff won, we'll stack to my right."

We twisted and reached and arm-crossed and stacked—and I suspected a deal of unnecessary touching went on. And when we'd finished, I was shocked. Manville was the only corporate winner. Three cases had been dismissed—by Judge Jurisa Haddes, no less, and all the rest were settled in favor of the mesothelioma victims.

"Well, good," I said. Though it was hard to believe. I'd been sure Donnettelli had some huge scam to benefit a lot of corporations on a large scale. That's the kind of thing people kill about.

"Looks like we need a new plan, Toots."

I nodded. My investigation had gotten shut down before I'd started, so I looked around for the law clerks, who were getting ready to leave. I told Hunter, "I'm going to have to dig deeper. I'll be up at the counter ordering copies of these files." And trying to overhear anything the law clerks say.

Hunter left me to indulge my natural nosiness, and I waddled up to the copy counter and needed a lot of time to make copies. One of the alien law clerks was from the Court of Appeals, and his buddy was clerking for a Supreme Court Justice. Seems they were hatching a foolproof scam to have some fun this weekend. Total waste of time. At least I got my copies.

CHAPTER EIGHTEEN

Back in my bedroom, I delivered a five-pound goose-feather pillow and tossed off my disguise. I was disappointed the clerks divulged no useful gossip. Whatever was going on with the asbestos cases, they weren't involved. Otherwise, the courthouse visit had been productive.

By one o'clock, I entered the salon through the rear and headed straight to Trisha behind the reception desk, where she updated me on the day's doings.

I pointed to the appointment book. "Is it possible I'll have uninterrupted time today? I have evidence to study."

Trisha's mouth opened, but words failed to form. I followed her gaze above my head, turned, and caught my breath. I'd rounded right into Hunter. He touched my chin with a manly finger and gently lifted my face to his.

Our eyes danced.

"I need a quickie," he said.

I suppressed an inner-spark-shiver left over from our past, and we walked in silence to my styling station. I snatched a clean cape from my stack and pointed him into my styling chair. "Are you here to ogle or to help with this morning's copies and develop a plan?"

Hunter's six-and-a-half feet flowed into the chair. "I'm here to protect, guard, and shield your true identity."

"Funny." *Yeah, I'd really shown him who was boss.* I cinched the cape around his neck too snug for comfort.

Like the snap of a crocodile, his fingers clamped my wrist. His voice lowered a few notes for privacy. "As much as I like your naughty-Judge side, don't jeopardize your life." After a momentary wrist massage, he released me, and I loosened the cape. The indirect eyes of my staff burned my backside.

I ran my comb and fingers through his hair and said right out loud, "A cut like the old days? I can shave in the team logo." I met the light in his eyes in the mirror. "Or, have you moved up—Glock, Taser, or spyglass?" Then I leaned in and whispered. "I didn't risk my life. I was in disguise. I was in a public courthouse."

"Where there had been a murder. Where the killer could use you for target practice. Where you are not supposed to be."

"I was careful." His cologne weakened the fight in me, and my voice wasn't as firm as I'd meant it to be.

Hunter scoffed. "You've never visited the neighborhood of careful. Sassy, yes; careful, no." He looked around the salon, checking the digs out like a hired inspector. "Salon's classy. Triple-framed mirrors—nice touch. You were *Quickie Cuts'* best stylist."

"Those *Quickie Cuts* days were great." I whisked the chair around. "About this hair." I wanted to avoid our history rewind, for now.

"Nothing funky, edgy, or colorized." Hunter's voice was deep with a hint of playfulness.

"My gut says the clue to the shooter is inside Donnettelli's chambers and courthouse gossip central."

"You do have a great gut." Hunter winked.

I ignored the wink, and in the mirror secured my eyes onto his. It was nice. But I reached for my prized scissors, razor, and trimmers and opened my drawer. Stuff—a lot of stuff—a shiny, rainbow of stuff burst up out of the drawer: springs, confetti, circles, stars, and dots of all sizes.

I jumped and screeched.

Flying bits of colored paper, paper clips, tiny rubber balls, and colorful candy sprang up and showered my station and the surrounding area. I felt shrunken and trapped in an arcade game on crack. For a second, I thought about switching to Depends.

Hunter morphed into Investigator-Tickle-me-Elmo, all giggles and grins. But staff and clients were in a tizzy—or they would be if anyone still said *tizzy*. A few had their hands up, others protected their heads with their arms. Carlye dropped to the floor.

She raised her head and looked around and seemed to think she was safe. "Who had a piñata? Why didn't I get a swing? What we celebrating?"

"Oh, brother." Margo frowned, fists on hips. "Find me a bigger dustpan." She bent down for a closer look. "What a waste of perfectly good Skittles."

On his hands and knees Hunter used a pair of tweezers to lift the cloth-covered springs that had boinged out of my drawer. He flipped them until he found the manufacturer's label, righted himself, and lifted a sexy-detective eyebrow. "Who'd you piss off in Taiwan?"

I gave him the long, slow blink. "Droll." From my workstation cupboard, I grabbed latex gloves, snapped them on, and studied the remaining contents of my drawer.

Hunter hunched over me. "Don't touch anything."

"I have visited a courtroom once or twice," I said. "Likely some screwball's idea of a bad practical joke." But I couldn't ignore the timing. I'd learned through repeated testimony: timing meant something.

I searched my drawer for a clue. Saw it. Stopped.

Hunter saw it, too. I sent Carlye back to her client, and Hunter whipped out his phone and took photos from all angles.

I tossed latex gloves to him, and he put them on.

"Try not to fret, my little nose-flaring Toots."

"I'm not anyone's little anything. Toot that." I froze my uncontrollable nose and shook my hands to prod him along.

He reached into the drawer and pulled out a gavel with a note tied on by a blue-silk ribbon. "Recognize the gavel?" Hunter asked. He turned it, and we both saw the imprinted name.

"Not mine." I had a sick feeling. "Untie it already."

I peered as closely over Hunter as I could without touching him or the evidence. "Open and read," I commanded.

Scrawled in blue crayon on my former judicial stationery:

> *Follow the money. I cannot help directly. They watching me. It is not safe to tell more now. Read, listen carefully. Everything become clear: follow the money.*

I felt gut-punched.

"Money?" Hunter tilted his head like a huge but confused German shepherd.

I shook my head. "It's like Deep Throat, but with bad English, a blue crayon, and Woodward and Bernstein lurking close behind." But for the first time since being arrested, I felt hopeful. This could lead to the real killer. The judicial stationery confirmed my hunt was inside the courthouse, but the dead body had already clued me in to that. I had the correct starting place. But Hunter didn't look hopeful.

"Sorry, Toots. Donnettelli's gavel places you at the murder scene." Hunter's voice was at the seductive-whisper level. "You and I both know killers like to keep mementos."

"And leave myself a blooming-blue note with it? Not likely. Not credible. Not common-sensical. Okay, that wasn't really a word." I had to get as creative as this message maker.

Hunter was documenting everything. (I did love a man who knew his job.) "Besides staff, who has your stationery?" he asked.

"My personal staff, but they all work here. Any number of people in the courthouse would have had access to it. For all I know, that stationery could have come out of courthouse recycling or the print shop who made it." I rubbed my temples.

"And the cryptic 'follow the money'?"

"*Follow the money* is a commonplace theme in any corruption scheme. When my law students don't understand why laws are slow to change, or there is a wrong outcome, I say: 'follow the money.'" With the promise of buying Margo a colossal dustpan, I asked her to help Hunter put all the drawer shrapnel in one bag and seal it, and then wash his hair.

I needed a shot of espresso, hairspray, and a new plan.

CHAPTER NINETEEN

My immediate plan was to develop a list of everyone who had access to Donnettelli's gavel. But the likelihood of developing a narrow list kept swirling around my brain. Gavels are generally left atop the bench, and security cameras would've captured the pilfering. It was clear the gavel went missing after his murder because otherwise it would've been missed. And, it must've been swiftly swiped by someone with knowledge of courtroom security. That narrowed the suspects to those who also had access to the Judge's suite, which included court security, cleaning people, each Judge's staff, and attorneys who hung around Judge Donnettelli's suite.

This task was formidable, but I was up to the challenge. I had no choice. I twirled my stylist chair round and round and let it mesmerize me long enough to confirm that I was capable of solving this murder one logical step at a time.

Everyone in the salon made a collective gasp. The sound broke me out of contemplation mode and into surprise mode. I looked up and saw a familiar face.

No wonder there was gasping.

The newcomer lifted a little three-finger wave like a timid second grader. He was male, yet strikingly female—more female than at our last encounter, when I would not have guessed he was gay. It was clear now, and I was happy he'd found himself. Blue-black hair, with a royal-blue streak in it, pale flesh, naturally dark-red lips, Mediterranean-blue eyes, and lashes longer than Carlye's on her best day.

"Davis?" That was the only name I could remember. It had been several years since he'd—or was it now she?—completed my Deferred Felony Drug Probation program.

"Honey. I can call you that now 'cause you're not my Judge, right?" He paused, tucked down his fingers from princess-wave position and continued.

I wanted to explain *Nicoletta* was preferred, but he wasn't in listening-stance and danced forward.

"That's why I'm here, Honey." One hand dropped to an uber-mobile hip and firmly rested there. "I owe you for believing in me after my little drug oversight."

We shared a few reflective seconds about his blip of felony drug possession and use, but he'd worked hard, gained amazing insight, and earned a nonpublic record.

Davis set down a large, professional black bag. He appeared prepared to move into a station.

"You changed my life, Honey. I'm here to assist you as long—as you need me."

He touched a joy-spot in my heart. "You've blossomed!"

"Davis isn't my first name anymore, Honey. It's officially my last name." He fluffed up his silk royal-blue-and-white scarf, coordinated perfectly with white t-shirt, black vest, and skinny royal, blue leggings. A diamond stud in each ear sparkled.

I watched his confidence with the same heartfelt pride I had for my own children. "And your last name—"

"Dropped it, legally when I came out. When I announced I'm a gay man and proud of it, there was a lot of abandonment, so that's what I did, too." He tucked one foot behind the other and performed a primo curtsey.

My grin couldn't stay hidden. "Makes sense." On probation he had been practical, used common sense, and enjoyed humor. He'd outperformed.

"Dawn Dinkie-Do Davis, at your service. Everyone calls me Dinkie-Do."

"I'm delighted," I said. "Ah, can I ask you—why Dinkie-Do?"

He blushed and bent his head toward his right shoulder. "I earned that name working on hair in New York. Anyone in New York who wanted hair that stands out adopted me as their stylist because I don't create any dinky hairdos. It just stuck, and it's me." He twirled.

"Makes sense," I said—again. And for him it did.

"I owe you. I got a future 'cause of you." Dinkie-Do batted his lashes and came in closer.

"You earned that release," I said.

"It's like this," Dinkie-Do said. "You told me I could overcome, but I had to release my secret. You saw it. I'd been hiding behind my drugs. I came out and became who I'm supposed to be. Then I fled to New York, where I am accepted." He gave *accepted* its full three syllables.

"All good," I said. I listened more closely.

"I graduated design school," Dinkie-Do said. "Got into fashion. Worked at *Marie Claire* and *Cosmopolitan* magazines." He did a charming modest head tilt. "Jobs in fashion didn't work because they figured I should be Queen of the hair and makeup team."

"Then should it be 'she'—I mean, what's your preference?"

I saw Hunter enter the workspace and sit at my station. I shot him a sharp look and hoped he understood not to comment.

Dinkie-Do didn't miss a beat. "I'm a 'he' with a flair, but I take no offense if anyone refers to me as 'she.' Like you say, it's all good." He did a demure little face side-turn and enlarged his eyes for a second. His face was like an amusement park full of motion and surprises. His fingernails fluttered in glittery royal blue that matched his hair.

"You're here." I raised both hands as if my team had just scored a touchdown. Maybe we had.

"I returned to school for hair, makeup, nails. Honey, I do it all," he said. "Jobs waiting for me on Project Runway and at *Marie Claire* magazine." He paused and swirled an index finger around the room like his private magic wand. "But when I read about you and your oh-so-elegant salon and the oh-so-large murder headlines, I knew you needed me."

Just then Carlye huffed in from the back entrance and tossed her satchel bag on her station. She gave Dinkie-Do an exaggerated once-over with her eyes, but somehow her whole body was involved. "Can't turn my back for one minute. Competition for clients is stiff, just like the streets."

Dinkie-Do side-winded a coy look to Carlye and proceeded. "Honey, you need my Dinkie-Do magic til you're finished with this here murder mess."

I couldn't help but give him my warmest expression. Eye wrinkles be damned. He was here to help. "Magic?"

"To be legit I need salon hours and a portfolio of pictures, so I get the big New York gig, not just because the editor-in-chief personally adores me."

That made sense to me. *He was adorable.*

He pointed at the station next to Carlye. "Gotta do things right. You taught me. No short cuts. I'll help you not worry about this fine salon. Together we'll make sure you turn a profit."

"Uh-uh, whoever you are." Carlye punctuated each syllable with a jerk of her head that made me fear for her neck. "That there's a bona fide working woman's station. And it's all mine. Hand's off."

"Settle down. No one's taking your station. There's an empty station next to you." I wanted to avoid a Technicolor catfight.

"Thank you, Honey. That's awesome." His voice flowed like warm cream rinse. He and his bag boogied to the station.

Carlye pointed a long finger at Dinkie-Do. "No, you did not. No one calls our Judge *Honey*. Least of all you."

Dinkie-Do stepped between stations and stood within Carlye's space. Eye to eye, he kept pace with her. The dual head-bobs were impressive.

"We'll work out your employment terms—" I called over.

Dinkie-Do and Carlye were facing each other in eye-dueling mode and ignored me. I decided the new station-mates would have to work it out and was confident they would when I heard Dinkie-Do, exclaim.

"My working with you is all set." He snapped his fingers, twirled, and opened his bag before Carlye could breathe out a vowel.

It was useless to give direction. The magic of the black robe was gone. Considering flying drawers and staff hiring themselves, my control was sketchy at best.

CHAPTER TWENTY

"Welcome, Dinkie-Do." I handed him a contract I'd quickly asked Trisha to print, then grinned. "Where are you staying?"

"I don't have me a place yet." Dinkie-Do batted his lashes and puckered his lips, then placed the paper across his heart.

I gripped the back of my stylist chair, where Hunter relaxed. "You let me know if I can help you find a place or if you need help with anything else to get settled."

"You are too kind." Dinkie-Do not only brightened, I swore he grew two inches.

"Carlye, you'll assist Dinkie-Do."

She harrumphed, and he smiled at her. "You have space," Dinkie-Do said. "I have time, know-how, and need. Win-win-win-win. Love it." He clapped his hands, unleashed his black bag, signed the contract, and handed me his framed license.

"Dinkie-Do?" Carlye faced him, one finger on her right hip, head-to-toe in leopard print. "I heard a lot of names on the street, but there ain't no one who'd survive a day wit that name."

He didn't look at her.

Dinkie-Do curtseyed to me. "Everyone in style in New York wants a Dinkie-Do."

"That's just silly—a grown man going around with a name where everybody thinks he ain't got a package to play with." Carlye shook her head. "Now that just ain't right."

Hmm. It's all about perspective. The world saw *me* as a killer. I studied the room. And right on time Margo, red gum a-crackling, returned a freshly shampooed Hunter to my station.

"Think of Dinkie-Do as one more person for Shazam to love," I said, then returned to the towel-headed Hunter.

Carlye mumbled toward Dinkie-Do, who was already fully engaged in decorating his station with all the elegance of a ballerina.

Time to focus on Hunter's hair and work *my* magic. I combed through it.

"I know you have a plan," Hunter said.

I snipped, combed, snipped some more.

My brain curled. "I have a plan to become a free woman." Finally, I could get to the real business of the day. "The records I—" But Detective Grayson suddenly loomed large in my airspace—and I dropped my shears and stooped to retrieve them.

"Which records would those be?" Grayson fist-bumped Hunter. Since my arrest, the arrival of *Detective Anyone* was a bad hair day walking.

Hunter spoke up. "I like my ears where they are." He took the shears away from me.

Like new-found brothers, Hunter and Detective Grayson aimed their collective boldness at me. Their bond electrified my tether. Damn.

Carlye swirled a hip at me. "No fair keepin' alla those men to yourself." She pouted red lips at two silent officers hovering behind Grayson.

"Dropped something." Detective Grayson reached under the edge of the floor cabinet, picked up a rolled paper tied with ribbon, and handed it to me.

It reminded me of a graduation diploma. I was just thrilled to be handed any paper that wasn't another damn warrant. It must've popped out of my workstation drawer with the rest of the mess.

"Thank you—" But as I spoke, my throat seized.

"What brings you here?" Hunter asked.

Grayson avoided Hunter and homed in on me, leaning forward like he could get me to confess something by his sheer intensity. "Strange activity on your GPS."

Before I could reopen my mouth, Hunter answered, "Can't be. I'm on guard duty, and I can show you a log of where she's been."

Detective Grayson squinted and scanned me head to toe and back. "Really?" He still didn't look away from me to Hunter. "Our transmission and the report suddenly had cyber-brain farts."

"Her ex hired me to watch her." Hunter mirrored Grayson's tone. "And, I can testify to every minute if you want to challenge her moves."

I needed to get into protective mode with an anti-crazy-male-banter cloud. I grabbed my hairspray and sprayed a cloud over me.

"You've been here all day?" Grayson pointed at me and twirled his finger to indicate the general area.

Ugh, I needed a hot shower to erase his over-obvious *have you had sex with her* tone. I sprayed more hairspray.

Grayson coughed and finally focused on Hunter. "She hasn't been anywhere but here?" He removed his yellow sports coat, revealing a white muscle shirt. He draped the jacket over his left arm, coughed again, and covered his nose.

Hairspray fumes. Good for evacuating vermin—I hoped.

Grayson reached into his inner jacket pocket and slapped a folded paper into Hunter's hand. "GPS printout."

"So what? You spot checked and found an inconclusive time period." Hunter returned the paper. "That error is on the tracker, not Nic."

"My job is to warn her." Grayson turned to me and spoke slowly. "Consider yourself warned."

"I was meaning to ask you, detective, isn't it a tad convenient that only my DNA was found on Donnettelli's gun?" But I buckled my lips before more spurted out.

"Negative. As expected, Donnettelli and his assistant's DNA were also found. We know assistants touch everything. You are a suspect, so confirmation of your DNA on the gun wasn't any surprise."

Inside behind my grown-up poker face, I was making a mocking ugly face at him.

He headed toward the front door but stopped and turned back to me. "You wouldn't know anything about exploding garbage behind Peter Dune's house—I mean the same night Donnettelli was killed?"

I told Hunter that Peter Dune was Donnettelli's Law Clerk and barhopping sidekick, and the objectionable detective got only: "Negative."

He looked at me like a fed-up dad looks at a misbehaving teen and left.

I pointed Hunter's butt back into the stylist chair. "You two are friends?" I asked.

"Promise you'll shear a straight line?" Hunter got comfortable. "Grayson and I have worked together some, and he drives a mean golf ball."

"I can live without him and his cronies." I untied then unrolled the paper Grayson had handed me. Two documents. I set them on Hunter's lap.

"By Jove, I spy a clue," he said.

I peered at the papers and lifted the top one. "Looks like a copy of Donnettelli's docket. A list of cases he would've heard that day."

"Meaning?"

"Law clerks use the docket list to note the final decision on each case to ensure the day's outcome is properly input into the Register of Actions, which becomes a public record." I took a closer look at the paper. "That's why the page is marked-up." I pointed to the handwritten notes.

Hunter peered closer at it. "There are marks like the paper has been crumbled. But who pulled it?"

I shook my head and pointed to the corner with the date.

"It's from a few weeks before he was killed. Looks like there were no criminal cases before him that day," Hunter said.

"Exactly right." I frowned. "This list is weird. Every one of these cases are big money or high profile."

"Doesn't sound weird. Rich people like to sue," Hunter said.

"But cases are assigned randomly," I explained. "On any given day, you'd expect to see a variety of kinds of cases. I don't think this many big, corporate money cases landing on one judicial docket could happen by accident."

"So Donnettelli's mess with the Manville case wasn't just him trying to bully you."

"Donnettelli's bullying, like his gruffness, allowed him to maneuver almost anything without further question by anyone." I grabbed the paper underneath. A copy of a bank deposit with my name on it. "One hundred thousand dollars?"

Hunter reviewed the slip, and his brows did something complicated. "That bank deposit with your name on it could point to motive—yours or someone else's. The docket could, too—if you were upset about it in any way—or maybe there is something that calls you into question."

"Not my motive—not my account."

"Maybe the bank slip was planted here to goad you into action?"

"Goad me into cleaning my drawer?"

"Maybe to upset you so much you'd do something to incriminate yourself," Hunter said.

I tossed the papers back onto Hunter's lap.

"I want to be clear." Hunter studied the pages. "You've never seen either document before today?"

"Never."

"You've said Donnettelli wasn't the brightest candle on the cake." Hunter waited.

"Even so, he wouldn't leave a bank slip around for anyone to pick out of the trash," I said. "We have a main shredder—budget didn't allow judges to have their own, but it's on next year's budget list to have one for every suite of offices. I know because I've asked for one every year and was denied." None of this made sense.

"Who has access to the shredding pile?"

"Just about everyone in the courthouse," I said, but decided to contemplate that answer more fully later.

"So, Your Honor, what does this tell you?"

"Multiple cases link Donnettelli and me together because they were assigned to one of us and then reassigned to the other. Essentially that means we both touched the file and it's likely we each made rulings, but that depends on the file. The bank deposit slip is ominous because it fits into 'follow the money,' but the money isn't mine." My head shook, my stomach turned, my mind wandered. I was anxious to compare the docket with the copies of the files I'd made. I needed to get inside Donnettelli's chambers to tear it apart.

Hunter leaned forward and whispered so only I could hear, "If this slip ties to you in any way, it's evidence that leads back to you being the murderer. It will look like you are part of a scheme to silence Donnettelli, so you could continue to profit from whatever he was into."

"That slip says nothing to me, means nothing to me, and it's not mine."

"It says payoff. It's circumstantial. And, it has your name on it, which speaks to ownership."

As soon as Hunter's haircut was done, I told Trisha where I was going and swore her to secrecy. Without interruption, Hunter and I would study the evidence until Sebastian joined us.

I had asked for evidence. Note to self: must be more specific. Damn it. Find evidence that leads away from me, not back to me.

CHAPTER TWENTY-ONE

Four city blocks from my salon, I slid into a booth in the Dublin Square Diner, and Hunter sat across from me. It was almost three, and the lunch crowd had dispersed, leaving the place quiet and private. We needed to scrutinize every possible way to interpret "follow the money" and where money and Donnettelli and I intersected.

The docket and deposit slip looked damning; could they have come from a friend? I had to figure out which money the mystery-clue-leaver meant for me to follow and whether it would lead to the real murderer. Sebastian had promised to text me as soon as his morning trial concluded, and I intended to have a plan in place before we next spoke.

Ever powerful, Hunter aimed a spoon at me. "You have a knack for trouble."

I bugged my eyes at him, and the waitress sauntered over, pad and pen in hand. We ordered food, she ogled Hunter, and he settled all his male boldness back in the booth. One nod from him dismissed her.

Back to me, he asked, "With Donnettelli—exactly what did you exchange?"

"A few ugly words—regularly, but nothing else—ever."

"His staff is still employed by the court?"

"They're assisting visiting judges with Donnettelli's docket until the election in November. The County will fill his position then." I made a mental reminder to charm Donnettelli's former judicial assistant. We'd always gotten along. I'd ask her about enemies, stalkers, and threats. And I'd try to get a copy of his schedule book. But I knew she was loyal to him, even dead. To get her to help me I was going to need some serious chocolate.

"About this exploding candy and confetti," I asked, "was this docket and deposit slip a real clue from someone trying to help me?"

"If it were an enemy, Toots, it wouldn't have been flying Skittles. You're a pariah. Nobody but me is willing to get close to you," he said.

I gazed past him and smiled at solid muscle under Australian leather, my Sebastian, in rapid approach. He slid in next to me, kissed me, and said, "Good to see you."

Hunter gave me the grown-up equivalent of the teenage *whatever* look.

Sebastian tossed his briefcase onto the seat, then placed a curious manila envelope in front of me. He pointed to the envelope. "Doll, that's a gift from the prosecutor in my current trial." His Australian accent warmed me in every situation. I introduced the men, chugged ice water, and focused on the envelope.

After Sebastian tipped his Crocodile Dundee hat toward Hunter, and the men conducted a brief male-bonding ritual, Sebastian looked at me. "I've got good oil."

"How good is this information?" I lifted the envelope.

"Buffet first?" Sebastian grinned.

So not that good. I set the envelope down.

"I'm hungry," Hunter said and spoke pointedly to Sebastian. "There's a free parking space out front where you can park that hat." He stood and headed for the buffet.

Sebastian made his eyes big at me. "A hat hater?" He removed it and tossed it atop his briefcase.

Sebastian's Australian accent and musky Dior scent soothed me; still, I needed a little ice water, not necessarily in the glass.

As we walked toward the buffet, I whispered, "You didn't text. How'd you find me? Slip my staff truth serum?"

"Trisha caved like a newborn joey." Sebastian grinned.

We filled plates and bowls, and back at the table, we all arranged our plates around the envelope.

Sebastian dipped his head at it. "Open it."

I picked it up, reversed the metal prongs, flipped the flap, pulled out a smaller envelope with a stack of papers, and thumbed through them. Bank accounts. Bank deposits. All in my name. All opened in the six months before Donnettelli was killed.

Just then the server clattered in with drinks, Sebastian helped distribute them, and the server melted over him with giggles.

Hunter crushed a bag of oyster crackers and dumped it atop his bowl of broccoli soup. "Crocodile's staying?" Hunter jabbed a fork into his salad.

"We've attorney-client business to discuss." Sebastian popped a grape in his mouth.

When Hunter's wandering Nike pressed up from my ankle to my knee, I crossed my legs, and the shoe disappeared. He wasn't playing fair; he'd said he didn't mix business and pleasure, so why the sudden touching? But I was so hungry I wanted to dive into my soup and cry *yippee,* while someone shredded the obnoxious paper in front of me. All mouths but mine were filled, and all eyes were focused on the papers in my hands.

Sebastian donned his take-charge lawyer face and asked Hunter, "Think you could rack off for a bit? I need a moment with my client."

Hunter leaned back and stretched his long arms across the back of the booth. "Relax, chew, practice wearing a real man's hat."

Sebastian tossed a grape onto Hunter's salad plate.

Before Sebastian could toss another, Hunter pulled up a one-hundred-dollar bill and slapped it in front of Sebastian. "Count me into the attorney-client relationship."

I was witnessing a boy version of a girl fight, but I felt more like turf than a girl.

Sebastian squeezed my knee under the table, and I relaxed some. His steady gaze triggered me to check my clothing to ensure it hadn't evaporated. His voice was low. "Any conflict I should know about?"

Between me and Hunter? "Nary a discouraging word." I looked back and forth between the men, our booth a fog of pheromones.

Sebastian pocketed the bill. "Consider this lunch meeting a confidential chinwag."

"Excuse me?" Hunter asked.

"Aussie slang for a chat." I shifted uncomfortably, and it wasn't because my interpreter skills were getting their usual workout. "As for these bogus bank accounts, I have no explanation." I thwacked the pages onto the table. "These were invented." I picked out the tossed-in grape from Hunter's salad and popped it into my mouth, and I prayed.

My man friend didn't miss a beat. "Your name, address, and Social Security number appear on each account."

"One hundred thousand dollars?" Hunter reached into his pocket for the marked-up docket we'd found. He held it so Sebastian and I could see it.

"The docket shows the result of cases," I said. "The writing in blue ink notes what happened in court. It's used to update the Register of Actions."

"The official record," Hunter said, as if maybe Attorney Sebastian didn't know what the Register of Actions was. *Ass.*

Hunter pulled out the bank deposit slip we'd reviewed earlier. "I'm curious why these deposits were made on the same day a few of these cases were dismissed."

I studied the docket and the bank slip. "Coincidence?" I hoped so.

But Hunter frowned. "In the clerk's office, Nic and I looked up these files. Plaintiff in each case seemed to have a viable case. But the cases were dismissed by the Judge."

"Judges don't always get it right. That's why we have a Court of Appeals." I wanted to state that for the record, but my voice was half-hearted because the dismissing Judge was Judge Jurisa Haddes. And I was biased.

Hunter handed the papers to Sebastian, who turned toward me and had the nerve to ask me, "Payoff?"

"How could it be a payoff to me when I was already gone, couldn't make any judgment for or against them? I've never willingly associated with him. Besides, Jurisa dismissed the case, not me." I pushed the papers away. "Trust me or leave me. Both of you."

Sebastian reached an arm around my waist and squeezed me closer to him. "We're on your side, but the tough questions need to be asked by us, not those fool detectives."

"Think about it," Hunter said. "Your case. Your decision. Someone was made very happy—winner pays you off—even if it takes him six months to do so. That's what those detectives are thinking."

I covered my face like a small child in hiding. I wanted my protective hairspray, and for a few silent seconds, I imagined spraying it all over me.

CHAPTER TWENTY-TWO

Sebastian studied the paper and bank deposit slip we'd found at the salon, and Hunter reviewed the documents Sebastian brought.

"Obvious pattern." Hunter flipped pages. "This prosecutor's gift feels more like a noose."

"Blimey, at least we didn't have to wait for it."

"Twelve accounts with one hundred thousand dollars in each. One account opened every other week for six months. And, this took a lot of planning and coordination because each account was filled over eleven weeks to avoid the IRS rule about reporting cash deposits over ten thousand dollars." Hunter finger-pounded the pages. "Toots, you haven't missed a bank within a mile." There was admiration in my keeper's voice.

"Prosecutor could make the argument that this money came from Donnettelli in some kind of scheme, and when he wouldn't pay you more, you shot him," Sebastian said.

I grimaced. "Not mine." I tried not to wail. "Banks have cameras. Check them."

"Wire transfers," Hunter said. "And eleven of these accounts were opened before Donnettelli's murder, the final one the day he was murdered."

"Then check all my phone lines, computer lines, whatever you want. Not mine," I said with less force than I'd hoped to exude.

"No need to sound deflated." Hunter whistled. "This date, four weeks before his death, does match Donnettelli's deposit of one hundred thousand dollars."

Okay, inflated again. "One hundred thousand dollars? But it was just one deposit, not eleven, like my fake accounts?"

"Right, likely because he deposited a check or some other instrument, not cash." Hunter lifted the bank papers, nodded and set them back down.

"Still the amount, one hundred thousand dollars is just like the fake account in my name." To frame me? For what? By whom and why? Donnettelli wasn't about to give me a thousand large. He was too cheap, unless maybe he had a million reasons to give it to me, or maybe needed me out of the way? I shivered to the core. "Donnettelli wouldn't tie me to him, and that's what this money does."

Hunter cleared his throat. "Makes Sebastian's theory more than likely. I bet that's their game plan; the deposit slip in your name and this deposit in Donnettelli's name gives the appearance you two were in cahoots."

"Look again. No cahoots. Not a single cahoot. No proof our bank accounts are tied." I folded my arms and waited. I said what the men were thinking. "Except the like deposit amount." And there it was: a cahoot, that led to me.

"Setup. Smells like a deal between accomplices, and that would leave a trail." Sebastian sounded lawyerly. "We need to find that trail."

I choked, and Hunter offered me his water.

"Bank accounts are opened, cases are shuffled, and somehow, money is made—lots of money." Sebastian looked at me. "If the scheme falls apart, you're set up to take the fall. Doesn't matter how many crimes. They've stacked it all on you."

"Murder, too." I lowered my voice. "Makes 'follow the money' more meaningful."

"Right. The setup is for every crime associated with the scoundrels." Hunter looked satisfied with his summation.

"Hey." I used my own attorney voice. It was nice to have a variety of tools to pull from. "We need to get bank video, analyze signature cards, talk to every damn bank employee, and now, or I'm dead behind bars."

"Too right," Sebastian said.

Hunter rubbed his jaw as if I'd punched it. "But how do they profit from a dead Donnettelli?"

My turn to point silverware. "Donnettelli wanted me to change an Order. If I didn't, it would cost a large corporation millions of dollars." I spoke quietly.

"They'd already let people die, so I refused to change the Order." I paused.

"Donnettelli changed it anyway," I said, "but left my signature page attached to the Order."

"Both the corporation and their insurance company saved millions," Sebastian said.

Hunter jumped in. "And I bet Donnettelli scored a bonus under the table and branded you as the one who signed the offensive Order."

I agreed. "That's the name the media prints. The rest isn't seen. He gets the payoff and the goodwill in an election year."

"But if Manville was paying off Donnettelli," Sebastian said, "I'm betting this wasn't the bloke's first buy-a-verdict rodeo."

Hunter winked at me. "Maybe some victim figured it out and got mad."

"A victim couldn't get into Donnettelli's chambers without being captured on the video," I said. "A victim wouldn't have a way to save that video of me shooting Donnettelli with my finger gun."

"It had to be someone who works in the courthouse, who could get into the judicial wing and knew how to avoid the cameras," Sebastian said.

"But according to the papers, everyone with access was accounted for—at the poker party-turned brawl, was with a spouse, or was sunning on a beach." Hunter leaned over the table at me. "I mean except you."

Ass. "That's the reality. Nobody could have killed Donnettelli," I said.

"It was right rude to bury the bludger, then," Sebastian said.

These guys were going to sit here and crack wise until I shuffle off to the big house. Time to step up the pace. "We need to do a few things: police can get video of anyone who entered the building that day. If we can get a copy, Hunter can interview half, and I can interview half. One of us needs to contact the ME and find out how he placed the time of death."

"You can't flit around Lansing like you're Wonder Woman," Sebastian said.

I figure he chose Wonder Woman because we both have hair that doesn't move. "I don't flit." I gave him my serious face. "I stroll elegantly. And I intend to get answers before I get locked up."

Hunter said he should be the one to talk to the witness since he was "a man of the people," but he allowed that Sebastian and I could come, too, if we wanted.

Not a trace of humor remained in Hunter's handsome face. "If Donnettelli was killed by a corporation covering its greedy tracks—maybe you're next."

We sat in silence for a minute and reconsidered possibilities. Then from inside his jacket, Hunter pulled out the evidence bags from my workstation-drawer explosion, and I told Sebastian all about it.

Hunter crunched down more salad. "Some people like to believe the worst about others." He waggled his be-spinached fork at me. "And someone wants judges out of the way."

On overload, I didn't want to digest that conclusion. "But I'd already left the courthouse on my own."

Then I saw it. "If I report the Orders were changed and someone in power believes me, then whatever Donnettelli's *scheme* is could be exposed. And even if I was right, these twelve bank accounts discredit me as a Judge who was bought, and it will look like I got paid off to kill Donnettelli. Either way—I get a lifetime of lockup." Refusing to blubber, I picked up the smaller sealed envelope, ripped it open, and spilled folded pages from AOL.

A subpoena fulfilled by AOL. Kikkra@aol.com with a list of corresponding emails from the twelve bank accounts. "I use Yahoo. I don't know anything about AOL. I have no password to this account." I flung the pages at Hunter. More lies.

He compared the twelve bank statements with the emails. "These begin *January through July*—" He tapped a note into his phone as he spoke. "My IT man will link these to a computer."

"Forensic study will take time and cost a fortune," I said. "I walked out mid-January."

"They wouldn't have opened accounts earlier because of tax filings and year-end statements," Hunter said.

"The accounts and AOL are too obvious, too coincidental. Planted," Sebastian said. "Leave that task to law enforcement and their warrants."

"Unless we can prove they're planted, they're hair-frizzing, media-frenzy, put-me-behind-bars-for-life evidence." Those people who liked to believe the worst about others were going to be ecstatic.

CHAPTER TWENTY-THREE

It was well after five o'clock when I sneaked back into my office, back into my chair, and Trisha was already plodding toward me. I swiveled, crossed my legs, pasted on a grin. Seeing her open smile made me feel good all over.

"Was your disappearance okay?" she asked.

"Like removing nail polish by taking the whole nail, without anesthesia."

She placed her hand on her heart and fluttered her long fingers. "Oh Judge, I know just how witnesses feel. Attorney Pearce is a holy show. Why don't you just run off with him and forget all this business?"

I controlled my face. "Charms the words right out of you, doesn't he? I've seen you with Sebastian." I tried not to laugh.

She pressed an age-spotted hand to her cheek. "He gives me a bit of a reddener—I mean to feel that raw sexual ride. 'Tis lost on you young ones." Her shoulders rose, and she wriggled. She was about to liquefy.

Okay, now parts of my brain needed to be poked out. I grabbed a comb and mirror to realign my natural thought process. I backcombed my bangs, held the red-and-black can, hit the nozzle and sprayed. Ahhh, back to reality.

"I didn't tell anyone else where'd you'd gone," Trisha said. "Judge Haddes and her Law Clerk Keldon McKean stopped in 'to pay their respects' and say they 'know you didn't kill Judge Donnettelli.' Reception still smells like her *Chloe* perfume. Why can't she spray just a smidge? But still, I refused to say where you'd gone." She looked quite proud of herself.

I wondered what kind of omen that was. Jurisa had never bothered to cross the hall to see me before, and I didn't have time to think about her now. "Trisha, we need to figure out how and why I've ended up with twelve new bank accounts times one hundred thousand dollars."

She did a no-brainer shrug. "Himself—your benefactor."

"Ex-benefactor. Take Dex off the table. Think murder setup. Tomorrow, we research the accounts." *Who better to save me than me*, I wanted to add, but decided I needed to spare Trisha any more worry. She accepted the account list, tucked it inside her sweater, and returned to the reception desk.

Before I could start on the next task, Sebastian phoned. He and Hunter had met with the Medical Examiner to garner the details I'd wanted. Sebastian said, "ME began with the room temperature—then added 1.5 degrees per hour until 98.6 degrees was reached."

"So he determined time of death with certainty?" I was trying to head calculate, but my brain was rejecting the numbers; I needed a calculator, graph paper, and caffeine.

"Yes and no," Sebastian said.

"Excuse me?" My brain screamed: *Hairspray please.*

"Some factors can speed up rigor mortis, like extremely violent exertion prior to death, and alkaloid poisoning."

"Unlikely, unless lifting extra cream cheese on his bagel counts as exertion."

Sebastian cleared his throat by way of objecting to my interrupting him. Then he said, "Heat speeds up rigor mortis and cold slows it down."

"I always complained the damn courthouse was either too hot or too cold." I'd try again. "Was the ME able to determine time of death?"

"Given those and other variables, he placed death between two and five in the morning. Gunshot was heard at approximately four."

"Bring your math skills and show me all this on paper." I beat my nails on my lips to stop my mouth from spewing vulgarities at the dead bully, the legal system, and the medical community. The night Donnettelli was killed, like most every night, I'd been in bed and sleeping long before two and long past five. Damnation, my boyfriend was out of the country and my only alibi was Jimmy Jack.

CHAPTER TWENTY-FOUR

The next morning, I'd barely gotten myself in and shut the door to the parking lot when Carlye appeared wearing an expression that said: *Threat level Orange and rising.*

"There's an unmarked car parked out front, and I started thinking dirty words like *search warrant*—"

My hand shot up, palm forward, and I knew Carlye was familiar with that silent command. But she had a nose for police. In her former work, she'd had to be careful.

"I'll shear those detectives." I grabbed my phone from my back pocket but wished I could use it to ask Scotty to beam me up.

"I ain't fond of most cops," Carlye said. "But the salon is already full of paying customers, and my nose hairs are activating." She scrunched her nose as if to prove it. "My nose don't flare like—"

I texted Sebastian and instructed Carlye. "Keep the search-warrant rumor tucked inside that tingling nose. If you can't hold back, stay in my office." I unlocked it for her.

Sebastian returned my text. *Anything you say or do can and will be used against you. Behave.*

Damn lawyer.

Don't cause bond revocation.

Mmmm. Good point.

I texted Rosa in the café to see what was happening over there and didn't receive a response. Damn.

Carlye pointed at her chest. "Look at me. I'm breaking into one big hive." She twisted outstretched arms. "I don't own any clothes that match hives."

Stomping back toward her station, she called over her shoulder, "Dinkie-Do's in here offering ever'body a *Dinkie-Do Special.* And I ain't never seen so much white around customer eyeballs."

I refused to worry until those eyeballs fell out, and the inmates used them to shoot marbles. After asking Trisha to organize the mob, I sneaked out the back door and aimed my boots toward Hunter's Escalade.

I tapped on his passenger window. By the time Hunter opened up, my insides were marshmallow goop. I climbed in and shut the door. "Not a social visit."

Hunter locked the doors. "Some serious suits have stormed your place of business. Shall I hit the gas, Mugsy?"

"Why didn't you swoop inside to protect me? I escaped before they were able to serve me, but I have no doubt they are searching every crevice. They could be in there for hours. You had time to intervene and stop this nonsense." I folded my arms and leaned against the door to face him.

He thrust his chest out and imitated my voice. "You're in total control of this investigation."

"Got it." My pride scratched like a prickly pear going down. "You officially have my permission to assist when needed. I'm not sure who to trust. If it's a question of money—"

He wide grinned. "Acknowledging trust. That's a start."

I decided to invent an all-purpose attention getter, the new *hit-slap*. Not to be confused with the old standby *bitch-slap*. It would go on the books as a new kind of assault, and by the time anyone did anything about it, the *hit-slap*s would be delivered to the obnoxious males who needed them. "Let's just say—no reason not to trust you."

"Your ex pays me plenty, Toots." Hunter intentionally drew out his voice, so every syllable resounded in me.

In his soft manly gaze, I saw the teenager I'd loved. His casual seated position was one that, in my youth, I would have climbed upon and begun a welcome makeout session. I was happy with Sebastian, my adult choice, despite Hunter's constant reminders of how good we'd been together. And I couldn't get it out of my mind that I wouldn't have bolted to Dex if Hunter and I had been right.

Hunter squeezed my hand.

But I freed it, pulled back, and stuck it underneath my knee, between my crossed legs. Damn. Chemistry as good as I remembered. We had a good history to remember together.

But I was too comfortable, and the longer I sat, more old memories flooded in. Hunter and I ended up talking an hour and a half, and I felt drained, but in a good way. Way more peaceful. After another minute, Hunter squeezed my knee and reached for his door.

"Let's find out what the detectives want." He opened his door, rounded the truck, and opened mine.

I'd be okay never finding out, but I hopped out. "This is harassment." I wobbled, and Hunter grabbed my arm to steady me, and we crossed the street. "Maybe they just need haircuts," I said half-heartedly.

"It's a battle of misinformation, you know," Hunter said. "On purpose."

I'd heard testimony like this in cases before me: Someone was purposefully misdirecting law enforcement. I knew enough to be a quasi-detective, conduct my own secret search, plot my own strategy to save my destiny, but the bad guys had an advantage. They knew no restraints. Without the lying and stealing and killing, I wondered how well I could penetrate their defenses.

"Let's walk slowly so we don't look like we are trying to interfere or give them any reason to think I'm worried," I said.

Hunter stopped walking and turned toward me. "Toots, you're not worried about them finding anything are you?"

"Seriously? Whose side are you on? If I was worried, I would have stayed and watched instead of hiding out with you," I said. "I know the turbo streak that runs inside these pastel detectives. They solve crimes first and look at evidence later. I can't, I mean we can't, do anything that might trigger them to dance down a wrong avenue."

"Okay, Toots. Baby steps." He looped his arm through mine, and we strolled toward the salon.

When we got inside, the place was in full gab-and-glam. Eight stylist chairs were working, and the waiting area was nearly full.

Trisha handed me a mug of coffee. She had a line of paying and scheduled customers. Margo was refilling the coffee station. Hunter, one step behind me, placed his hand on my shoulder. And from a corner in the reception room, a pair of detectives surged toward us.

I had a sudden urge to pee, but managed to turn off the neon *OPEN* sign. I wanted scheduled business to continue without the disruption of any more walk-ins while I dealt with the detectives. Before I could speak, the pastel-green-jacketed detective fluttered a paper in my face.

"Search warrants."

"Maybe you should consider search warrants for the courthouse and leave me the hell alone." I thin-lipped the detectives.

All I wanted was for them to disappear, and if that didn't work, I wanted them to get done, get nothing, and get out.

Deadish eyes fired back at me, and the detectives flashed badges—like I might have not recognized them from the hundreds of times I'd seen them in court, and—oh yeah, they'd arrested me on Friday.

"We've conducted numerous interviews. You are the common negative thread in the Judge Donnettelli scenario." Detective Grayson's voice was monotone. His face was expression-free. "Search applies to the whole building. Uniforms are searching the café, too. In your absence, we served your manager. We've just finished." He chin-nodded at the reception desk.

Poor Trisha.

Hunter stepped forward and grabbed the ugly documents.

The men jungle-glowered at each other, and Detective Grayson re-flashed his badge *to his golfing buddy*. "Official business." In case Hunter had been napping half a minute ago.

"Make a wrong turn on your way to Hollywood?" Hunter tossed the search warrant back at Grayson. "Your talent's wasted here."

"Go re-roll your PI license in Silly Putty. If you interfere in this investigation that's all it's going to be good for." Grayson returned his attention to me. "Maybe you want to tell your sentry here the felony penalties of obstructing. You used to be pretty good at that."

Hunter had it right. Hollywood was a good name for Detective Grayson, in his Miami Vice, Sonny Versace knock-off suit. Fredericks, in his black leather vest getup, remained curiously silent. He was Tony Baretta minus Fred the Cockatoo. I needed to find a channel that played '70s and '80s detective shows. That and throwing buttered popcorn at the screen was on my secondary agenda for fun.

"Do what you will, but don't interfere with my customers, ever." I emphasized the 'ever.' I felt taller. And in control. A little.

But the detectives ignored me, poked about the salon, and eventually headed to the café. Grayson called back to Hunter, "We're still on for the Traverse City Open, right?"

Hunter nodded. The detectives disappeared into the café. Uniformed officers followed, and anticipating a mess, I wiggled a finger at Hunter—*the traitor.*

But before we could go to the café, Trisha cackled loudly and pointed me to the opposite end of the reception area, near the end of the product shelves.

I joined her and found Dinkie-Do had commandeered a table and turned the end of the room into a makeup counter. A camera and a small printer sat on the corner table ledge. And a large photo album lay open. I hadn't had time to fill it with opening-day photos.

I hugged Dinkie-Do. "Aside from pilfering from my office, how'd you do all of this so quickly?" I flipped through several pages in the album of before-and-after customers who'd scribbled-in reviews. Dinkie-Do and Margo planned to enter them in my new website. "You're miraculous."

"It's been a busy day, and this is just a little distraction from the Domineering Duo," Dinkie-Do said. "Trisha and Margo helped." Dinkie-Do shoulder bobbed. "Every waiting customer got a free makeover." With a ta-da flair, he showed off his talent one woman at time.

"Incredible." Dinkie-Do was to makeup what Edward Scissorhands was to hair.

"Honey, you'll need to reorder items, but not too many. I've decided to develop my own makeup line, and you'll want to stock it. I've been thinking on it for a while."

"Let me guess, shadows to match your blue hair streak?"

He waved and swiveled his hips, and five ladies giggled. "Of course, and you'll carry it here. And on the website."

Eventually I'd regain full control of my salon and my life, but it wouldn't be now, and it wouldn't be soon. Seeing every female in the salon jumping up to ensure her place in line, I realized just what a gem the idea was and wanted to recommend Dinkie-Do for a Mensa membership.

"Trisha can schedule as many makeovers as you can fit in." I wondered what a Dinkie-Do color pallet would look like. I envisioned the Tiller Girls, flamingoes, peacocks, and a sandstorm with a rainbow in the bluest sky. If anyone could sell it, Dinkie-Do could.

My immediate secret need was hairspray, a pedicure, and a total-body massage while eating a barrel of chocolate-covered coffee beans frozen in coffee ice cream. I had to stop my inner screaming.

Trisha nested a mug of coffee in my hand. "Dinkie-Do is his own fierce force." She popped an earbud in one ear for music and a small blue earplug in the other ear. No wonder she could work in chaos without distraction.

I distracted myself by chitchatting with customers before Detective Grayson swaggered back into the salon swinging a sealed evidence bag, and Hunter shadowed him. I felt like a client suffering serious perm burns.

I fixated on the evidence bag.

"Finished? Curfew comes quickly." I purposefully had a deep sneer in my voice as a reminder of how inconvenienced I was. Even if Grayson didn't get it, I felt better. And sometimes it was just about a girl feeling better.

"Pocket calendars." Grayson held up the bag.

I waited for the brilliant explanation that was sure to follow.

"Calendars from the banks—the hundred-thousand-dollar account—banks," Hunter said.

"Not mine," I said.

"They were under your magazines on your tables in your building," Grayson said. "And we all know criminals like mementos. On your way out of the bank—easy to grab."

"We hardly ever strip-search patrons." I set my mug down with a clunk and asked Trisha to lock up tonight because I had a thing for the afternoon. I ignored the Hollywood Twins and the mess they were making, then returned to my office, grabbed my bag, and exited stage left.

The near-sighted creeps would soon search my car, my home, damn, even my underwear drawer. My immediate mission was clear: find out who planted the damn calendars.

I needed a step-by-step plan. It was someone who knew me, could plant evidence, *and* was linked to Donnettelli. My first thought was Jurisa. She and Keldon had both been there, but surely Trisha would have watched them the whole time. I'd scour the appointment book to consider everyone who'd entered my salon.

How the hell was I going to find whodunnit?

CHAPTER TWENTY-FIVE

When I returned to work the next day, my poor Ratification Hair Salon looked like the countless before-and-after search warrant photos I'd seen. I texted staff about restoring the salon to order and discovered they were already en route.

Soon the place was salon professional enough to satisfy Vidal Sassoon.

I stepped into the hallway and smelled familiar cologne.

An Australian-flavored whisper came: "Doll, is it safe to join you, or are you still in clean-up mode?"

Sebastian's timing, like his looks, equaled perfection. Mine, disastrous. I grabbed his oversized manly hand and silently led him behind the door into the secret hallway between the café and the salon. I turned the lock and flicked on the lights.

Sebastian faced me with a hair of space between us, an arm raised over my head, and his fingertips resting on the wall. "Miss me?" He grinned and bent his head toward me like a date that ends in breakfast.

My mind was in sync with his; my body had been there for hours. But the lawyer-wants-to-stay-out-of-prison side had serious issues to resolve and control to regain. "Have you found any evidence to show detectives those bank accounts aren't mine, and the bank calendars were planted?"

"Negative." He ran the tip of a finger over my bottom lip.

I forced myself to concentrate on staying out of jail. "I mean did you point out the obvious, like the money had been wired, so I wouldn't have stepped inside their damn banks? And if I were that stupid—which I'm not—why risk twelve banks? It's over ten grand, so I might as well put it all in one account."

"Doll, to open the accounts you had to sign the signature cards and present your ID—in person." His brows wrinkled up like waving flags, and he kissed me. "Somebody had to have an ID card with your name on it."

I came up for air with new hope. "Forged signatures. We'll be able to see the culprit on the bank video they recover."

"I've requested the bank videos," Sebastian said.

"But this AOL email was used to open the accounts, so all the monthly bank statements are going to the perp. Can we put a stop to that?'

"Right now," he said, "we could discuss the consequences of taking responsibility for those email accounts—together in the shower."

I reached up, snatched his Dundee hat from his head and ran my fingers through thick waves of bleached-blond hair. "I'm ahead of you."

Sebastian grabbed my hand. "Doll, you know my motto—next time you dare to travel under the hat, there are other things that come off, as well."

"You know my motto—everything that stands up must be sprayed down." I giggled. His Dior blended perfectly with my Lauren. "Care to check the appointment book with me in my office, call Hunter—?"

"I can check things all by myself." He ran his fingers over my t-shirt outlining my breasts.

I tingled hot and cold, up and down, and he kissed the side of my neck.

But then I remembered my priorities. I barely pushed him away and let my hands drop. "Imagine me and you when I'm tether-free," I whispered in his ear. "Right now, you're my lawyer." I ran my nails up the back of his shirt and stepped toward my office. "And later tonight we'll explore other roles."

"Cops are obligated to turn over every piece of evidence." Strong arms pulled me back and held me. "Think like a lawyer, not a defendant."

I wanted to turn myself completely over to him, but if we missed a step, I could end up wearing an orange jumpsuit. There'd be plenty of playtime, I hoped.

He finally filled me in on the guys' plan to meet the witness the police had interviewed—the one who claimed to have heard the shot that killed Donnettelli. Sebastian answered a few minor questions on our way downtown.

We met Hunter outside Troppo's Restaurant—a great place to eat—and we sauntered casually down Michigan Avenue toward the front of a large, well-kept brick building, where people assist the homeless and others who need help. The men had tossed their jackets and ties in the cars, and I was in jeans, t-shirt, and cowboy boots.

It didn't take long to find Stella—the witness in the police report who'd heard the early morning gun shot. Grayson had further described her for Hunter: just over four feet tall, and dressed all in white, including long sleeves in the July heat, long blond hair, and a gray and white puppy in an oversized shoulder bag. She spoke loudly to the pup. Yep, we weren't going to miss her.

Right away, she took an unexplained dislike to me and cussed me out in some language I couldn't identify, so I stepped back. Diplomat Hunter—man of the people—strode in to try, but she accused him of letting his eyes wander. I nearly did a jig when it became clear she liked my Australian man. We were jointly relieved.

She said that on the fifteenth, she'd heard a shot fired inside the courthouse at about four in the morning.

When Sebastian asked what she was doing outside before sunup, she said she lived on Kalamazoo near the courthouse, and her puppy needed to relieve himself. In the early morning darkness she let him run around her yard, enclosed by chain-link fencing. While waiting for him to do his business the shot rang into the quiet of the night causing her to grab her puppy and lock herself inside her home. Sebastian certainly couldn't argue with that. He thanked her for her candor, handed her a card attached to a wad of bills to buy puppy food, and left.

Hunter had tried to suggest someone offered her money to tell that story, but that's as far as he got before she thought he was calling her a hooker, and she tried to sic her puppy on him.

We retreated to my office, and I asked Hunter to find out for me where Stella went to eat, shop, or hang out. Meanwhile, Sebastian and I spent hours researching names from the appointment book, and he called Trisha in and out of my office to decipher her shorthand.

When Trisha began to wring her hands, I asked her what was wrong and she said, "We've had a bubble of birds and blokes from the courthouse make appointments like you wanted, but they're not all polite."

"Who's been rude to you? I can still give a good straighten-up talking to."

"That Noel, he's a quick-talker. He acts like it's my fault I can't understand him because I'm too old. He's the one who mumbles."

"Noel Lemmon?" I peered into the book. "Noel's okay. He was Donnettelli's court reporter. He just talks fast to hide his lisp." I thought of my own disguise. "Trisha, think back, is it possible anyone from the courthouse has been here in disguise?"

"Judge, the people we see usually receive multiple services. Wouldn't a disguise be discovered?"

"Not if they just stepped in to check the place out." The truth in Trisha's question and the concern in her voice made me worry she was doubting my sanity. I made a mental note to visit anyone from the court system I could find in the appointment book.

Sebastian and I used Facebook, Twitter, Foursquare, and Instagram to research salon clients with any connection to the courthouse or Donnettelli. I hired *InternetCheck*, a search service that had access to otherwise inaccessible information. All roads may lead to Rome, but the evidence still led to me.

Sebastian and I kept at it all day, and by nine thirty I was exhausted and barely wiser and headed home—alone. One must have priorities.

CHAPTER TWENTY-SIX

The day's stress always melted away when I pulled into my driveway. My home. My space. My sanity sanctuary.

The house was a hundred years old, historically intact, but I'd modified it to meet my needs. Where the horse barn had once been, now stood a big attached garage with ample loft storage. Some of the neighbors still maintained a horse or two for their grandkids, but I had neither the temperament, nor the desire. I did, however, love the attire, and my closet proved it.

With the press of a button, the garage door lifted, and I searched the area. All clear. I pulled in for the night. I hoped to toss my boots and climb into bed before anything else went wrong. A refueling night's sleep is what I needed. I'd mount my investigation tomorrow.

Once inside, I could take the hallway to the kitchen and the back staircase to my bedroom, but I liked to walk through the house before I retreated to my private space. I pulled off my boots and my socks, wiggled my toes, and giggled at the furry tether that glinted back.

Jimmy Jack purred and nuzzled the fluffy interloper. I dragged the cat on my ankle along the hallway into the kitchen, through the family room, around another shorter hallway that led to the foyer and headed for the front stairs that led to my retreat on the third floor.

But the doorbell had the gall to chime, and of course my intrepid guard cat immediately investigated.

I so wanted to ignore the door. Nobody on this planet would have the nerve to drop in on me when I was this tired. But a second chime sounded, and my curiosity bested me. I grabbed my phone and went to the door. When I mustered the energy to peek through the door hole, an eyeball looked back at me. Only someone I knew would be goofy enough to do that. I looked through the side window at the familiar silhouette and opened the door.

Dinkie-Do gave me the princess wave. "Honey, I am so glad to be here. I heard you have a lot of empty space, and I'm willing to grace a room or two with my presence."

There he stood in all his New York audacity. Colorful bags, swinging hips, expressive hands, and kind eyes.

I wanted to scream. No, no, no. I must be alone.

"Honey, you won't even know I'm here."

"I'm pretty astute."

"Who is this sweet thing?" Jimmy Jack climbed onto a Dinkie-Do bag. My traitorous cat reached up, arched his back, and rested two over-fingered paws on Dinkie-Do's chest. Purr.

He stroked Jimmy Jack's back and scratched in all the cat places.

Turncoat. "Jimmy Jack is my faithful companion. You'll have to find your own boy toy."

They rubbed noses.

I heard two purrs and shuddered. I had to interrupt this love fest. Mental note: next acquisition, female kitten to remind Jimmy Jack of his primal urges.

"This is the friendliest pussycat I ever met," Dinkie-Do said. "A Hemingway pussy—look at all those fingers."

"Keeps all twenty toes to himself, and they're mine." My voice was a little edgier than I'd intended.

I walked around Dinkie-Do's piled bags. "How did you get here with all of that?" I inhaled and exhaled without waiting for his answer. "Exactly how long are you staying?" Instead I stuck my head outside and double-checked. No parked car in my front circle parking or side drive. But a dark Camry, like the one parked across the street from the salon all day behind Hunter's Escalade, sat across the street from my house. I closed the door and reset the alarm. I'd have to ask Hunter about that.

Dinkie-Do perched on the largest of his bags and crossed his legs. "Is there a problem?" He rested his chin on one finger.

Somehow, I was beginning to feel safer with Dinkie-Do inside my home. "Uh, you need what exactly?"

"A room to sleep in and organize my garments. And a creative area for my makeup line to develop my colors."

"This house has survived three boys and an ex-husband, so I'm guessing it can endure a bit of makeup." Surely, a little Dinkie-Do couldn't unravel the whole house.

"Thank you, Honey. Behind the black robe, you're not so tough." Dinkie-Do hugged me.

"About this Honey thing—"

"Oh, you're so sweet. Honey, I only mean it with the best intent. I refer to my best friends that way. Now, show me to my room."

I stifled any comments. Control. I had lost it. I switched off the downstairs lights and grabbed a bag in each hand. "Follow me." We climbed to the second floor. "I'm on the third floor. Off limits to everyone. To the left are my kids' rooms. Off limits. To the right, four guest rooms. Take your pick. I'm not your cleaning lady or your maiden aunt with time on her hands. My cleaning crew is a middle-aged husband-and-wife team, and they don't need extra work, extra gossip, extra entertainment—"

"Oh, Honey, I bet I could show them how to step up their pace and brighten your whites." He waggled his head. "I saw a man on a horse down the street. Do you have—"

"No, and don't bother my neighbors or their horses. Don't play loud music. Don't let me know you're here."

"I'm as quiet as a curling iron." He shimmied his hips. "I was just going to say I use to ride when—"

"And Jimmy Jack sleeps with me. Not negotiable." I cleared my mind of unwelcome images.

"Oh, Honey, understood. I wouldn't dream of sleeping with your pussy." Dinkie-Do blinked quickly and a smile crinkled up.

I ignored the poor word choice.

He put out his hand, and we shook. "Deal, Honey."

We set his bags in my former master bedroom, and Dinkie-Do marveled at the view, the closet space, and the bathroom. I turned to go, and somewhere amid his swirls around the room, he handed me an unopened *Wall Street Journal.*

"It was still under your welcome mat."

I took it and pulled his bedroom door shut behind me. I'd never subscribed to the *Wall Street Journal.* I bought it from the newsstand or read it online.

With Jimmy Jack attached to my side, I climbed to the sanctity of my third-floor space, locked myself in, and cradled my phone in its charger. I turned the TV on and tossed the *Journal* on my bed. My suite was an apartment hideaway. With everything in it, I could hibernate for weeks.

After stretches and sit-ups to keep me limber, a steamy shower, and enough olive-oil lotion to slalom my way into my sheets, I plumped my pillows, climbed into bed, and unwrapped the newspaper.

By newspaper standards, this copy of the *Journal* was near-ancient. The date was highlighted yellow: one week before the murder, but six months after I'd left the bench. Tiny Donnettelli ghosts tiptoed down my spine. I pulled the soft sheets up, grabbed my phone, and positioned it between my breasts. If I stopped breathing, it could jumpstart my heart.

I pulled apart each section of the newspaper and eyeballed it. When I reached the stocks, I did stop breathing. Highlighted bank stocks. I counted. Twelve. There was that nasty number again. All twelve stocks were up. A good bet they were the same twelve banks where I now happened to hold large sums of money. Others were down—another good bet I didn't hold those. I'd have to report this to the SEC.

I couldn't release the paper until I found Manville Corporation. The stock was low. I'd have to check what it was before Donnettelli changed my Order. I bet myself the stock price had gone up. In the moment I couldn't recall other asbestos case names. Releasing the newspaper, I was drenched in cold sweat, intuition, and gut fear.

At the foot of my bed, Jimmy Jack purred off-key. Intuitively he sensed something wasn't right in the world. I needed a few minutes to calm, to think. I needed help to sort this mess. I texted Sebastian and Hunter, got up, and grabbed my robe. I plucked out the Taser I kept hidden in my updo and set it on its charger on the bedside table, fluffed my hair a bit, and grabbed a mint. Who was doing this to me?

CHAPTER TWENTY-SEVEN

Half an hour later, buttoned and knotted into my long, crimson-and-gray jersey robe, I sat with Hunter on the family-room loveseat. A fresh pot of Chai tea and butter cookies sat in front of us.

Someone was trying to help me, scare me, or confuse me. We had to find out who was planting evidence. Preferably *before* jury selection.

Hunter devoured butter cookies as quickly as I refilled the plate. The sugar helped him process the highlighted newspaper. Tossing it onto the coffee table, he settled his shoulder behind mine and rubbed my hand in his. "Toots, somebody is trying to tie you to rising stocks and big bucks in the bank. This ain't good."

"Oh, if I only had a mind like yours." Like a curl on a muggy day, I'd lost my bounce.

"Where's your high-priced lawyer?"

I couldn't tell if Hunter was teasing or being sarcastic. "In a meeting."

Hunter popped the last cookie into his mouth. "Are ballistics in?"

I shrugged. "No idea. Are you replacing the keypads in the house?"

"Upgrading as soon as Dex wires the money. He's been a bit distracted by all this and is not his usual prompt-paying self."

I wanted to offer to pay, but with the salon startup, my finances had taken a hit. "I want every keypad to glow in the dark, especially the one in my bedroom."

"Moonmen will be able to see it." Hunter traveled his talented fingers from my hand to my arm. I liked the mini-massage, but I needed to focus. I pulled away, grabbed my mug, and gulped too-hot tea.

"I can provide personal in-home security."

"Someone knows how to find me, so added home security, yes—personal in-home, no."

"Your security's already damn near perfect."

"Planted calendars, a gavel and letter, and now an old newspaper? It's not perfect enough."

"Calm down, Toots." His voice flowed like melted chocolate. "Tell me about this Jurisa person."

How did he go there? "Okay. Haddes. Judge Jurisa Haddes. She'd do anything Donnettelli wanted. Hated me, Laurel, and Palene. She's what I call a "P" girl: A prissy who pays attention to anything in pants with power."

Hunter's face crinkled all over.

Hit-slap to him. "No, you can't date her; she's married to a retired detective."

"I didn't say a word." He squeezed my wrist. "But your jealousy takes me aback."

Anxious hot flashes kept me in the present. I ignored his side-tracked commentary. "Whoever delivered that paper was here." I brought my voice down an octave. I wouldn't wail. "On my porch. Do you have video?"

"I'll check." Hunter texted and scanned his phone.

I almost planted my eyeballs on his phone's screen. "What?"

We saw it together. No mistake. A black Labrador Retriever dropped the paper on the stoop. "Guess we could check for paw prints."

"Toots, I've been doing this a long time, and I've never seen delivery by dog." Hunter dropped his phone into his shirt pocket.

"So these fancy cameras and all the security equipment are a bust." I tried not to cry.

"We'll figure it out." Hunter breathed in the scent of my hair. The doof. "We're installing more strategically placed cameras for you."

"Damn it. You need to take pooch-deliveries seriously. I refuse to land behind bars."

"The only stripes on your body will be swim-team wear. Promise."

I blushed.

He grinned.

Our eyes held.

I hadn't thought about those red-and-white-striped swimsuits since Hunter and I left the less-than-hallowed halls of high school. We laughed.

One summer I'd worn a teeny string bikini in our school colors—until my father took scissors to it. My scrapbook revealed pictures of us together in my barely-there suit.

"You promised me another bikini." We laughed again, and tension easily slipped away along with the years.

"No expiration date on that promise." He virtually turned back the yearbook pages, and we were together again; his fingers outlined my face, my lips. "After you ran off and married Dexter, didn't his barrel of money buy your every wish?"

"No one was happy about us eloping in high school, especially since I was at the top of my class, even while I was in cosmetology school. They figured cutting hair was my only goal in life—well that and marrying money."

"You leaving stung me deep."

A youthful, hurtful mistake. My fault. "I was young. We were young."

He let his eyes close. "I often wonder—"

"I was always happy I'd gone to hairdresser school when I was a high-school senior. I was able to work and support us. Dexter's family was more than generous after I bore him three sons. You, I mean, we, weren't meant—"

"We could've—"

My fingers hushed his lips. "I focused on work, school, experimental baking, anything that directed me away from the havoc I'd caused. Kids came along, and I was happy." I lifted my chin to face him. "I'm sorry."

"You should be. It'll be a great story to tell. One day." Hunter winked.

I finger-smacked his bicep. "Don't be an ass. Our history belongs in the past. I said *I'm sorry.*"

"Show me." Another wink.

I tightened my robe. Now was no time for complications. Now was the time to discuss evidence and paperwork. Time to find out who'd set me up.

Jimmy Jack jumped in between us. I could always count on my feline friend and his timing.

My focus returned to Hunter. "Did you run a check on the black Camry—"

"—parked across the street at this moment and several feet behind me at the salon?"

Damn. I hated it when he finished my sentences. It was bad enough his pheromones erased whole thoughts in my head. Good thing he was on my side. "I've been so distracted I forgot to ask you."

"My extra eyes."

"Who is—are—who's in those vehicles? How many vehicles are there? Every superhero has a visible sidekick."

He winked.

No on the winking. No winking. I didn't approve of damn winking.

"No one meets my sidekick, Toots. Not even you." He set his thumb under my chin and raised my head until our eyes met. "For safety my backup crews stay in the shadows."

My temperature rose, and Hunter's night beard brushed against my cheek—

"You go, Honey-girl, I'll be outta here in just a minimoo." The sound came from somewhere behind me.

I jerked and struggled to sit up straight. *I won't even know Dinkie-Do's in the house.* Right. It was time I pressed Hunter for a hard look at my paperwork. His mere flippant glance was less than pacifying. "Okay, private eye, I need your viewpoint on my work so far."

Jimmy Jack leaped over the back of the loveseat, circled around Dinkie-Do, and zigzagged between his legs.

Hunter and I, in unison, turned our heads and tried not to gawk. With his fluffy pink bathrobe, matching slippers, and hair wrap, Dinkie-Do looked like he'd swallowed the Pink Panther.

I carefully modulated my voice. "What happened to unpacking and taking a bubble bath?"

"Dinkie-Do is organized. I did me all that. It's tea-and-me time. I need to plan my makeup line and enjoy my beauty sleep. Tomorrow is a very full client day. Business is rocketing; word really gets around in this tiny town." He snapped his fingers, bent, picked up Jimmy Jack, wiggled over to the stovetop and heated water. "Tea?"

I eyed Hunter but spoke to Dinkie-Do. "We're good. There's a tray on the counter. Take it all up to your room. Remember, no maid service." Damn his bad timing.

"And no pussycat." He released Jimmy Jack and arranged the tray as the kettle began to re-boil. "Sorry, Pussy JJ. DD will make it up to you."

"He's on the second floor," I whispered to Hunter. "I'm in my third-floor suite."

"Can't wait to visit the third floor." Through my robe, he squeezed my knee. "For security reasons. I'm sure it's cozy compared to my high-rise loft." He paused and slid closer. "The night-time-city-lights-view is something you'd enjoy."

Chills spiked through me from ground zero.

Silently we watched Dinkie-Do clatter toward the stairs, tray in hand, beam on face, wiggle in caboose.

"Bed and breakfast?" Hunter's eyes crinkled in the corners. "Let me know when you have openings on the third floor. Room with the best view—"

I punched him in the shoulder. "I'm certain it's no match for your high-security, high-rise bachelor loft overseeing the city. No visit needed. I'll live with your description."

"The comforts of a real home are missing." His fingers walked up my thigh, outlined my cheek.

At the sudden thought of wearing prison gray, my insides recoiled. The grit of my attorney-self rose, and its armor shielded me. I mashed the papers into his nose. "Your opinion now. I'm not sleeping until I find something, anything."

"My clue to leave. Time, distance, space," Hunter said. "This is going to take time to sort out. Toots, you've pissed off a lot of people."

And at least one of them wants me behind bars.

CHAPTER TWENTY-EIGHT

Thursday just as the sun rose, Hunter and Sebastian sat across from me in the café. My daunting task after onboarding a rush of caffeine was to convince them to help execute my plan to let the Security and Exchange Commission (SEC) know about the bank accounts with the rising stock. Immediately.

The three of us filled the posh, corner café table I'd designed for private meetings, the drive-thru line outside was moving quickly, and most of the inside tables were empty. Nice and private.

Rosa Abigail Parks, a third-year law student (of the rare straight-A variety), swung her hoop earrings and supplied us with a large carafe of coffee and a platter of sweet beginnings. Her stunning African-American eyes were wide, and I knew she was about to burst into some awful rap. I signaled her to wait and introduced her to Mutt and Jeff.

"Rosa's name and initials are no coincidence," I explained. "They were thoughtfully chosen by her mother, who spent summers engaged as a blues singer and the rest of the year singing opera."

"Music and law." Sebastian grinned at her appreciatively.

"Her grandfather and father were well-known lawyers with high expectations of Rosa." Her long curly hair swung in rhythm with her pencil-thin hips and shoulders as she returned to the counter. When she was out of earshot, I told the guys Rosa played piano, guitar, and drums—and claimed a heart filled with rap, despite a lack of talent for it.

She was very intelligent, but common sense needed to mature in her still-developing brain. Until then, she agreed to help me manage the café at least til she made up her mind what her chosen profession would be. She spoke and thought in lines of illogical rap and a touch of law. But the conflict rarely led to depth of song. *If only her vocabulary had a dash of that rhythm.*

But who was I to grumble about mangled rhyme schemes? I just wanted to cut hair, show a profit, and stay out of prison.

I'd listed asbestos cases, decisions, and affected parties, and the internet and Facebook filled in some of the gaps, but not enough. Images of rich corporations against sick, impoverished employees and customers strained my heartstrings and pointed toward motive. But those damn banks stocks fit somewhere, too.

I needed more eyes. I pondered what the angles of surveillance video would show from any cameras located in and around the asbestos-selling corporations and at the banks.

Sebastian refolded the special-delivery *Wall Street Journal* and chewed the corner off an egg-croissant sandwich. "We've a dilemma."

I flashed disbelief. "Only one?"

"This outstanding brekkie can't delay turning over the evidence to police and prosecutor." Sebastian's table-side manner was curt.

"And the SEC." I needed clarity. "The SEC comes down hard on people who use non-public information to make themselves rich." I needed them to see my point of view.

"If you go to the SEC right now—"

"Hold up Aussie-Down-Under." Hunter pawed a bagel like a hockey puck. "I thought you lawyer types were cautious and confidential?"

Sebastian coffeed down his bite. "We don't operate in porky. Legal process works best in every country when everyone operates with clean hands and absolute truth." He focused on me.

Sebastian's damn accent and Australian slang messed with me every time. When I added gorgeous looks, law talk, shots of coffee and hairspray, erotica trumped my common sense. Both men studied me. I jumped in. "You're right; we keep our cards hidden inside the cashmere, but there's the right time and the wrong time to give information." I eyed one man and the other. "We need to strategically determine what information we release when and to whom. And we need to start with the SEC."

"If we bring in the SEC and the Feds," Sebastian said, "jurisdiction may be lost."

"You're dating Aussie-the-Obvious." Hunter smirked. "And you know he's right about sharing information."

I blinked. I was trying to recall what he was saying. Damn. This nest of testosterone was causing me to lose focus.

"So, do you, agree?" Hunter looked frustrated. "You, having served as a—"

"It's my duty to inform the SEC. Not anyone else's. Mine," I said. "I need all my actions to show my innocence."

"The detectives may suppose you planted the newspaper, like they did with the calendars," Hunter said. "That you are trying to send them in the wrong direction by making it look like you're being set up, when in fact you're the murderer."

"Ridiculous." I ran my hands through my hair to keep from punching something or someone. I needed calming hairspray.

"We all have a duty," Sebastian said.

I bit my thumb knuckle. "So far I haven't done anything wrong. But I may run out of time. And, if I start hoarding evidence—"

"Even with speculative tidbits, they can revoke your bond." Sebastian suddenly looked all lawyer. "If the court gets new evidence, or evidence shows up that leads them to conclude you are a target, a tether and high bond won't keep you out of jail. You'll be behind bars for your protection."

Piercing panic caused sweat to bead in uncharted body parts. Hell, I'd just talked myself into being too scared to function. So much for my plan to come clean with the SEC. I reminded myself I was in control, and I'd rethink that plan and put it on hold.

"We need these detectives on your side." Sebastian stuck up his pointer finger. "Let's verify the information and make it easy for those blokes."

"Now that the Crocodile agrees—" Hunter turned his full attention to me. "Toots, make a list, where the number twelve attaches itself to you, no matter how remote."

Sebastian obviously approved. "Good oil, mate." He turned toward me. "Start with asbestos cases—civil and criminal. If that doesn't pan out, we'll expand the list to include other money cases like banks or insurance cases."

"When Donnettelli shifted the asbestos cases from his docket to mine, and there were a few hundred of them, mostly old, but a few new ones, he cherry-picked cases he wanted from my docket," I said.

"Could there be twelve solely related to one type of case or issue?" Hunter asked.

Sebastian placed his napkin on his plate and asked me, "Did you check?"

"Could be." I shrugged. It was worth checking, but even if I found twelve cases on the same issue, how could that necessitate twelve bank accounts? What I really wanted to do was question everyone who'd entered the courthouse the day Donnettelli died. Police could get a report and share it with Sebastian.

Hunter was fixed on agreeing with Sebastian. They'd oddly bonded somewhere among coffee, insults, muffins, yellow highlighter, and me. I needed another undercover trip.

"Look," I said. "We've already said that—based on alibis—nobody could have killed Donnettelli."

They both agreed, but in a patronizing way that made me want to kick them.

"Here's what we're going to do." Invoking Judge voice. "Assume all the alibis are hokum."

"Hokum?" This from both men at once.

I nodded. "Hokum. Malarkey. Shit."

"Ah. Hokum," Hunter repeated.

"So the guys weren't at the poker party—"

"We can't imagine away the newspaper article breaking up the brawl and showing them being arrested." Sebastian was trying to sound gentle. "Things we can challenge include star- witness Stella, maybe time of death—"

"There's really nothing else to work with, Toots. The bastard's dead. You're the only one with motive and without an alibi."

I've heard the expression "I saw red," but I'd never experienced it before, and I wasn't liking it now.

Sebastian quickly stood and nudged the galumphnik next to him. "Hunter and I will work the Donnettelli angle."

I stood. "Noted." I snatched my cup and the last egg croissant and made for the secret door into the salon. *Meeting with these guys was as stressful as a judges' meeting.*

CHAPTER TWENTY-NINE

Time to work my magic on my friend Laurel. At my station, I wished I could order an infusion of revival chemicals before I began to work. I promised myself that every pump of my stylist chair would include pumping clients for information. Every move I made had to count. Laurel had information or access to it, and I was thankful she was willing to snoop and share the wealth.

"About time," Laurel called from the reception area.

Seeing her brought feelings of being home, and hearing her voice calmed me like a drug.

Laurel (in her usual designer dress and dark nylons) was from old money. While in court, I'd made sure my robe was floor-length to cover my jeans and cowboy boots, but her robes were cut three inches below the knee. At sixty, she was still beautiful. I'd heard talk that attorneys took nylon bets while they waited for her: *was she wearing plain, fishnets, lace, or back seam.*

She hugged me. "I need a new look."

"I need answers," I whispered and released her. "Follow me."

I seated Laurel in my stylist chair and prepped her as we absorbed the light-rock music streaming in above the hum of blow dryers and scents of ammonia and candy-apple shampoo.

About half the staff was in, so what Laurel and I did and said would likely go unnoticed.

Dinkie-Do stood at his station and peacefully added highlights and lowlights to his client's hair, while entertaining her with stories of New York's nightlife. Carlye wasn't at her station, so for the moment, peace reigned in their part of the stylist world. Margo's headphones sound-secluded her while she stacked towels. Trisha answered phones, and for the first time since we'd opened, she was too busy to give me a *good-morning, Judge* shout-out.

From under the nylon cape, Laurel slid out her extra-large oversized bag, unzipped it, and pulled out something. Her brown eyes were wider than normal. "For you."

I intercepted the flat, wrapped package. Red, white, and blue starred-and-striped paper tied in a turquoise ribbon. "It's not my birthday." It didn't look like Laurel's choice of wrapping paper. "From you?"

Laurel lifted her chin and lowered it. "Palene and I have missed you. Something to ponder now that you have time and *questions*."

The emphasis on questions was my answer. She was here to help. I secured the package in the cupboard at my station. "I am working the biggest puzzle of my life." I stepped behind her chair and connected with her via the mirror. "What are you thinking hair-wise?"

She ran her hands through her hair, as if seeing it in a new way. "Every year on Michael's birthday, I surprise him with a new woman. Well, this year it's a double surprise. It's not his birthday. He thinks he's too smart for me to pull one over on him. Humph."

I rotated the chair, so we were face-to-face. "Still volumizing your hair with orange-juice cans?" I pulled out a few hair clips along with my client notebook. "We'll shock your husband."

Laurel fanned her face with her hand. "I'm a not-so-old southern girl who knows what she likes. Michael better like what you do, or one of us will be sleeping in a big empty room in your big house."

Just that moment Dinkie-Do strolled by with a bowl of color. "Do we have us another roomie?"

Laurel couldn't croon toward Dinkie-Do fast enough. "Why haven't we met?" Wide-eyed, she goggled as if she'd just unwrapped a Christmas and birthday present all in one.

Oh boy. "Just girl talk." I motioned toward his client. "Mrs. Ashton's calling for you."

But Dinkie-Do focused on Laurel. "Honey, I've got to get this color on the beauty at my station, but when you're finished, we'll talk about a Dinkie-Do makeover—my treat." He scurried away, swaggering in his slim black jeans. He wore magenta socks, and a vintage tie poked out from under the protective smock.

"You can't miss the bench. This is too much fun." Laurel folded her arms. She expected a response.

"I'll enjoy it after I dispose of Donnettelli's revenge." I combed through her hair.

Laurel reached up and patted my hand. "You were a wonderful, thoughtful Judge. It's a good closed chapter. The murder chapter will close, too." She looked around the room and motioned me closer. "You've been such a good friend to me," she began. Then motioned me still closer.

I bent down, and Laurel whispered, "The courthouse is eerily quiet."

With a little privacy, Laurel would talk. "Hint?"

Her eyes focused up and slightly over toward my cupboard, where I'd put the package.

"Thanks." Tonight, would be interesting. I debated whether I should open the package alone or include the Thunder Twins. I protruded my lips toward one side and waited. Face motion helped me think.

Laurel whispered, "Donnettelli's sidekick, Peter Dune—"

"Clown-about-town and Law Clerk—"

Laurel raised a hand as if swearing. She was serious. "The same. Only redeeming value is that he writes damn good legal briefs." She sat back. "But the twerp's been following me. Palene, too. We've stayed away from you out of fear someone would plant evidence on us, maybe kill us." Her voice trailed.

I was pretty sure no one ever said *twerp* in this century. I plunged in. "You don't think *he* killed Donnettelli? I happen to know that beady-eyed/scowl look he puts on is just a mask. The freckle-faced boy sends half his paycheck to his elderly parents. He was the surprise for his mom's fifty-second birthday." I removed my fingers from Laurel's hair and walked around to face her again. "But he might know something."

Laurel blinked toward the wrapped package in the cabinet. "I never liked waiting through the twelve days of Christmas."

Twelve? I waited for her to say more. But she didn't. Seemed interested in her nails and the tips of her shoes.

She wasn't going to explain. So I returned to her hair while the sting of the word *twelve* whitened my roots. Had she said that on purpose? Was she trying to tell me something else?

I turned fully intent on asking her directly but was stopped by a from-behind hug attack—unnamed arms wrapped around me; an unnamed short person clung to my backside.

"Judge, I had to see you." It was a youngish voice.

I wasn't happy being the huggee, and I didn't recognize the voice of the hugger. But when she released me, I turned around and recalled the angelic face. Purple-spiky-hair girl with the exasperated mother. A former defendant, who'd had Easter-egg-colored hair and pierced everything.

Now, a combination purse/diaper bag hung from her shoulder. Beside her was a stroller with a sleeping auburn-headed girl. "Oh my, you look gorgeous."

"It's my daughter's second birthday. If it weren't for you, I wouldn't still have her. And I had to show you and say, 'thank you,'" she said. "I got early release from probation and started college classes, where I also earned my high-school diploma."

"Congratulations." I was genuinely elated.

"That's not all." She lowered her voice and inched closer to me. "I work for a bank. I pay my mom rent and day care. No new piercings, and I don't use the ones I have except for my earrings. I'm even getting my own place."

I motioned, and we walked to my station while she told me about her work, her apartment, and her future plans. Then she handed me an envelope. "I read about you. I might get in trouble for this," she whispered. She didn't blink until I grabbed the envelope. "I don't care. That is how much what you did for me means to me, especially allowing me to earn a non-public record."

"You did all the hard work. I just steered you a little."

She bent over her daughter and wiped the sweaty bangs out of her eyes.

I ripped the envelope open and unfolded a bank statement. Donnettelli's bank statement. Three accounts totaling just under two million dollars. That wasn't including what was in his retirement accounts. Damn. I slid it back inside the envelope. "How did you get this? You could get fired for this."

Unconcerned, she shook her head at me. "I got to thinking about how you told me you were a Judge and taught law school. You work hard to earn money. And I got to wondering how that Donnettelli Judge had so much. It didn't fit," she said.

"You're brilliant. You graduate college and add on to that brilliance. I'll keep watching as you make your mark in the world." I refused to give her a lecture on employee theft. I wished I could give her a raise.

She hugged me again, and I reached into my back pocket, grabbed the bills I had, and snuck them into the pocket of the diaper bag. Damn. I felt like I was paying for stolen information.

CHAPTER THIRTY

Three hours later, a ten-year-younger version of Cybill Shepherd emerged from my chair and entered the wild world of Dinkie-Do.

An hour after that, Cybill Shepherd wished she was Laurel Briggs. Laurel pulled out her bankbook, bubbled like a schoolgirl, and patted a large bill into Dinkie-Do's palm.

When she grabbed a stack of his business cards and promised to spread the word, his pupils enlarged. I worried what exactly might accidently pop out of Laurel's mouth.

I wanted to believe her arrival, friendship, and gift were omens she'd turn out to be my inside-courthouse informant, but her blurting that *twelve* at me had me wondering.

After she left, a river of clients kept me stylist-busy and information-dry until mid-afternoon, when Hunter phoned and said Stella usually dined at LaVerne's between five and seven, but don't bet on it, and he couldn't get over there tonight. But soon.

Trisha appeared and announced that Judge Donnettelli's Law Clerk Peter Dune had come in to support me and she thought I'd squeeze him in. Without waiting for a response, Trisha pointed Peter toward my chair and trotted back to the reception desk.

"I heard your free-haircut offer on the radio." Peter eased into my chair and swiveled to face me, and he grinned from his GQ hairline to his chin. The grin seemed to be a whole-body thing.

My cringing body wanted to backflip away from his meticulous, but masculine presence, and my thinking switched to black-widow-spider mode. My empathetic-mom side reminded me Donnettelli's staff were not Donnettelli, and I should be flattered Peter thought enough of me to trust me with his oh-so-perfect hair. Looked as if it hadn't been cut in two whole weeks.

"Judge, it's cool to see you leave the bench and start your own business. And you manage to outshine even trumped-up murder charges."

"Call me Nicoletta. It's good to see you again." Hoping God wouldn't strike me with a bolt of liar's lightning, I gestured to get Peter to face the mirror. "I'm sorry for your loss." Well, I *was* sorry for Peter—just not for the absence of Donnettelli. I busied myself scrutinizing his hair. "You did good work for him as his Law Clerk." I wanted to shout out: *you must have something to tell me*, but I restrained myself.

"Judge Donnettelli was an ass in the courthouse," Peter said. "But away from it, he had a human side. He liked to laugh. Still, that didn't make up for his cruelty on the job. Actually, this haircut's on him."

I stepped back. "How's that?"

He reached into his pocket and pulled out a couple of Visa gift cards. "He was never good at gift giving, actually gift buying." Peter laughed. "Visa cards. His choice of the perfect gift." He showed me one. "I thought spending them here would brighten your day." He set one on my counter. "Poetic justice."

His words felt right. Peter had always gone out of his way to make people smile. I explained what cut I'd like to see on him, and Peter agreed. Talking, draping him, and washing his hair gave me time to formulate questions. Tact was going to be my challenge.

"My last day, Judge Donnettelli and I had a sort of weird elevator ride. On my way to the parking garage, we ended up together on the judges' elevator. I thought he was headed there too, but he exited on the second floor. I watched before the elevator door closed and saw you standing a few feet away. At that time I figured you were waiting for him—but before he reached you, you turned back and handed something to Judge Haddes. Do you recall what you gave her?"

Peter shrugged under the cape. "Nothing. She was the one waiting for Judge Donnettelli. He'd told me to meet him at the elevator bank. When he saw her, his mood turned sour, so I told him I'd meet him in his chambers."

"I'm sorry, I thought I saw you hand her something. Maybe you shook Judge Haddes's hand." I tried to press for answers without making it feel like an interrogation.

Peter reddened. "You wouldn't know this, Judge, but Judge Haddes likes bodily contact and initiates it directly or accidently, if you know what I mean. She'll use about any situation to get close, to touch." He fake-shuddered all over. He wouldn't look at me, but I didn't think it was because he was lying. If it was, he was really good at it.

"So she reached for your hand, to touch you, for the thrill of it?"

I thought he was going to cry. "Yeah, I'm a hell of a man."

"That's her problem, not yours," I whispered. "I've seen her actually rub herself up against men. I've always thought it odd." I made a goofy face at him. "Lots of times she's rubbed herself against Judge Donnettelli."

My inner screwball seemed to put Peter at ease, and he croaked out a laugh. "Both Judge Haddes and Judge Donnettelli have that in common, they rubbed a lot of people the wrong way."

Peter did like his wordplay.

I lowered my voice. "Did you ever hear any of the rubbees, or anyone else for that matter, threaten Judge Donnettelli?"

Peter guffawed. "Yeah, all the time. But not seriously. Last time I heard a threat, it was at an after-hours poker game. He raked in a bundle, and Wade Mazour slammed out with a scowl. If he'd looked my way, it would have singed my eyebrows."

"Did you play?"

"I'm into making money, not losing it. I'd been working late and walked out after Wade."

"But the infamous poker party was at your house."

"By judicial order," Peter said. His whole body tensed, and I could hear the resentment. It was as if fun Peter had left, and whatever remained spoke up. "I had played with the Judge once, and he owed me a bundle. I mean a Santa's-bag type bundle. Donnettelli had always made good with other judges, but the lowly help didn't rate with him."

"So you quit playing." I tried to pack all the approval I could into that sentence. I did everything short of saying *atta boy*.

Peter ripped the cape off and turned to face me. His usually handsome face was contorted into an angry sneer—a mask for obvious pain. "Since I refused to play, the bully rubbed my nose in it by ordering me to host the game at my house from now on."

Peter sounded sincere, and he didn't hesitate a bit to answer anything I asked him. That last evening in the courthouse, my mood had been seriously tainted by elevator time with Donnettelli. I must have seen Peter through Donnettelli-stained lenses. Now, he looked like he still wanted to say something.

I'd had lots of practice making my expression accepting. A learned trait from having three sons.

A whole minute passed before Peter stood and leaned down to speak right into my ear. "You probably read in the paper that Judge Donnettelli phoned me around two in the morning—at the poker party."

"Come here a minute." I led him into the not-so-secret hallway, creating us some instant privacy, and Peter stood with his back against the door and looking altogether grateful.

"You told the police Judge Donnettelli was ranting about me," I said.

Peter was the picture of a man with a guilty conscience. "They asked me directly what he'd said." He scratched the back of his neck. "But they never asked me what else I heard, so I didn't tell them. I haven't told anyone."

I subtly nodded, secretly willing him to trust me.

Peter looked me in the eye. “I heard a woman’s voice in the background.”

I must have looked like someone had flipped my off-switch. My thought processes shut down and my mouth hung open and my heart was making a hard drive to the finish line.

“I just wanted you to know,” Peter said, “that I don’t blame you.”

Somewhere in there, while I was still lost in my private episode of *Black Mirror*, Peter left. He didn’t say another word. He didn’t let me ask if he recognized the voice, or if he somehow thought it was me.

He just disappeared.

Damn.

CHAPTER THIRTY-ONE

I was sure Peter thought telling me was the right thing to do, but it rocked me from the soles of my cowboy boots to the final layer of spray on the top of my hair. What if the police got ahold of that? And who could it have been? Jurisa?

Every now and then a girl needs to go home early, and for this girl, this was the day.

Carlye promised to give Dinkie-Do a ride home. (She'd named her car Herbini. I was okay to miss that ride.)

Armed with the house key and alarm code, Dinkie-Do promised a quiet arrival, and I had my own quiet arrival to make. I hit the reception desk first to let Trisha know I was leaving, and I could tell she was upset—or something. "Spill it, my friend," I said. "What's bothering you?"

"My old eyes must need a check-up, Judge. Peter Dune came here by way of Uber-Haddes."

"No way," I said. "That's too far-fetched even for those two." We giggled.

I had to get out of there.

On my way home, I stopped at the Salvation Army store, picked out a couple outfits, took them into the parking lot, and stomped them good. I already felt better.

It was barely five when I got home, so I dove into my closet for another makeover. I took my hair down, teased part of it and glopped on styling gel, went a little crazy with some bright lipstick and blue eyeshadow, and dressed in the battered, baggy khakis and a shirt.

Within ten minutes, I was on a stool at LaVerne's Café and ordered the soup of the day. Two stools down, sat tiny Miss Stella dressed in pristine white.

After I'd been served and had a couple mouthfuls of what I hoped was split-pea, I pulled out ten twenty-dollar bills. I grinned and smiled and tried to ooze pride.

When Stella didn't bite, I started sorting the bills into stacks and laughing out loud. Of course, the server came to shush me—all part of my master-sleuth plan—and I bragged like a banty rooster that I'd earned this money, and all I had to do was talk. I told the waitress I'd easily earned stacks of cash that totaled two hundred American dollars just for telling a guy I saw the other guy go through a red light. HA!

That did it. Stella was gesturing and scoffing and cussing in some language I didn't know. I told her to step off, old bag—okay, so I'm not up on street talk—I told her she couldn't make ten cents if she tried.

Right away she was in my face boasting about a whopping five-hundred dollars she'd gotten for saying she'd heard a gunshot when she was walking her dog. She punctuated the sentence by giving me the finger.

That I understood. But, I was too happy to let one little finger deflate me. I phoned Sebastian and filled him in. He was on it. I was exhausted and zoomed home staying five miles over the speed limit so I wouldn't get pulled over and arrived in record time.

When I finally entered my home, I didn't stop for anything except to toss my clothes and crawl between my sheets. Propped up by pillows behind my back, I jotted down my Stella contact, including her finger, and everything Peter said into a bedside notebook and tossed it back on the nightstand. The pictures of it all were filed into my brain's solitary confinement until further notice. I had other things to think about.

Top of my agenda: to open Laurel's package.

Jimmy Jack seized the other half of my king-sized bed, where he batted about the turquoise ribbon curls on Laurel's package.

"Sorry, my boy." I tossed the ribbon off the package. He leaped toward it and tangled all four paws.

Jimmy Jack could always take my mind to a joyful place. I tore off the wrapping paper and focused on the thick manila envelope inside. Unmarked. I opened it and pulled out a stack of paper. Court documents. Register of Actions.

"Jimmy Jack, look at this."

The furball ignored me.

I flipped through dozens of pages, scanned rows of cases. Docket entries of my cases and Donnettelli's cases. I didn't mourn his passing. I didn't kill him; I didn't even hurt him. Okay, I'd admit to *thinking* of ways to make him suffer, listed alphabetically, and cross-referenced by location.

For nearly two hours I worked through the papers and hadn't realized any time had passed until I plugged my phone into the charging stand on the night table.

Two years of docket. Frenzied worry ran through me. What was Laurel saying? On a legal pad I made columns: *Donnettelli Docket, Kikkra Docket.* Under each heading, I entered cases, and I searched every page. Some cases were short, barely started. When I compared them, I came to the words: *Cases Transferred.*

I drew a third column, but something was missing, so I halved that column: *Donnettelli to Kikkra* and *Kikkra to Donnettelli.*

I reached to the stack of copied papers—the asbestos cases. I added a fourth column to isolate those.

Donnettelli had told me he was transferring all the asbestos cases. High-stakes cases for both sides. If he'd found a way to profit from them, who killed him and framed me? Why? Did he have an accomplice or an enemy or both? If somebody wanted him dead, oh well, but why involve me? All the shooter needed to do was cover his own tracks.

I needed to go back farther in the files, copy more, and determine how many more of my Orders he had changed. Damn, how long had he been changing Orders? He'd been a Judge for decades.

CHAPTER THIRTY-TWO

I'd like to think I remembered every decision I'd ever made, but there were too many to remember without looking at each file. Damn.

We had no process to transfer cases all over the place like this.

Wait. Untrue. Chief Judge could transfer cases under the radar. I'd thought it was only the asbestos cases he'd transferred. But—no—he was moving all kinds of cases. The freak was controlling decisions.

I never imagined he had that kind of audacity.

I sat back. Was that enough to get killed for, or to kill for? Who stood to gain? The asbestos cases are linked to me because they were on my docket; it could make me look guilty. If some of them are linked to Laurel or Palene, should they be suspects? Are we all targets of Donnettelli's assassin?

A siren seared the air; red lights above the doors flashed. The smoke alarm! I snatched up the papers and my cat and dashed out the door toward the stairs. Wait. I ran back into my room, threw the closet doors open and grabbed my favorite three pairs of cowboy boots.

Jimmy Jack squealed.

I hugged my treasure to my chest, dashed to the stairwell, leaned on the oak banister and slid down to the second floor. Rounded a corner. Mounted the banister. Down to the first floor, through some bizarre cloud of blue-and-purple into the garage. From somewhere in the kitchen area, Dinkie-Do shrieked. Jimmy Jack scurried under a couch.

God help him! I dropped the rescued items. Without missing a step, I turned and shot back through the door, shut it tight behind me, and ran into the cloud.

"I'm sorry," Dinkie-Do wailed. "I'm so sorry."

I sneezed hard. Was the ceiling going to cave in?

Through bursts of smoky blue, gray, and purple, and glitter clouds I ran toward the sound of Dinkie-Do's panicky voice. The odor of burned chalk jumped up and smacked my face. My eyes prickled, and I sneezed again.

An enormous cloud of blue-and-gold smoke mushroomed at me. I lunged backward, blinded. With both hands I sheltered stinging eyes, and my lungs strained for air. More sirens blasted outside.

But inside, silence settled on the room. I blinked and blinked. Glistening bits of dust flitted through the air, and it tasted like burned Kaopectate. I grabbed my cell. "Dinkie-Do, can you move?"

I thought he answered, but his voice was drowned out by the blaring horns of three very expensive pieces of heavy equipment that belonged to East Lansing's Finest First Responders.

I ran for the front door before real-life heroes knocked it down with their real-life axes. As soon as I released the lock, three large men in heavy yellow coats dashed past me into the cloud.

I pointed the Chief toward the kitchen, and his crew charged forward. When he asked me what had happened, I was no help, and he followed his men. They'd find Dinkie-Do. He had to be okay. Police and EMS would help, too.

The final firefighter warned me to stay back, but I followed him toward the kitchen. My ears hurt from the blaring alarm. I couldn't see Dinkie-Do. I couldn't see more than a foot in front of my face. I couldn't see my formerly immaculate chrome appliances. I blinked again, let tears wash the grit from my eyeballs, and gingerly wiped under my eyes.

Frozen bodies sat on the stools at my island. This mess felt and smelled like a Dinkie-Do fiasco. He'd conjured something, or it was another attack on me. My house could survive almost anything, but I couldn't survive another arrest. Damn.

A firefighter appeared, cradling a glittery blue Dinkie-Do. A wheeled gurney received him, and an oxygen mask was placed over his face. The firefighter would survive despite glitter falling off his uniform. It was Dinkie-Do who worried me.

I fought hard not to bawl: *You must be all right, Dinkie-Do. You must.*

The large firefighter barked at me. "Outside. Now." His voice was powerful, but not unkind. "Now."

Normally not one to submit to masculine barking, I made an exception for the giant firefighter with the sharp ax. After all, they'd saved my . . . my Dinkie-Do. I snagged a tapestry, wrapped it around myself then ran into the front yard. Despite their distance, the neighbors—even one on horseback—were in full curiosity-mode.

I enjoyed watching law enforcement shoo away the gawking neighbors. I didn't enjoy all the amused faces witnessing the chaos called my life. It seemed like longer, but within half an hour, after instructions on how to properly clean the vents and air out my house, a reminder to close all the open windows, and a vehement colorful refusal from Dinkie-Do to go to the hospital for a check-up, all uniforms were seated in their vehicles in various stages of egress.

The burly Fire Chief chuckled and waved from the high fire-truck window as the rig heaved out of the drive.

"Oh, Honey, your beautiful kitchen has a new glow. I'm so sorry my electric-rainbow-blue eye shadow exploded." Dinkie-Do shuddered and glitter rained off him. "My new makeup line, well, developing is not an exact science, you know."

I wrinkled my forehead at him.

"Too much glitter and a pinch of this and that—who knew?" Dinkie-Do shook his head. Glitter fell onto the driveway all around him. "Homemade glitter bomb. My bad."

Bad may be useful. I wrapped my arm around Smurfie-Do. "Clean up the mess, and save me a few vials of the exploding blue stuff, will you? Guess my burglar alarm placed your new shadow in questionable-prowler category."

"Honey, I'll save you all you need as long as you promise to be extra careful." Dinkie-Do clasped his hands together. "Those city employees are my new best friends. They all want salon appointments."

"You scared my gizzard into the next county." I couldn't get enough air to yell. I suddenly realized I was dropping glitter of my own.

"Honey, that blue looks divine on you. Definite fashion yes-yes."

I hoped it looked good with neon-orange jumpsuits. "I'll contemplate that as I go to the garage to rescue my things and find Jimmy Jack." I stopped and faced him. "When you figure out what caused this, let me know—without duplicating it."

"Honey-girl, I'll try."

I circled back. "Any new guests you want to disclose before we return to inspect?"

"Ah, yes. My practice gals." He grinned. "Such a treat to glam them up at your kitchen island."

When I returned to the remnants of my kitchen, Smurf King was surrounded with cauldrons of color, spiked heels, and six inflatable adult-sized Plasti-gals in wigs. The island sat ten. I guessed two were a couple and the other four were awaiting dates. The "ladies" sat aligned in audience forum, and there were easels—some with paper, others with mirrors. The Plasti-gals were covered, a few bent.

My fists clenched as tightly as my teeth. "Mistook my gourmet kitchen for a Technicolor science lab, did you? We're not zoned for Experiment 420." I was already wearing the world's biggest *Fashion No-No* on my ankle. "My house is a no-cloud zone."

"Jiffy clean up," Dinkie-Do said. "Pay me a no-never-mind." Left hand on hip, he lassoed his right hand into his dimpled cheek. "No worries."

"I've got nothin' but worries." My vital signs were heading home toward normal, and I thought it best to insert some space between my new boarder and moi. From the freezer, I grabbed my emergency box of Thin Mint Girl Scout Cookies. I'd brew tea upstairs while

I steamed in a hot shower. My teacup bottom needed a crust of Australian Fairy Bread to dazzle me while I pondered and drank.

"Honey, before you depart," Dinkie-Do's voice dropped an octave. "There's something you should know."

He was entirely too serious for this to be anything good. "Is my life in imminent danger?"

He shook his head. "No, Honey."

"Is your life in imminent danger?"

"Uh-uh." Another negatory.

"Then this woman is headed to the third floor." I strode toward the stairs, turned, retraced my steps, and scooped up Jimmy Jack. "What I need to know can wait til morning."

Glittered blue shoulders drooped, he turned his back to me, and I gave in. Better to clear the air all the way. "Okay, spill. Two minutes."

"Honey, this is probably not the ideal time to be bringing you my personal problems—"

Longish pause.

I gave him the finger-twirl for *get on with it.*

"Honey, it's your friend, Laurel. The Judge," Dinkie-Do said.

Now a long pause, given I was covered in Technicolor dust, and my eyeballs were melting. I willed Dinkie-Do to speak.

"Judge Laurel has a bit of a problem." Now the Smurf was speed talking. "I mean, being your friend, I'd never officially report her."

I thought about falling to my knees. "Have mercy on me, I beg you. Get to the point, please."

"Your long-legged friend stole two pairs of my best heels, size ten." Dinkie-Do's bottom lip quivered. "Royal blue and passion fruit."

Now a long pause. I heard what he said. "Okay, that's the downside. Is there an upside to this issue? Maybe a punch line?" I'd seen his station decorated in shoes, flowers, and an array of oddities. But Laurel could buy a shoe store; he had to have it wrong. She didn't have the mind of a criminal, except in fantasy talk.

"No upside, no punch line, no kidding." He was serious.

"Then please explain; don't just complain. I need details."

"Honey-Judge, you need evidence? My workstation's outfitted in the color palate I am planning for my line. My shadows will match my beloved shoes and a few of my favorite things."

I squeezed my sore eyes tight for a second. Nobody wanted to learn about the secret faults of the people they love and admire. Only one thing to do. I stepped toward the cupboard above the desk, opened it, and pulled out my recipe box. Behind divider M, a money clip held, two thousand dollars in twenty one-hundred-dollar bills. I drew it out. But now there were only six bills.

An invisible somebody dragged the tip of a popsicle down my spine.

A non-invisible thief had been in my house. In. My. House. But how, who, and why? And why not pilfer all twenty bills?

I'd somehow been transported to the East Lansing Twilight Zone. But I couldn't deal with missing money until I'd saved my vision, my complexion, and my mind. I replaced the empty clip, returned the box, and closed the door.

"Take these." I set the six bills on a be-glittered patch of kitchen table. "You keep Laurel in shoes. Not one word to anyone. I'll keep the two of you in shoes. Deal?" Two judges arrested I didn't need. I guessed lifting shoes was Laurel's way to relieve stress.

Beyond the glitter, Dinkie-Do's face glowed, and he grinned like a woman on a liquid diet, who'd just been given a chocolate bar. "Honey, definite upside. Deal." He twirled, stopped mid-snap, crooked lipped. "Honey, why trust a friend who steals?"

"She doesn't know she's stealing—shoes calm her." Like hairspray calmed me.

"Like dressing my Plasti-gals calms me." Dinkie-Do batted his lashes.

I trusted Laurel with my life. Until that moment I hadn't thought about her stealing anything but hearts. A lot of things about Laurel made sense to me. Laurel liked wearing shoes that stabilized her and made her feel pretty, regardless of where they came from. She wasn't really stealing from me; for many years we'd shared so much. I understood. I needed to steal into my bath.

CHAPTER THIRTY-THREE

Exhaustion numbed me into a sleep so deep it felt like it had never happened. When the alarm clock intervened, I hit the snooze. I pressed repeatedly. When the ringing continued, I finally comprehended it was the telephone and opened my eyes.

Everything was very dark. I focused on the time. Not even midnight. Not getting up, not answering the phone.

Damn. Ringing again. I rolled over, smacked the landline next to my bed and lifted the receiver. I sang in my kindest voice. "I'm not in violation of tether—you are in violation of my sleep time."

Dexter spoke. Barry White low-and-soft. "Lover, you need a visit from me."

"Like I need an arsenic cocktail."

"The boys are fine. They'll stay here. A sort of management test run for a week or so."

"Need sleep—" Dex wasn't fooling me. His money was his fourth child, and I was still somewhere in the running for fifth. By now, sixth or seventh place. He continued to try to save me by spending greenbacks, clear reminders of our marriage failure. And I don't wear failure well. Prison would be my ultimate failure.

"I booked a flight," he said. "I'm staying at the house—" He spoke louder, faster. A clue I couldn't talk him out of it.

The house. "*My* house?" I felt as if wet hair color was dripping down my face, and I could neither wipe it off, nor scratch the itch. "When we were married, I didn't need you to rescue me. I don't need you to rescue me now." Dex loved to rescue me like Rapunzel from the tower. Sometimes I'd loved to let my hair down with him. *But that was a different problem.*

"Lover, I've missed seeing you. You always look like a million."

"Now I am a million."

"Warm my million percent cotton sheets. I'll be in tomorrow." And click, he was gone.

What was it about men and hanging up?

I hung up and plopped my pillow over my head. After a minute, liking to breathe as I do, I rethought the pillow thing. I lifted it long enough to spy the alarm pad by my bedroom door. The house alarm was set, but that didn't satisfy me. I texted Hunter to review Laurel's home security and wondered if that would alleviate her sudden fondness for other people's footwear.

I plunked the phone back into the charger, and Jimmy Jack drifted from the foot of my bed, curled himself against my chest, and purred. Mmmm, my kind of guy. Time to recharge my brain with a game of *Connect the Courthouse Files.*

CHAPTER THIRTY-FOUR

Sebastian came by early, joined me for breakfast, and filled me in on the Stella debacle. He'd persuaded Grayson and Fredericks to meet him at LaVerne's for a chinwag with the witness.

Stella suddenly forgot to speak English, but the server remembered me and reported the whole conversation. Sebastian said Detectives particularly enjoyed the physical description of "the other crazy woman" at the counter that evening.

Now both sides knew what I'd known all along. Somebody had put some effort into planning to murder Donnettelli and frame me. Detectives said it didn't make any real difference, but I knew it did, and before I was done, they'd know it, too.

When Sebastian dropped me at the salon, Hunter was there and escorted us to the table in the break room. He had printouts spread across the table, and at a glance I guessed they were profiles of corporations involved with asbestos litigation.

Hunter asked how he could identify the primary bank for each asbestos company, and Sebastian told him to check the appendices to their annual reports, Form 10-K.

"You can find those at sec.gov," I said helpfully.

Hunter stood and gathered his paper products. "If I had an oversized ostentatious hat, I'd tip it. See ya." He turned and left.

Alrighty, then. Sebastian kissed me warmly and said he'd return to pick me up whenever I texted him—unless he was busy, in which case, he'd call an Uber. Funny man. I was surrounded by funny men.

The day was a Macy's-worthy parade—one talkative client after another, and a half dozen of them were from the courthouse. They all got free haircuts, but they left generous tips, and it was truly fun to see them away from that den of drudgery.

Late in the afternoon, Trisha took me aside.

"Judge, you remember Wade Mazour, a Law Clerk for the State Supreme Court. Nice fella."

"I've seen him in our courthouse from time to time." I remembered the last day I worked there, Donnettelli had been demeaning Wade and had shoved him into the breakroom, and that infuriated his friend. "Most recently was when he was picking up case files marked for the Court of Appeals."

Trisha glowed. She was one person who thoroughly enjoyed people, and she welcomed all signs of individuality. "He's looking for a change." She did an exaggerated shrug-thing with her mouth, and her joy spread to me.

I welcomed Wade just before six o'clock with an open arm. (I didn't want to scare the guy.) When he crossed the room, Wade might have seen Carlye or Dinkie-Do, but he was so focused you couldn't prove that he'd noticed anyone but me. He was an eyes-straight-forward-focused kind of guy. Stocky, sturdy, and staid.

"Good to see you." I motioned him to sit in my stylist chair, clipped the cape around him, and smiled up at him in the mirror. His intensity made me want to check my lipstick and respray.

"Here's the thing." Seemed like he was trying to get a running start on this conversation. "Last year I got divorced."

"You just joined a huge club. I'm divorced, too."

"My ex thinks that at thirty-four I have no style, no taste, and no vision."

"Ouch."

"Next month I'm 35. I want you to morph me into a guy she won't recognize, and women will want to date, and that causes her to approach me in the bar—"

"And she won't realize she's approaching you, and you can give her a one-liner she won't forget—and walk away?"

Wade relaxed. "Call me Mr. Transparent."

I ran my fingers through his hair and saw the possibilities. "You're just honest. Most divorced people would cheer you on for daring to do what they've dreamed of."

Now Wade fully relaxed.

"I'm thinking low skin fade with brushed-up fringe and highlights and lowlights."

"I'm thinking one step at a time."

"I'm thinking, you're my last client of the day, and I have all the time we need to morph you into such style your ex won't recognize you, and when she does she'll be jealous. If you don't like it, it's free." I met his eyes. "Then, you let your beard grow, and next week I'll have Carlye clean it up and teach you how to maintain a roguish, professional style. Carlye has a way with the men."

"I like the way you think."

When we were done, he liked the way I styled hair, too. He bought two bags of product and made another appointment.

I locked up, grabbed Dinkie-Do before he began to redesign his station, and we sped home. Dinkie-Do complimented me on the Wade transformation but scolded me for not giving him a row of blue tips. I clicked on Pandora to my dance-music station, and we stopped arguing and danced and sang until I turned off the key and hit the garage-down button.

When piled out of the car, and before I could insert my key, the door swung open wide.

"Lover—" Dex held the door and waved us in.

"Need a ride to a hotel?" I entered. Noted: golf pants, golf shirt, bulging muscles. As firm and chauvinistic as I remembered. The few gray hairs in his sideburns and at his temples were perfection brushed on. Damn, he aged well.

Wide-eyed, Dinkie-Do seemed unsure whether he should come in, then in a timid hip-swinging gait, he followed.

"I'm comfortable right here, Lover. I've taken over the lower-level suite. I knew you wouldn't mind."

Can't know what you didn't care to ask, just like our married days, is what I wanted to shout, but my caffeinated, sassy self, took over. "D-I-V-O-R-C-E. Remember?" I kicked off my boots. I wished I could kick him, but there was a witness, and only an ingrate would toss the guy out after he'd posted a million-dollar bond.

"Got a million reasons and three great sons to remember. Besides you need the added protection." His eyes rolled toward Dinkie-Do.

"Meet Dinkie-Do Davis. He's perfecting his makeup line here." I stepped back.

Dinkie-Do grinned, popped his shoulders up and down a few times, and offered Dex his hand.

Of course, Dex gripped Dinkie-Do's hand and pumped expansively. He'd always been a people person, and he'd been a money person. He just hadn't been a husband person. "Ah, I met your friends—in the kitchen," he said.

Dinkie-Do blushed. "Tonight after dinner, I have to beautify my ladies. I promised makeovers with my new colors. After I prepare us a welcome-first-night-roomie dinner."

"Make that for two. I'm going up." I turned toward Dexter. "I agreed to security from a distance, not up close and personal." I disappeared to my sanctuary, and I wasn't coming out until Monday. I needed sleep and quiet and privacy.

CHAPTER THIRTY-FIVE

Our seven o'clock meeting was early, especially for a Monday, but early was essential for Laurel and me because our time together always slipped by faster than hair color in a box faded.

Always classically dressed, Laurel was easily recognized in her sling-backed red-and-blue multi-stitched heels coordinated with the lightweight knit shell, sweater, and just-at-the-knee skirt. We had our usual *purple eye,* because three shots of espresso had become as mandatory as hair spray, and added a slab of lemon pound cake smothered in whipped cream. We sat at our usual corner table near a trash bin at the end of the café. We positioned our chairs so that we faced the wall with a window overlooking a corner of the parking lot.

We wore oversized sunglasses and silk scarves, but Laurel's words didn't make me feel better. Dressing to hide in public to meet with a friend was like wearing an annoying hangnail. But Starbucks was centrally located between our homes in absolute avoidance of everything downtown. Since that included the courthouse and Donnettelli, who'd preferred bagel shops, this had become our caffeinated safe haven.

Laurel said her morning docket began at ten, so we were good, at least until we were discovered. I needed to talk with her about the envelope she'd left with the record of actions.

"I've put the information you left to good use. It raised questions." I sipped coffee and watched her reaction. "But it didn't provide any real answers."

"I already told you the Chief Judge asked me to cover hearings and sign things when I was his Pro Tem CJ. Initially, we were true to our normal personalities: I was eager to please; he was overbearing."

"Always?" I took mind snapshots of every word.

"Donnettelli got worse with age," she said. "I carefully reviewed everything. When I refused to sign because I disagreed with a decision, he became irate." She sounded more sad than angry.

I tried to read between the lines. The significance didn't click. Did this relate to me? "Signing for him wasn't your responsibility," I said.

"No. He needed distance from the issues, my name on documents instead of his to avoid direct association with the final Order, so he could blame me, if necessary." She jiggled her plate back and forth.

"And you've been bullied ever since," I said.

She broke off a corner of the pound cake and held it. "Gang bullied. He used his power to turn others against me. Except for you and Palene." Laurel took out a tiny white linen handkerchief, embroidered in red and blue.

He'd done the same to me. I asked, "Did you document?"

"I have every email, every exchanged paper." Laurel's tone was low but serious.

"Ever do anything with it?" I knew the answer. I needed the confirmation.

"I'm not strong like you, but I reported him." Laurel balled her fists. "And I'm not sorry he's gone. That was a golden bullet."

Surely, she couldn't believe I'd done it. "It wasn't me." Could she have done it? Nah.

Laurel stroked one eyebrow. "Let's face it. We all wanted him dead." She laughed, and it was clear it was meant to cover the awkwardness of judges agreeing that someone should die.

In that moment, I felt relieved. But she did have motive.

Laurel whispered, "There's something else that has always bothered me. Donnettelli regularly had the ability to charm Jurisa Haddes. When I wouldn't sign, he appointed her Pro Tem CJ. She belly-laughed at everything he said, even raunchy, sexy things about her. Her Insipidness signed whatever Donnettelli put in front of her."

Judge Jurisa Haddes wore bottle-burgundy hair in a perfect bob and perfectly tailored suits. It suited me not to see her at all. "Her Insipidness is a perfect name for her," I said, and we giggled. "Laurel, did Donnettelli ever change any of your Orders?" When Laurel started nodding, I stopped talking.

"Like I said, I reported the bastard," her voice hardened. "The State Court Administrators Office did nothing. Judicial Tenure believed him over me—said I'd forgotten what I'd signed." Laurel gulped but stopped short of crying. "I directed my staff to allow only you and Palene to sign in my absence. Remember, that was when I told you I would only sign for the two of you and warned you to do the same."

"I played nice and signed for everyone," I said. "Even him. Shame on me."

Laurel shook her head at me with a half frown.

Small pieces were falling into place. I patted her wrist. "Could Donnettelli have done something to Haddes to make her mad enough to kill him? Can you search for other modified Orders? Maybe recheck your file?" My excitement made my nose flare.

Laurel shrugged.

"I've found a possible link to the moved cases, to Donnettelli's sudden infusion of money, and possibly to my changed Orders, including whatever you signed for him." I handed her the pictures on my phone.

"Really?" Laurel asked with uncertainty.

"Look at these charts I've made. Enlarge them, and you'll see," I said.

"Immoral is not illegal." Laurel touched the screen. "I own some of those same stocks."

That's interesting. "Me, too. But I haven't sold any." I explained my theory to her and decided to leave out my decision to contact the SEC about my twelve bank accounts.

"Michael manages our money; I spend it." Laurel sounded as grim as she looked. "Who do you think is involved?"

"Someone upset with both Donnettelli and me." I gazed up at the ceiling.

Laurel ran a stir straw through her lips.

I leaned into Laurel's space. "Can you review files of asbestos cases where there is a possible high payout?"

"Mesothelioma cases are big money, but a chunk of any settlement goes to medical bills." Laurel paused. "No way they could result in a big payoff like the lottery. That would be a dead end." She looked so sorry for me.

And I hated being pitied. We sat in silence until I looked out the window and tilted my head for a better look behind Laurel.

Something was moving outside the window. Just loud enough for Laurel to hear, I said, "Why is Peter Dune snapping pictures at us through the window? Damn stalker."

"He's just talking on his phone." Laurel bent her head to her chest and raised her eyes to peek at him. "He may be talking with Renée Reed—Donnettelli's Judicial Assistant. Rumor has it they've been on-again/off-again for a while."

I was more overt. I wanted him to know I not only saw him, I recognized and scrutinized him. "Nope. Look how he's holding the phone."

Laurel squinted. "Maybe he's reading something."

"The instant he realized I caught him, he stopped and fled."

"Probably made him mad that you were so brazen about it," Laurel said. "He's got his share of hothead in him. I mean—I've heard."

What was Laurel doing? In less than the time it took to down her Venti Caramel Cloud Macchiato, she'd pointed the finger at Jurisa and Peter. I asked another question, but Laurel seemed dazed.

Suddenly, she gathered her things and couldn't get to her car fast enough. I guessed seeing Peter spying on us had creeped her out.

By the time I got to my car, Laurel and Peter were out of sight. I was left with a bag of unanswered questions and a half-eaten slice of lemon pound cake.

CHAPTER THIRTY-SIX

I clicked on my office light. Rainy days, mad money, mad men, the benefit and the burden—they ran together, collided, and pointed a guilty finger at me. I intended to squash *them* before *they* squished me. Problem was: who were *they*?

At my desk, I reached into the drawer for highlighters, pens, and everything else I could think of to complete a moveable office.

I dialed the front desk. "No one leaves tonight," I told Trisha. "I want you, Carlye, Dinkie-Do, Margo, and Rosa to meet me in the kitchen area for a meeting. Lock up. No one else is invited. Tell no one about the meeting."

"Yes, Judge."

"Answer no questions; take no excuses. We've no time to waste. I have tether curfew. Meeting's nine o'clock sharp, earlier if you can pull it off."

"Highly unusual. Yes, Judge." Trisha clicked off.

The knots inside me loosened, but they didn't untie. I organized supplies and doodled random thoughts in a notebook until Trisha buzzed me to remind me my client was due in an hour—meaning I could only meet with Hunter until then.

Damn. Had I forgotten a meeting?

Somebody tapped on the door.

"Enter," I said.

"Toots. I see you've locked yourself away. Practicing dance moves?" He grinned and sat in the chair across from my desk.

"Droll, even for you," I said and sat in the chair next to Hunter.

"I've just come from police headquarters," he said. "I thought you should know that there are no fingerprints on anything in Donnettelli's office."

Damn. "Nothing? Not even a partial print on anything we turned over either?" I knew the answer before I asked it.

"Nada."

I raised my shoulders and felt them deflate with each word I uttered. "The absence of prints is evidence and makes me more convinced someone in the courthouse is guilty of murder and framing me."

"There are gloves in every courtroom, right?" Hunter said.

I realized he was making a statement, not asking a question but I answered it anyway. Sometimes talking out loud helped me think more clearly. "Yes. They are used when officers or anyone else testifies about evidence they have to touch for any reason."

"The availability of gloves would be known by personnel, but it's also known by the public." Hunter stared at me. He always had the ability to read my mind.

"I doubt any of the public would touch the gloves." Hearing those words out of my mouth caused an interesting thought: what about court cleaning staff, outside repairman, mail personnel, and other delivery persons who frequented the courthouse?

The rest of the day I kept busy with clients making mental lists of accessibility to gloves and the important issues I needed to discuss with my staff at our meeting.

CHAPTER THIRTY-SEVEN

Shortly after nine with the café in full brew, the salon closed for the night. Rosa, in fresh-roasted-bean scent, had her night shift in order and her evening tasks finished. She and the salon staff sat around the kitchen table with a spread fit for pastry connoisseurs.

For a fleeting second the silence was so daunting I felt as if a bailiff had just called, "All Rise," and I'd forgotten my robe. I had to build a team and launch them into action—all in forty-five minutes

"Honey-girl." Dinkie-Do wiggled his way around the table to my chair and returned me to reality. He pushed it behind me. "You're not looking well. We've been neglecting you. Honeeey, it will never happen again." He put a hand on each of my shoulders and pushed me down into the chair. Then he bent, eyeballed me, frowned, and shook his head. "Have some water?"

I pasted on a happy face. "Hairdo, go. Sit. I'm fine." I crossed my legs, bouncing one knee over the other.

Dinkie-Do sat, but Rosa and Carlye simultaneously opened their mouths.

I grabbed a thick red marker from the table and drew a happy face on the water bottle. Then I inked a big red X over the mouth and pointed it at them. "No one speaks. Listen. Okay?" One at a time, I met each pair of eyes until all signaled agreement.

Carlye put her hands over her mouth, and everyone followed her lead. I was suddenly sitting at a table of speak-no-evils. "Thank you."

I air-plumped my cheeks because a whole large piece of me felt numb. Finally, I got up and stood at the back of my chair. That felt right. Okay.

"It's obvious my *trouble* is escalating. I don't know how or why. But before I say anything else I want to make sure you know I trust you. All of you. And secondly, I need your help. And, the third thing is, well—things might get dangerous—okay—more dangerous. So, if you want to get out, take leave, vamoose down ol' Toledo way, now's the time to go. I don't blame you, and nothing will be said. I thank you all for everything you've already done."

"I ain't going no wheres," Carlye said. Her mouth free, she grabbed a cream-cheese Danish and waved it. "I been through worse than this. Heck it's just getting good. And my Shazam is a great watch bird. He can scare off any kind of evil-doer." She bit into her pastry.

Trisha chuckled. "Judge, I've told you before, I'm going to crack on with you no matter what. I'm too old to feck off."

Dinkie-Do flapped his hands at me. "I'm in this to stay. We're roomies. We have work to do."

Rosa shook her head. "You know I came to work, and you're here to shine. I got no time to whine, and you've got no time to stunt. I'm here to learn, and you have still to teach." She paused and blurted. "Do I get to carry a gun?"

I was sure she was going to say I had to punt. Bad rap was back and with gun-desire.

"Duh. Bond conditions," Dinkie-Do said. "No weapons around our Honey-Judge. Besides, it's just not fashionable."

Seeing their loyalty, I wanted to cry, but didn't.

"QVC carries purses with side zippers for guns," Carlye said. "I know about these fashion things. A girl has to stay on top of fashion *and* protection. Besides you can put protection in there, both kinds."

Margo's eyes brightened. "I'll bedazzle holsters."

Carlye fanned her face. "The truly great thing is that the purse and the protection come in matching colors."

"I'll absolutely check that out." Dinkie-Do scribbled a note. "Matching essentials with eye shadow is a must have."

"Can we stay on topic?" I straight-armed Mr. Water Bottle zip-your-mouth face at the group.

All eyes again on me, I said, "Okay. You can't discuss any of this with anyone, even among yourselves, unless you're with me. You all know Hunter's adding to our security. He's also been checking for bugs."

Dinkie-Do shuddered from head-to-toe. "Call the Orkin Man—"

"Chill, Fashion-King Gumby," Carlye said. "She means listening devices, like the ones used by the CIA and FBI and politicians."

"My bad." Dinkie-Do re-focused on me. "Go on, Honey-Judge."

I tossed Dinkie-Do a water bottle. He opened it and guzzled.

"I'm not sure who to trust—except for us." I looked at each of them again and hoped nobody would jump up and confess they'd been spying on me.

Carlye snatched the happy-faced bottle from Dinkie-Do and tossed it over her shoulder into an open trash bin. "What about your ex, or your guard that Hunter fella, or your lawyer-hunk-uh boyfriend?"

"Three white knights." Dinkie-Do twirled his pointer finger. "Just like in the fairy tales they'll come through."

Subtract two detectives who've already convicted me, and I'm still up one knight. I'm not good at math, but I liked the odds of enjoying my man, preferably in the bedroom, while I handled my life. That scenario hadn't failed me—yet.

"Margo, buy everyone—including me—untraceable disposable phones."

"Drug-dealer phones?" Margo said.

"I'm going with," Dinkie-Do said.

"Avoid predictable routines," I said. "Travel different routes to and from work to avoid being followed."

They nodded at me.

"My big request—" I hesitated. "When courthouse people come in, I want to be notified. Always. While you shampoo, I'm going to search anything not attached to them."

"Gossip's glam, but an illegal search?" Dinkie-Do looked shocked.

Margo flushed. "Not illegal if you're not a government agent."

"Miss Judge doesn't have time for an expensive lawsuit. She has all of us," Dinkie-Do said.

"Gossip is hair salon's first language," Carlye said. "I bet there's an Official *Rosetta Stone: Speak Hair Salon with Confidence.*"

"Not," Dinkie-Do said.

"Maybe I'll get rich writing it," Carlye said. "Since I don't lack imagination like some people who work here."

"Some people who want to continue to work here will listen up." I tried to sound playful and got right back to serious. "When we're finished, we'll send each client café-side with coupons for coffee, bagels, yogurt, and the works. Rosa will arrange extra staff and shifts. Margo will assist—salon and café."

Thankfully, Rosa agreed without rap.

"The next three days will be grand for listening. You're all going to be too busy to do much else but have wee talks with clients. If there's even one walk-in we'll be overbooked." Trisha cackled. "It'll be a savage time."

This plan was strengthening my resolve, and I had new hope. Busy was fantastic. Busy with gossip and many pairs of inquiring ears was profoundly encouraging. Busy just might slip me through those ugly prison bars.

CHAPTER THIRTY-EIGHT

Almost a week of nonstop clients, my scribbling names, possibilities, and theories, caused the time to zip past. I was thankful I hadn't seen hide nor ballcap of the Hollywood Twins. By Thursday evening, I wanted nothing more than to get into the house, up the stairs, out of my clothes, and into a tub.

When the garage door rumbled down behind Dinkie-Do and me, I unlocked the door to the house, and we entered. The aroma of marriage swarmed me: dinner. I hadn't cooked a full meal since my night in jail. I dropped my stuff, lost my boots, and headed toward the enticing classic-French-chateau fragrance. Dinkie-Do sniffed along right behind me.

"Mmmm," Dinkie-Do said. "Is that chicken?"

Dexter fanned a spatula toward Dinkie-Do's Plasti-gals. "The Stepford pageant and I have prepared parmesan-encrusted chicken, smashed potatoes, green beans with almonds, and cherry-and-blue-cheese salad. Plenty to share. They're on diets."

"Cute as always." To stop myself from dancing to the aroma, I pinched my earlobe. "I'm on work overload." I really needed to be alone.

"I'm about to faint from famish." Dinkie-Do smoothed down an intense auburn Plasti-gal ponytail and gazed over his Plasti-harem.

I glared at Dex, who might as well have been a prancing peacock on the make. I wanted to slap his I've-got-you smirk.

"Alas, I'll accessorize my dollies best on a full stomach." Dinkie-Do looked to me for approval.

Deflated, a looming headache now replaced hope. I had to give in to food. It would help. "Speaking of chickens, where are your two cockerel companions?"

Dex flipped the chicken onto a tray. "They're mapping out a next step."

"This is my life, and I'm in control of it—"

"Trust yourself, Lover—that's right, and trust what you know, but for cryin' out loud, trust who you know."

He was right. I had good family and good friends and a good Sebastian. I was glad for the help.

Dexter tilted his head for a better view of the kitchen table and then looked back at the island and set the chicken down. He grabbed place settings and rearranged everything to seat us all at the island with Dinkie-Do's dolls.

It was, in some bizarro world, more fitting.

"Wine?" He opened the refrigerator wine door and gasped.

"No alcohol; on bond." Words I hated reciting.

"Okay, Coke with lemon it is." He opened the lower vegetable bin and grabbed a lemon.

"Ditto. No alcohol in recovery, lifetime." Dinkie-Do glided into a chair, next to one of his girls. The way he put an arm around her reminded me of Tom Hanks in *Castaway*, confiding to his volleyball companion Wilson. "The colors are all so much brighter without it, aren't they, Sugar?" he said thoughtfully. "It's like a brilliant gift."

I was proud of Dinkie-Do for making it through that wall. I didn't want to get smacked by that wall. And I didn't want to end up on my face under that wall.

Dinkie-Do handed me a tin.

Perplexed. Again.

"Blue shadow sparkles for you, Honey." Dinkie-Do thumbs-upped me. Then he whispered, "Like from the little mishap the other night."

I tossed it in my bag. An explosive gadget that couldn't get me in bond-violation trouble. I liked it. I directed a permissive nod toward Dinkie-Do, who mouthed *wow* at the meal. I slung my bag over the back of the chair next to him and sat. I had to admit, it was nice being served a homemade meal.

"This just tickles my taste buds," Dinkie-Do said.

"I'll tell the chef you approve." Dex licked his lips.

I was hungry enough to eat kitty treats. The thought of cat food sent me swiveling to figure out what corner Jimmy Jack had curled into. With food steaming through the house, it wasn't like him not to be the center of attention.

"Jimmy Jack?" I called.

Dinkie-Do set his silverware down. "He just rubbed through my legs."

Not exactly what I wanted to hear, but at least I knew he was afoot. Jimmy Jack hissed; my nose and arm hairs bristled. My body stiffened. I reached into my updo, grasped the hard handle, and slipped the Taser out. "Get back." I aimed. "Jimmy Jack isn't afraid of anything." My voice was firm, but the sound of it unnerved me.

There were growls and hisses. Then, near the pantry, a high-pitched meow sounded. The hair on his back stood up, and his tail puffed out.

I saw it. Since screaming is a one-way ticket to out-of-control, I clamped my teeth hard. A really big serpent with a nasty attitude slithered across my shiny kitchen floor. The creepy reptile was as thick as my wrist and coming straight at me.

I centered the red light and fired. Stepping back, I shot again, and again. Okay, it was like the clay pigeons. I'm happy the court issued all the judges a state-of-the-art repeater Taser—I did eventually hit the target, but other casualties happened, too. I didn't care.

The final shot had Dinkie-Do yelping and shrieking in sobs as he held his now-shrinking pony-tailed Plasti-gal. Jimmy Jack gave a final screech and sprinted as if he'd been sprayed with dog food and was surrounded by wolves.

Dex pressed me against himself.

I wasn't sure if he was scared or trying to protect me after the fact or trying to restrain me from further plasticide. At this point—if he didn't let me go—the onslaught would be against him. I peeked up at him, sure my face was more contorted than angry. "Your point in restraining me?"

"What the hell?" Dex released me. On the floor lay a stunned, hopefully dead, eight-foot-long, black rattlesnake, and it was sporting a black bow. The bow held a paper.

Dex gingerly removed the Taser from my fingers. "You can't have a Merlot with dinner, but you can carry a concealed weapon?" His voice had a higher pitch than I was used to.

"This is a no-rattlesnake zone." My jaw tightened and my back teeth ground together. "The Taser is court-issued, and they never asked for it back. At least my shooting lessons finally paid off."

"Airhead lady might disagree." Dex chin-pointed toward teary Dinkie-Do.

I grabbed my phone, snapped photos, and pulled a paring knife and kitchen scissors from the utensil drawer. Armed with adrenaline, I tiptoed toward the reptile.

It wasn't moving.

Dex said he'd get the note for me, but he didn't come any closer.

I snipped the ribbon and snatched the note. "Dinkie-Do, pull yourself together before Sir Hiss-a-lot wakes up. Get Animal Control over here. Dead or alive, it's their issue."

Dinkie-Do rubbed his cheek against the doll. "She was so beautiful."

With my eyes on Dex, I hugged Dinkie-Do. "Dex is magic with airheads."

Dex summoned the Bangles and walked like an Egyptian. "If I can find the old bike-repair kit, and you don't mind a little patch, she'll be upright by the time you fill your bubble bath."

"Oh, Mr. Dex." Dinkie-Do released the doll. "Thank you."

"Patches, garage, upper closet shelf." I turned to Dinkie-Do. "Dress her in leathers. It'll complete the look."

"You two are the best." Dinkie-Do swished to the kitchen desk for his phone.

Dex focused between the note and the snake. "Well?"

I waved the paper like a white flag, and he followed me. "At the salon and café doors—I think we need to add a metal detector."

"Right," Dex said. "The next snake might be carrying."

Ass. We sat at the kitchen table away from the chaos. The note, like the ribbon, was different from the others, like its sender. Plain white copy paper and oddly printed text. I read it aloud.

> **YOU SNAKE. KEEP YOUR MOUTH CLOSED FOR A CHANGE.**
> **STOP NOSING INTO OTHER PEOPLE'S BUSINESS BEFORE SOMETHING WORSE HAPPENS.**

This was like a bad dream. I was naked. In the dark. In a pit of rattlesnakes. And everyone was watching.

CHAPTER THIRTY-NINE

After I single-handedly mastered the rattlesnake, the evening passed without incident. Fresh from the night's sleep, I entered *Feather-rap* Café. Rosa, on a stepstool, armed with coffee beans, was refilling a coffee machine and mumbling bad rap lines. My charmingly organized café had morphed into a fourth dimension where rules didn't exist and pandemonium squawked.

Carlye gushed toward me with hugs, as if I'd disappeared and reappeared before her eyes, and she wanted to ensure my physical presence. "Great, isn't it?"

I stepped back and frowned. "Are you confused? Café. Not a pet store," I whispered. "People eat here. I could lose my license. Health Department citations—"

"Federal law. You can't discriminate. I did me some research. Talked to an old lawyer-john of mine."

I shook my head in long negative sweeps. "About working at the zoo?"

"My baby needs changes of scenery." Carlye shot two fingers out and Shazam climbed on. After rubbing nose-to-beak, the parrot perched on Carlye's shoulder. "See how well behaved my baby is in here? Shazam is calmed by the smell of coffee and the grinding of roasted coffee beans."

Ironic that Feathers and I were calmed by the same thing. I wondered how many shots of hairspray Shazam could handle. I had to get back to my staying-out-of-prison, clean-souled life.

Carlye pulled out a tiny orange vest and placed it so close to my nose I saw double. "Service animal. Vest says so."

Damn. "You and Rosa manage Shazam, scoop poop, clear feathers, and monitor his squawk."

"Shazam won't make any more mess than Dinkie-Do."

No time to argue. I called over to Rosa, "I'll fill the corner booth in two hours. Fill the table with edibles. I'll need privacy." I stepped toward the linking door into the salon. "Bird-mama where are you working today?"

"My next client ain't for half an hour. This here is Shazam-and-me time." Carlye ordered a scone, and I exited the café before anything I'd regret exited my mouth.

When I sat at the reception desk, I told Trisha how I'd fearlessly protected my menfolk against a malevolent reptile and searched the internet as best I could. I had one lead on a local exotic-animal dealer and discovered no animals were missing within a three-hundred-mile radius.

I decided to give up on that mystery and finger-scrolled through the appointments, while Trisha looked over my shoulder.

"Some people from the courthouse have made appointments," Trisha said. "I'm being careful not to schedule a blunder. Who'd blather with their boss in the same room? Coworkers together, now that'll be fiercely productive." She pointed at my column in the book. "You have clients most of the day, but if you work fast with your next client there's time for a break when Wade's with Carlye."

Trisha was right up there with Sebastian, hairspray, and coffee. If she kept this up, I might have to adopt her. A good chance to be involved in the chatter was busy hands and open ears, but the chance to wander and chitchat might even be better.

Trisha tapped at a name and said, "Wade Mazour is coming in for his beard; he's becoming quite the professional man." She cackled.

I knew she didn't mean to sound sinister, but her laugh had undertones of maladjusted Joker attacking Batman.

"Let's hope Wade talks." I'd try to talk him into highlights or something else that would cause him to linger and loosen.

Trisha pointed to a name in Dinkie-Do's column. "Judge Laurel Briggs' Law Clerk Zena Royale is in for a brow wax. That Wade runs the lot of them over there. Like gang-leader of the law clerks, he is. And Zena is as much of a fashion queen as her Judge," In Trisha's world everything was shamrocks and lager.

I'd never seen the law clerks congregate. I told Trisha, "The only time I've seen them all together was at a Halloween party." Noel was the perfect Frankenstein's monster and Zena Royale came in burlap and a Mess America sash. None of them seemed capable of dastardly doings.

"If Wade leads me to some answers, I might join his gang," I said and pondered open-ended questions. Cross-examination was where I shone, but in the salon, leading the witness would be frowned upon. I vowed to be as subtle as low-lights while Carlye pruned him. I had to wonder why Laurel didn't tell me Zena would be in.

"The salon's brilliantly filled." Trisha gestured wide. "Everything's prepped for gossip. Rosa has a grand man delivering pretty pastry trays, carafes of specialty coffees, and bottles of juice."

I flipped a thumbs-up and went to get my station ready. Striding toward the work-floor center, I stood toe-to-toe with Carlye, her wacky parrot balanced on her forearm.

"No pets in the salon," I said in my best matter-of-fact tone.

"Shazam fits right in," Carlye wailed. "I know what I'm talking about. He'll keep everybody talking and wanting to come back. They'll bring friends in for services and to see him."

Drat. I could imagine that happening. I rubbed my temples. "Okay," I whispered. "But any calamity, any mess, any Amazon bird flu, it's on you." I might never be able to hire new stylists into this nest of renegade hens. I crossed the room to my station.

Squawk. "Nice rack, Jack."

Damn straight.

Carlye set up a bird swing next to her station, and I made a mental note to check my insurance, my business license, and the city animal ordinances. Dinkie-Do bounced and twirled, rearranged his station with new heels, scarves, flowers, and accessories.

His station looked like Hawaii-meets-New York on steroids. Shazam did seem to fit in. I focused on

Margo's station. She maintained it right out of a Paul Mitchell School award-winning *How-To* book.

My station was classic. I'd rethink my look, but not now. I sat, crossed my legs, and closed my eyes for calming seconds. My every-day-is-wedding-hairspray-day would get me through.

Distracted by the jingle of the door, I saw Wade Mazour enter. Carlye engaged him in conversation and escorted him to her chair, claiming master expertise at men's facial hair. Wade complimented Shazam and offered to babysit him anytime. Carlye danced around Wade, who was now seated in her stylist chair, and then handed him a feather from her collection. Wade slid it into his shirt pocket.

"Oooey. You a man of men, putting Shazam's feather next to your heart."

"I'm a vegetarian," Wade said. He paused, fixed his eyes on Shazam, then met Carlye's. "I can't stand the thought of any animal being harmed. Shazam is proof of how intelligent they are. I love hearing him talk."

"That's my baby," Carlye beamed.

Had I heard that right? Vegetarian? Lover of all animals? I had to rethink the rumors I'd heard about Wade bar hopping with Donnettelli, making midnight runs for Coney dogs, and crossing the entire city in search of the best bar-b-que. Not being a vegetarian wasn't illegal, and Laurel and Palene liked Wade. But, he was at the notorious poker party the night of *the murderous deed.*

I was on edge, confused, and still pondering Wade's inconsistency when the next jingle of the door sent me into grappling mode. My heart, mind, and body prepared for the next shocker. My intuition had vanished.

I was more than a little surprised to see my friend at the door.

Margo offered Shayla Hoffman, the Probate Court Administrator, coffee and a scone, and they headed toward my corner.

"Welcome. I don't usually hug, but I've missed you."

We hugged. Shayla sat in my chair; I caped her and met her eyes in the mirror. "Very happy to see you."

"Couldn't pass up a free haircut." Shayla grabbed her coffee and scone and took a large bite and a long sip. "You've caused a lot of talk."

"Gossip?" I raised a tell-me-more brow.

"Same courthouse since—" She blushed.

"Since I tossed my robe for hairspray and was arrested for murdering my nemesis?" I grinned.

She chuckled. "I've missed your style. But Donnettelli's grouchiness is not missed."

"How's Probate Court?" I kept my voice light. Shayla had been a good gal-pal. We'd shared lunch and confidences. When things were bad, and neither Laurel nor Palene were available, I'd hidden in Shayla's office. I didn't want to abuse our friendship, but I didn't want to be anyone's jailhouse friend.

"Palene's threatening to join you." Shayla announced like it was a done deal.

"That would be a treat." Palene had mentioned the idea, but never seriously.

"She's looking into massage-therapy schools. Says she's kept up her nursing license, so it won't take much to get certified." Shayla lowered her voice and looked at Wade Mazour. "You keep big company," she said.

"Friend of yours?" I whispered. "I didn't realize he was an animal lover." The pair turned and watched Shazam sitting on Wade's shoulder.

"Who knew?" Shayla was trying hard not to laugh.

"Bird whisperer. Until now, I've only seen Shazam that content with Carlye." I tried not to watch too intently, but the scene melted my heart just a tad.

"He isn't in our building very often," Shayla said.

I tried to watch him and focus on Shayla, as I combed through her hair. "What were you thinking? Color, cut?"

"Update my style." She tossed out the command as if she were invoking wild abandon. "I can't toss anything black and flowing and walk out of my job, but I can walk in a new woman."

"Understood."

"I trust you." She settled. "In fact, I've wanted to tell you something. I'm not sure if it's important." Her eyes darted to Wade, like maybe she didn't want to talk in front of him.

I handed her the hair-color wheel with attached hair samples. "Follow me."

Shayla leaped off the chair and shadowed me into the mixing room.

I closed the door behind us and faced her.

"People think Donnettelli had a lot of money." Shayla paused for effect. "Not true."

"I don't understand."

"Several years ago, his parents died within a year of each other," Shayla said. "The estates barely covered the debts."

"He has siblings." I'd never met them. I figured they were also scary.

"Younger brother and sister, penniless until after their parents died." Her voice got somber.

"Life insurance bypasses Probate." I ran through a laundry list of ways to inherit money both in and outside of an estate.

"Nope." Shayla shook her head. "There was a creditors' hearing. And there was only enough insurance to cover the funerals. His parents' home was sold to pay the debts."

"Your point?"

"I'm nosy. Everybody knows that about me," she said as if she were proud of it. "The estates were filed months apart but were open at the same time, so after a joint hearing to close the estates, I wanted to take a peek, but both were closed and ordered sealed."

"Sealed? That's odd."

"Agreed. It's extraordinary. From what I saw there was no reason for that. Violation of court rules, as you know files are difficult to seal without good reason."

Violation, yes.

"I'm the last person who ever sees the files in the Probate office before the final hearing—just before they go to the Judge. I personally checked each of those files for all closing documents and organized what the Judge needed to review and sign. Nothing special. The estates were short of money."

"So?" I inspected her face. Shayla was serious, but a visible uncommon blanch ran through her.

"Look, all I'm saying is Donnettelli started showing off and acting like he was from old money." She rubbed her fingertips together. "Almost immediately, well close in time after the closing of the estates, I heard he began supporting his siblings. I didn't think much about it because he's a Judge and makes good money. But I was struck by it when you were arrested."

I waited.

"Then I thought back to the money and the file being sealed."

"No one complained about a conflict when the files were sealed? Any possibility of a trust?" I asked.

"No objections, no assets, no trust." Shayla didn't blink. "Judge, you know, when there's no objection, closing the file is acceptable, even if it is against the rules. There's no one to complain about it."

"What's your pleasure?" I asked.

She handed me the color wheel with three hair samples plucked: blond, sable, and copper. "Surprise me."

"Got it." Thoughtfully I pulled a mixing bowl and hair color from the cupboard.

We returned to my station, and I began her new look by separating sections, painting her hair with color, and enveloping it in foil. Adding her info to what I already knew—nothing wrapped neatly together.

While they were in the salon, Wade and Zena didn't say anything about anything, but they suddenly disappeared together. Were they dating? Were they up to more than beautifying? Were they reconnoitering? Nothing matched, which was beginning to be too usual.

Shayla's updated look left her delighted and talkative. Before we were done, she'd told me about the trouble with her car, the problems with her neighbor, the new shoes Laurel had worn last week, and a date—with the potential for a second date—during which she'd seen Judge Donnettelli and Renée Reed at the Crowne Plaza in Detroit.

I reminded her it was a convention center, and there was probably a court-related reason they were there, but she pooh-poohed that and explained that Peter Dune hadn't thought it was court-related—when she'd helpfully told him about it. Evidently—according to Shayla—when he'd heard the news, Peter turned an interesting shade of purple. Did I smell motive?

CHAPTER FORTY

By Saturday afternoon, the vastness of Donnettelli's arrogance had set my brain to reeling, and I sat at my station making notes to organize what I'd learned. Just how many court rules could he have violated? Had a broken court rule gotten him killed and me framed? Or had he violated one too many social rules? Nah. If it were old-fashioned jealousy, I wouldn't be headed for the slammer on a frame-up.

Laurel appeared at my station, placed a note in my hand, hugged me, and beelined to Dinkie-Do's station. I flipped the note inside my notebook. "You look beautiful as always," I called over to Laurel and secured my notes in my station cupboard.

"You look distracted," Laurel said.

I wanted to tell her she looked distracted, too, and ask her why, but there were too many people within earshot. Laurel always occupied a room. At her last weekly appointment, she and I had agreed that Dinkie-Do would highlight her hair, and I would cut.

She waved me over to his station. "Heel-toe it this way. Let's chat."

Laurel's energy always reignited my own. "Yes, ma'am." I stood and saluted her.

When I landed by her side, Laurel asked, "Sleep much? Sorry, but before you take the scissors to my scalp, you need to pull yourself together."

"I can cut hair in my sleep." I shot her a stern look. "You look like you're not sleeping, either. Everything okay?"

Laurel smoothed her dress over her knees. "I'm not facing murder charges. I'm just working in a not-nice place."

Dinkie-Do began his hair-dance while he draped, snapped, and played with Laurel's hair, lifting one length at a time. "We'll get your glam on. A third color will make a much bolder statement. Your high-cheek-bone structure can handle it, and I have the perfect makeup, too."

"It's like you read my mind." Laurel shouldered in and accepted a cup of coffee. She drank a long sip and marveled over the new Dinkie-Do shoe display. "What fun."

I crossed to the serving area, grabbed a cinnamon roll and placed it on a china plate that matched the coffee cup Laurel was holding.

"You all make me wish I could quit and join you," Laurel said. She eyed the pastry I placed in front of her with longing.

Dinkie-Do grinned, with a quick showroom gesture toward the new shoes he'd purchased courtesy of my cash flow. The missing fourteen hundred dollars popped back into my memory. I still had to deal with that mystery.

I scooted over to Carlye's chair and sat there while Margo swept the floor. "I have an odd question." My voice was low, my eyes focused on Laurel.

"Shoot." Laurel's voice had a teasing edge. "Not literally."

"Funny." I swirled Carlye's chair toward Laurel and motioned to Dinkie-Do. He pumped up her chair to exactly my seated height, swiveled it to face me, and excused himself to mix color.

"How did Donnettelli get all his money?"

Laurel shrugged. "His parents' estate, a few big cases from when he was in practice, and good investments." She studied me. "Why?"

"Because no seated Judge in recent years becomes rich on a Judge's salary. But Donnettelli did."

"He clung to people who had money." Laurel added, "His buddy Judge Haddes has money. We all spent money on our kids, but Jurisa and her husband saved theirs."

"He was a bottom-feeding sucker-fish," I said.

Laurel chuckled. "Jurisa was his insipid algae."

Dinkie-Do set the color down on the cart beside his station and organized foils.

Jurisa Haddes walked every lunch hour, heat, rain, or bad hair, and was married to a now-retired detective, thirty years her senior. She openly followed Donnettelli's lead, no matter how revolting, and soaked up the attention of men like dermabrasion sucks up dead cells.

"Donnettelli had no real respect for her. Ever notice her lioness-in-heat moves? She is famous for touching every male around her and freezing out every female," Laurel said. "And her lame excuses to rub against Donnettelli! Kept me looking for wear-spots on his clothing."

I fake-frowned. "You're horrible." I was hoping for something, anything to latch onto.

Laurel sipped coffee.

"Our feud was so widespread," I said, "attorneys didn't even mention Donnettelli's name to me."

"They were afraid of him," Laurel said. "If they didn't laugh at Donnettelli's jokes, he'd even take it out on their clients."

"He threatened attorneys, too." I said.

Laurel slapped her hands against her cheeks. "Judges, too."

Now we were into it. "The bastard did something to you that you haven't told me. Give."

Laurel gripped her saucer with both hands. "Like he did to you in the elevator—liar's blackmail. He wanted something signed and said he'd let Michael know about—Donnettelli and me—as if."

This was it. "What did he want you to sign?"

"I don't remember. I sign so many things." Laurel set the cup on the counter and turned away from me. "I know I'm going to love these colors."

Had I been dismissed? Or had she really forgotten? Alrighty then. Maybe Laurel was hiding more than chronic klepto-shoe-mania.

I strode back to my station. "I'll keep asking questions. Somebody's going to replace me on that suspect short list."

Within minutes, Trisha appeared with a box of pretty pink glass vials trimmed in silver and placed one strategically at each station. I didn't recall such dainty packaging on any recently placed orders. "Did I order those?"

Trisha fingered the ribbon on one she'd placed next to her register. "Sample box. There's a number to place an order."

"Those are big sample bottles, and pretty."

"Highly unusual name," Trisha said. "New company: *Gamba*. Better whiff as good as it looks."

"We'll see Monday." At the end of a full Saturday there were too many fumes to get a good scent. I had to keep all my senses on alert in every way. Two perfumes in one day, a definite fashion don't, as dangerous as having two men in one day. It could wait.

Margo's bedazzled nails sparkled as she rapidly tossed a pile of gum and Blow Pop wrappers into a garbage bag, tied it, pulled it from the bin, and released it with a thud.

Dinkie-Do cleaned his station and put his sample bottle next to a silver-toed pump. "Oh, you all, go on with yourselves. I'll spritz it if it's a sweeter, fruitier scent—"

A sour-lemon wince embodied Carlye's whole person. "You had to go there. Can't you just let things be—tap dance quietly?"

Dinkie-Do ignored her. Nose up, palms up, rotating hands up, he magician-swirled. "As I was saying, I do not like those ones with peppery, cotton candy, cinnamon notes. I cannot wear them, I cannot stand them, I cannot sell them." Finger snap. Twirl.

"Look Sam-I-Am, finicky scissor-clipper, glitter shadow, primper-man, maybe you should come out with your own perfume line. I might even be your tester." Carlye rocked her hips and planted herself between their workstations.

Dinkie-Do wiggled back and forth, snapped his fingers again and then aimed a sly half grin at Carlye. "I'd ask you in a scented note."

"I can smell it already. Just find me a scent that doesn't offend my Shazam." Carlye positioned her backside to Dinkie-Do and exited for her weekend. Dinkie-Do was staying late to work on his product line.

I locked up and called it day. I made a list of discussion points and was anxious to meet with my male trio. Dex was cooking, and I was hungry.

I entered my house to the sound of male banter and a set table complete with flowers and appetizers. The thought that I never had to leave my home with this kind of care crossed my mind, but it simultaneously occurred to me I'd be in another type of prison. I needed to stay in control.

That evening over dinner, we four shared new information and a horde of hypotheses. Hunter had followed Jurisa Haddes more hours than he'd cared to and now hypothesized she had a sister, and that sister had perished when—during a tornado in Kansas—a bungalow landed on her. I couldn't argue. When the man's right . . .

Sebastian was up to his sexy calves in profit-by-case-manipulation, and he was certain it was the reason Donnettelli had been killed. Dex—shy as ever about me and my career and how outspoken I was—thought Donnettelli had been killed just to get me to stop talking in general and about the Manville case, to be specific.

But I had the real deal: Donnettelli owed Peter Dune poker money, and not only didn't he intend to pay Peter, but humiliated him by forcing him to host the poker party—on an ongoing basis. Not many men endure someone's sadistic degradation without contemplating payback.

Peter had been at the party, sure, but once Donnettelli phoned and made it known he was at the courthouse, Peter could have easily slipped away. The man lived seven minutes from the courthouse. He parked a rental car down the street from his, slipped out, killed Donnettelli, and the next morning, he messed with the card-swipe and camera software to make it useless in an investigation.

I asked Hunter to find proof that Peter had the skills to modify the recordings and to get a copy of the video of me in the hallway, finger-shooting Donnettelli.

The men didn't agree with me, but they had the decency to try to hide their patronizing attitudes. If I waited for them to bust a move, I'd be rooming with twenty-one hundred women, courtesy of the state of Michigan.

CHAPTER FORTY-ONE

Monday morning, in an *I'm a free American* mood, I clad myself in red Ariat Western boots, blue bootleg jeans, and a red-and-white lace-cutout shirt. It was August first and about a month until my pretrial hearing. I awoke firmly committed to an added motto: "Every day is Independence Day."

I entered the salon—ready to tackle the day. All I wanted was one quiet business day to review everyone who'd been in the salon, who'd had appointments, and who might have set me up. Were there any unique intersections between the courthouse and the salon? Dinkie-Do followed me inside.

Carlye eyed Dinkie-Do. "Twenty minutes til we open. You sure is cutting it close."

Dinkie-Do ignored Carlye.

"My first client is already waitin' at the door," she said.

Sure enough Donnettelli's Court Reporter Noel Lemmon was hovering around the double doors. "He must be in a hurry. Carlye, go ahead and let him in, please."

Dinkie-Do raised both hands in his half celebrating/half take-charge way. "I've got it." He flipped on the *OPEN* sign, unlocked the double doors, and flung one open wide. "Welcome to the land of luxury. Miss Carlye awaits you."

Noel smiled warmly at Dinkie-Do, who wiggled up to his station, pulled a few combs from the sterilizing solution, and laid them out on a towel.

Carlye met Noel, escorted him to her chair, and introduced Shazam, who was parked on his perch. "Ranger coming." *Squawk*. "Pic-a-nic baskets. Hot man." *Squawk*.

"That's a discerning bird." Noel climbed into the stylist's chair and let Carlye cape him.

"Hey, no on-duty vest, no pets," I called out.

"That vest crushes Shazam's stunning feathers," Carlye said. "And this here beauty salon don't want a bad rep for anyone having a bad hair day."

Noel raised his hands. "No bad hair day for me, please." His voice was kind and accepting.

I sidestepped the hair-versus-feather issue. "And just what is the reason for your service bird?"

"You ain't allowed to ask that. And you're stressing me out with the goings on around here."

Great, something else to be blamed for.

"Bird feathers," I said. "He wears the vest, or he flies home." I folded my arms and stood in solid judicial stance.

Carlye harrumphed, grabbed Shazam, and slipped his vest on him.

"We're having a no-catastrophe day here," I said.

Noel laughed. And Shazam occupied himself quietly by picking at his vest. Finally, a good thing.

The front door chimed, and Hunter and Sebastian sauntered in and huddled with Trisha for a minute to get the scoop on my mood. There was so much swagger as they crossed the workroom and camped at my station, I expected to hear a chorus of "Howdy, Miss Nicoletta."

But before they could acknowledge me, through the not-so-secret passageway, Rosa came in, too. "The latest bank deposit." She handed it to me. "I mean in your dream, you might want to scream, because that bird, ain't no nerd."

I blinked at the revenue column and held back a *yahoo*. Hearing between the lines, I figured she thought Shazam was bringing in customers. "Impressive. I'll set aside a portion in a Health Department Defense Fund." It wasn't easy to remain stern when profit was grinning up at me. Rosa gave me an understanding smile and headed back to work.

I called after her. "Hey Rosa, grab a few of those pretty sample perfumes from Trisha. Today's special. You and the café staff should try it out."

She accepted a handful of bright pink bottles and headed for the café. Hunter and Sebastian settled in at my station, and I stepped over to Carlye's to speak with Noel and sent her for a short break.

"I'm sorry for your loss, Noel." I pocketed my fingers. "I know you worked for Judge Donnettelli for a long time."

"The bastard had it coming," Noel said easily, without any hint of malice. Like he was just acknowledging the inevitable.

"Any idea who shot him? I mean if we stipulate I didn't do it." That's me—Subtle Nicoletta, they call me.

Noel clowned it a bit, stroked a pretend beard. "If—and it's a huge if—we stipulate you didn't shoot him, then I'd have to say it's someone Donnettelli was too fucking stupid to listen to."

Colorful. "And you deduce this from—"

"Why else would anyone take the trouble to shoot him in the ear? Come on. That had to be somebody sending a message. And think of the number of women roaming the town, freed from visiting his majesty's chambers in the middle of the afternoon. Yikes!" He made an exaggerated scared face.

I laughed. "You're assisting the visiting Judge now?

"Until the November election," Noel said. "Then I'm going to take some vacation time—somewhere you don't have to scrape ice off your car for thirty minutes before you can run to the market five minutes away." He laughed.

"People like to make fun of Michigan weather." Carlye was back. "But me and Shazam, we like the seasons, and we like snow, and we like—"

Trisha interrupted and handed Carlye one of the free samples, a pink perfume spray bottle.

"Oh! I likes me some pretty perfume." She spritzed herself, and Noel pulled the cape up over his face.

Hairdressers and female clients spritzed. I sprayed my forearm. I sprayed again. Rosa stopped and sprayed her neck just before she opened the door to the café. I breathed in a long whiff. Not much to it.

But Shazam cawed and cussed and demanded pic-a-nic baskets. With a long, loud screech, he flapped to the highest point in the salon and perched and draped his left wing over his face, but he kept screeching. It unnerved everybody. Had he become so bonded to Rosa that he demanded to join her back in the café?

Sebastian called, "Dogs' balls."

Margo snatched a bottle and spritzed me, and then Trisha. The room wobbled as if our feet were planted on trampoline tarp.

From high above the chandeliers, Shazam squawked, "Dogs' balls."

Everyone seemed momentarily stunned until bewilderment spread. The spritzing and sniffing and nasal assault morphed into cognition and congestion.

Faces contorted.

There was gagging, coughing, jumping up-and-down-ing and harmonized nose-holding.

Ugh. The perfume was a definite *Fashion Don't Ever.*

Carlye cried loudest. She performed a kind of tribal-looking rain dance with eyes closed as tight as old raisins. "Ooowhey. I'm blind." Her tone ran up and down the scale. "I've smelled that stench before—under my tires. That there bottle has a skunk inside." She peered through one eye. "Dead molted skunk." She swung around. "My baby! Where's my baby?"

Squawk. "Dogs' balls."

Rosa returned, holding the bottom of her blouse over her head, her eyes blinking faster than a high-speed chase.

Sebastian and Hunter burst into uproarious laughter.

"How'd you let this happen?" I headed toward the pair of guffawing goof-offs.

His shoulders quaking, Hunter showed me palms up. "We use this scent to hunt. Like Carlye said—skunk. It's bottled for hunters to hide human scent."

"Holy shit—Gross." Profaner words escaped me along with clean air. "Hard to take an adversary seriously when he has to resort to kindergarten stunts. What's next? Fart cushions on the chairs?"

Hunter fashioned his hands into some kind of long gun and pointed it into the air.

Noel was laughing so hard, his chair shook. "I guess this cut is on the house." He pulled off his cape and laughed all the way out the door.

"Your fancy perfume won't hurt you." Sebastian laughed out loud. "Some dunny rat replaced the perfume with skunk juice." His face was actually wet.

"Didn't hurt me." But someone was making it clear he could get at me if wanted to. If Peter Dune had taken revenge on Donnettelli, would he take to harassing me? "Calm down, everyone. It's just a manufacturing mix up." I made it up as fast as I released words.

"Perfume got mixed up with animal hunter's camouflage. Trisha's writing coupons for free services. Go home; we're closing for the morning." I motioned Trisha to attend to the front. She was vibrating her head and muttering *highly unusual*. "Did anyone in the café—other than you—get sprayed?"

Rosa shook her head *no*. I was happy to avoid hearing rap—maybe some good came of this mix up.

Careful to avoid contact with my total stinkiness, Hunter leaned and spoke into my ear just as I was rationalizing this would quickly pass. "Toots, there's one other thing."

Yeah, he needed a *hit-slap* after I showered. "I'm listening." I clamped a towel over my nose.

"The scent tends to get much worse as it ages and is exposed to the elements."

Ugh. Great. Before removing the towel from my face, I inhaled a deep breath, and clapped my hands until the room was quiet. "Everyone please exit. We need to clean up before the Health Department gets wind of this. Okay, poor choice of words." I returned the towel to my nose and breathed. Hunter was right; the stench was already more robust. I couldn't imagine it getting much worse.

Shazam eventually calmed, but he clung to Carlye like an additional appendage, and she blamed Sebastian for teaching him a new bad word.

Flinging the phony perfume bottle into a trash bin, Rosa turned down the hallway toward the back exit. Trisha grabbed a stack of towels and passed them out until everyone had one.

Two of the three other clients left peacefully with their coupons. But the third demanded cash for time and ruined clothes. Trisha folded a one-hundred-dollar bill in half and tucked coupons inside the fold, handed it to her, escorted her out, and locked the door behind her. Pulling the shades, Trisha chortled *highly unusual*.

I could live without ever hearing those words again.

I had a strong impulse to spray Hunter and Sebastian so they could join in the fun, but I didn't—only because I'd lose precious time. I'd have to find another way to skunk them, so they could share nature with us.

Just as I thought my deep-woods day had ended, there came knocking on the front window, Trisha unlocked the door, and bells jingled.

"Guess I picked the wrong day to run away from my docket," Palene said. She removed the knotted scarf from her neck and held it to her nose with one hand, the other held a rolled magazine. "Business reorganization?" She laughed and her short chestnut-brown bob seemed to laugh with her.

"Fumigation day, girlfriend." I held my nose and promised to hug Palene another day. She slipped the magazine to me. I unrolled the latest *Cosmopolitan* magazine.

"Shayla said you'd be interested in this," Palene said. She rolled her chocolate-brown eyes sharply toward the magazine and up to me.

I felt something bulky in the magazine and tightened my grip on it. Must be the Probate estate verification. Friends and hairspray, equally reliable.

"Are you here to fill out an application? Heard you want a job as our masseuse." I loved to tease her.

Both hands covering her face, Palene cleared her throat and stepped back to the front door. "First find a giant air freshener." From a pocket, she pulled a red envelope and handed it to me. "As I was getting out of my car, a little girl handed me this and asked me to give it to you."

Pressure like thick fluid drained rapidly from temples into my gut. "Thanks." I couldn't pull off a smile, so I palmed her a stack of gift certificates, showed her out, and locked the door again.

Fully aproned, masked, and gloved, Margo slipped around the room with an industrial garbage bag and tossed everything that couldn't be laundered. She passed out smocks to replace tossed-off clothing, zipped one sample bottle into a Ziploc bag for police and prepared a duplicate for Hunter.

She gathered the remaining bottles and double-tied them into a separate garbage bag for police. With both arms straight out, away from her body, she set the police stuff aside and walked the rest out, I guessed to the ugly dumpster that rested under a gnarly cherry tree in the corner of the parking lot.

Even with a mask, Margo couldn't hide her grin.

Carlye, who'd tossed her bra and her blouse into the garbage bag, bounced up to Margo, arms firmly crossed over her smock-covered, free-floating cleavage.

I waved Trisha home and Margo toward airing the salon. After that, she'd help out at the café.

Dinkie-Do pushed out his quivering bottom lip. "I need a ride home." He was near tears.

Carlye interrupted. "Oh, no you do not. I'm not going anywhere dressed like this alone. I dub us book-ends." She pushed her elbows into her sides and clasped her palms together. "You're with me and Shazam. I'll take you wherever you needs to go."

"Thank you, Miss Carlye." Dinkie-Do sounded sincere.

She said, "Grab some garbage bags and towels because no vermin stench is touching my sweet car."

I shooed them out. "Vamoose."

Wide-eyed and pale, Dinkie-Do followed Carlye. Within three minutes the salon was quiet.

"You men have to withstand my reek, and I don't care how raunchy I get as it ages on me. I fear prison stench will be worse."

Their joint eyes danced in sync as they mutely undressed my smocked body, and I got uncomfortable. It reminded me of the mini-dresses I used to wear and tried to ignore just how much of me was showing. I pondered why, as competing male predators, they didn't spar over the single girl carcass. Women would simply tear each other's hair out.

"Your work calls," I said. But they couldn't take a serious order from a smocked skunk. And the irritation heat from my body caused a rise in potency. Okay, I'd find the funny later, much, much, later.

Sebastian scratched his chin. "Shall we meet in the woods, where you aren't sooky?"

"You think you smell great all the time?" He did, but I wasn't going to admit that after he just told me I stunk like a wild animal. *Sooky—my ass!*

Skunk smelled sweeter than whatever was looming inside the courthouse, and it was safer in the woods than whatever was looming here. "Another clue." I showed the men the red envelope.

Ripping open the evil envelope, I found a newspaper cartoon—main attraction: a guillotine. The note that came with it said:

THIS IS THE LAST TIME WE ASK NICELY. KEEP YOUR MOUTH SHUT.

Deep calm—bordering on catatonia—spread through me, and it seemed someone had turned down the volume on my life. I saw people moving, but the room was silent.

Sebastian took me home.

CHAPTER FORTY-TWO

Late that afternoon—soaking in my third hot, scented bath—my skin was scrubbed raw, my rear was slightly numb, and my right foot was less than comfortable sticking out of the water to avoid short-circuiting the tether. It was supposed to be waterproof, but at this point there was little I trusted. If I was going to get electrified, it would be by Sebastian.

My brain surged through the competing teams of haters aimed at Donnettelli, but I kept coming back to Peter. The challenge had become how to get him to admit he'd shot Donnettelli.

My emerging defense was convoluted. But my reputation needed a solution, not a defense.

I submerged my thoughts and my body, sans right foot. Despite the hot water, a cold chill ran through me, and I pulled the plug. I raised and dried my pruny hide. It was time to sift fact from fiction and map out a plan to get Peter to come clean.

My phone vibrated on the countertop. Barely towel-headed, I growled at the phone and tapped speaker.

Sebastian. "Before my meeting, I dropped off the phony perfume bottles to Hollywood, and I filed your report."

"And?" I wanted to click off.

"Bloke didn't think it was much of a corker. Needs your statement. He questioned the integrity of your business circles and scoffed it off as a competitor's prank."

I moaned—not the kind of moan Sebastian preferred. "Let me guess. Big fun at my expense." I heard silence.

"We'll have a ripper when this is over."

"Palene dropped off verification from Shayla that Donnettelli didn't inherit much from his parents."

"Good oil." Sebastian whistled. "Get some clothes on."

Phone silence.

My cheeks burned. Damn man could sense my bare flesh. I double-checked my phone to ensure FaceTime was off. I needed serious playtime in an evidence-free playground. I wiggled my ring finger. It was bare. Still my decision to remain single. I couldn't hairspray myself to one man just yet, not even Sebastian.

I needed some serious me-time to contemplate everything that had happened with everything we'd compiled. Now was the perfect time. I double-checked the lock on my bedroom door. It would stay that way until I smelled dinner fumes that called me downstairs.

Strong hunger pangs growled when I reached the bottom of the material I'd compared without success. The aroma of a warm meal filtered in from below and distracted my frustration. Was that apple pie in the mix? I tumbled down the stairs and happily took my place at the table. I was getting accustomed to three-male pampering. That was probably not in my best interests, but I decided I had more immediate problems to address.

After dinner, Dexter, Hunter, Sebastian, and I talked about everything but the immediate problem. We cleared the kitchen table and were reseated, enjoying warm apple crisp and ice cream with the late-arriving Dinkie-Do. We were enjoying second helpings when the front doorbell chimed. "I'll get it," Dinkie-Do offered—only to shortly return, flanked by Team Hollywood—again.

"Sorry," Dinkie-Do said.

"It's okay. Care to join us, boys?" I pointed to the empty chairs and the sweet cuisine. Tweedle-Dee and Tweedle-Peach clambered in and joined us.

Grayson focused across the room on the island. "Are Barbie and company joining us, or are they waiting for Ken and Allen?"

The fact he knew Ken's friend's name was disturbing. I clasped my hands in front of me, Godfather-like, with matching voice tone. "Unless you depose me, I'm not answering." Damn it. *I* needed answers.

Grayson sat between Sebastian and Dexter. Fredericks sat between Hunter and Sebastian. A full house. One, I hoped, that wasn't near collapse.

"Search warrant, Detectives?" Sebastian asked.

Grayson pulled up a leather portfolio and unzipped it flat on the table. He took a file folder and handed a report to each of us. "A fresh release from the Prosecutor's Office."

Sebastian squinted. "Without your yabber. Tell us."

Grayson began. "The ME completed Judge Donnettelli's full autopsy. Ballistics and toxicology reports are attached." Grayson flipped pages. "Page three, no toxins found. Page four, two different bullets.

Two shooters. One when he was alive, and one—when he was dead."

"Hot damn." Amazement struck me. "An enemy invasion against Donnettelli."

Sebastian cleared his throat. I understood and stopped speaking. I wanted to happy dance, remove the tether, and oust my tenants, but I knew anything I said and did could be used against me.

I also understood Grayson intended to stay a while. He poured himself a cup of coffee, stirred in cream, and slurped.

"So, were you Shooter One or Shooter Two?" Fredericks snapped a large grape from its branch and rolled it between his fingers. "One is guilty of murder." He popped the grape into his mouth and chewed. "Two, likely guilty of nothing." He broke two more grapes free and popped them into his mouth. Then two more. Slow, methodical. Like he was the frog crushing a fly; like I was the fly.

"Charging on the second bullet is the prosecutor's call," Grayson said.

"We're focused on bringing this first bullet to conclusion." Fredericks shot me a cold look.

"Conduct a real investigation, and arrest the real culprits," Sebastian said.

"Like the Ouija board, we go where the letters direct," Fredericks said. "Letters spelled your client's name."

The coffee, like my mood, had cooled.

Hunter shook the paper. "Wrong game, Vanna—these letters spell *autopsy*. Try Game Changer for a thousand. Who's the second suspect?" Hunter pointed his fork at Fredericks and then Grayson. "Wrong category, wrong answer. Nicoletta's not either shooter."

"Your client had an ongoing feud with the victim, and that's motive. Your client is caught on courthouse security footage having what look to be arguments with the victim on more than one occasion, evidence of that motive. Your client knew her way around the courthouse, that Donnettelli had a gun, how to gain access to the gun, knowledge of his schedule—all of which enabled her to plan, scheme, and perfect her design to murder her adversary," Fredericks said.

Grayson picked up a cannoli and used it like a cream-filled pointer. "And surveillance footage shows you and Judge Donnettelli getting into the judicial elevator together and not leaving for several minutes," Grayson added. "A rather long time for two enemies to spend together."

"Just when did you determine my client knew his schedule or wanted to be trapped in the elevator with him?" Sebastian asked.

"We checked the elevator records. There was nothing wrong with it. Somebody pushed the stop button. You two stayed inside, doing what?" Grayson let the question roll off his tongue smooth as cannoli filling.

"Wasn't my doing—" I began, and Lawyer Sebastian cut in.

"I want to see those records and footage," Sebastian said. "My client has nothing to tell you except *go find the real killer.*"

"We've conducted interviews at the courthouse. Seems the Circuit Court Judges maintained similar schedules and could watch each other on the courthouse security cameras," Fredericks said. "She knew exactly when to corner him off-screen in the elevator. She knew exactly when and where to shoot."

I'd heard similar arguments by the People during criminal trials. I barely heard Sebastian ask the Hollywood team to leave and sank into my chair.

"Wrong information," I sighed. "I steered clear of him and his schedule. I didn't press the elevator stop button; he did."

CHAPTER FORTY-THREE

When the Detectives were safely outside, I tossed the Autopsy Report onto the counter. "Let's divide our work to cover more ground more quickly. I'm their bull's-eye; I not only want them to step in bull crap, I want them to eat bull crap."

The men guffawed, but there was no comfort in that. I felt like bull crap.

Hunter winked at me. "Let's begin with the suits who've been hanging in your café. They're not SEC."

"How sure are you?" I asked.

"My guys got DNA from your café, and we ran checks. The suits work in the movie industry. They're bonded, so their DNA is on file." Hunter pushed away from the table, walked to the kitchen desk, and reached into a soft, fat briefcase I hadn't noticed.

Despite the heat outside, I felt like flakes of Christmas-tree snow just whirled down my spine and left a nagging pinecone needle in my throat.

"The suits are diverse," Hunter said. "Everything from making movies to alleged money laundering. But no criminal records I can find."

"Maybe not those two, but some of the people they work for sound like nasty whackers." Sebastian pretend-played the table as if it were his personal piano.

"Money laundering is not a clean business." His Australian accent stroked another chord with me, and I shifted.

Hunter returned with a red file folder. "Money is in the forefront of everyone's mind, not murder." He opened the folder and pulled out two pictures. "I got LEIN information—you know, like when a cop runs your license—"

"Law school, professor," Sebastian said. "Get on."

"The suits fund legit movies, fine restaurants, and fine jewelry stores. But with their success travels, rumors of ties to illegal gaming and low-rise and high-rise housing scams. Rumors aren't unusual when people have a lot of money." Hunter folded his arms.

"We're losing focus." I wasn't sure how this news fit, how the money tied in, or how these men had done anything wrong. And I was still tethered. "We have to solve Donnettelli's murder. Someone wants to push a quick trial and conviction." I sat back. "We need to follow the money, not let it lead us around by our noses."

They needed to hear me. "I found an odd asbestos case, and I need copies of the file, but the Register of Actions indicates it's at the Court of Appeals."

"Odd how?" Sebastian asked.

"I know at least one bank in a building filled with asbestos. That lawsuit ended in a settlement. And the insurance company paid big. Employees got sick, and some have died."

"If Donnettelli messed with these cases," Hunter said, "someone might have decided to knock him off."

I picked up a table knife and held it like a gavel. Props were good. My knife extension became an immediate focal point—one I might need to use more often.

"I need a copy of the witness lists. One of those names may be useful. And a list of all court personnel who touched that file. I want to see if there's any overlap."

"Let's get in there and get copies." Sebastian pulled out his phone and typed a note to himself.

"While we flounder about, someone in the courthouse knows something and may be manipulating files." I pounded the table with the butt of my knife prop. "The case I just mentioned links all our issues. I hope it'll clear up some of the damned confusion."

"What's clear is that you're targeted. I don't want that bull's-eye on you," Dex said. "Death will not become you."

"In prison or dead, there's no difference." I thought back to the snake note. "Someone wants me to stop complaining about Donnettelli changing my Order."

"Hollywood and Company need to investigate Donnettelli's enemies, including his staff," Sebastian said.

"What do you think about Peter Dune?" Hunter asked.

Funny you should ask. "One. I saw him—at the end of the hall—the last time I saw Donnettelli alive—same day I walked out. Dune had just handed an envelope to Judge Jurisa Haddes and shot me a snide look I can still feel. It was weird. Two. The day I snuck into the courthouse dressed as a pregnant hippie, that day—he gave me a long look."

"He could just have a thing for women with big bellies," Hunter said.

Sebastian ignored Hunter. "Another reason for you to stay away from the courthouse."

I tried to remember I was feeling empowered and hoped it would last. "Three. Peter didn't tell cops he'd heard a woman in Donnettelli's chambers when Donnettelli phoned Peter at two in the morning. Four. He was photo-spying on Laurel and me at Starbucks, knew I'd caught him, and he stopped and fled. Five. He hates Donnettelli for demeaning him, for not paying his debt, and for forcing him to host the poker parties."

Dexter looked frustrated. "What does all that add up to in evidence terms?"

"No evidence Peter has any special skill with video or computers," Hunter said.

Sebastian suddenly looked more lawyerly. "How this is handled is key. Privately. Quietly. Between us. No accusations should be verbalized to anyone until there's hard evidence."

Hunter was already nodding. "Yeah. Make Peter mad, and he's liable to remember to tell the Detectives about the woman he heard in Donnettelli's chambers."

"We need a plan. Let's meet in forty-eight hours to compare and trade information." I stabbed a strawberry, and we watched it ooze. There was a metaphor in there somewhere, but I didn't want to think about it.

When we left the table, I headed toward the stairs and my bedroom, but Sebastian stopped me. He stood silently next to me until Hunter and Dex walked out together. They had business to talk about.

When we heard a car start, Sebastian leaned in and kissed my forehead, then took my hand and led me up the back stairs.

CHAPTER FORTY-FOUR

In less than a minute, we were in the bedroom.

I toe-kicked the door shut.

When Sebastian wrapped his arms around me, I nestled into his chest and let the lump in my throat and the day's frustrations leak all over his shirt.

After a few minutes, I looked into his eyes. "What's that look for?"

"I'm gobsmacked I haven't been sent packing." Sebastian squeezed his arms around my waist and held me tighter. I heard his heart quicken.

I found his hands and led him to the bed. "If you're complaining, find the door, and lock it behind you," I said while I unbuttoned my shirt. I kicked off my boots and tossed open the bed covers.

Sebastian swiftly dropped his clothes on mine and sent exploring fingers down my shoulders toward my waist. "I intend to hold you til you sleep, and I'll be grinning like a shot fox every second."

How did I deserve such a wonderful boyfriend? I recalled kissing him, and the next time my eyes opened, my body announced the need for caffeine. Strong espresso was needed for me to face lack of sleep and the early morning. Damn, for having so little sleep, I felt rejuvenated. I grabbed the remote and flicked on the news.

Sebastian kissed the top of my head. "Sleep."

"Not until my sudden-onset, gray-stripe phobia goes away." I turned up the volume.

"Holy dooly. No drama, until after we're naughty." Sebastian kissed me hard and rolled on top of me.

I dropped the remote.

CHAPTER FORTY-FIVE

At eight, I dropped Dinkie-Do at the front door of the salon. I circled around the building, parked in back, gathered my things, and got out. I strolled through the parking lot, unlocked the salon's back door, and stepped in. I just had to get past the kitchen and the supply rooms before I could hide in my office.

I stuck my arm out the back door, clicked the lock symbol, and listened for the locking beep.

Damnation.

The explosion ripped from Elvis with a deafening *BOOM!* It shook the asphalt and the floor under my feet. I gripped the doorframe and held on. Red-yellow flames blasted into the sky.

The stench of burning rubber and gasoline stung my nostrils. My eyes teared from billows of smoke. I couldn't pull myself away.

My beautiful blue Elvis was an inferno of shattered glass, twisted metal, and smoking leather.

Miraculously, there were no bodies in the scattered parts. Only me. I trembled from the inside out, while some survivalist part of my brain took over, and I slammed the salon door and locked myself inside. Unsteady, I dialed 911. They said they already had the call.

Sure enough, I heard sirens. Déjà damn.

From both sides of the building, my staff sprinted in, and I opened the door again.

All around me, patrons made noise. Some darted away; some dashed toward the blaze; some snapped pictures; others held up their phones filming. It was like watching a mixed-up screen—like I'd played with my remote and set slow motion and fast-forward at the same time.

I punched in Sebastian's number. But Hunter's voice echoed behind me. With Sebastian in my ear, I couldn't concentrate on what Hunter was shouting. Male potency reached around me, grabbed my phone, demanded Sebastian's immediate appearance, and clicked off.

Sirens nee-nawed into the parking lot, and I knew just how they felt. I bent, rescued my keys, and tossed them into my bag. Police arrived first with the fire truck. EMS pulled in from the side street. At least I wouldn't meet the crew from the kitchen fiasco—different jurisdictions.

I hung my thumbs from my jeans pockets to control my emotional reverberations. If only I could get to my office and shut myself in. But Hunter slipped my phone into my bag and his arms around my waist. In unison we made for the table in the kitchen area.

Thankfully, it was only a few paces. I could have been right next to the car. I could have been inside the car. I could have been fused to my car's innards. Forever.

Voices pelted at me like oversized hail. I wanted to duck, but I sank onto a chair at the kitchen table.

Hunter grabbed cold bottles of water, set them in the center of the table, opened one, and handed it to me. "Rehydrate," he said. He grabbed another bottle and sat next to me.

I was still trembling.

Hunter wrapped an arm around me again and held me. It morphed my shakes into small quivers, but I felt numb. He kissed my temple. "We'll figure this out." He squeezed my hand. "Promise." He handed me another bottle of water. "Drink."

"Im-press-ive," Carlye said with head-bob punctuation. "You cleared this place faster than a SWAT team in a hand-job joint." She sat and studied me from across the table. "Way I see it, there's a higher power telling you to get yourself one of those high-powered military vehicles."

Dinkie-Do stood behind Carlye, his concerned eyes fixed on me, his hands on Carlye's shoulders. "Oh, Honey, our beautiful blue Lincoln Continental."

Carlye scowled up at Dinkie-Do and shrugged his hands off her. "You two get married or something? That Lincoln Continental ain't no child, and it sure ain't yours and hers. You just better get a grip."

The Grim Reaper took Donnettelli, he took Elvis, and he had a grip on my throat. I decided to listen to the first responders in search of a clue, any clue.

Trisha could have been the new Ratification Salon bobblehead. I hoped the car bomb hadn't left her with a permanent twitch.

"Judge, I have phones to answer, and you have new staff to hire. Three chicken-feathered stylists flew the coop—for keeps." Trisha tried to laugh, but she sounded like a chicken with a half-wrung neck. She disappeared quick as hairspray mist. Addressing her bobblehead issue would have to wait.

"Honey-girl, never you mind, we'll all help you," Dinkie-Do chimed in.

"Those ungrateful stylists didn't fly the coop; the rats abandoned the ship," Carlye said. "Bunch of deserters. You'd think they never seen a car bomb before. I'm thankful my little Shazam is safely at home."

Everyone focused on Carlye. Nobody noticed Hunter's arm around my shoulders or his fingers circling the center of my back. His magic worked. No more trembling.

"Hunter and I will protect everybody." I doubted my half-smile convinced anyone—ten minutes after I'd almost been blown into a firefly. "And Judges don't break promises."

Dinkie-Do snapped his fingers. "They'll have to firebomb me out."

"Keep your wishful thinking to yourself," Carlye said.

Under the table I patted Hunter's thigh, stood, and faced the back door. He followed my lead. I called back. "Everybody up front. Business as usual. Please." I head-gestured to Hunter. "You're with me, Hulk."

Firebomb-ready, I opened the back door. First responders and a news truck huddled around my charred Elvis like so many chiefs at a hero's powwow. Damn, Sebastian parked next to the Detectives. Better him than me.

I stepped out and shut the door. Okay, I slammed the door. Time to grill the investigators.

"Look at this, Toots." Hunter drew me back, bent, and picked up something—a note wrapped around a brick, which Hunter promptly liberated.

Letters cut from newspaper and magazine headlines:

> SERIOUS ENOUGH 4 U? MYOB BITCH!
> KEEP YOUR MOUTH SHUT.

Hunter quietly rewrapped the brick; I'd never seen him so sad. He wrapped a strong arm around my shoulders.

I decided it might be safer not to get too close to Elvis. Despite needing information, I needed my body parts intact to solve the murder mystery. The note jellied my insides and evaporated my confidence.

I stared at the uniformed officers, in their bomb-gear. They crawled over, under, and through the remains of my Elvis. A few checked the perimeter of the parking lot.

Someone wanted me dead—as in not talking. Shut up? About what? Did I know something?

"Sebastian's covering Hollywood and his buddy," Hunter said. "Let's escape to the café."

I still that loved that man.

CHAPTER FORTY-SIX

Once police and fire cleared a lane and taped off the crime scene, there was no shortage of gawkers. I struggled to control my face. I thought of Peter by the elevator, Peter spying on me and Laurel, Peter under my Elvis. Damn. I had to reign my face in and calm my thoughts, but I could only do that if I discussed them with my three protectors. The drive-thru window had steady business, and the café was standing room only.

"Hell of a marketing move," Hunter said, but there was no mirth in his voice, and he signaled Rosa to negotiate a place for us to sit, which she did without benefit of rhyme.

I ordered myself to use my nice-Nic-voice. "We'll have to wait for a seat in my own café unless you think we should go elsewhere."

"Toots, you know as well as I do, we need to stay where the action is. Look around and tell me if you see anyone out of place."

I had to agree and tuned in my eagle eyes.

Half an hour later, just as we'd snatched a back table, Sebastian came in looking for us.

"Crickey deadheads out there don't know what to do with that vehicle of yours—or with you." Still standing,

Sebastian grabbed a muffin. "Orange-Cranberry. Good for the blood." He sat across from Hunter.

I grimaced at Mr. Manners and went to the counter for a trayful of bribery for the menfolk. The guy in front of me was Peter Dune. I couldn't believe it. I hadn't seen him come in. My metabolism and my mouth kicked into overdrive. "Are you here just to gloat, or are you going to explain why you needed to blow up my car?"

He stepped back and looked surprised as if I'd smacked him, and I might have—if I could have reached that high.

"It's time to come clean, Peter." This tyranny had to stop. I got in his face as closely as I dared, without having assault charges added for touching him. My audacious move lost some oomph because I had to crane my neck back. "Your intimidate-the-Judge tactics aren't working. It's over—as of this moment." I pointed my finger in his face. "And, stop taking pictures of me and Judge Briggs, or we'll ask for stalking charges and a personal protection order, and you'll be out of a job."

He snickered. "Isn't unlawful to take pictures of you in public. Your notoriety brings in big bucks for each picture." He guffawed. I wanted to punch him and his pasted-on smirk. His cold eyes chilled down the full length of my body.

I pointed his frigid face and hot coffee and chocolate croissant toward the booth where Hunter and Sebastian waited. "Trot over there and tell those men how you got out of that poker party—and I already know how you did it—and how you killed Donnettelli." I stood my ground and didn't blink.

For a half-second he tipped his head like a big Irish Setter with a tough puzzle. Then he gave me the finger, grabbed a lidded cup of coffee and a bag of pastries from the counter that weren't his, and walked straight out of the café. I'd add arrogant thief to his column. Meanwhile, I apologized to the confused customer who'd just watch his order get heisted.

It was a tad anti-climactic when I returned to the booth schlepping a tray of banana frappés, one coffee, and a single chocolate croissant. I sat next to Sebastian. Wisely, neither of the men thought it necessary to discuss the persuasive power I'd obviously lost since leaving the courthouse.

I made it clear I didn't want to talk about my near-demise-by-explosion. I explained what just happened with Peter and convinced Hunter not to go after him. We had bigger things to discuss. Grabbing last night's envelope from my bag, I waved it. "Discussion materials."

Sebastian put his hat on the back of the chair and reached for the envelope, but he murmured, "The bomb squad recovered some kind of homemade incendiary from your trunk."

"But my car was in the garage last night and this morning."

"I'm installing more cameras with added angles inside your garage and a list of everyone who has access," Hunter said.

"All my codes have been changed, and except for my houseguests and cleaning crew, no one has access."

"Some chump is watching you." Sebastian sunk a straw into his banana frappé.

"Do the Detectives understand this happened because I'm innocent?"

"They traveled the conspiracy theory path." Sebastian slurped frappé. "In that moment it was easier to lose a car than your freedom. I listened, offered alternatives, and they went away."

Hunter slammed his mug down. I believed he intended that slam for Sebastian's face. "Did you tell them they're playing with nuts and have no screws to tighten into them?"

Someplace deep inside, I sank. Scowling, I eyed the manila envelope. I wanted a full, complete, intact life. And I meant to have it. With an open palm, I smacked the table.

Both men jumped.

"Those misguided Detectives had better get a bottomless gas tank and steer their attention elsewhere. I'm off the map." I pointed to the envelope. "I think I know what Peter and Donnettelli were up to."

Sebastian opened the envelope and handed me the papers. I spread them out. "Copies of the past two years' Register of Actions. Cases Judge Donnettelli and I had in common."

"How can two Circuit Judges have cases in common?" Hunter frowned. "You don't appeal to each other, do you?"

"Not in any sense of the word. But when there are conflicts, Judges recuse themselves, and those cases go back into the random pool for reassignment."

Sebastian agreed, nodding. "And there are other special circumstances," he added.

"Like case consolidation." I said and pulled out the notepad with the columns I'd made. I set the notepad next to the computer printout between the men, and then guided them through the cases with my walking fingers while I explained the ways the Chief Judge can transfer cases.

"Donnettelli played with the natural order of case assignment. Right?" Sebastian asked.

"It was supposed to be random," I said. "But he was moving cases all over the place."

"The poddy-dodger was controlling outcomes."

He was getting his own way with other people's lives. I put the copies I'd made on top of the Register of Actions.

"You discovered Donnettelli's trail." Hunter flipped through the papers. "It makes sense that someone who was negatively affected also figured it out and got upset."

"And plunked a bullet in Donnettelli, and you are the next target," Sebastian said.

"No. I'm convinced it has to be an insider. I'm also convinced it was Peter," I said. "No one outside the courthouse could get into the Judges' area, and even if someone did, the shooter knew how to avoid the cameras."

"And how to finagle the keycard software—or at least the report."

"Who cares about a case getting reassigned?" Hunter studied Sebastian and both men turned toward me. "I mean who benefits from a reassignment? People just want their cases resolved, right?"

"When there's true impartiality." I focused on Sebastian while I spoke for a sense of whether or not he agreed with me. "However, a biased Judge—who wants to direct an outcome—cares."

Sebastian didn't blink. "There could be appeals, but asbestos companies could have moved out of the US by then—hard to get at them internationally—more years of delay. Cases could outlive the interested parties." Sebastian looked disheartened.

Hunter bent nose to paper and studied the notes. He was in his own zone for several minutes. Back in our air space, he shoved the pages at Sebastian. "So the twelve bulging bank accounts were meant to frame Nic and confuse Detectives."

"While Donnettelli hid really big money somewhere—in other accounts or offshore maybe," Sebastian said.

Our corner of the room went silent as we pondered the information. But all this had me thinking back to how I'd missed what was going on right around me with Donnettelli's case maneuvering.

Of course, Palene, Laurel, and I hadn't been involved. Donnettelli extra-bullied us to ensure we stayed beyond arm's length away, so we wouldn't suspect anything. We just wanted to do our work and get the hell out of the building and away from him. Which was what happened. Damnation. We'd been played—unknowing and disposable pawns.

"It sounds like multiple angry victims with motive to kill Donnettelli," Sebastian said.

My guess was somebody had threatened Donnettelli, making the asbestos cases too hot for him.

Hunter sour-faced me. "Some suit at Manville is trying to scare somebody?"

I shrugged. "I'm convinced Peter Dune is behind the mess."

"After Nic resigned, Donnettelli phoned my office several times advising me that I'd better tell her to let the issue with the Manville case drop," Sebastian said.

"He was a polite scoundrel with an evil tone. I told him to rack off or I'd report him."

"Judge Briggs and Judge Field might also be targets," Hunter said.

"Anything is possible," I said. "Worst-case scenario: it could look like we were all working together."

What a mess. I un-papered a peach-pecan muffin, split it in half, and smeared it with butter. I deserved some butter. Not a lot of butter. Just a taste. Sometimes a girl needs butter.

Still, I recognized the bottom line problem. Even fine-tuning the picture, the guilty path still led to me. I called over to the server, "More butter, please."

CHAPTER FORTY-SEVEN

Just before two, I was surprised to find Carlye at Dinkie-Do's station. I stood and listened to her laugh with Dinkie-Do and Shazam. I was glad they could still laugh. Dinkie-Do had changed his color scheme and quietly replaced the shoes Laurel had found interesting.

"Boss-man." *Squawk*. "No horny dolls. Pic-a-nic basket." *Squawk*.

Slapstick Hair Salon wasn't going to derail my investigation. I intended to find the smoking documents to prove Peter Dune was sabotaging my life. It was time for another visit to the courthouse.

Carlye was eyeing a row of nail polish. "Matching bird-toes and gal-nails are to die for."

"Hey—watch your language." Margo chewed her Blow Pop and pushed the broom in between the stylists. "*Die* is a *don't* term here."

Carlye shot her a five-finger flick-off.

Dinkie-Do spun his client to face the colors, selected a bottle of polish from his upper shelf and pushed one hip forward. "Stunning blue." He lifted it in Shazam's direction. "Wonderful."

Dinkie-Do's client was smiling at me. She was Judge Donnettelli's Judicial Assistant.

"Hi, Judge." Her enormous brown eyes shone, and uncertainty flitted through them. "I've wanted to stop in, and well, here I am." She twirled a charm bracelet around her wrist like a three year old with a wind-up toy, despite being thirty-something.

"Renée Reed!" We'd never been besties. But she must want to talk—or she needed a free haircut. I knew she'd come eventually, and I was ready. From my upper cupboard I pulled a be-ribboned box of Godiva signature chocolate truffles and handed it to her. "Welcome to my new life."

Dinkie-Do excused himself to mix color.

To put her at ease I tried to soften my face and my voice. "How've you been?"

"Scared for you. For us, too." Renée tilted her head.

"You've lost your boss. I never had a chance to tell you how sorry I am." I kept it formal.

"I worked for him for fifteen years."

"I know you served him well," I said gently. "He and I didn't get along, but I know you two were close."

Barely five feet tall, she'd always reminded me of a Russian doll because her sense of fashion was a cross between mountain girl and JC Penney's. Her long vest atop a clingy shirt and flowing skirt with mixed patterns hurt my eyes. I wondered whose side she was on.

"While Judge Donnettelli was alive, I wasn't able to think of you as a friend. I—" Renée's cheeks pinked. "I don't believe you killed him." She paused. "I'm keeping an open mind." Her eyes dropped to her lap.

I reached for her hand. "I appreciate that more than you know. I didn't murder him."

"I miss him." Renée squeezed my hand hard. "He was funny. But lately, he was a little grumpy. In fairness, something was going on that didn't involve you."

I held her gaze. "How do you know?"

"I didn't ask," she said briskly. "I know you two stayed away from each other. The few weeks before he died, there were lots of phone calls, staying after hours, locked doors—"

"Everyone has moods, gets behind with work. No offense, but I bet he had more bad moods than most." Seemed like a safe road to take with her. I stepped back.

Renée's face relaxed, and she eased back into the stylist chair. "These moods were out of character."

Geez, were we talking about the same guy?

"I was scared, but I wasn't sure why."

"Did you tell the police?"

Negative head shake. "I tried. Sure. But they didn't care. They only wanted me to answer questions about you."

"Any clue—maybe any gossip—why?"

Renée rubbed her hands together. "Rumors are you couldn't handle taking orders from a man."

If I'd ever met a man capable of giving orders—

"I witnessed the police search and endured thousands of questions—" Renée stopped abruptly. "Honestly, I'm confused. If the prosecutor has doubts about you, I mean, of course you know, it's rare for anyone charged with murder to be out on bond, even a million dollars—"

Ah, a woman with common sense. I might like her after all.

"—and there is doubt, since you're free, the killer's lurking. And I'm afraid just because I worked for Judge

Donnettelli, I'm targeted." Renée's words ran together. Tears welled. "I don't want to die."

I kept my voice to a whisper. "Follow me." A few minutes later we were in my office seated at the chairs across from my desk. "Are you willing to help me?"

Renée looked around the room. She didn't say no.

"Can you pull courthouse records, files—confidentially? And make copies?"

Affirmative nod. "Whatever police didn't seize." She seemed a tad relieved. Women generally needed to be active to feel safe.

"Did police remove his schedule book?" I tried to hide mounting exhilaration.

Renée fingered her earring. "They took this year's. It was only half full. I offered past years', but they declined, said something like it was too far removed."

"I need the past two years' schedule books. Personal ones, too."

"No personal books. He had one oversized red schedule book with every hearing, appointment, holiday, birthday, meeting, and occasion. If it wasn't in there, he wouldn't remember."

"Did you schedule his personal appointments?"

"Rarely. Anything Judge wanted private, he noted with his own shorthand, usually initials. My job was to respect his privacy." When she spoke of Judge Donnettelli, her confidence shone.

"The cardinal rule: Judges are always in; our personal schedules are never released." It was a standard line, necessary for safety and privacy. But Judges like Donnettelli took advantage and were away from the courthouse too often during work hours.

I noticed Dinkie-Do peeking around the corner and waved him forward. He was ready for Renée, so she and I followed him back to the workroom, and Renée took her spot in Dinkie-Do's chair.

"Was your Judge friends with Wade Mazour?" I tried to ask about him casually, as if I were asking if she liked cheeseburgers.

"Judge Donnettelli got along with the law clerks of other Judges. When we were behind, he would borrow them."

"That's odd."

"No, Judge Haddes's clerk liked to stay busy, and they were friends, so he offered to help."

"But Wade Mazour is a law clerk from the State Supreme Court, so that would have been a conflict—helping out on your Judge's docket."

Renée smiled. "Nothing for the docket, but when we were very busy, and Judge was stressed out, they all went out for boys'—uh—men's night. It relaxed my boss. He always came in the next morning whistling." She paused. "For anything that looked like a conflict, either Peter Dune or I handled that. We insulated our Judge from any perceived problems."

It was likely his night to cheat on his wife. I wondered what problems they handled for Donnettelli.

Renée bit her thumbnail. "I'm sorry you're going through all this."

"Can you—confidentially of course—pull all the asbestos cases for the past three years—no matter on whose docket?"

She tugged her earring and jiggled a hot pink nail-polish bottle at Dinkie-Do as he neared.

I guessed the earring play was spy code for *yes*.

"Can I get an emergency mani-pedi today?" she asked Dinkie-Do, pulling out a Visa card and setting it on the counter.

"It's proven, God's creatures bring in business," Carlye said. "Uh-huh."

"Blue balls." *Squawk.*

"Your mani-pedi's on me." I stuck her Visa card in her side purse pocket. "A bottle of polish, too. Dinkie-Do will take phenomenal care of you. We'll talk soon." I gently patted Renée's nails. I hoped this was the beginning of an alliance.

But, if she followed through, her information from Donnettelli's schedule book would hotwire my investigation. I dove into my office to plan my strategy.

For almost an hour I studied notes and made more, focusing well until raucous sounds behind my office door distracted me. The noises were so loud they trampled my nerves.

I jumped up and jerked my door open.

My entire staff stood united in an attack on my fearless door. I blinked, brought both hands up in a commanding stop position, and pictured myself as a stiffly hair-sprayed Wile E. Coyote. But my staff Road-Runnered right over me in high-definition quad speed.

"Whoa." Until that moment I'd never contemplated the intensity of their caring or our Muppets-meet-Cruella-de-Vil dress code.

"Judge?" I could always count on the matriarch of the crew to toe-test the warp level of my mood. "Are you feeling all right? You look flushed."

"For some reason, I'm a little distracted."

"Uh-huh" Carlye shook her head and waved her right hand, a ruby dangling from the center of a fingernail. "Now I know that's right, and I know why."

Dinkie-Do slammed his hip up against her. "You know so little, it frightens the shadow right off of my tender lids."

"Hey, watch it, Gray Matter, or I might flatten your color wheel to a platter of white," Carlye said. "Don't need a fancy degree or nothing to understand her stress."

Dinkie-Do frowned. "She has good friends at home that keep her calm. Me and Jimmy Jack."

When Margo handed me a bracelet-sized, white leather box engulfed in white ribbon, her bedazzled fingernails shone, and her bedazzled toes peaked out of her bedazzled pumps. "Ignore Frick and Frack." She smacked the box into my palm. "Open it before I hot glue those nose flares."

I refused to acknowledge the threat. Nose flares had been embedded in me since I was a child and couldn't get what I wanted. Like frayed underwear, I tried to hide them, but when words failed, my inner child flared. "I'll hibernate more often if it results in gifts." I turned the box over to spy every angle for markings and found none. "Where did it come from?" I placed it near my ear. No ticking. No vibrating. I sniffed it. No scent.

"It's not from us," Margo said. "But next time you lock yourself in your office, I'll bring you a giant candy bar."

I unleashed the ribbon and opened the hinged box. A BMW remote key with note attached. Kryptonite. I felt vomitus.

"Least you could do is read it out loud," Margo said.

I followed orders. *"Grab your purse and your phone. Walk to the back lot. Time to drive home."*

"I know taste when I see it," Carlye said. "You got some sugar daddy on the hook I don't know about? 'Cause that just ain't a good idea. I know about those things." Carlye bent over the box and studied the key so closely she looked cross-eyed. "It's real. I got to see this. I'm going out there with you." She grabbed an oversized umbrella from the stand beside my door and held it up. "Uh—things might go flying. Girl's gotta be prepared. Don't have to tell me nothin' twice."

Dinkie-Do raised both hands. "Hallelujah, we have a ride."

"Short-pants, *we* ain't got nothin'," Carlye said. "Cinderella got herself a slick man with a hot ride, and all she got to do is press the key."

"My Honey-princess takes no ride without her boy-guide." Dinkie-Do dismissed Carlye with a downward hand wave and wiggled away. "Follow me." He pushed his chin up high and confidently jiggled toward the back door and the parking lot.

I remembered courtroom days when Dinkie-Do, Carlye, and the gang were ordered to follow me. I'd command that control over my life again. Someday.

Trisha put her arm around my shoulders and squeezed. "You all right, Judge?" She whispered, "Must be you-know-him. Brace yourself."

"Can you lock up? I'm curious, but I can't handle another 911." I tossed my phone into my bag, double checked my desk was locked, snapped off my office lights, and locked my office door.

I pointed at Margo. "If it's a car, if it's safe to drive, if it's not a joke, on my way out I'll honk the horn. I'll give you a ride tomorrow. Tonight, it's a direct drive home. Help Trisha close?"

A corner of Margo's mouth ticked up. "Sure thing, boss."

"It's Nicoletta. And lose the gum." I waved goodbye and treaded down the hallway toward the back lot, where my day had begun.

I could hole up in my room and work on that tonight. The kryptonite was working. I felt weaker already. Every nerve was on fire, and I wondered what occupied Hunter and Sebastian. Their silence was as unnerving as this walk.

I didn't have a chance to ponder long, though. With Dinkie-Do waiting at the back door and Carlye sauntering behind me, I clutched the knob, closed my eyes, and flung it open.

In the exact space where my antique Lincoln Continental had melted now sat a royal-blue BMW Convertible M6. When I was married, my ex had been hardwired into anything on wheels, but I—being of a more discriminating nature—remained a proponent of the classics and wheels *made in America*. This backhanded dig was wrapped in a pink ribbon larger than the Easter Bunny Parade. Yep. A love bouquet from Dex the Ex.

Carlye whistled. Dinkie-Do said something about a new hue. It must have cost a year's salary. I snapped a picture with my phone, unzipped my oversized shoulder bag, plucked out my hairdresser travel pack, and pulled out a blade. I cut the ribbon and returned the blade to my kit. "Stand back." I held up the key fob.

"Let me," Hunter said and placed his hand over my fingers.

I smacked his bicep. "Where have you been?"

"Checking out the premises and the new delivery," Hunter said, all business.

"Too late," I said and clicked the door unlocked. I didn't need a last-minute rescue. I clenched teeth and fists and buttocks and opened the passenger-side front door. No kaboom.

"You ain't driving that spectacular possible death trap, are you?" Carlye's eyes were as round as prism hubcaps. "It'd be shameful to watch such a splendiferous ride blow up."

"Duh?" Dinkie-Do rolled his eyes at her. "How else is she going to drive me and her home?"

"I can drive you home," Hunter said and grabbed the keys.

I blinked. "I will drive me home." Okay, I had to admit the thought of even riding a bicycle was scaring me. A little bit. Actually, being blown apart was the thing that scared me. Twice in one day didn't seem possible except in special-effects movies. But, pressing my ignition fingers into a new engine to find out didn't make me eager to bust a move toward another liftoff. Still, I had enough dignity left to snatch the keys back from Hunter.

"You almost became a thousand-piece jigsaw puzzle. I wouldn't be jumpin' into an enticing car that ain't been inspected." Carlye eyeballed the white-leather interior. "I love me the smell of a new car. But we need Inspector 99 or someone like that."

"Inspector 99 works for Fruit of the Loom," Dinkie-Do said. "Where do you get your information?"

Carlye stepped closer and bent toward Dinkie-Do. "Your Fruit of the Looms are so dried up, Inspector 99 has retired and is looking for work in another field."

Dinkie-Do glided past Carlye with an exaggerated head bow and curtsey, topped with an extended hip swag toward the driver's side. He opened the door, ran a finger over the steering wheel, seat, and console. "Like the afterglow of fortifying hair treatment. A gift from a man who knows you well. No jigsaw worries."

I half smiled. A gift from my placebo husband. Trisha's guess was right. I gave Hunter a sharp look, and he remained silent. "Take cover." I pressed the remote twice. Like magic, the engine turned over; the radio came to life. We might as well hear music while we waited for the explosion.

Dinkie-Do snapped his fingers like a Greek dancer. "Drive'll be smooth as styling gel. Let's ride." When the engine roared, he twisted himself around the car and slid a finger along the paint and chrome. Dinkie-Do had rounded first and second base, and I was waiting for the BMW to say *yes* to a date.

My choice was clear. Leave Dinkie-Do alone with his date or drive home. "Hunter, go back to checking the premises." I grabbed my phone and punched in my ex. The car music was replaced by ringing, and I turned around to face it.

"Lover, it's about time." Dex's voice boomed through the car speakers.

I leaned into the front seat. "How the hell are you on the speakers?"

"Technology. Latest Apple iPhone in the glove box for you to swap with your phone."

"Chauvinist bastard." It was all I could think of. I had a limited vocabulary these days, but I could take care of myself, replace my own car, upgrade my own phone.

"*Thank you* would be nice. That particular BMW's overloaded."

"BMW—Bowel Movement for Women."

"Nice." Dex drew the syllable out. "Lawyer potty-mouth still intact."

"Buy American."

"BMW—Best for My Woman. Be safe in style. Hunter programmed it with your garage and alarms. Equipped with everything you might need. Lover, it's even outfitted with under-the-seat fire extinguishers and blankets."

"Droll." I shook my head. My staff heard every lover-laced word. "Not the time or place."

Dinkie-Do and Carlye ogled me.

I wanted to drive over the new iPhone, but the visual would be lacking, and I wasn't sure my contacts were backed up. At least it was safe to drive. I should've realized Hunter's first call would've been to Dex. Of course Dex would have a hero's reaction.

"See you at home." Dexter's voice stung me. "By the way, you're welcome." He clicked off, and the radio clicked on.

At home. My instinct, heart, and impulse ping-ponged between nesting and hiding.

I barely had time to absorb and sort Dex's words.

No, damn it. I have to control this mess. No, no, no. I had to interrupt myself. It was less than professional for the boss to throw a hissy fit like a tired two-year-old. I couldn't expose the extent of my loss of control.

Carlye rounded to the front-passenger side and opened the door. "Sounds like Inspector-Ex said the ride's good to go. You gotta realize you earned what that man just give to you. I have no problems taking gifts. It's not like you asked for it. It's like your car burned up, and the sky rained a new one." Carlye looked pleased with her logic.

Her rationalization actually made sense to me. Scary. I needed to go home and find my lost control under the dust bunnies.

I checked under the seats. Using my phone as a flashlight, I found under each seat a small fire extinguisher. I wasn't amused. It was time to get revenge for the demise of Elvis and the wrongful charging of me. I needed a plan to rearrange the freckles on Peter Dune's face. I might even take before and after photos.

CHAPTER FORTY-EIGHT

Early that evening I hid in my bedroom sanctuary, where I'd removed all the art from the wall and hung dry-erase boards. Over the next three hours I poured over paperwork, took an emergency ice-cream break, drank a pitcher of caffeine, and sat cross-legged on my bed.

It was time to state my case—beginning with a timeline. It began the last day I saw Donnettelli: the day he threatened me verbally, physically, and with his gun. The day I'd walked out: early January.

I moved forward to the day I was arrested: July fifteenth, then arraigned, tethered, and bonded: July sixteenth. Into the timeline I added the twelve bank accounts, case maneuvering, planted bank calendars, notes about alibis, highlighted newspapers, missing money, spying at Starbucks, the rattlesnake, skunking, and car bombing.

I studied my work. Everything that had affected me since my last encounter with the Chief Judge now had its spot on the board.

How could I make it work for me?

When the doorbell chimed, I cursed Hunter or Sebastian or whoever thought ten o'clock was a fine time to visit. Where had Dinkie-Do and Dex scurried off to? I recalled Dinkie-Do saying something about taking a bubble bath. Regardless, I'd have to answer the door. When it chimed a second time, I went down and discovered it was a very pale Renée Reed, Donnettelli's JA.

"Renée?"

Shaking, she stepped inside, watched me close the door, pulled out two red, legal-sized schedule books, and handed them to me.

"It could have waited," I said. "Why are you quivering like that? Are you cold, maybe getting sick?" I held the heavy books next to my chest.

She hugged herself.

Something was very wrong.

"Did someone follow you?" I asked. My brain went right to Hollywood and their antics.

She shook her head *no*, and I led her to my family-room loveseat. I set the books on the coffee table and sat as close as I could. And I waited.

"I adore my makeover." She sounded like a terrified six-year-old. "Everyone treated me so kindly I was so eager to thank you. So, I drove right to the courthouse to grab the schedule books for you—but I found—" She shook uncontrollably, and one shoulder jerked.

"Take off that long purse strap before you strangle yourself." She removed her bag and set it near her feet.

With two fingers, I stroked her forearm and waited.

"He's dead." The words seem to erupt. "I just saw him before I left for my hair appointment. And now he's dead."

"You're going to miss Judge Donnettelli," I tried.

Headshake. "Peter Dune, our law clerk." She had to push these words out. "He's dead."

Frost iced over me from the inside out. I remembered the confusion on his face when I accused him in the café.

"Why would someone want to hurt him? *Who* would want to hurt him?" I felt my innards panicking. "I'm so sorry." I had to get into his office. *I'm a bad person. Entirely selfish.* I should be concentrating on Renée. Another death churned my stomach into a whirlpool of fear. Many years on the bench had taught me to hide my emotions, so I squeezed Renée's hand.

I'd been locked in my room all evening. And Dinkie-Do, well it had been hours since I'd seen him. No alibi for me. Again. Hollywood would remind me I knew my way around the video, ugh.

When did Peter die? There was a murderer in the courthouse, and Peter's death only helped me if I could prove it wasn't me. *Nic, don't be a beast. Renée needs you.*

She sobbed. I grabbed a box of tissue and a quilt from the back of a couch and murmured something about deep breaths.

"Half our office is dead." She full-out bawled. "Our court reporter Noel Lemmon and I are the only two left. Some crazy defendant out there—"

"Sh. Sh. You'll stay here," I whispered in a firm-Judge tone. But I was struck by what she'd said. Was there somebody mad at Donnettelli *and* me *and* Peter? "You won't go back to work or to your apartment until we find the killer."

The panic drained right out of her. I expected to see a puddle at her feet. When she began to breathe easier, I gently asked for details—from the beginning.

"In my office," Renée said, "I opened the closet across from my desk, pulled the schedule books from the shelf, and set them on my desk. As I was closing the door, I glanced inside Judge's office and noticed the light coming from the door they shared."

"Peter's office?"

Nod. "He's been closing files and drafting proposed Orders." Renée sniffled. "Peter wanted the new Judge to have a clean docket."

I sent the silent go-on vibe, slowly nodding that I understood.

Renée rocked forward and back. "I yelled into Peter's office and asked if I could help, so he could get home." Her tone sounded as if she were accusing herself of stupidity.

"But he didn't answer," I whispered.

"I figured he didn't hear me, so I went in. It smelled like he'd spilled a bottle of Chloe and didn't get it cleaned up. He was hunched over his desk. Then I thought he was sleeping." She struggled to stay in control. "I started to tease him." Tease drew out like another accusing wail.

"I—walked—saw a line of blood on his desk. I peered under him. His shirt was red, and the blood was from his chest—more on the floor. A big pool." She breathed funny. "He looked white. I touched his forehead. So cold."

She shook her hands hard as if to rid herself of the touch memory. "I *knew* he was dead. I grabbed the books. Ran here."

"Did you call police? Security? 911?"

Renée focused her attention on me as if I'd thought up some brilliant new idea she'd missed. "No."

Shit.

"I totally freaked out. I thought of what had happened to you and wondered if I'd be arrested too for something I didn't do. Actually, I'm not really sure what I was thinking, but I was terrified and ran out, and once I was in my car, all I could think of was coming to you for help."

"Anything else you want me to know?" I waited.

A few seconds later her eyes glazed like she couldn't see right. "I think there was a gun in his hand." She closed her eyes and whispered, "Suicide?"

Only an autopsy could determine murder, suicide, or accident. I wasn't about to discuss anything more about that in her current shape. I forced my voice to remain even. "You understand Peter will be found." My insides trembled for both of us. "You, running down the hall—you're likely the last person who'll be seen on the courthouse video—that may make you a suspect."

My brain raced. I avoided saying: *aside from me.* I wanted to finish the sentence shouting: *and if we're found together, the damn Detectives won't wait for your explanation or mine.*

I reassured myself she wasn't the killer by taking a moment to inspect her. I hoped it was suicide, but the tangle in my gut hinted otherwise. My quick inspection revealed no visible sign of blood on her. She didn't smell freshly showered, and I'd never thought of her as the actress type. I elected a different tactic. "You need to explain to police what happened before they make assumptions." *I was living the nightmare.* "Wait here."

I darted through the house—to the kitchen for the teakettle and a notepad. I ran upstairs and rapped on all the closed doors and called out for Dinkie-Do and Dexter. After a few minutes it was clear that Dexter wasn't home. Dinkie-Do opened his bedroom door. His face was covered by a green mask, and he was wrapped in his fluffy pink robe. I pointed him downstairs and told him to peel his face and get dressed. Texts to Hunter and Sebastian—to find Dexter and get here now.

This was about to get ugly. Okay, uglier.

CHAPTER FORTY-NINE

It took me several minutes to change into jeans and t-shirt. When I reappeared downstairs, color had returned to Renée's face. De-masked Dinkie-Do had set the table, and a pot of tea, another of coffee, and a carafe of water stood in the center.

"I'm afraid of jail." Renée sipped her tea, and when she raised her hand, I noticed the edge of her sleeve was bloodied.

I didn't blame her.

Dexter, Sebastian, and Hunter walked in through the garage door, and I whispered to Dinkie-Do to bring a large plastic bag and grab anything he could find for Renée to slip on. I pointed to her sleeve. I figured she'd freak out the minute she saw the blood.

When Dinkie-Do returned with his fluffiest pink robe, I thanked him and restrained myself from commenting.

With help, Renée changed and washed a blood smear from the back of her wrist, while I grabbed her blouse and zippered it into a gallon-size plastic bag. I directed her to the kitchen table and introduced her to the guys already seated there.

Dexter was scooping ice cream from one of three containers in front of him. "I had a craving. Didn't think you'd miss me." He handed out dishes of ice cream.

When the doorbell rang, Hunter escorted Detectives Grayson and Fredericks to the table as he'd done fourteen hours earlier.

"Confession time?" Detective Grayson looked bored.

They sat. "What's so urgent you demanded to see us a second time in one day?" Fredericks said.

"You invited yourself earlier." I was out of patience with them.

Swiftly Dinkie-Do reached around Grayson and Fredericks, filled their coffee mugs, then quietly retreated with Jimmy Jack.

The Detectives shifted their focus to Renée.

I scooted my chair, so it almost touched Renée's and patted her hand. After re-introductions, reminding the Detectives they'd interviewed her after Donnettelli's body was found, I said, "Renée, tell the Detectives what you told me."

"I thought I forgot my checkbook at the office," she said. "Peter Dune is—I found him dead, lying there."

Detective Fredericks immediately pulled out a notepad. Grayson folded his hands, scrutinizing her with his super-cop vision. Her blood couldn't travel through a vein without his permission; neither could mine. Except for the occasional blink, the Detectives' expressions were closed for business.

I wondered if the courthouse footage would catch her in her lie. She was carrying the oversized schedule books. Surely they'd write checkbook. Ugh. I'd have to think about that tomorrow.

"Last to leave your office?" Grayson finally twitched his upper lip. "Besides you."

"I was the first to leave, so I don't know who left when. I worked a few morning hours." Renée hesitated. "Afternoon hair appointment."

Grayson looked at me. "You can verify that appointment?"

"Yes," I said.

"Keeping it all in the family," Grayson said. "Your salon? What's it officially called?"

I knew both Detectives had the answer memorized, but I told him anyway. "Ratification Hair Salon and Café."

Fredericks scratched it down as if he'd never heard it before.

"Dinkie-Do styled her hair," I said.

"You found a dead man and didn't think to call anyone? But you were calm enough to drive over here—to the woman accused of murdering your boss?" Grayson reached for his phone.

"Check out courthouse videos," Renée said, but her tone lowered as she added, "There are no cameras inside Judges' offices—just the hallways and the courtrooms. But I didn't do anything wrong. Time it out; I didn't kill anyone."

"Could be a simple case of suicide," I said. I added nothing about the gun Renée said she saw. If she wasn't mentioning it, neither was I.

"I didn't kill anyone," Renée repeated.

I felt her mantra, as it was my own.

Sebastian jumped in. "Don't be a bounce. She doesn't have to say word one to you blokes."

Bounce was *jerk* in Aussie. I liked the sound of it. I agreed and snapped my scone in half. Okay, it didn't make a loud crack, but the visual helped; it was the best I could do with what I had. "No need to bully her. Seeing a dead body, especially a friend, is difficult."

Sebastian looked from Renée to Detectives, and then centered on them. "She'll be apples because in a few minutes you two fine Detectives will be returned to the street."

Grayson hit a speed dial, spewed in a few numbers, acronyms, and orders, clicked off, and slid the phone back into his pocket. "The whole damn force is on its way to the scene." He scooted back his chair and stood. "Let's join them."

Renée frowned. "Judge Kikkra and Judge Donnettelli barely spoke—"

Grayson interrupted Renée who winced hearing his sniping tone. "And you're about to tell us she didn't commit either murder? Did you? Murder all in the family; you two did it together, maybe?" Grayson looked at Fredericks, then me and Renée. He swayed his pointer finger back and forth at her. "You and your boss had a fight? Right? About what?"

Renée stiffened. "I followed orders. We never fought."

Sebastian pushed his chair away from the table and stood. "Holy dooley. Your accusations just struck time-to-leave."

Grayson softened his tone. "Anyone having problems with Peter Dune?"

Sebastian signaled Renée to proceed.

Renée started to look at me but stopped herself. "Not aware of any."

Grayson wagged his finger at her. "You two friends?"

Renée remained still, eyes focused on his finger. "Peter was a bit of a loner but liked by everyone. Close to Judge Donnettelli."

Grayson swigged his coffee and stood. Probably some attempt to assert control of the situation. "Did you touch anything in the office when you found Peter?" His voice was deep, but not hostile.

Renée looked at the ceiling. "Light switches, closet door, my desk, the body." She released some air.

I guiltily handed the bagged blouse with the bloodied sleeve edge to Grayson. I didn't want to be charged with interfering with an investigation for not turning it over. "For you. A bit of blood got on her."

"How?" Grayson asked. He sat. The one-word question sounded like a dare: try to explain *that*.

Renée began shaking again. I wrapped comforting arms around her.

"I used my keycard to get in and out." Renée sounded deflated.

"Whoa. Let's start from where you touched the body, and you bloodied your shirt." Grayson set the bag beside him.

"I wanted to check—to help him—but he was cold."

Grayson dipped his head toward Fredericks. "If that's true, the coroner might place time of death early-to mid-afternoon."

Grayson dagger-eyed me.

"I was at my salon, and here, video surveillance and GPS tether. Check out all my alibis," I said. "Don't go there unless it's dismissal dialog."

"I forwarded the phones to Peter just before I left at eleven," Renée interjected.

"So it's safe to say Peter Dune was murdered when he was left alone in the office." Fredericks rested his pen under his chin.

"That means someone was there watching—waiting for an opportunity. Check out the security cameras," I said.

"Why do you suppose the cleaning crew didn't find Mr. Dune?" Fredericks asked.

"It's Friday. They clean inner offices twice a week: Tuesdays and Fridays," Renée said. "Either they were already done, or they hadn't reached our suite, yet."

Grayson read a text on his phone before he addressed Renée. "I want you downtown in the morning to make a formal statement, or a squad car will escort you in pretty silver bracelets."

Fredericks jotted a final note and closed his pad.

Renée and Sebastian went silent. Hunter stood and directed the Detectives to the front door.

"No one here has a problem due to this Peter's demise," Sebastian said. "I'll be at Police Headquarters, and by mid-afternoon I'll have something."

Renée leaned toward Sebastian. "You're not going to leave me alone with those Detectives, are you?"

"I'll have you packed up and at home long before I meet with them." Sebastian stood and with two fingers snatched his keys from his front jeans pocket. "Uh, but it may be a conflict for me to actually represent you."

"Please represent me. Conflicts can be waived right?"

"Let's see how this goes and not get ahead of ourselves," Sebastian said.

"Not home—here, please." Renée was near tears again. She turned to me. "Judge Kikkra said."

I confirmed. Renée conveyed her appreciation, and we went up to her new digs and left the men behind with Dinkie-Do.

About fifteen minutes later, I returned to a clean kitchen with the guys and Jimmy Jack seated at the kitchen table. Dinkie-Do transferred Jimmy Jack to me.

When I turned toward Sebastian my face flushed, and I tried to simmer it down. "When do you plan on sharing the information we've gathered? Obviously, the Detectives have no apparent interest in clearing me. I need to report what we've found to the SEC in the morning. We need all the help we can get."

"Peter's demise has got some spunk into you. You wear it well." Sebastian's eyes traveled around my face, and he grinned. "Now's a perfect time to trade information. If these Detectives don't see their case against you falling apart, they're dim."

Hunter frowned. "The courthouse investigation has landed on Nic."

"I'm not in the courthouse."

"Exactly," Hunter said. "Peter's murder is an eye-opener."

A bit of the fog cleared. "All those warning notes—I'd thought they were from Peter. Someone is willing to blow up my car and kill people to get me to abandon the asbestos victims and go to jail."

"My men will be on you and Renée like your best mascara," Hunter said, "but that court reporter—Noel Somebody?—he's an open target."

"Is Renée—trustworthy?" Dinkie-Do asked the question, but eight eyes put me under glass.

I didn't blink, breathe, or speak. She could be a spy; she could be the murderer; she had blood on her; she could know the killer; she could be afraid to admit it. Renée could help to clear me. I'd have to ponder all that and who to trust later. "I think so."

Dexter rubbed his hands over his face. "My money stops on you." He held both hands up as if to say he couldn't help it. I didn't like to see him so uncomfortable.

"If she needs it, Renée can be appointed an attorney," I said. Dex and his money had spoken.

The scene of me yelling at Peter in the café, commanding him to confess—in front of a huge roomful of people—it replayed in my mind. His head tilt. "I have to go to bed," I said.

And they let me go.

CHAPTER FIFTY

At five-thirty, after a few hours of agitated sleep, I dragged myself out of bed and through my morning routines, which ended with double-duty hairspraying. I turned on the television and grabbed the schedule books Renée had brought, highlighters, pens, and a notepad. Everything went onto the table near my bed. My laptop hummed, and I sat crisscross applesauce.

After several minutes of turning schedule-book pages, warm realization spread through me. I verified the Detectives had been sloppy in not retrieving these schedule books. I also understood why I was the strong suspect—other than the obvious corpse, my DNA, and my fingerprints. My initials appeared throughout Donnettelli's schedule book.

Monthly meetings between JNMK and JWED. Sometimes the meetings included CCHS. JNMK: Judge Nicoletta Marie Kikkra and JWED: Judge Warren Edward Donnettelli, but who was CCHS? Not many people had four initials. It couldn't be that hard to figure out. And why was that person only at about a fourth of the meetings? And, I had to figure out how Donnettelli was able to bank almost two million dollars.

It seemed there may be two million reasons to want to point the trigger finger at me, but why? The beneficiary would be his wife. Wouldn't Detectives investigate her first? Why me? That question nagged at me two million times.

I opened the second schedule book. Same pattern. And it likely continued in the third schedule book, the one in police custody, the one logged in with all the other bogus evidence against me. The one I didn't get to see. But the past predicted the present.

Law enforcement hadn't shared this discovery. I wrote WHY on my notepad underneath WHO. Were Detectives trying to figure out who CCHS was before they shared the pages? Why hadn't Detectives asked me about those letters? I deflated. The answer led to me.

After two more hours, my eyes bulged. I headed downstairs, schedule book in hand. Seated across from the Plasti-gals, I inhaled my first sip of coffee, and Dinkie-Do and Renée strode into the kitchen.

"Breakfast for all in a Dinkie-minute," Dinkie-Do said.

When Renée joined me, I showed her the schedule book and asked if she knew what the initials meant.

She scanned the entries. "I wrote those in at Judge Donnettelli's direction. I figured as Chief Judge, he was counseling you about something."

"Did he say that?"

Renée shook her head. "Nope, I assumed from your initials."

"Recognize CCHS?" I circled it.

"Figured those were from someone with the State Court Administrators Office or some mediator or counselor assigned to you two," she said. "SCAO did things like that when Judges had issues. No secret you two didn't get along."

"Anything you remember about those meetings?"

"At first, I didn't think anything about them. But later, when he returned in a bad mood, I wondered, especially when he began to return early."

"What did that mean to you?"

"I remember thinking: *these meetings are going to give him a heart attack.*"

"Did you ask about them?" I knew it was a long shot. Staff rarely questioned Judges.

"When he *did* return, he often slammed himself inside his chambers. When he didn't return, he'd call and tell us not to expect him til morning."

"If he returned upset, would he calm down?" I felt myself on the edge of cross-examination mode but couldn't stop myself.

Renée thought for a moment. Dinkie-Do placed a fresh mug of coffee, an empty plate, and silverware in front of each of us and returned to the stove.

"Eventually," she said. "After he locked himself in his chambers with coffee, bagels, and a stack of newspapers, he'd take the bench in a decent mood. We figured caffeine and carbs worked, so we kept them around." Renée sounded much calmer than the night before.

I was suddenly curious whether Donnettelli ever gambled. "Sports fan, was he?"

Her mouth puckered. "When I'd bring him his coffee and signing file, I'd set the mug in front of him and sit with the file until he read the headlines first and then the stocks; the sports page was last, if at all. Actually, I have that backward, *unless he was* the headline because of a big case, he read the stock pages and then headlines, local and state news, and sports. Finally, he'd stick out his hand, and I'd give him the pile of documents for his signature. I generally watched him sign, to answer questions or schedule anything he needed."

"He made you sit and wait while he read the paper?"

"His routine. I respected it." Renée took in a breath and released it loudly to make her point. "You Judges are all predictable, even if you think you're not."

I had to ask, "How much did you know about his personal business?"

Renée frowned. "He didn't keep much away from me. I practically ran his life, well, you know what I mean, so he could be free of worries."

The Donnettelli I knew ran his own show. Was she aware he was manipulating case decisions? I dove into my immediate issue with her.

"Renée, you told Detectives you'd forgotten your checkbook."

"Yes," she blushed. "Quick thinking."

"The footage will show you carrying the schedule books. If they think you are lying, they might ask the prosecutor for obstruction charges." I sighed. I hated this discussion.

"My coat is a bit roomy. I tucked the books under my coat and walked out with my hands wrapped around my belly. And actually, that's not accurate. I ran out. Couldn't get away fast enough."

Geez, Renée was pretty crafty. Apparently she was able to think two steps ahead. Was there anything else she'd planned ahead? I added that to my contemplative list.

At nearly nine, Sebastian arrived to take Renée to see the Detectives after breakfast. Over a second cup of coffee, Sebastian promised Renée that the minute she wanted to leave police headquarters, they'd disappear.

Everyone blessed Dinkie-Do for his breakfast art while sharing kitchen clean-up duty. Dex planned to drive Dinkie-Do into the salon for his ten o'clock client.

When the doorbell clanged again, I opened the door to Hunter—bright-eyed and smiling.

"All sexed-up for a busy morning." He winked.

"Grow up." He looked damn good.

"I recognize that zoned-out look of yours from high school physics class." He almost touched noses with me, his favorite form of emphasis—ever—since we were kids.

I pressed my palms against his chest and pushed him back. "It's my less-than-intrigued look. Why are you here?"

"Aside from protecting that end zone of yours, I'm here to block anyone from gaining home-field advantage."

Touché. I spun to exit the foyer.

Hunter caught my wrist. "We need to chat with Donnettelli's court reporter."

He had a point. Half of Donnettelli's office had been murdered. The other half may be targets. I feared for my staff, too.

"I have a little show-and-tell before you two leave." I deepened my voice to show just how serious I was. I needed their full attention.

In the kitchen, Renée was slipping on lipstick. Sebastian had keys in hand and sent me a meaningful half nod.

"Sit." I pointed to the schedule-book pages I'd flagged. "Note the meetings and initials in the schedule book."

Renée looked concerned but remained silent. She and Sebastian turned pages, read it in tandem, flipped pages, seemed to compare, flipped back.

Sebastian's face creased into concerned lines. "Nic, have you checked your schedule against his?"

"I don't have to. I never met with Donnettelli alone, ever. And he never asked to meet with me alone. Had he even hinted at a meeting, I would've refused to meet without a witness and hit record on my cell." If my own attorney asked about private meetings between me and that oaf, if Sebastian even thought it could have happened, what would others think? "Damnation, if there's anything that indicates we agreed to meet and did meet, it's a bold-spray lie."

"At trial—" Sebastian began.

I cut him off. "No trial. No plea. Dismissal, with prejudice, so I'm free for life, not behind bars. You promised." I turned to Hunter. "And you promised." I gave credit to every syllable. "I didn't murder anyone. The pretrial, where I'll turn down any offer the prosecutor makes, is scheduled for the day after Labor Day. And I'm damn scared. This mess needs to be dismissed immediately." I couldn't feel myself breathing.

"We've got fewer than four weeks to gum up their investigation. For dismissal by pretrial, we need to counter their evidence." Sebastian key-pointed at me.

I steadied myself. "My lawyer brain is blaring: find the killer, or I'll be convicted by Halloween." I refused to be scolded.

Hunter hovered over the schedule book, flipping pages back and forth. "CCHS. Could the initials stand for Computerized Criminal History Search?"

Renée's mouth dropped open. "Like for applications for guns or other clearances?"

"Lots of reasons. Did Donnettelli request them?" Hunter asked. "Did you?"

"Not that I recall." Renée didn't flinch.

A defense-witness answer. We needed one-on-one girl time for a reality check. Donnettelli's office held secrets. And my gut said Renée had secrets of her own.

It was time to clear out my house. I owed my staff a sense of normalcy and my clients service with an unencumbered smile. I retreated to my sanctuary, turned up the music, filled my coffee cup, and danced while I readied myself. My fully charged Taser tucked in my updo and my softest boots on, I triple-checked the locks, set the alarm, and headed to my car.

I hardly remembered the drive to work, but I still felt the vibes of the tunes I sang. When I entered the salon workspace, I had to wonder if Dinkie-Do had heard my blaring tunes. He was dipping, nodding, and snapping while combing, clipping, shaving, and styling *Dexter.* I blinked quickly to see if the vision was real or if it would fade. "Are those highlights?"

"I told you no teenies and no tinies." Dinkie-Do pirouetted and landed flat-footed and toe-tipped. His navy, stone-washed jeans and triple tank top had me wondering, but I was certain his wardrobe had something to do with this morning's shadow mixing-and-matching. These past four days, his colors had become brighter and bolder. I decided I didn't need that much information.

"I get it. Latest boy-band look. I've just never seen it on Dex." Somewhere there was a group of elder Breckenridges ordering a hit on me. I was glad I'd kept my maiden name. Near the front door, Trisha waved her come-hither hand, so I asked Dex to meet Hunter and me at Sebastian's office in an hour and headed back toward Trisha.

And Carlye (who'd strategically strapped her girls in an inoffensive pink, nylon-lace tee) was clad in a black-and-white-leopard-print skirt with a silky pink sash at her waist and peppermint-pink heels. She promenaded to the rinsing bowl with her client, but mustered a loud, "Uh huh, I told you." And completed it with a hip exclamation point.

Dinkie-Do shunned her with his backside.

Appearing by my side, Trisha whispered, "Judge, Sebastian better move into your house to protect his investment." She understood me like only a good friend could.

I told her I'd be in Sebastian's office the rest of the afternoon. I met Hunter in the parking lot and thanked him for putting extra inconspicuous cameras around the building. I wished I'd thought to ask if the back parking lot had any dead zones. *That's a damn stupid term: dead zones. Geez.*

CHAPTER FIFTY-ONE

In the conference room adjacent to Sebastian's office, a bevy of beverages said, "Welcome to a tiresome-but-friendly-and-necessary working meeting."

The trouble with meetings and men was lack of focus. Women fought it out. And it could be an ugly battle, but we got resolution and a makeover. Men just made ugly battles uglier.

Right now, I needed their focus on me. But being in a room with three men you've had sex and long-term relationships with was like asking a hungry snake to contribute to strategy while not scarfing up the single, chocolate-covered mouse at the table.

I sat at one end of the conference table, while the men shook hands and exchanged ESPN-like noises. Sebastian sat to my right, Hunter and Dexter to my left.

I knew these guys. I knew they were thinking past my eyes. I knew two of them were going to be disappointed. I yanked the envelope from my bag.

Sebastian declared the "chinwag" was about the research I'd done, and I proceeded to control my presentation. First, I showed a copy of the Register of Actions. Sebastian explained to Dexter that the register reflects everything that happens in a court file's life, like a public diary. Evidently, he was going to help me control my presentation.

"In the suit against Manville, the corporation took a huge financial hit. The way I'd decided could have put them out of business. When Donnettelli changed my ruling, the outcome of the ruling actually made Manville financially healthier than ever."

"And one of the banks on our Most Wanted list was a party to that action," Sebastian said.

I named the twelve banks highlighted in the gifted newspapers—the banks I now had a stash of cash in. "It looks like I took a payoff to abandon the mesothelioma victims."

The men sat back and leaned forward like crash-test dummies.

"Walk us through," Dex said.

"The computer assigns me a case by random draw. Even before I know it's assigned to me, on the QT, the Chief Judge decides he wants it and immediately reassigns to himself—"

"How would Donnettelli know a case is assigned to you before you know?" Hunter rubbed his chin.

"Any clerk in the Clerk's Office could monitor case assignments, as could the Court Administrator. I think one of them informed Donnettelli, and then he changed the assignment. The clerks can monitor Orders getting filed, too. That's how Donnettelli was able to change my Order on the Manville asbestos case. He had an informant who notified him of everything I filed. I can't imagine how many of my Orders he might have changed—or of any other Judge for that matter." I paused. "Like Laurel. He told me she had signed some self-serving Orders."

"Donnettelli wouldn't go to all that trouble to cover up his own murder," Hunter said. "Do you think Laurel is involved?"

"Only like me as an unwilling victim." I hoped I was right.

Sebastian agreed. "There was originally some other end goal, but someone—the co-conspirator maybe—kept the 'score' for himself, offed Donnettelli, and framed Nic. Highly efficient scoundrel."

Sebastian flipped through my notes. "You've looked into anyone related to Manville?"

"I have. And the time has come. I can't delay reporting this to the Securities and Exchange Commission." I winced just saying the words.

"The SEC may arrest you," Sebastian said. "It looks like you got paid off to rule in Manville's favor."

"It's my duty," I said.

"It'll be harder to prepare your defense if you're in lockup," Sebastian said. "After my secretary makes us working copies, these documents will be in my safe."

Dex squished up his forehead. With his new hairdo he looked like an out-of-control meteor. "What's it going to take to keep Nic safe and out of custody? Guard lions? Add it to my tab."

Here it came. Prisoner in a free world. Toss the Constitution. Checks and balances be damned.

Hunter cleared his throat. "She gave me a glimpse of this the other night at her house—"

Like an aggravated Jedi, Dex scorched me with his laser-light, blue eyes. "Just how many men are waltzing through my house?"

"My house," I whispered. "I hear a house in Colorado calling you."

He faced the other men, shoving my end of the table into a *the ex has to have last word* sinkhole. Another *hit-slap* for him.

Without so much as an eye crinkle (no Advance Anti-Aging Cream for him) Hunter continued, "Think about how Judges' cases can be turned into profit."

Dex hovered over the table. When he smelled money, he took the lead. I followed his body language, and we huddled like the Detroit Lions at fourth and ten. At least the guys had stopped arguing about the SEC.

Dex whipped out his smart phone and used the calculator. "Just about any event with two sides can be turned into a profit-loss event, legal or illegal."

True Dex. He loved the *Hunt for the Wild Greenback*.

Hunter looked damned serious. "My team compared Donnettelli's financial picture of several years ago with his recent finances. He went from comfortable middle income to lavish upper crust."

"Blimey, in two or three years?" Sebastian asked.

I tucked my hands underneath my rear and gulped. "Yeah." Humph. "And from the little *I* put together, let me guess: The oil on this financial canvas drips so close to my docketed cases, I could be wearing stripes til I'm laid out in velvet and lacquered oak."

The men looked grim.

Not the response I'd hoped for.

With a flourish, Sebastian wrote the number twelve and circled it. "You have a mere fraction of the funds Donnettelli has."

What better reason to kill the guy? It looks as if he were holding out on me. I knew that was a problem. I'd heard enough murder trials to know it before I heard the word.

"Motive," Sebastian said.

That's the word. Damnation. Motive is listed under: plan, scheme, design, clearly meant to mislead, and find me guilty.

Sebastian drew darker circles around the awful number.

"But I didn't make a penny," I said a few notes short of a wail.

"A case could be made that you were involved, and they cut you out," Sebastian said.

Now Dex wanted to help. "Or you got greedy and wanted to run the operation, which is why he shifted the asbestos cases to you—any number of scenarios."

"Revenge is as good a reason for murder as any," Hunter added matter-of-factly.

"I never had that kind of cash. It's so obvious they set me up." I consciously kept my nostrils still, cleared my throat to underscore my point, and yanked the marker from Sebastian. I couldn't look at it anymore.

"Whoever *they* is, *they* are still out there." Hunter looked past me at Dexter.

"Look at the worst-case scenario," Sebastian said. "You and Donnettelli hated each other. Add money in the mix—"

I held my hands up, and Sebastian stopped speaking. I could see it from the other end of the table. Hell, somebody on Alpha Centauri could see it. I scooted my chair back, stood, and paced. I thought back to Laurel, to other dockets, case-code types, the civil cases involving asbestos. The rewritten Orders.

"My research." Sebastian untied a brown portfolio and lifted out a manila file. "I found a way to get good oil, if you agree."

I snagged a couch pillow and clutched it against my chest. Resting my chin on it I said, "Agree?" I studied Sebastian. I wasn't ready to exchange my designer wardrobe for a Crayola-colored jumpsuit. "To what?" The crinkles above Sebastian's brow, told me there was trouble brewing.

"You could consider testifying and going into protective custody." Sebastian paused and seemed to be looking for his next words on his male teammates' faces.

This couldn't be good. "I'll contact the Securities and Exchange Commission now. I discovered financial manipulation after the bank records and the newspaper appeared and my car blew up. The SEC will—"

Sebastian interrupted me. "—ask questions after you're behind bars and watch how this plays." He frowned.

Hunter stood in front of me. "There's a hell'uva great case against you. You jumped off the courthouse bandwagon when things began to fall apart—that's what they'll say."

Sebastian appeared to agree, and Dexter was rubbing his eyes.

"The three of you want me to ignore my integrity and evidence that could free me?" I bit the inside of my cheek.

Sebastian shook his head. "Before you crack a fruity, we need to strategize, plan, have a serious chinwag—"

"Before you get all Down Under on me, just remember I'm an honest, innocent, cowboy-boot-wearing, Levi-clad American with rights."

"Look, Judge—" Sebastian closed the file and folded his arms. "You know that if the SEC takes you, the Feds get interested, your bond will be revoked."

I stood. "Hiding facts from the Feds smells like federal time, even if I'm found *not guilty* of murder—I'm gone. Plus—it's wrong. I have a legal duty to report it." I grabbed my bag, and flashed Hunter and Dexter each their own familiar *stay-away* glare. With the toe of my boot, I pushed my chair in at the table. "True as ever: 'these boots are made for walking.'" And I walked.

CHAPTER FIFTY-TWO

Out on the sidewalk, I dialed the salon and told Trisha to have whoever was in-between appointments come pick me up. Pronto.

Twenty minutes later and several blocks from Sebastian's office, my sparkly blue BMW pulled into the Taco Bell lot and parked a few feet in front of me. Carlye jumped out of the driver's side and flailed her arms, as if it were possible not to see her. Several cars honked at her.

"Well, I guess I still have it. It's a gift. Once you're a people person, you never lose it." Carlye flashed a glorious grin, dropped the keys into my open hand, wiggled her hips, and waved to the passersby.

"Thanks for coming," I said. "Let's go."

"I appreciate you letting me drive this fine vehicle. I didn't believe it when I was ordered to pick you up. Why you walking, anyway?"

Carlye's lack of diplomacy was never disputed. I opened the door and slid into the front seat next to a wide-smiling Dinkie-Do.

"Hey," he said. "I joined in for the smooth ride and to see if I could help." Dinkie-Do batted his lashes.

Carlye arranged herself in the backseat and slammed the door. "Well, are you going ta spill? Something big must've happened for you to be walking. We can't have you running the streets. You're not like us. You can't take care of yourself."

I turned sideways and scowled. "Excuse me? I didn't get where I am—where I was—without hard work." Avoiding specifics was fine with me.

"Yeah, I hear those paper cuts can hurt." Carlye glanced over at Dinkie-Do, who shrugged, but remained wisely silent.

Paper cuts, my big-toed Aunt Anna. But I used my nice voice for my friends. It wasn't their fault I was headed due south on Shit Creek. "I need to get back to the salon." I had to refocus on finding an insider-information plot.

"Alla this ain't right," Carlye said. "Why is Margo working next door?"

I nosed out of the Taco Bell driveway onto Grand River, and both passengers whimpered. Loudly. You'd think I'd sat on their puppy. "Now what?"

"It's Taco Bell," Dinkie-Do said. He cocked his head and gave me a big clownish grin.

"Yeah, TB," Carlye said.

Now they agreed? "You're hungry?" It was almost one. I should've guessed.

"It's un-American to pull into a Taco Bell and not order something." Carlye over-blinked. It was her tell.

Dinkie-Do bobbed his big black hair with its new brighter-blue stripe. I backed up into the drive-thru, and a few minutes later we had a dozen hard-shell Taco Supremes, Mexican pizzas, burritos, slush drinks, extra napkins, and sauce packets galore. I pulled over, hit the top-down button, and gave the "*no mess, no smell, no crumbs, I am not maid service*" instructions I'd given my kids. I had to admit Taco Bell was instant food comfort. It settled me down. For the moment.

"Thank you, Mommy," they sang in unison.

I groaned. "Stop. You two getting along is suspect; tell me what's wrong at the salon." I gunned the engine, squealed away from the parking lot, and (I hoped) my horrible afternoon.

"Well, it's like this—" Carlye paused to wash down a taco with her strawberry slush. "Rosa was talking with Trisha two separate times, and I couldn't hear anything over the blow dryers, but she looked upset."

Dinkie-Do interrupted. "So we—"

"You came along for the ride." Carlye's voice was opera sharp.

Without unbuckling, Dinkie-Do spun toward the back seat so fast he almost hit me in the cheek. "*I* talked *you* into going with me to talk with Trisha, uh-huh."

"Little Tango." Carlye bit into her burrito. "After Rosa left, we talked with Trisha."

Watching Carlye, I almost hit the curb. I had to quit looking at her in my rearview mirror. "Your point please?"

"She sounded like a long-legged leprechaun and muttered something about some tools catting around the café to make us the Muppet. And she sent Margo to help Rosa." Carlye slurped the bottom of her drink and tossed the cup into a paper bag.

"Between bad rap and Irish slang, we're not sure of the specifics, except in any translation it equals *problem*." Dinkie-Do neatly rolled his empty taco papers, wiped each finger on a napkin, and tossed the paper into his bag. He snapped his fingers and rested his head on his right hand. "That's all we know." He beamed. "Thanks for lunch. It was delish."

Driving one-handed eating tacos over a lap of napkins while listening to this strange turn of events had me thinking back to the meeting I'd just escaped. And within minutes we were safely back at the salon.

I thanked and dropped off Carlye and Dinkie-Do and told them I'd be in the salon soon. I'd noticed my sister's vehicle in the lot and decided to figure out where she'd landed and curtail the chaos and Animal Kingdom she usually brought with her. Like me, caffeine would be her first stop, so I headed toward the café. Within seconds, my mirror image approached, clutching a super-sized cappuccino and the messenger bag that held her furry pal.

"No dogs allowed," I said firmly. I put my arms around my sister, Nella, and pointed her toward the back door. She planted her face nose-to-nose with mine, like when we were kids. She tried to mesmerize me with big, hopeful-sister eyes.

"No issue." Nella always minimized my concerns. "I stopped in to tell you that I'm going back to Europe to meet our parents and talk them into returning for you. Thought you might want to know."

I agreed with her, silently. My parents, my family, should be here instead of hiding between European ports. I just had bigger sharks to harpoon. My smile said *thank you*. But, I knew there was more to her story because a call or text would've sufficed. I waited.

"I was hoping you could babysit Starfire."

I found my voice real fast. "No way, sister. Bon voyage."

Nella looked forlorn.

Oooh. "Look," I said. "I'm a hot minute from having bond revoked. Think about it, I can't leave Jimmy Jack and Starfire alone without extra insurance on my boots." I hugged her. "Besides, I'm not painting your pooch's nails."

Nella patted my arm understandingly, returned my hug, and left with the promise of sending postcards. I grinned.

Now I finally had a minute to check on the café. Before I could say *banana-cream croissant*, Rosa and Margo nearly bulldozed me. I spun halfway left and right to spy the whole room. Everything appeared in order. "What's this about, and why aren't you making coffee?"

"The pair of suits, taking notes." Rosa mumbled through one side of her mouth. Subtle.

"It's a coffee shop. Meeting place. So what?" *Relief.*

Rosa mouthed words just loud enough for me to make them out: "They're not meeting. They're not greeting. They're memorizing this place and you."

"Reporters?" I shrugged. "Sadly, I'm a hot topic."

In unison the young women grimaced.

"Do they speak?"

"Coffee. Croissants. Phone calls."

"See the earpiece." Rosa lifted a finger and tugged at her right earring. "Been here on their dime, all the time, since your Elvis blew."

My life was becoming Hitchcock-worthy.

Two close-cut, clean-shaven men didn't appear to notice me. Were they trying too hard not to notice me? They were wearing standard issue: navy-blue suits, white shirts with blue ties. Lawyers, law enforcement, CIA, FBI, legislator—my brain ran through a long list of Brooks Brothers' jobs. And I clicked into my earlier meeting—SEC.

"Update me." I tried hard not to display concern. Hmm.

Full of information to ponder, I headed over to the salon. I needed respite from my life, and hair had always been able to give my brain a vacation from anything difficult in life. I'd hoped the rest of my day would be smoother. I wanted it to go smoother. I loved smoother. But no. It was an entire afternoon of the opposite of smoother. The wax pot exploded and spewed hot goop over cupboards, wall, mirror, chairs, and floor. Carlye got a little burn and had a meltdown of her own. Dinkie-Do encouraged her a bit too optimistically, and when I left, that over-loud discussion was still going on, complete with competing head-bobs so vigorous, I feared for their vertebrae.

The un-smooth didn't end there. I was safely in my car when I remembered I was all out of coffee-bean ice cream. Going home without restocking was unacceptable. Nothing would stop me from stopping by Target on my way home.

Once in their parking lot, I reached into my bag, flipped my debit card out of my wallet, then left my bag and phone locked in the car, and ran inside for frozen therapy. I whirred the cart toward the backwall freezer section in the almost empty store, filled it with every available ice cream carton labeled *coffee*, and made for the open cashier lane. At full speed, I smacked right into Wade Mazour.

The clang of the crash ping-ponged inside my skull. Damn. It took the better part of a minute to recognize the young woman with him. It was Laurel's law clerk Zena Royale.

"Judge Kikkra," Wade said. "I know Judges aren't likely to get speeding citations, but if you don't slow down, you could be banned from late-night Target shopping." Wade laughed. "I'd hate to see all that ice cream melt."

How did I explain coffee-ice-cream stress eating? "Nice bumping into you both." Damn, did I say that? "How are you doing?"

"Enjoying our ice cream, just like you." He held up an enormous container of Neapolitan. "Target sells the hard-to-find original with real pistachios and cherries. I'm a regular." Wade grinned, and Zena tried to hide her irritation. Evidently, she had places to be, cold stuff to eat.

"Happy to know you're not depleting that stock," Wade said.

"Coffee's my thing." We strolled to the cashier, paid, and they not only walked me to my car, Wade loaded the bags of ice cream into my trunk. I thanked him and hoped they didn't see me palm a pint.

I always kept a spoon in my bag, and the carton was finished before I got home. My mug of joe was made in the kitchen and emptied again by the top step.

When my sugared, caffeinated feet plodded across the bedroom threshold, I'd planned on a few hours of review. What I didn't plan on was falling asleep in my clothes and waking up surprised that sunlight was streaming in.

Time for amends—okay some atonement—mostly reality-revisions. I sat on the edge of the bed and sent my three unruly bodyguards a we-need-to-talk text. I needed assurance in triplicate that I was in charge, I had a voice, and we were all aimed in the same direction. This would work best if it seemed like their idea—a daunting but worthy task.

I believed in preparation and feeling good all under, especially when seething emotions weren't easily hidden. I sprayed *Michael*, donned my favorite black thong, and zipped soft leather Prada boots over my straight-leg black designer jeans. The feel and smell of fashion were first-rate medicine.

An oversized lace tee over a black string tank completed my clothing, but I wasn't done until I teased, styled, and sprayed my hair repeatedly to ensure my every-day-is-wedding-hairspray-day look. I confirmed my makeup and descended the stairs to settle my life. I had to make the men understand my position.

When I turned into my kitchen, the scents of flowers, bacon, eggs, and coffee transcended the next vision: Dexter and Dinkie-Do fussed over a bright-yellow, white, and royal-blue daisy tablecloth offset with red dishes and bowls of fresh-cut fruit and flowers. Side by side in tune with their feminine sides, the sight warmed my inner girl.

Hunter and Sebastian were sharing the morning newspaper at the kitchen table. A low hum of Elvis, songs from his early years, sounded in the background. I heard Sebastian call out appreciation for Dinkie-Do's culinary expertise, then he explained that in Australia, if a guy was called *Dinky-di,* it meant he was genuine.

Dinkie-Do thanked Sebastian, then wandered into the cooking area toward a frosted treat in the cinnamon-roll family.

Dexter had read my mind. "We four need to get back in sync."

I opened my mouth and got as far as, "In sync means I'm in control," when Dex planted his brawny body in front of me.

"And you need to listen." Dex pounded gorilla fists on his chest.

Damn. I wasn't prepared to swing through trees with him.

He dug up his Tarzan voice. "Force me to make you listen. Bond be recalled. You in protective custody. Locked up in cell." He looked serious. "We're all on the same side, the only side. Your side."

"You three may have had a pre-morning meeting," I said, "but whether I'm with you in spirit or in person, I remain in control of my destiny—"

From the corner of my eye, I saw Hunter. He didn't look away from the paper, but he straightened and stuck his chest out, and I puckered hard to keep from laughing.

I judicial-eyed the men. "I agree; we're all on the same side."

"As long as you heard me." Dex folded his arms.

There was my choice: I could wear the latest Catherine Malandrino designer jumpsuit or inmate classic wear. "Well played, Ape Man."

He flashed me the briefest look of genuine gratitude, and I sat at the kitchen table.

I poured coffee, and Jimmy Jack jumped onto my lap. Deep, very deep inside, I warmed. Life was damn complex. But the men understood: I was in control. I was sure they understood.

CHAPTER FIFTY-THREE

About eleven that morning, Hunter and I found Noel seated at the private corner table of the café, awaiting our arrival. I didn't know how to peg Judge Donnettelli's Court Reporter Noel Lemmon. He was nice enough, but he was a weird bird. I'd never forgotten the words of my favorite law professor: *Money makes people funny*. And there was plenty of money floating around among these murders.

Noel lounged with his legs crossed, bouncing an agitated foot clad in an expensive running shoe. A thick shadow of facial hair was visible, something I'd never seen on his Courthouse face.

He raised both his hands—surrender style. "You got me. I killed the bastard. And I'm glad he's dead. Can I go now?" Surly seemed to emanate from his core. Something had changed since the day Carlye had cut his hair, and we all got skunked.

"We'll be brief. We're sorry about Peter." I motioned to a plate of scones. "Try one."

His navy-blue-and-white running suit explained his fit exterior. In his mid-forties, I guessed, he'd never married, but was rumored to juggle many relationships.

"I'm investigating this whole ordeal," Hunter said. "Did the police talk to you about Donnettelli or Peter?"

Noel snapped, "Ask them." He broke off a corner of a cherry scone, pushed it between taut lips and chewed open-mouthed like the cartoon of an insolent thug.

I averted my eyes until he swallowed.

Hunter matched Noel's glare but kept his tone level. "Look, drop this hard-ass act of yours. This tiny inconvenience might just save your inconsequential ass. Nicoletta didn't kill anybody, but someone interested in seeing her convicted might see you and Renée as interesting targets."

"Peter was my friend." Noel refilled his mouth, but then it seemed he just gave up. I don't know what his inside struggle was, but he'd just resigned, and now he knocked his knuckles impatiently on the table. "Let's get this over with. I have a life."

"For the moment." Hunter picked up his keys as if it were time to leave. "It's Renée's worry, not mine."

"Wa–a–ai–t," Noel said in an elongated contemplative tone.

Hunter made I'm-listening and I'm-willing-to-stay moves, with a don't-tempt-me-to-leave look. "Do you know why Renée is terrified? Somebody made good on a threat to your Judge?"

"No." He chewed with his mouth closed.

"You're not being disloyal," I said. "You could save lives—yours included." To punctuate, I finger-tapped the table in front of him. Like a hand-pat, but with distance.

"You can take your chances with some crazy defendant out there and an overwhelmed law enforcement department." Hunter held his hands out, palms up. "Or you can play nice, help us, and help yourself."

Noel scratched his stubble and stopped his neurotic foot jiggle. His eyes clipped to mine. "Prosecutors have their prime suspect."

Did he really think I'd shot his boss?

He cocked his head to the side, the way a gangster holds his gun. "All I know is—you won the feud." He aimed his pointer finger at me.

The rat learned that move from me. That's what I used when I sentenced killers to life.

"Then why kill Peter?" Hunter said. "This Judge has an alibi as solid as your court-reporting fingers are attached to your hands—no matter how temporary that may be."

Noel didn't respond at first, but then he seemed to erupt. "If you killed Peter, too—"

"Whoa. You are out of line. This is what's going to happen," Hunter said. "I ask a question, and you answer it."

Noel did a shrug-nod thing. Wouldn't want us to get the crazy idea he cared.

Silence was my friend here.

Hunter got ready to write. "Comprehend this. Just like those words you take down in court, the truth saves your life, but a lie rolls the dice. Understood?"

Noel grunted. "Snake eyes."

"Look, no one's paying me to protect you. But you tell me the truth and keep me updated, I keep watch. You disappoint me, I turn my back." Hunter flipped Noel his card. "One thing pisses me off. Liars, which includes anyone calling my Judge a murderer."

Noel scooted his chair up to the table. "Let's get this done." His voice was louder, but not entirely as surly.

"You review the docket. Begin with asbestos cases, especially ones that include banks. Think specifically about those and any other cases with big-money judgments. List any Donnettelli transferred from Judge Kikkra's docket to his docket."

"Donnettelli had authority to do that." He sounded as if he were answering an accusation.

"I need those transcripts faster than expedited and at no charge." I watched Noel. Transcripts were his livelihood. But protection wasn't free either.

Hunter held up two fingers. "Work backward, two years."

Noel's body stiffened. On his face, surprise collided with realization and morphed into fear, but it seemed to happen in slow motion, like his personality batteries were running down. He knew something. And I needed to find the lever that would cause him to spill. Noel kept watch on the café entrance but spoke to us. "You need the rulings or the whole transcripts?"

"Rulings are the quickest, right?" I said.

Noel agreed.

"Four pages on one. With the index in the back so I can review quickly. Then the whole transcript must follow." My jaw stiffened.

"Most of those cases have been appealed. I'll run a list and change the format to the four-up and hit print," Noel said quickly but in his professional voice, like he was answering a request from a paying lawyer.

This high-tension question-answering continued for two hours. When Hunter and I were satisfied we'd gotten all we could expect, and Noel was clear on our meaning of *transferred cases*, we thanked him. He stood and even shook our hands, promising to keep us informed. Noel left the café with the gait of defeat.

I groaned at Hunter. "Sometimes Noel is as bizarre as his former owner."

Hunter chuckled. "He looked too scared not to give you the transcripts. Still, he held back. Hopefully he trusts us more than he trusts Hollywood and Company." Hunter winked.

"Please do something about that annoying wink."

He grinned. "If I winked at someone else, you'd be pissed."

Arrogant as always. A *hit-slap* was coming his way. I stood. "I've got to get to work." I grabbed my bag from the back of the chair, slung it over my shoulder, and walked away.

I intentionally swaggered in that effortless take-me-now way. Two can tease. I disappeared into the secret salon hallway and didn't turn around, but I felt Hunter's eyes burn my backside until the door slammed. Damn.

For the rest of the afternoon, I holed up in my office. The business of saving my backside meant I needed to organize my growing list of questions according to priority. Danger increasing around me was complicating my usually methodic process. I noted Donnettelli's surviving staff in the suspect category. Money makes people *funny*.

Funny, yes, but insane? It had to be more than money. Then it struck me like a bolt of peroxide. Jurisa Haddes.

Not only did she loathe me, but she also adored Donnettelli. Framing me for murder fit within the evil fabric of her soul. Did murder fit?

If Donnettelli and Haddes had a falling out, could it have escalated to murder? Was I taking the fall for killing my enemy—at the hands of my enemy? But why would Jurisa murder Peter?

Because he'd heard her on the phone when Donnettelli had called during the poker party.

That fit. And there was something else that had made me think of Jurisa the night Peter died, something Renée had said. I hadn't wanted to interrupt her at the time to ask about it, but I meant to remember to ask later.

I kept at it—creating and answering questions, cross-examining myself until Sebastian came to pick me up.

When he and I got back to my house, it was almost eight. Right away, Hunter took me aside and slipped me a thick yellow envelope, which I dropped into my shoulder bag.

My kitchen table was piled high with oven-barbecued ribs and a giant colorful salad. The whole crew was waiting with smiles. I so needed a bath and a bed and aloneness. But I resolved myself to basics of decent society. *Must eat supper. Must be polite. Must say words to people.*

CHAPTER FIFTY-FOUR

Early the next morning, I woke with specters of Hunter's big yellow envelope haunting me.

He'd gathered reports showing major purchases made by any Michigan law clerk, court reporter, court administrator, or judge. As soon as I was ready for work, I sat on the bed, and I plowed into the envelope's contents, coffee in one hand, yellow highlighter in the other. I might be able to see who'd been spending on a level with Donnettelli.

Judicial salary was no secret. Every judge had income and investments. Every judge on our bench, except me, was currently married, a few more than once. No judge had been divorced and married more than Donnettelli.

The financial check the Detectives had pulled on me wasn't enough to prove I'd opened the twelve bank accounts. It wasn't enough to show motive. Not by itself.

But it wasn't enough to clear me of murder. I had traced and explained my holdings, but the detectives weren't satisfied. If there was a clue on my evidence boards, I didn't see it.

I needed a boot of coffee, a boat of chocolate-covered coffee beans, and a bottle of *19 Crimes* wine.

Maybe one of the old criminals on the label had advice about whether or not I should trust Laurel or Renée.

Renée had said Donnettelli showed a clear change of lifestyle, beginning with the loss of his parents and his most recent marriage. And Shayla was sure the money hadn't come from Ma and Pa Donnettelli.

Most men can't survive five wives, yet Donnettelli was able to support them and flourish—despite alimony and child-support payments, college bills, and repeated property division. He'd been frugal until his last wife. And he'd been a successful criminal-defense lawyer before he was appointed to the bench.

And then there was the bully side of Donnettelli. And one of the wives could be deadly mad at him; ex-wives added onto my suspect list. Would he let an ex-wife into his chambers? Hmm.

Jurisa's purchases were few and modest, and she'd sold property up north and a boat this year. Was she stockpiling cash?

The breakdown of Donnettelli's stock portfolio wasn't here, nor did I have any judicial retirement investment account for him. Stock portfolios were much trickier to obtain, but not impossible. Stocks could be clearly and quickly identified.

There was my own stock portfolio; I've always held several thousand shares in four banks: one local, two national, one international, and no asbestos or insurance companies that I recalled. I'd held the same bank stocks consistently for fifteen years.

I thought back. I'd held my bank stocks since before my divorce, and I invested some settlement monies into the same stocks I'd held—ones that had produced well.

That was before I was a judge these past eight years, through high and low investment periods.

I rubbed my temples. I needed information to save my freedom, and I counted on the truth to revive my integrity.

I forced myself to dig deeper; my wall chart needed to compare the growth of judges' retirement accounts: which stocks, how much, and when. In the bank papers Purple Girl had brought me, I found Donnettelli's Social Security number.

I needed to review my own investment portfolio, too. So, I got into the storage closet behind the bookshelf there, picked my way over boxes and bags to the aging filing cabinet, did some concerted looking, and yanked out my investment portfolio. I was glad the judicial retirement system used only one investment company.

Back in my room, I phoned the number shown on my papers. But when the recording began asking questions, I punched in Donnettelli's Social Security number and zip code.

Hmm. I needed a four-digit code. Donnettelli wasn't that savvy. I'd read his schedule book and seen the initials he'd used over and over. One set of them were his: JWED. I checked my telephone for the corresponding numbers: 5932.

Donnettelli was both consistent and predictable in his actions, which gave me the intuition he would use something easy to recall. After having raised three boys, numbers corresponding to letters on the phone like a child's first secret-decoder ring made sense to me. Not exactly obvious to all, but easy to remember, fit into Donnettelli's worldorder. I punched it in. Hot damn, I was good. Out came a series of choices. I hit the automated response for copies of 401(k) and 457 retirement account statements and clicked off.

They'd been frozen, but thankfully his wife kept the same information. I'd guessed probate was still open since he was murdered, so access hadn't changed. It struck me—maybe they were considering his wife or an ex-wife as a suspect? Wishful thinking.

Hunter would have to intercept the mail from Donnettelli's house. A little federal offense to free me wasn't going to cause my hair to fall out. I blew out apprehensive steam and texted Hunter and Sebastian: Meet in café. 10 a.m.

CHAPTER FIFTY-FIVE

At ten, armed with notes about Michigan court employees' financials, I returned to Rap-and-Squawk Central, where the men were already seated at the private corner booth, the table heaped with carafes of coffee and plenty of pastry. Sebastian stood, which strategically placed me in the center of the men. I wasn't sure who was in more danger.

"Need legal advice on your bird sanctuary?" Sebastian sat and stretched his arm around the back of the round leather booth and me.

"Hey, Kangaroo, let's hop to important issues like freeing our girl." Hunter winked at me and rested an arm in front of me.

Squawk. Squawk.

Damnation. "Another word from either of you, and I trade baked goodies for bird food." I hiked the large yellow envelopes from my lap onto the table and thumped my fingers on them. "Judges have similar retirement accounts, which is not illegal. I need to have the exact stocks to figure out if there has been any colluding or conspiring with any specific stocks in their retirement or personal accounts."

"Having a retirement account is part of the job benefit," Sebastian said. "Don't judges receive matching funds?"

"Yes, but not the point. What I'm thinking goes well beyond the legal retirement account. Judges are not allowed to be in business together or with other judges at different levels or with attorneys who appear in front of them."

"Unethical may not be illegal." Hunter unwrapped a muffin. "No such thing as a morality court."

"Are the judges accepting gifts or taking bribes?" Sebastian rapped his fingers on the stack of files in front of me.

"That's what we need to figure out," I said. "We know Donnettelli was taking bribes and making threats. I wouldn't put that behavior past Jurisa Haddes; she fits the same mold."

I spoke low. "Hunter, I need you or your trusted ghost staff, the guys I'm not allowed to meet, to pluck the mail from Donnettelli's house and pilfer the duplicate retirement papers I just ordered from his retirement account."

Hunter's grin slid clear off his face. "How did you—?"

Sebastian began. "Ah, federal crimes—"

I cut them off. "We needed access to Donnettelli's retirement accounts. And there has to be a critical examination of any big-money cases Donnettelli transferred to himself."

Hunter whistled at the chart I'd made. "Parties, attorneys, witnesses?" Visible excitement rose from his neck to his cheeks. "Are these related to your twelve overfed accounts?"

"Can't tell, yet." I held my coffee in front of my uncontrollable, inconsolable nose. Maybe I could freeze-spray my nostrils into place. "Follow the money." Finally, the men were finally more interested in my paperwork than their appetites. Good.

"It'd be quicker if I asked Detectives to subpoena material," Sebastian said. He kept studying the information across the table. "And it will be valuable at trial."

"There's not going to be a trial." I folded my arms. "I want the paper trail that gets charges dismissed."

Sebastian put on his lawyer face. "Trial is set two weeks after September's pretrial. Huge gamble obtaining information by means other than lawful—"

"My life. My choice. Until these detectives shift a gear up a different road, you two need to pop a wheelie and help me investigate." My head revolved between Sebastian and Hunter. "Dexter's paying big, Colorado-resort bucks. Let's use them." I did not wear orange well.

CHAPTER FIFTY-SIX

Two hours later, sitting on my bed, Renée at my desk, I questioned her. "Renée, I'm curious about the relationship between Donnettelli and Jurisa Haddes."

Instant recognition flamed in her eyes. "We didn't talk much about them. I mean if—"

I interrupted with a stern voice. "You're being loyal to Judge Donnettelli by helping to find his killer."

Renée focused on the ceiling. "They spent time together, sometimes behind locked doors for hours." Her neck muscles stiffened in the vein of a jilted woman. I tossed that thought like expired hair color because staff loyalty was inbred, and I couldn't knock her for it.

"Did you ever hear anything behind those doors?"

"We tried," Renée said. "Speculated, about something intimate." Her voice was almost inaudible.

Renée clamped her body, and I wondered if she was in pain. "Judge Haddes is like starched laundry. A whole box of fabric softener sheets wouldn't soften her." She pronounced Jurisa's name as if it left a bitter taste in her mouth. "She acted as if the Judge was her personal property." She was quiet for a few seconds.

"And her law clerk talks too loud." Renée sounded full of resentment. "And he skulks around the security monitors."

"But to his credit, over the years, Keldon has discovered a few deviants who've snuck in behind someone who was buzzed back and jurors who didn't stay in the jury room."

"Yeah, but he really seems to care about what women wear." Renée giggled but not like it was funny. I think she was embarrassed.

I wanted to keep her talking. "He does constantly praise the women about their fashion sense. But he also filled in for my law clerk lots of times and did a great job every time."

Renée half smirked. "Judge Haddes despises other females. And around men, her eyes glaze over. Especially Judge Donnettelli."

"Did his wife ever visit the office?" I asked gently.

"No. Judge Donnettelli gave me a special credit card to use at his direction. I'd make regular dinner reservations for them." Renée half smiled again. "I arranged delivery of jewelry, flowers, a tableside violinist."

I'd never considered Donnettelli a romantic. "Like for anniversaries?"

"Like make-up sex," Renée said. "It was make-up jewelry."

I asked her if he had other women, and she said he was trying to be faithful, but his wife was happy to wear expensive-jewelry blinders. He said their marriage was basically over.

The Court Administrator had directed her to clean out Donnettelli's office, and she boxed up the contents of his desk, his books, and his personal papers. It only took three boxes, and those were still in Noel's office.

I ducked into the closet and came out wearing a Blonde Ambition wig. Renée helped me find makeup and clothing to match the wig and agreed to meet me at six in the morning dressed for work.

"Wear your courthouse-entrance badge. We're making an early morning pickup," I told her. Time to get me some evidence.

CHAPTER FIFTY-SEVEN

Seated in my BMW, I felt like Barbie's new older sister. I glanced in the rearview mirror. Nobody would recognize me. My lips and brows were painted larger. I shadowed my nose to elongate it. Spiderlike lashes were glued on, and I modified my gait. Layers of heavy foil encased my GPS tether. I'd be home before my GPS had time to show error, different location, or tether interference.

Close-up camera resolution didn't worry me—the courthouse didn't have top-of-the-line equipment.

But once at the courthouse, Renée's keycard didn't work. She'd been turned off—like a County shunning. Fortunately, she knew where Noel lived, and fifteen minutes later I swerved the BMW into the driveway of his Cape Cod. "I expected some swinging bachelor pad."

Renée was in the know here, too. "He inherited the house from an old spinster-aunt he used to help out."

I cut the engine and opened my door.

"Are you really going to wake him up? The house looks dark."

"I just hope he's alone." I scrunched an exaggerated YUCK face and stepped out of the car.

Renée made big eyes. "I hope he's dressed." She jumped out the passenger side.

I pressed the buzzer three times to ensure Noel understood the urgency of answering. Door chimes brought out the small child in me. I pressed the buzzer until I heard angry barking on the other side of the door.

Silently facing each other, Renée and I waited.

Seconds later the door chain rattled. Noel—barefooted, plaid-robed, scowl-faced—appeared and opened the screen door, his collie behind him. "Been working the streets for extra cash?" His morning breath vapors evoked recent skunking reflexes. "I think you being here is a tether violation."

A hand strategically over my nose, I said, "I'm not here to ask for your opinion. I need you dressed and downtown with us." I maintained judicial-order tone. Years of habit would cause him to comply. "Box pickup from your office."

"*You're* taking the boxes to the Judge's wife?" Noel tried to shut the door, but my well-placed boot slowed him down. Noel's collie growled. "No way." Noel's voice was lower than his dog's growl.

Under another circumstance I might have offered to babysit the beautiful collie. "You have a ginormous target painted on that balding pate you strive to hide. I intend to deliver the boxes. I need access to get them, and you are it. It'll go better if you're dressed when you swipe your badge." I detached my boot just before the loyal collie sank his teeth into my boot tip.

"That's my delivery," Noel snapped. "Donnettelli's wife wants to go through them."

"She will. In the safety of her home. Are you intent on sporting a designer body bag?"

Blotches flushed up Noel's neck toward his hairline. He didn't speak, but I could see in his face this wasn't the first time he'd thought about being cast as the target in this drama.

"My car, ten minutes, bring your courthouse keycard. Don't call anyone. I'm your ride to work; find a ride home." Acutely aware I was at risk, I swiveled to fresh air. Noel's front door slammed, and I retreated into my BMW with Renée.

After nine minutes I revved the engine. At eleven minutes Noel appeared, opened the back-passenger door, slid inside, and forcefully slammed the door.

He made a show of turning his face away and glared out the window.

I shrugged his foul mood off and chauffeured to the beat of my Pandora tunes on Charlie Puth Radio.

Six songs later, we were in Donnettelli's suite, where three boxes were piled in the corner. Noel handed the first box to Renée, but dropped his keycard. I coughed, bent, picked it up, and shoved it inside my boot.

Noel huffed at me. "If you're getting sick, don't breathe on me." He shoved two boxes into my arms, whipped open the office door, and ordered us out with a grin at Renée and a mumbled *see you in hell* in my ear.

CHAPTER FIFTY-EIGHT

In my bedroom, Renée sat on the floor. Cross-legged, I sat next to her. I'd blackened her name from the suspects list. She was more target than suspect, but I'd keep her floating on a mental list in case her status changed. I popped the lid off box one. "Let's inventory."

She said, "Shorthand's quick. I'll write; you peruse."

I peeked into the box. "I have no idea what I'm looking for—so editorialize as I lift?"

She looked reluctant to go on. "Judge was very private. Going through his stuff is like visiting Casper the friendly ghost."

I looked at her, willing her to say more.

But whatever it was, she shook it off and said, "I'll tell you what I think and what I know, and I'll document what you pull out." Renée showed me her pad and pencil to prove she was on the job.

"Deal."

Renée pointed the pencil at each box in order. "Box order: *one* his desk; *two* his office; *three* his bench."

"Perfect." I exhumed the contents. Touching his things felt as grimy as being in his presence. I scanned the pile. "That square box is uncommon. Doesn't look made in America with its detailing and pretty colors elevated in metal."

"From Germany. He ate the cookies, saved the tin." Renée opened it and dumped it out.

"Are those football triangles?" I hadn't seen those since fifth grade. Boys made them out of notebook paper and played games whenever teachers left the classroom.

Renée chuckled. "He hated long phone calls. He used speaker phone and turned off video conferencing."

Mmmm. I did the same thing.

"Between taking notes, he made footballs. I'd find them flicked all over the floor, toss them back to him, and we'd joke about my bad aim."

"I can relate."

Renée chuckled and covered her mouth with her hand. Her spirit was lighter.

"Football triangles. Interesting stress reliever." Explained why he was such a misfit; the guy was stuck in fifth grade.

"I didn't realize he saved them." She returned them to the tin, pulled out a smaller tin and grazed her fingers over it. Small tears filled the corners of her eyes. "Same gift basket. Hard candies were in it. We cleaned that tin out together."

Did Renée have a crush on her boss? Ugh. She put the tin down and picked out a can of pepper spray.

I picked up the box, opened it, and dumped out lapel pins from organizational meetings. I had a jewelry box full of them. I dropped them back inside the box and then yanked out a business envelope tucked in the bottom and what looked like Jurisa's Courthouse ID badge. What the hell was that doing there? Just how involved was she? I snapped the lid on the tin and slipped the envelope and badge into my back pocket.

Renée was occupied reading the back of the pepper spray can.

"I'd feel better if you kept the pepper spray," I told her.

She quietly placed the slim can between her pretzeled legs and grabbed the next stack of files. "These are personal letters, thank-you letters, he'd saved." She handed the pile to me, and I reviewed it quickly. Just when I was ready to return the pile to her, a white linen handkerchief fluttered to the floor. I quickly retrieved it and turned it over. I recognized it as one of Laurel's. How did her hanky get mixed in with Donnettelli's collection? I shoved it in my back pocket with the envelope and returned the letters to the box.

My hope of more rose and fell quickly. Nothing. Box one held a few curiosities but was overall as bland as the soles of his demonic shoes; if a clue was festering in there, it was well-hidden.

"Box two, primarily law and personal books. I shook each one as I packed. No loose papers. He was orderly—as you can see from his desk." Renée lifted the lid and pulled out a book.

"Return it. For completeness, make a list later."

She put the book back, applied the lid, slid it over, and opened the final box.

She handed me his Taser with its charger. "I have the pepper spray. You take this. I should've turned it in, but no one asked."

We'd all been trained on Tasers and pepper spray. "Thank you." Now I could keep one in my updo and one on the charger. It would mean I would be prepared at all times. I'd charge it after she left. Damn this was lucky.

Except for the Taser, box three was as boring as my own bench drawer. "Renée, did you remember to pack your Judge's gavel? I'm guessing his family would want that."

"Sure did." But she frowned. "That's odd." She studied the list and scoured back through each of the boxes. "The gavel isn't here."

"Did it look like the tape you sealed up the boxes with had been broken?"

"No. But it was the standard packing tape we all have, and it could have been easily removed and replaced with a new piece." Renée bit her bottom lip. "Why would anyone want his gavel?"

"Good question." I bet I had the truant gavel. "My gavel was made of olivewood." I pointed to where it lay in front of a stack of books on a corner shelf in my room.

"That's beautiful," Renée said. She walked toward the shelf for closer inspection.

"How would you recognize his?"

"Dark walnut, with a beautifully carved handle. His initials were cleverly burned in the design, so you'd need to know what you were looking for," Renée said. "A gift from his father when he graduated law school. I think I have a picture of it on my phone."

She plucked the phone from her pocket and tapped 1111 to open it. She realized I'd seen the code and recognized the question in my eyes.

"Passwords are hard to remember," she said. "And every crook knows nobody is dumb enough to use 1111, so it's safe." She made a sweet half-smile, half-shrug, but her aura was tinged with deep sadness.

"I can't picture Judge Donnettelli as a young lawyer." Had he always been ornery?

"Look," Renée said. "It's in almost mint condition." She showed me the photo. It looked the same, but I couldn't swear to it.

"I wonder if his gavel was an antique, like mine, since it had carvings."

"One day, when he was very upset at a defendant, Judge pounded it so hard there's a slight dent in the mallet."

And just like that, confirmation. I remembered that dent, though at the time I wasn't focusing on it.

Renée teared. "A fond memory, now."

"I'll carry the boxes to the garage later. It's nearly noon, and we should get to the salon." I didn't want to show her my secret closet, where I'd store the boxes until delivery time.

"Noel said Mrs. Donnettelli wasn't ready for the boxes. Truth is, I'm not ready to talk with her about Judge." Renée sounded sure of herself for the first time today.

"When she's ready, Dinkie-Do can drop them off."

Keeping the boxes a few days was wise—despite our differing reasons. "All this needs to settle in my brain. Sometimes nothing is something."

There was a ghost in those three boxes, and there was nothing friendly about him; I just couldn't see what I was looking at—yet.

CHAPTER FIFTY-NINE

Before sunrise, dressed in clothing like I'd seen José and his staff wear when they cleaned the courthouse and a men's wig from an old Halloween costume, I drove to the courthouse. A travel tool kit hung from a shoelace around my neck under my shirt. A roll of duct tape and a package of baby wipes were stuffed inside my waistband.

If Noel had reported his keycard missing, it would have been cancelled immediately, and I'd be done before I started. I parked on a side street away from cameras, walked up the staff ramp, and swiped the keycard. Magically the door clicked open.

Head down, I hurried to José's cleaning closet, which was never locked because it housed the massive shredder used by facilities. I pulled on a cleaning shirt and pair of vinyl gloves, filled a pocket with disposable gloves, and wheeled out the cart.

As I entered Donnettelli's chambers alone, I held my breath and inspected the room from closet to desks to shelving units. Nothing. Damn.

I sat in his chair to engage his aura. There had to be more. I snapped pictures just in case I missed anything. I couldn't risk a second entry.

I twirled in his chair. Why hadn't the idiot ordered a new chair? It was old, uncomfortable, and provided no support. Like Donnettelli.

I had to get out of there. I stood, I gave the chair a twirl, and it leaned awkwardly. I patted the seat and found a lump in the corner. Quickly, I flipped the chair on its side, removed the fasteners, and reached inside for the padding. I pulled out a wad of bills.

Jackpot.

Money that didn't lead to me. Except that I'd found it. Damn.

I felt the old buzzard's evil ghost laughing his ass off at me finding evidence that could lock me away for good.

The Hollywood team would assume first that I had returned to retrieve my stash, forgetting to allow me to explain that I just got lucky, and it wasn't mine. They also might accuse me of planting it. No way was I risking their bumbling creativeness interfering with my freedom.

I laid the bills out in a plastic garbage bag, wrapped it around my waist, and duct taped it on me like a bomber about to detonate. I realized I wasn't wearing gloves and gasped. Damnation, this was how real criminals got into trouble. Hadn't I learned anything?

I smoothed down my shirt, grabbed one of Donnettelli's robes from the hook, and used it to wipe down everything I'd touched or looked at real hard. His robe would erase me and spread around his DNA, double bonus.

I used the robe to re-stuff the chair. After I retightened the nuts, I toe-kicked the back of the chair to knock the stuffing right out of his lingering wicked presence.

As soon as I'd returned the office to pre-search condition and the bin to the room in the basement parking garage, I dropped the key card on the garage floor, and strode out a little heavier than I'd entered.

Making it home without being stopped was key. I double-checked my gauges and ensured my lights were turned on. Fingers tightly gripped at 10 and 2 on the steering wheel, it was time to drive home like the secretary of state was giving me a road test. The streets were filling up.

When my own garage door finally lifted, I pulled in and sealed myself inside, rested my forehead on the steering wheel, and calmed myself enough not to scare Jimmy Jack.

Then, I raced up to my room. Who needed a work-out-club membership when racing up three flights of stairs had become easier than an eyebrow wax?

In my bedroom, I sat in the middle of my bed and counted my loot, knowing that it would not only trail back to me, but I'd just amped up their case against me. I had to remain calm and not overstress. Just over a million-and-a-half dollars. Gigantic, dead-president reasons someone wanted Donnettelli dead.

I removed the storage drawers from underneath my bedframe. There was an empty area behind the drawers, which had struck me when I'd bought the bed. I'd joked that it was too small for me to hide in.

I layered the bills in that empty space, and it couldn't be seen unless the mattress, wooden platform and drawers were removed. I'd never seen any search warrant locate evidence from a bed in this spot. But if it was found and linked to Donnettelli, I'd face any number of obstruction-of-justice charges.

Had I found more than a million reasons that got Donnettelli killed or reasons that would get me convicted?

CHAPTER SIXTY

A few hours after I'd peeled and parked my megabucks, I got ready and headed to work. I needed some alone time in my office, and it wasn't a long drive.

Within blocks of the salon, I realized Hunter's black Escalade lurked closely behind my rear bumper.

I swerved into a parking lot and turned off the engine. My anger rose like humidity in a Michigan summer. While I waited for Shadow Hunter to slink over, my hair probably frizzed. By the time I skimmed on a layer of lipstick, he'd bent forward, rested one arm on the roof, and knuckled Shave-and-a-Haircut on my passenger window.

I rolled it down.

He leaned in. "Looking good, Toots."

Unblinking, expressionless, not one movement. My Snow White move. But I was curious about what was so urgent it couldn't wait until I reached the salon.

Hunter tried to unlock the door. "My client—"

Buzz—wrong answer. I rolled the window up, but he stuck his fingers in the way, and I had mercy on him.

"Don't get those flaring nostrils stuck before we talk."

I overtly flared my nose.

Hunter begged for two minutes, my curiosity tricked me into opening my door, he crawled into the car, almost touched noses with me, and said, "Judges know stuff."

But why were we talking about it now on the side of the road, when I ought to be at work? I demanded details.

Hunter's eyes smiled. "Judges make decisions that allot money to one party and take money from the other."

I closed my eyes. "Wake me when you get to the part that keeps me from going to prison."

"A body in the know could cash in on that sensitive information," Hunter said.

Why did he have to say "body?" I detected a hint of arrogance in his voice. Okay, a glob of arrogance. I opened my eyes. I pictured the columns I'd filled in on my charts. "Someone more powerful than Donnettelli might kill him because he'd leaked that kind of information." I thought back to my research.

"Or because he'd refused to share it," Hunter said. "We need to know which side of that line he played on."

"It could be why he changed my Manville decision." I wove back to my asbestos cases. "If Donnettelli had changed decisions on Laurel's and Palene's dockets, too, that equaled one big reason he would want me, Laurel, and Palene to be afraid of him all the time, too scared to question him or even to be near him, his case files, and the truth. But that still didn't really add up to Donnettelli being killed."

"It could if we found out who was interested in that information."

He had something. "But his changing my Orders still meant motive and guilt that led to me."

Hunter agreed.

I clutched the top of the steering wheel.

"Let's wait and talk this over with Sebastian and Dexter." I waved goodbye.

Hunter leaned close. I could feel his warm breath. "I like it better when we're alone."

"It's always about sex with you, isn't it?" I tried not to notice how hot he smelled and the fusion of his scent with my sex-zones. Damnation.

"Toots. Why would your mind go there?" He leaned even closer. "I was talking about the investigation."

"Out!" I ordered and pointed at the door. I hoped my firm tones didn't alert him that my order equally applied to my rampant hormones.

"You're sure? We could discuss your fixation on me."

I revved the engine and glared. Or tried to. It's hard to glare when your Victoria's Secrets are melting into a leather seat, compliments of your ex, and you're seated in close proximity to another ex. Damn hormones. I'd have to work through my want-to-have-sex-now yearnings and figured as busy as we were on Tuesdays, getting myself into the salon would dump a cold bucketful over my unsatiated desire.

Minutes after arriving at the salon, despite wanting to, I couldn't just return home to further investigate and consider my plight. No way I could justify spending all day at home frittering with Donnettelli's boxes now hidden in my secret storage or thoughts of his money-stash—correction: my money stash.

Renée was wearing an apron and working with Margo. I was proud of Renée and her blossoming confidence. I wasn't sure if it was because we were becoming friends, she was away from the courthouse, or she was carrying pepper spray.

That evening, after the salon doors were locked and all the staff exited, I had just enough time for a meeting with Sebastian and Hunter. I sat at my desk, and the men pulled up the chairs so closely to the front desk edge that they could rest their elbows while they watched me lay the contents of the envelope I'd found tucked in the bottom of Donnettelli's lapel-pin box in the center of the desk. There were a dozen Visa cards and a county ID card for Jurisa Haddes. More inside puzzle pieces. Somebody needed to give me a corner piece or at least an edge piece.

The Visa cards reeked of a move Donnettelli had doubtless learned from criminal testimony: spend large amounts of money by buying reloadable credit cards used as debit cards. No wonder he liked to buy his wife fancy dinners and gifts.

Was this asbestos company payoff money? The credit card Renée had used for the missus's apology gifts must have come from this pile.

Hunter dialed Walmart with the last four digits of the first Visa card, the code on the back, and his phone number. A few minutes later he got the balance. Nine thousand dollars. He did it for all the cards. Two hundred and sixteen thousand dollars. Damn. Money grew from everything Donnettelli touched. We had to find out who was in it with him.

Sebastian was convinced the detectives would dig deeper if we simply showed them where to start, so

Sebastian tried to arrange a meeting with them. They couldn't be persuaded to come to the salon or to set a time tomorrow but were willing to see us at 8 p.m. at the station.

But when Sebastian, Hunter, and I arrived—on time—we were shown into an interrogation room and left to wait so long, I started to worry about getting home before my tether turned into a pumpkin and exploded orange mush all over my ankle.

When the pair deigned to show up, they'd left their brains behind.

"Basically, there's a tie to changing Judges' Orders in multi-million-dollar asbestos cases," I told detectives.

Sebastian showed three solid cases that should have gone to trial but were dismissed. And it looked as if no one complained. "Something's rotten in Ingham County."

"Try this," Fredericks said. "Chief Judge found out this twelve bank scheme of yours to hide your payoff bucks, and before he had a chance to report your misconduct, you shot him." Fredericks flipped through his notes. "You had everything to lose."

"Why else murder the Chief Judge and stop the perfect stream of illegal income?" Grayson asked.

I knew these guys. I'd seen them do outstanding investigative work, they were smart, and their testimony was always professional. They had to be deliberately being obtuse.

"I'm out." I stood. I was weary. Detectives heard what they wanted to: the evidence pointed at me instead of away. This meeting absolutely affirmed that I had to solve this murder.

Sebastian tipped his hat to the detectives. "A bit of hard investigative work and less double talk might put us on the same team and the killer behind bars."

"Video of your client in and out of the courthouse the week Donnettelli sucks his last breath is a gotcha, counselor." Grayson gripped the back of the chair.

Fredericks jabbed his pen in Sebastian's direction. "You've watched the footage."

I crossed my arms. "I picked Judges Briggs and Field up to visit my new salon."

Fredericks pretended to write in his notepad and mumbled, "Judges forgot how to drive."

"Ah, Judge Briggs." Grayson's voice could blister the paint on the wall. "She's not a Judge Donnettelli fan."

"A million people in the naked city are not Donnettelli fans," I said. Talking to these guys was like a bad Brazilian wax.

"Read this." Fredericks passed papers around the table.

I shivered. Cold familiarity. I'd read hundreds of similar reports. *Coroner's Report.* I scanned it. It referenced *Peter Cedric Dune*. Cause of Death: *Undetermined*. "It hasn't hit the news, yet. A coroner's inquest needs to be scheduled." Fredericks paused and scanned the table.

Our silence spurred Grayson to interject. "Perhaps you and Judge Briggs conspired to murder Dune? You've each heard enough cases to be educated on the how-to."

"We'll figure out your scheme," Fredericks said.

In my head I recited the Bill of Rights. *Congress shall make no law . . .* Bags in hand, I turned toward the door. "Judge Briggs is not in the General Trial

Division. She's in the Family Division. You can't tie any case manipulation to us, and we've declared every earned dollar to IRS."

Fredericks pen-clicked. "Even though Judge Briggs was Chief Judge Pro Tem under Donnettelli? Even though you have twelve cash accounts?"

I ignored him. "Line up dates, deaths, and court files, and watch those flipping dominoes do the wave." I strode to the door.

Sebastian scooted his chair back, jumped up, landed in front of me, tipped his hat again, and opened the door.

My boots clicked through the open door and down the worn terrazzo in the old police station. I heard Hunter's voice trail back at them. "You upset our girl. Be wise about what you do next." His voice wrapped around me like a warm blanket. But the heavy door creaked and banged shut. And I shuddered.

CHAPTER SIXTY-ONE

When we reached Hunter's Escalade, I couldn't crawl into the backseat quick enough. I snapped my seatbelt and sank into the soft leather. "Step on it before tether curfew blows my ankle off."

I wasn't worried about Hunter's speeding. My overwhelming need was simple: home. As we whirred through the streets, I counted trees, electric poles, hookers . . .

Suddenly a jolt crashed through me.

My body jerked forward; the seatbelt cut into my chest; even my voice hurdled into waves. Damnation. We'd been walloped, and my nerves unhinged.

I felt my head, stomach, and legs. I was intact. I reached into my bag and latched onto a can of hairspray then patted the Taser in my updo. I twisted around toward the rear window as much as my seatbelt allowed and peered into the shadowy night. "Get that damn beast."

A black truck with monster wheels loomed over us.

My insides stiffened into a corset of terror, a lack of oxygen disoriented me, and I couldn't get any air.

Dark-tinted windows, thunderous motor. Again, it rammed and jolted me into airplane-crash position.

"Hang on," Hunter shouted.

"Seriously?" I shouted with full-on, no-regret, sarcasm. "Hit that ogre with all you got."

"Stay down." Sebastian's voice was commanding and detached. He pulled out a silver, long-barreled gun from somewhere and propped it between the seat and his legs. He grabbed a black Glock from inside his jacket and aimed it at the rear window. "Arseholes' unlucky day to want a burst up."

I shrieked. My bags had slipped to the floor of the truck and were covered in broken glass and bullet casings. Shattered glass bounced around me. "Aw, hell no," I screamed up from my crouched position. "Swiss-cheese his wide ass." My voice curdled, rendering me unable to speak as another spray of bullets fired at the truck and return fire whizzed through our vehicle above my head.

I checked myself for wounds and ratcheted up just enough to verify Sebastian and Hunter were without holes and spattering blood. My heart was exploding with such gusto against my inner chest wall, I ached. I kept reminding myself to breathe in-between making a pact with myself to either obtain a concealed weapon permit or connect a long hose with a sprayer attached to a vat of super starch hairspray.

My body lurched forward again. The last time I felt like this I was at the carnival with my sons on the egg-beater ride. My back jerked away from the seat and slapped back again. I grabbed onto the seatbelt strap, but it didn't stabilize the body-in-a-blender feeling. "Damn this villain."

I hit 911. "Pull the damn trigger and make a U-turn before he shears us."

A barrage of bullets bombarded us.

Sebastian fired the Glock. He blew out the rear window. "Fang it." Two more bullets blared from his Glock.

"He means turn!" I shouted up at Hunter.

Between me and the world hung a shroud of high-pitched squeals. A whole new level of supernatural. My goosebump-fear mixed with my adrenaline-rush caused me to spew with impatience. "Rotate the damn steering wheel before we get killed or drive over the SOB," I screamed. I had sons to see and a life to live. I was truly scared.

"Gotcha covered," Hunter yelled back, screeched the tires right, turned down a dark alley and thudded into and over worn boxes, bags, and other trash piled next to overstuffed dumpsters. Rubbish ricocheted in every direction, spinning like smacked pool balls. Refuse crash-landed on the roof of the SUV and slid off. The sudden stench of unleashed molten garbage immediately sifted through the unglassed windows, and I winced.

I couldn't see if he'd struck anything else or what kind of minefield the boxes had left in our wake, but the rear-end jolting stopped.

Neighborhood dogs barked; a few howled. On both sides of the alley, windows lit. For a second I could see inside our vehicle. Apparently my 911 call couldn't locate our moving target. Now neither could the shooters.

The Escalade made several more turns through the maze of tight apartment alleyways, finally cracking out the other side onto Brindle Road, which was well lit and full of vehicles. My cocky men actually laughed.

Although I was grateful the thugs were vanquished, I was angry, nauseated, and confused.

"You okay back there?" Sebastian asked.

I looked up into the rearview and caught a glimpse of light in his eyes that comforted me. "I'm buying boots to match my joyride bruises."

Sebastian set the safety on each weapon, tucked them discreetly away, and turned back to face me for a few seconds. "But you are okay?"

"Define okay?" I didn't mean to sound angry, but I felt battered. I knew it wasn't his fault, but *okay* wasn't in my momentary vocabulary.

"Debrief at home," Hunter said. "Your bewitched ankle needs to return." Hunter turned toward Sebastian. "What did you see?'

"Blokes' dark-tinted windows in their truck obstructed my view," Sebastian said. "I did catch a quick glimpse through the window I blasted out. Two men, ball caps, ski masks."

"I need five seconds to recuperate from flying glass, shrapnel, and garbage stench." I was overwhelmingly appreciative, but I needed to climb into my bathtub and bawl.

Hunter maneuvered the last corner into the long road that led to my home.

"Nic, did you see anything else?" Sebastian asked.

"Seriously?" I gulped. "There's some popcorn under the seat."

Hunter turned back at me and winked.

We approached my house, and two black-and-whites clogged my front drive. "Now what?" *Could the thugs have beaten us here? Am I under arrest for being with men with guns, a clear bond violation? Damn.*

CHAPTER SIXTY-TWO

Renée and Dinkie-Do stood in my front yard facing off with three uniformed officers. A fourth uniform sat in one of the three police vehicles that flocked my driveway. He spoke into his radio.

There was no time to replace the Taser in my updo, so I buried it under my hairspray cans in the bottom of my bag.

Sebastian volleyed me a stern look. "Use your right to be silent."

Like Old West sheriffs dismounting their horses, the men stepped out of the truck and slammed their doors in unison. I imagined Ole Hunter and Ole Mr. Sebastian, hands on holsters, spurs jangling, with dusty jeans and day-old beards. Maybe I needed a *hit-slap*, or at least an ice cube between my breasts.

I fished my house key from the zippered compartment in my bag, balanced my things on my arms, and slid out of the truck. At first I had a bad case of Bambi legs, but I commanded them to get it together. I wasn't sure how to pull off the silent-woman bit. I voted for woman power and made a power line for Renée.

I focused on her forlorn presence.

A young, stubby-ponytailed female officer stepped aside to allow Renée to wrap her arms around me.

I separated myself from her long enough to hand my shoulder bag of contraband to Dinkie-Do. He absconded inside my house and quickly returned. What the hell were they doing here? I hadn't heard helicopters filming our near-death experience, but then, my ears were still ringing.

Renée's smeared makeup looked like she'd just cleaned my chimney. "My apartment's been ransacked, plundered, and crunched into oblivion—my things are barely recognizable." She held up a phone charger. "This is all I could salvage, except for my clothes. They apparently didn't like my wardrobe." She tried to grin, but the corners of her mouth turned under faster than she could pull them up. A small, paisley pouch gathered by a ribbon at the top dangled from her wrist.

"Bag of magic tricks?" I smiled. Poor joke, but I was curious. What had she rescued that she hadn't listed?

"Magical credit cards. I hide them in a ceiling tile above my bathtub." Renée held up her wrist. "I only carry the ones I need. These are all my others." Tears fell.

"Smart," I said with applaud in my voice, but the curious Judge in me—who wanted to remain free—wondered if any of those cards were Visa credit cards from Donnettelli.

"Not so smart. I had another bag behind the toilet. It's gone."

After introductions with four onlooking officers, Hunter and Sebastian were motioned to the back of the running cop car. I waited until Sebastian, several feet away, finger-flagged permission to speak.

Relief crawled over me like the bubbles I hoped to sink into. Selfishly, I was jubilant this new mess wasn't about me, and I was immediately remorseful. My gut told me the break-in had to be related to my arrest or Donnettelli, or both. Were they looking for the money he'd hidden? Why would they think Renée had it? "Renée, begin further back."

"After work, Dinkie-Do and I stopped by my apartment to water my plants. We found the door unlocked."

"I didn't let her go in. Honey, I'm no stranger to this kind of thing. Learned all sorts of things living in New York." Dinkie-Do aired all ten fingers stiffly.

"How did you know?"

In the moonlight Dinkie-Do's wide eyes glowed. "Always push on the door, Sweetheart, before key insertion. If it's solid, check the knob. Make sure it's locked. Two simple rules. If either one is broken—it's a break-in. Run and dial, Honey. Run. And. Dial."

Renée jumped in, "Quick as his fingers turn the knob, he drops it, grabs my arm, and pulls out his cell. We run into the stairwell. He hit 911. When the scream of the sirens were close, two men ran out of my apartment."

"You saw them?" I couldn't believe their luck.

"We propped the door open just a crack with the operator on the line." Renée's voice squeaked.

I squeezed her hand.

"Oh, they were a definite fashion no, not ever, Honey. Dressed in baggy black sweatpants and black t-shirts with—"

"Black ski masks and ball caps?" Sebastian called over his shoulder.

"Good guess, attorney man. Guess you've seen a lot of bad men in Fashion Drab." Dinkie-Do said. "No passion for criminal fashion." He shimmied all over.

"No guess. We just had a run-in with those two. They've had a busy night."

I edged Renée toward the house. "Are any of those credit cards from Donnettelli?" My voice was low, only meant for Renée to hear.

"He never knew when he'd have to send me shopping, so he gave me a couple of cards to keep at home." Renée opened the pouch, pulled out a half dozen cards, and handed me the two gold ones. "Here."

I palmed them and wondered if she knew how much was on them. Someone surely did. "The others from behind the toilet?" I asked.

"About ten. I added one or two a month. He used them at Christmas for his family. Gave them to me to hold so his wife couldn't spend them."

Damnation, I wanted to scream. *Donnettelli and Renée are in this much deeper than I thought.* Instead, I wrapped an arm around her and squeezed. "Go inside. Freshen up." I motioned Dinkie-Do to follow her inside.

Dinkie-Do grinned. "I'm on it."

"Officers, would you like to join us inside?" I approached and round-robin shook their hands. "Your assistance is much appreciated." I paused. "One thing I don't understand. Why are you here instead of at Renée's?"

A stocky, tanned, crew-cut brunet, who appeared to be blond ponytail's partner, tucked away his notepad. "She was too shaken to drive. We grabbed a few bags of clothes she'd pulled out from the bedroom after we searched it, and Officer Stahl drove the victim's car here."

I frowned. "Anything missing?"

"We left CSI dusting for prints and snapping pictures. Ms. Renée promised she'd deliver an inventory list."

I wrinkled my forehead at the third, tall, curly-black-headed officer.

"My partner Officer Chard and I are regular patrol through your neighborhood. A radio alert advised us of a high-speed chase and gunshots headed in this direction." His eyes focused on our missing window. He lunged forward to investigate. "Bullet holes?"

"I'm Attorney Sebastian Pearce. We're working with Detectives Fredericks and Grayson."

"I'll radio them on scene. You can make a formal statement in the morning." Curly head's partner, who monitored the radio, motioned to him. "Gotta cruise. Good luck." He strode to the vehicle and slammed himself inside, his handheld radio to his mouth.

The danger was escalating. Had to mean we were closing in—but on what? Banded together, we got safely inside, but a few minutes later Carlye stormed the gates.

"My baby and I are here." Carlye's bag thunked on my porcelain-tile floor, which sent Jimmy Jack's fur airborne, his tail expanded three times normal size.

Shazam, perched on her left shoulder, bent his head forward. *Squawk. Squawk.* "Naughty dog. Ranger coming."

I'd clearly forgotten my front door needed a flashing neon *Bed & Breakfast Closed* sign.

"Renée gives me the frantic 911, 'bring my valuables and triple-lock my doors' speech. Says she's headed here, and could I reach you." Carlye fanned revival fingers over her heart.

Renée attempted an apologetic head bow.

"Well here I is because Renée's home's been looted. We gotta protect each other *and* you. I grabbed my baby." Carlye perused the table. "Mmmm. You eat like this every day? I'm gonna like this." She pulled out a chair, sat, and plated some goodies.

After a second, Renée confessed, "I phoned Noel, too, but there was no answer. I called police to check on him."

"Have you heard anything?" Hunter asked.

Renée shook her head. "No," she whispered.

Male sign language kicked in. In sync, Hunter and Sebastian's chairs slid back. "On it." Hunter gave Sebastian the after-you hand signal and followed him. Seconds later the front door opened and slammed behind them.

Around the table, no one felt like talking.

When my phone finally rang, everyone gawked. I met Renée's eyes before I answered.

Hunter's number. "Speak." I couldn't handle more syllables.

"Toots." A clear sign Sebastian wasn't within earshot.

I kept my face expressionless realizing the room had focused on me. "Tell me." I didn't know what else to say.

"Found your boy duct taped to his bed post."

"Is he—" I couldn't utter the rest of the sentence.

"Alive," Hunter said. "Police and Hollywood won't get much out of him until he mends a bit."

Okay. "Did Noel say anything to you?" I used my come-on, you-can-tell-me voice.

"He's been critically beaten," Hunter said. "Appears to have been like that for a day, maybe two. Ambulance to Sparrow Hospital. Renée likely saved his life by calling in a health, safety, and welfare check when she couldn't reach him."

"Geez." I was getting good with one syllable words.

"One other thing," Hunter said. "A rag was stuffed in his mouth, and inside the rag was a wadded paper—a note with pasted-on letters: MYOB. KEEP YOUR MOUTH SHUT."

I dropped into a chair, almost dropped the phone. Got it back to my ear in time to hear Hunter.

"—and Sebastian's with police. Double check you've set all alarms, cameras, and turned on all outside lights. Promise?"

"Done." I was officially scared.

"My man will be outside soon. Toots, I need you to see where Noel fits into that board you're building," Hunter said. "This attack on Noel says someone's getting desperate." He clicked off.

Not more desperate than me.

CHAPTER SIXTY-THREE

We survived the night, and I awoke early with conviction and a plan. I dug into the secret closet behind the sliding bookcases and grabbed an oversized metal whiteboard and its accompanying bag of magnetic alphabet letters and numbers. Memory lane threatened to draw me in and swallow me, so I got out of there. There was work to be done. I hated the feeling I was miles behind, lost in a dark forest without a guiding star. I decided to create my vision path and find answers.

The attack on Noel might be the puzzle piece I'd been missing. Donnettelli was killed; I got the snake and the skunk perfume and almost blown up and shot at. Renée got burgled. Peter got dead. My episodes arrived with direct and indirect warnings. Had Donnettelli and Peter been warned? I didn't want to wake Renée, so I sent her a text: *Important. Have you received any warnings, threats, or weird communication of any kind since Judge Donnettelli's murder?*

Back in the quiet of my room, I set the metal board against the wall, dumped the bag of magnets, and sat. I double-checked my letter list from the schedule book, even though they were hairsprayed to my brain.

I created one list in alternating colors and more lists in identical colors. But nothing jogged my brain.

JNMK CCHS JWED

I squinted, watched the letters shift out of focus and refocus. To the right, I placed a plastic dollar sign and then numbers.

JNMK CCHS JWED $12,000,000

Enough to kill for; not enough to incite my brain. My neck crooked, my heart arrested, and my blood heightened from simmer to boil. Who were the twelve bank CEOs? I booted my computer. Pulling mine apart first, I jumbled the twelve magnetic letters. Initials become branded on you just like lipstick.

Damn it. I was lipstick-thinking. I rebooted my brain. There was no logical reason my initials would be in Donnettelli's book. So—they're not my initials. I rearranged the initials alphabetically and added spacing.

C C E H J J M N R S W

I was reminded of my second-grade handwriting board. The letters didn't speak to me back then, either.

When the computer screen flashed, I Googled.

Half an hour later, I decided I might as well have spent my time tossing pasta on the walls to see what stuck because everything I typed in fell into outer space. No CEO bank match.

So what else could they be? I headed to the bookshelf to get the *Michigan Bar Journal* and a list of all the Michigan Judges.

My phone vibrated. Laurel. She had the day off, and joy flushed through me. I needed real conversation, real talk with a real friend, so I told her to hustle her high-heel-loving heinie on over.

CHAPTER SIXTY-FOUR

While I waited for Laurel to arrive, I prepared an inviting table. Half an hour later, she sat next to me at the kitchen table, and I explained the sequence of events that had me triple-checking my rearview mirror and using the Dinkie-Do doorknob strategy.

Over coffee, I described a hypothetical scenario in which twelve people inside the courthouse—from the cleaning crew to the Chief Judges—colluded to make untaxed dollars. I didn't mention the Visa cards specifically. But I let Laurel know the scheme could be worth around $1.2 million, likely more. I didn't want to give anyone an accurate count.

Laurel didn't blink. She set her coffee cup down. "Nicoletta, I've been your friend for a dozen years." I'd never seen Laurel more earnest. "I'm telling you—you can't let yourself get caught up in some fantasy conspiracy theory."

I refused to show the blast of resentment I felt, but I couldn't blame Laurel. After all, I'd been so certain Peter was the brains, and it could be that announcing it in the salon was what got him killed. "You know, with all the criminal intelligence that goes through the courthouse, and everything being computerized, somebody could make a lot of money. Honestly, now that we are talking about it, I'm thinking it's more than likely there are scams under our radar."

"I hope not. At this point I'm the target they'll pin it on." I rested my chin on my fist.

Laurel picked a Godiva chocolate from the nut-and-candy dish in the center of the table and unwrapped the chocolate. "Have you thought about Wade Mazour?"

Was she changing the subject? "Law clerk to the Supreme Court Chief Judge Belington," I said. "He's an ice-cream connoisseur."

"Judge Belington adores Mazour, despite his haircuts that yell: *I need a barber*." Laurel licked her finger. "He knows his stuff—except for grooming." She laughed. "He needs your touch."

I walked to the counter and fed the Nespresso a navy pod.

Laurel continued. "He's protective of his master—a bulldog in training without a care for common morality."

I wondered where Laurel was going with this. Was she trying to drop a heavy hint? If so, why? From what I'd witnessed Donnettelli had bullied Wade like everybody else.

She grinned with her eyes as if she'd cornered the bad guy. "Wade creeps me out."

Why would Laurel try to involve him? I shrugged. "Assume Donnettelli's playing for incredibly high stakes, and he single-handedly—"

Laurel corrected me. "Single-handedly—plus the guy or gal who shot him." She used her eyebrows meaningfully.

"Okay, *they* invented a way around the automatic scheduling of cases—big civil cases related to mesothelioma and asbestos, which involved millions of dollars." I knew I was right about that much. I looked for surprise on Laurel's face but saw none. Had Donnettelli been telling the truth in the elevator? Laurel was knowingly involved? I shuddered.

"Are you okay?" Laurel frowned.

"Except for the obvious, yes."

Laurel smoothed the tablecloth. "The intricate strategy and daily watchful planning of a conspiracy would take a tremendous amount of time."

"Agreed. The pair would've spent considerable time together outside the courthouse." I thought about the rumors of bar-hopping and skirt-chasing with Donnettelli and Noel and wondered if Wade Mazour joined them, or anyone else, for that matter. "Did you ever hear about Wade spending a ton of time with Donnettelli?" I placed the cup of coffee in front of her, and then sat across the table.

Laurel leaned back. I leaned forward.

"If Donnettelli wasn't with the wife, he was with Jurisa, sometimes his court administrator," Laurel said while slowly unwrapping a caramel-filled Godiva.

"We knew he loved to be surrounded by adoring women."

She tossed the Godiva into the steamy coffee and fished it out with a spoon that immediately crossed her lips. She slowly pulled out the spoon with a flutter of her eyes that spelled satisfied and spoke. "Someone very intelligent had to regularly direct Donnettelli. He simply didn't work that hard. Jurisa could have directed him." Laurel paused with a thoughtful finger on her lips. "Payoff had to be enormous."

"Do you know why Jurisa and her husband sold their property up north and his boat?"

Laurel looked sad. Embarrassed. "Derrick had a problem. He likes the casino in Mount Pleasant a little too much."

Ah. Jurisa needed money. Maybe that's why she fawned over Donnettelli. It couldn't have been his personality. "She wove a tangled plan to earn extra hidden money that quietly crept into place and poked like gray hair."

Laurel shook her head at me. "Whatever way you color the case-swapping kaleidoscope, making money outside of the norm, it's a dangerous scheme for any judge, especially for a chief judge. I have no connection and want no connection to whatever it was or is. Everything Donnettelli touched, he tainted."

I waited. Did she know more or not? Was I missing something? Laurel was the queen of innuendo, and with her, sometimes nothing was something, and sometimes something was nothing.

"You were smart to get out and start a new life. I'm envious."

"So smart I'm headed for a really long sleepover on the government's dime." I unwrapped another chocolate for Laurel, handed it to her, and grabbed one for myself. "Given the fact that Donnettelli willingly played with the court docket, why would someone want to murder him?"

Laurel grabbed my wrist and squeezed it. "Money. And, it must be about big money. Somebody was paying Donnettelli and his plus one to do something or profiting big-time from something he was doing."

I stopped my legs from shaking. "Then either the Somebody or the plus one decided Donnettelli was more useful dead. But then whoever it was also killed Peter Dune and tried to scare me into shutting up. Nothing fits cleanly."

"It fits when you think about it. Peter was Donnettelli's law clerk. He knew what the Judge knew. He had to go," Laurel said, looking quite pleased with her deductions. She pulled a tiny white handkerchief from her bag, carefully wiped the corners of her eyes, and put the hankie back.

"But that doesn't tell us who the co-conspirator is," I said. We were talking in chocolate-covered circles. "And it doesn't tell us why Donnettelli wore an expiration date—not if he was key to messing with the cases and profiting from it."

After a brief lovefest with the candy dish, Laurel's fingers plucked out a gold-wrapped chocolate-covered cherry.

I replayed the word *motive*. My brain clicked. Case-file maneuvering, changed asbestos Orders. Power and money: motive. But that wasn't really new was it? I sighed.

We turned the problem over for more than an hour. When Laurel took a bathroom break, I quickly rummaged through her enormous shoulder bag, picked out one of her white-linen hankies, pocketed it, and tucked in a pair of red-soled sling-back pumps under her bulky wallet. I would've enjoyed hearing her squeal of delight when she found them, but I found equal enjoyment in being knowingly ignorant of her Louboutin love. When she reappeared, I wrapped goodbye arms around her and walked her out.

CHAPTER SIXTY-FIVE

Out front, Laurel blew me a kiss, opened the passenger door, set her bag inside, and put on her driving shoes. She's the only woman I've known who swapped shoes to drive.

She started backing out, and I waved goodbye. The real uppers in life, besides hairspray and caffeine, were girlfriends and chocolate. A little girl-chatter could solve world problems. I wondered why the White House hadn't figured that out.

Just as I turned back into the house—firecrackers? I jumped. What the hell? Not again.

Crack. Crack. Crack.

Gunshots.

Screeching tires.

On no—

Laurel.

Inside the garage I hit 911. Through the front window, I saw the black demon-truck speed off.

Hunter's security guy tore into chase-mode after the truck.

Laurel's car rolled into my evergreen border, which thankfully stopped her. Running, I screamed into the phone for ambulance and police. Bullets had pierced her passenger door. I flung it open and dove inside. "Laurel." Her face was pale.

The dispatch operator asked questions I needed to answer, but the interruption just infuriated me.

Her left hand lifted. It was bloody.

"Where are you hurt?" I scanned her body, following the gush of red. I couldn't see where she was hit. Don't die. Damnit. "Laurel, I know you can hear me. We've got shoe shopping to do; get it together, girl. I need you. Michael needs you."

I hit speaker, dropped the phone, and answered dispatch. "Gunshot wound, one, maybe more. I've tossed a blanket from the back seat over her. Applying pressure on the wound I can see."

I pressed with one hand and hugged the blanket around my friend with the other.

It felt like seasons must have changed before I finally heard sirens. Then, within seconds, they were in the driveway. Here. Running toward us.

Relieved, I stepped aside for the EMTs and collected my phone. *Damnation. She had better live.*

"I'm locking my house and getting my bag. I'm right behind," I yelled back at a focused man hanging an IV bag. All with professional precision. Not one move wasted. *Was someone trying to shut her up because she knew something or because she was involved? Maybe everyone I loved was at risk.*

I squealed out of the garage and drove at a rate behind the ambulance that should have had me arrested. I didn't care. My friend was in trouble, and it felt like I'd pulled the trigger. I was so shaken, my welling tears were too shocked to drop. I pulled into the hospital emergency entrance, parked, and ran into the hospital behind the gurney. Despite the EMTs asking me to step aside, I grabbed Laurel's hand.

But too soon, I was forced to release her hand and let the professionals take her away from me. They whisked her down the hallway to the surgery floor. When the doors opened and released me toward the waiting room, I clicked in Michael's number. When he answered, I spoke as quietly and calmly as I could and headed toward the check-in desk. I enunciated each word. *Laurel has been shot.* Words I'd never imagined uttering. Words I'd never wanted to say to her adoring husband. Words I couldn't rationally explain.

Somewhere among tears, apologies, and reassurances—I made promises and mentioned God repeatedly—I convinced Michael to ask a coworker to drive him to Sparrow Hospital. My thinking and breathing signals were all confused. I thought about Laurel's laughter. I had to stay positive, or I'd cry and never stop. Laurel would never forgive me for not being strong for Michael.

Once she was checked in, I received a patient number and chose a corner seat with visibility to the surgery screen. Laurel was definitely in surgery. That meant she was alive. I gulped my fears down and then heard a familiar voice.

"My man radioed me. He lost the shooter truck, but gave it a good chase," Hunter said.

I was grateful it was Hunter who'd found me first. I wasn't ready to console Michael; I needed consoling. "That damn truck; it's like an evil elephant hiding in a rose bush."

"That elephant keeps reemerging without any thorns. Not just anyone can disappear in this town. We're on it, Toots."

"Like rain on bare hair, you're on it," I muttered.

"You're in shock." Hunter lifted my hands and pulled me up. He confiscated my phone. My hands were still covered in Laurel's blood.

"Let's clean you up." Hunter's voice was tender, and he heaved my bag and slung it over his shoulder.

It was like old times. Okay, I'd take a *hit-slap* back. He walked me into the family restroom and locked the door. He pulled up my sleeves, pumped the soap, and lathered my hands and wrists.

I looked in the mirror. Bright red streaked across one cheek. The warm, sudsy water oozed pink bubbles down the drain, and I was thankful I wasn't alone. I was even more thankful Michael hadn't seen me covered in his wife's blood. *Good move, Hunter.*

Fifteen minutes later we stepped out into the hallway, and I almost slammed into Sebastian.

"Jingoes. Double mates in the john." Sebastian tipped his hat at Hunter. "Fetching purse."

Hunter gave Sebastian the meekest smile and patted my bag like it was his own.

I marveled at their male bonding. They were good men. "I'm glad you guys are here," I whispered. Skunk-juice perfume was sounding like a step up, now. Damn it, how long could it take Michael to travel thirty miles?

Hunter twirled into the waiting room modeling my purse until I snatched it and sat in an empty corner cluster of chairs near the information station.

"Team Hollywood will arrive soon." Sebastian handed me a cup of cold water from the cooler. "Someone—who's not you—will be in the shit for this. It's time they used their cakeholes for a serious chinwag."

I crushed the emptied paper cup. "Not now." Besides, I'd heard that before.

Four scolding eyes morphed me into a child. I wished age-repair cream worked that quickly.

He's here.

I stood, tossed the cup into the basket next to the water cooler, and opened my arms toward Michael, who was running toward me.

"News?"

We hugged. My face was wet with tears. His was, too. I opened my mouth to speak and then closed it because I was about to wail as loudly as my free-flowing tears. I pictured Laurel. I held my breath and collected myself. Laurel would want me—no Laurel needed me—to help Michael through this.

Minutes later, I looped my arm through his, and in silence we headed toward the information desk, where Michael pumped the receptionist—unsuccessfully.

We sat and watched the electronic patient board flicker numbers, but not Laurel's.

Sebastian tapped my shoulder, and I backed up. Pastel and Leather stood on either side of him. I pointed, Michael remained planted in his chair, and I played follow the leader.

Sebastian dropped back. He stepped into me and wrapped his arm around my shoulder. "Those blokes double-timed it."

He was warm and comfortable, and I wanted to melt into him, but kept in step with him toward the detective huddle, where Hunter joined us in an empty family meeting room. We filed in and sat in unmatched chairs. The only thing I wanted to hear was Laurel's laughter in recovery with Michael.

Fredericks opened the notepad. Grayson wanted everything I'd seen or heard. And the questioning went on a long time. After three rounds of questions, I was frustrated.

"After the excised bullets are compared with the death shot of Donnettelli, the facade may change." Grayson's voice was stern.

I stood. "Add this to what I gave you at our last meeting: appealed decisions, asbestos Orders modified, and lots of money. Are you interested in being real Detectives and making worldwide headlines?"

Fredericks stopped writing. Grayson finally spoke in a bland voice with his palms turned up. "You know the ropes." They stared at me like I'd remained silent. "Did your co-conspirators shoot your friend?" Grayson very pointedly, very slowly, leaned toward me.

I backed up against the wall. I wished I could've flattened myself into it and morphed invisible, like I was being treated. "Are you effing kidding me, you bastard? That's my best friend in there, and I'm not only worried sick, I'm heartbroken! Something you two obviously know nothing about. What have Laurel and I ever done to you that causes you to treat us like this?" Ugh, I've turned into that defendant who lashes out at everyone. I needed hairspray mist to glue my emotions together and seal my mouth.

Hollywood stared at me and my emotional tantrum. A detective tactic I loathed being on the receiving end of.

"Would you just get your head out of your pompous ass for once and do some actual work instead of leaving it all to me?"

I couldn't stop myself. I ignored Sebastian's *remember your right to be silent* frown.

"Someone needed Donnettelli dead because he had been playing with them and then—maybe he wanted to quit. Laurel helped me piece this part together. And, yes there's likely more. Whoever is behind this just slowed Laurel down." I wouldn't entertain the notion of her dying or even losing a leg.

"We're working various angles," Fredericks said. "Like why not shoot you *and* Judge Briggs?" He pointed his pencil at me. "You keep ending up alive. Did you order the hit on her?"

"You don't deserve an adult pencil. Grab a fat kindergarten pencil and trade your pen for large Crayolas next time you play with the supplies."

I wanted to be crass but thought better of it since my life depended on being rational, and at this point I felt on the verge of irrationality. A deep, calming breath held me together before I continued. "Someone wants me in jail, and they want Laurel quiet about something. You're so focused on me, you're not seriously looking for anyone else."

"Only people close to you or in your way are dying," Grayson said. "Revolves the evidence pointer back to you."

"I think the killers wanted to frighten Laurel into playing their game like Donnettelli did." Okay, good lead—*play our courthouse-switch-Orders-and-case-file game or be the next body*? Had someone approached Laurel, and she didn't tell me?

Silence.

"Was someone trying to beat Noel Lemmon into submission?" Fredericks asked.

Grayson studied me.

Hunter interrupted. "Let's check on Noel while we're here."

I looked cross-eyed at Grayson and Fredericks. "Detectives, your investigation leaves a trail of unanswered questions." I tapped my watch.

Neither detective flinched.

Sebastian tipped his hat at the detectives. "We're finished here, detectives. We have friends to check on."

I felt like punching a city employee, but these guys had guns. I hid my hands in my back pockets to stop myself. I found Laurel's white handkerchief, pulled it out, opened it. Damn. "Yes," I said. "We have work to do and much to check on. I'm thinking you detectives have some real work to do. I can't imagine you enjoy our time together." I took a step toward the door.

"We're not finished here," Grayson said.

"Call me when you brush up on your training and get your uninformed lazy asses in gear." I turned toward the door, and my men followed me.

This was not how I wanted to spend a beautiful August night, or any other night of my life. I was beyond relieved when Michael texted me.

By midnight, Laurel was in stable condition, but not awake. Once she was transferred to her patient room, Hunter stationed a security woman inside her room. The detectives placed an officer outside her door. Sebastian had disappeared and used his lawyer magic to expand my tether hours and locations for safety to include the hospital.

Hunter squeezed my elbow and turned me out of the waiting room into a secluded area of the hallway. He fished a set of keys from the inside of his jacket.

"New car." He pressed keys into my palm that evoked an avalanche of chills into my toes. He'd found my inner crushed-ice button.

Without consulting me, Dex left me a key to a slate-gray Audi and directions to expect a surprise at breakfast.

CHAPTER SIXTY-SIX

The next morning after twenty sit-ups, a long shower, and getting dressed, hairsprayed, and caffeinated, I enjoyed a brief, reassuring conversation with Laurel. When I finally raced down the back stairs I couldn't imagine what package, prize, or punch line he'd surprise me with. I hoped it was evidence in the exculpatory category. And I rounded into the kitchen.

"Good morning." In choir, there they were. My boys with my—Dex.

Warm goosebumps and the memory of happy years engulfed me. Then a flood of relief encapsulated mother-bear fear, and I cherished the feeling of the warm bodies of my trio rushing into me, hugging me tightly.

My guys were nineteen, twenty, and twenty-one, born so close together, I felt like I'd delivered triplets. Eventually I got my hormones and my birth control right. After almost three years of continual pregnancy, I felt a kinship with female elephants.

Now I never wanted them to let go. "What are you three doing here?"

Dex made jazz hands and whispered, "Surprise!"

Jake knuckle-rubbed the top of my head. "Told Dad we were coming with or without him."

Josh squeezed my shoulder. "We're in this together."

Judd squeezed his hug on me tighter. "Missed ya, Mom."

I kissed my sons.

Dex made a fabulous breakfast, and I enjoyed every minute with my men. He explained that he and Dinkie-Do were rearranging room assignments, so the boys could have their rooms here at Nicoletta's B&B. And he filled me in on the new security measures at work. I would've liked to stay to discuss security and tactics. Instead, I hopped into my car and called him from my cell so we could continue our discussion on my drive to the salon.

I barely recalled driving. I could hear Dex loading the dishwasher dishes in the background while we spoke. Too bad he hadn't been this attentive when we were married. It was well after nine by the time I entered the salon. But once there, I reassured my staff that Laurel was on the mend, and we had new safety gizmos and additional security men from front to back to protect us at work.

Shazam squawked. In honor of Judge Laurel, Dinkie-Do's station was at "half heel"—half bare, single shoes with heels faced west. I delivered my best military salute toward the shoe shrine. Dinkie-Do grabbed a heel and returned the salute. I turned toward my station and watched Trisha seat a client in my stylist chair.

I recognized my first client, Jillian Wiek, a retired Court of Appeals Clerk, who I knew remained in close contact with her former coworkers. I remembered her and her Texan accent from practice, but we'd had no contact since I'd donned the robe. She was about to be mother of the bride.

"When I heard Judge Briggs got shot," Jillian said, "I had to come say how sorry I was. I knew you wouldn't shoot her or anyone else."

I pulled my fingers through her hair to avoid answering, and then clipped the protective gown around her. "You'll be stunning, second to the bride."

Jillian watched me in the mirror, while I combed her out. "How's Judge Briggs doing?"

I hadn't heard one breath in the media, and Grayson and Fredericks promised nothing would be released, pending investigation. We were all sworn to secrecy. "What've you heard?"

"She's not, I mean she'll be good as new?"

"Of course." I made myself sound so nonchalant, she'd think I was asleep. "How did you hear about Laurel?"

"When I dropped off cookies this morning to the Court of Appeals clerks, they were abuzz about the shooting."

I combed her hair. "Wonder how they heard."

"The Chief Judge's clerk was saying Judge Briggs got shot giving you confidential court information."

I handed her hair-color swatches. My look prodded her without giving away my anxiety.

"That Wade Mazour talks more than any woman I know." Jillian did a giggle-snort thing.

She chose chestnut brown and returned the color-swatch ring to me, and I headed off to mix the colors.

Inside the color room, I phoned Sebastian and let him know that Laurel being shot is the morning gossip in the Court of Appeals Clerk's office. Somebody there knew firsthand. He said he'd advise Team Hollywood to interview everyone in the Hall of Justice to determine who knows what and from whom. For the first time in days, Sebastian sounded excited.

Phone returned to my pocket, I had an instant vision of how the black truck had so easily disappeared: underground parking at the Hall of Justice where Court of Appeals and the Supreme Court Justices parked. I phoned Hunter and asked him to put a man on the justices' underground parking structure.

I was almost back to my station when Trisha handed me a manila envelope the size of half a file.

I accepted it and flipped it over. No markings, but it felt hard.

"Culver DeClerk's exact quote: here's a tip for you and one for your boss," Trisha said.

A present from my favorite courthouse security guard—at least I knew it was safe to open. Culver was a longtime friend. I broke the seal and looked inside. A folded note: *With the shooting of Judge Briggs, I thought it prudent to share what I know. Culver.* And a DVD.

Perfect bedtime movie with microwave popcorn and a caffeine chaser.

CHAPTER SIXTY-SEVEN

After dinner, in a small interrogation room, I again sat facing the not-so-dynamic duo. Hunter and Sebastian were with me. Thankfully, Dex had taken our sons out for the evening.

First, detectives passed out papers. "These are lists of people who hold Supreme Court, Court of Appeals, and Trial Court parking passes. No vehicle you described has a parking pass under any court building, and there's no security camera footage of such a vehicle," Grayson said.

At least they were finally interested. "As in no footage exists, or there's none with matching trucks inside or outside the Courthouse?"

Fredericks answered, "No to all." But he had his eyes on his notepad.

If there's no footage, somebody's gone and tampered with the cameras. "What did the security officers say?" I asked.

"They didn't say they'd seen a truck like the one you described," Grayson said.

Fredericks kept writing and didn't look up.

"And what he did say was—" *Come on, you can tell me.*

Grayson kicked one chair then slumped into another. "They all agreed that it's very easy to slip in and out of the underground garages without an official access card, and once you're in, there are known blind spots the camera doesn't cover. That being said, it's notable that these blind spots are comprehended by the younger generation, who have a strong grasp on how to access data and use technology. Deputies have rousted nappers there twice that I know of. There's also evidence that in the recent past someone has accessed the video and messed with it."

I couldn't find words. Hunter guffawed. Sebastian suggested we change the subject now, and let the detectives fill us in later on their plan to trap the malicious vehicle. A shootout down the middle of Cedar Street was a serious problem.

"This is known how?" Hunter finally asked. "It writes over, so you're talking within the past weeks? Right?"

Grayson shook his head in thought. "Over the years when we have needed to check the footage, there were blank spots. The Court Administrator chalked it up to needing better equipment and simple electronic error."

"In other words, the Chief Judge—as in the departed Donnettelli—stopped any inquiry." I paused. Hearing no acknowledgment of my comment, I pressed forward. "Alrighty, then," I said. "Next order of business." I handed Grayson the DVD. "I only ripped it open. I didn't touch it."

"Not a likely surface for prints." Donning latex gloves, Grayson set up the DVD player and pressed play. "I have a trade for you when we finish."

I hoped his trade wasn't my tether for handcuffs.

Fredericks was always ready—open notepad, pen in hand.

Dates appeared on the screen, beginning just over one year ago. It was Courthouse video—preserved, not written over. Somebody techy had captured and saved it. Images of Judge Donnettelli and Judge Jurisa Haddes—repeatedly. Holding hands discreetly. Reaching for each other, fondling, kissing, touching. Unmistakably they believed they were in private, outside of camera focus.

Jurisa, my former office suitemate, was a woman with a secret deeper than the number of her hair color. Her poor husband.

When the recording ended, Grayson stood and clicked on the lights. "Your security-guard friend, Culver DeClerk, will he speak with us? Testify?"

"Offer him a just-in-case immunity deal, so he'll feel safe to talk." I paused. "This evidence makes you look pretty silly for not fully investigating other assailants with motives. Jilted lover is an ancient motive for murder."

Sebastian scoffed. "Shonky investigation."

"It only speaks to motive for one bullet. We found two different bullets in one dead man." Fredericks stuck up two fingers.

"Yet you arrested only me. Either you find the two trigger happy-killers, or I will. My bet is on me." My voice firm, I ogled the detectives. "I understand the '80s big hair is reemerging. And I have a few salon chairs to fill; perhaps I can enroll you two in barber school?"

"Not so fast. I promised you a trade," Grayson said. He nodded at Fredericks, who swapped DVDs and hit play.

Sebastian leaned forward. "Evidence you forgot to turn over?"

"Evidence we just received via bank courier."

That had my attention. All eyes on the screen, I triple-blinked at a figure who looked like me, but wasn't.

Fifteen minutes later the DVD ended, but Grayson froze it on the last frame. "Here's your copy." He handed an envelope to Sebastian. "Care to explain?"

"I don't know who that was, but it was not me." I enunciated each word as slowly and clearly as I could and dubbed them with a dozen *hit-slaps* for thinking that disassembled mess looked like me.

"Your hair color and updo. Your jeans and cowboy boots. Your gait," Grayson said. "Fredericks and I have witnessed your various looks and moves in the Courthouse.

All three men turned toward me. I felt like I'd forgotten to wear undergarments. I pointed at the semi-fuzzy bank film. "Look at the cowboy boots. Not my boot bracelet. I make my own boot bracelets and spurs." I lifted my left boot and clunked it on the table. "One of a kind."

CHAPTER SIXTY-EIGHT

The next morning at Sparrow Hospital, I faced off with two more officers, one in plain clothes, the other in uniform, each conspicuously placed outside Laurel's room at the end of the hall. I flashed my driver's license and heard familiar laughter from her room, while the officers checked the approved-visitor list. I leaned in to see who was there.

Dinkie-Do in full glory: "Judge Briggs—"

Laurel showed her stop hand-sign. "Call me Laurel."

"Judge Laurel," he said, "my station is just not the same without you." Dinkie-Do wore tight, black, thin-legged pants with a black shirt striped in thin florescent colors and a skinny, lime-green tie. Silver loafers.

In a designer clay pot, a sturdy, four-foot-tall blue spruce with a star on top sat on the bedside tray table. Several sling-backed high heels hung at differing heights from the tree, and the mate of each shoe hung by its heel on the rim of the pot.

It was a beautiful sight, deserving of a New York Macy's window. Shoe frontals inward, heels pointed out, Swarovski crystal snowflakes hung alternating with pots of glimmering eye shadows and bedazzled needles.

Laurel's hands lay crossed over her heart. "I've never seen anything more beautiful except my husband and children." She touched the tree. Dinkie-Do turned it thirty degrees, and she gasped again. "Worth getting shot over."

"Miss Laurel, you're embarrassing me." Dinkie-Do lifted one shoulder to his bent head. "Ooooh, look who's joined us."

I entered the rest of the way, and he hugged me.

"Love the tree, but I'll be avoiding bullets, thank you." I removed myself from Dinkie-Do's grip, hugged Laurel, and then sat on the corner of her bed.

"I've got clients." Dinkie-Do princess-waved. "Keep pumping iron so you get outta here. You're in my book."

Laurel shone. "It'll take me a while to decide which shoes to wear." She laughed, and he wiggled out the door.

"You look radiant." I clasped her hand. "How's Michael?"

"My doctors ordered him to go home to sleep." Laurel could hardly keep her eyes off the shoe tree. "Michael left after the second officer was posted at my door."

"I feel so badly about—"

Laurel cut me off. "Feel the shoe leather, and the world is good again." She stroked a heel and a crystal. It scattered small rainbows around the room. "Truth. What caused this, and what rids us of this?"

She knew me well. "My new theory: Maybe Donnettelli was vying for a Supreme Court appointment."

Laurel didn't blink. The silence spoke for her.

Head tilt. "You knew?"

"I didn't know you hadn't thought of that connection. How is it you're surprised?" Laurel's tone made me feel like a third grader. "Donnettelli liked to play with the big boys; it made him feel bigger. He was all puffery. You know that. And think about it: why else would he spend his time rubbing elbows with legislators?"

Surprised? I felt small and stupid; I did know that. "Guess I forgot to look at what was right in front of me."

Laurel continued. "Political parties nominate Supreme Court candidates, which takes money, lots of money. Hence the case-swapping, so he could get the decision he wanted."

I winced. "Then somebody offs him and points the smoking gun at me. Why?"

"Well," Laurel said patiently, like the whole world, except me, could see what was going on. "If you're locked up for murder, Donnettelli's playmate can go on with the scheme, and nobody's investigating swapped cases anymore." Laurel looked quite pleased with her analysis. "When you spoke out about that Manville case, you may as well have ordered the hit on Donnettelli yourself. He had to go."

I felt as if I'd been backhanded, and I held onto the bed to keep from reeling. She was right. I'd denounced Donnettelli publicly for changing my Order. The letter Sebastian had sent to everyone was very clear. Any co-conspirator would have to do away with him. "I didn't know he wasn't acting alone." This was awful.

Laurel placed her hand over mine. "Of course not. You were doing what you always do—speaking up for those who couldn't speak up for themselves. Everyone's focus should have been on getting justice for those families devastated by mesothelioma."

Laurel made more comforting noises, and I realized she was showing signs of needing sleep.

"It wasn't supposed to be a stepping-stone for His Supreme Belligerence to the Supreme Court. Did you ever hear him talk about it?"

"I heard Noel on the phone the other day." Laurel's words were beginning to slur. "He told somebody you stole Mrs. Donnettelli's boxers. Isn't that funny?"

I numbly smiled in agreement, thanked her, and kissed her forehead. I couldn't head out of the hospital fast enough. I speed dialed Dexter as I walked, and when the call clicked in, I didn't wait for him to speak. "Meet me at the salon ASAP. Bring our sons. Please."

I had a horrid feeling that before I got to my house, the cops, the detectives, and the murderers would be there. I feared I'd hear: yes, there was evidence you withheld in your secret closet and in boxes that belonged to the man you killed. Damnation, I was tired of all that leading to me.

By the time the guys pulled up at the rear door of the salon, I was there and ready to brave that rolling den of testosterone.

Fifteen minutes later, we pulled into my driveway. I gave the boys a key to the secret closet and told them what to do. Each son marched upstairs and down again—a box in hand and loaded it into the Hummer.

I put the key to the Hummer on the island near the patched Plasti-gal, phoned Dinkie-Do, and asked him to take a break, get a ride home, and deliver the boxes to Mrs. Donnettelli. We didn't want her missing her boxers.

CHAPTER SIXTY-NINE

Late in the afternoon, I was cleaning my station when Sebastian came in and unexpectedly announced that the detectives wanted a word. Behind him, Hunter led Detectives Grayson and Fredericks. I reached for the red-and-black can, spritzed myself, capped it, and returned it to my shelf.

Just the sight of those two detectives annoyed me. I pointed the infiltrators to the back room, and followed them, closing the door behind me.

I sat at the head of the kitchen table and waited. And waited.

Hunter started. "Detectives are looking for a person of interest and want to ask you about it."

"Someone who's not me?"

Fredericks hunched over the table. "Not for publication." He kept his voice matter-of-fact.

I felt bound to quiz him. "Related to Donnettelli's murder?"

Fredericks kept it as bland as "shave it all." No creativity or inflection. I wondered what would happen if he sat on a wire brush in his boxers. "Judge Jurisa Haddes."

"You're searching near me? Seriously?" Not once did she ever travel outside her judicial suite to visit with me when we were colleagues, never sat next to me at one Judges' meeting, never made any effort to speak to me in the parking garage, elevator, or at social gatherings when our paths inevitably crossed.

Fredericks made like he was reading from his little notepad. "You were both Circuit Court Judges. You were both involved with Donnettelli."

"Not!" I felt faint. I never faint. But the thought that I was in any way involved with Donnettelli—I was about to faint.

"In a manner of speaking," Fredericks said. "There's big money here, and where there's big money, there's bound to be some action. We're looking for her near the action."

"No time for fighting." Hunter winked at me.

Ugh!

Grayson showed a police-stop hand. "Common ground is swelling. I'm leaning more toward your thinking."

Sebastian looked from Grayson to Fredericks and said, "So find Judge Haddes, charge her, and request dismissal of the charges against Nic."

Grayson scratched his ear. "Just where would you stick that into the Constitution, counselor? The magic word to charging is *evidence*." Grayson dropped his voice.

I raised my voice. "The magic word is freedom. Mine. You interviewed Culver DeClerk?"

Fredericks said they had, and that Culver would testify about the video.

An affair *was* a reason to murder, but there was so much more here. "Did you speak with Haddes's husband?"

Faces blanked, but I understood that silence. "They're missing together?"

"Dog's balls. Offer some lollies, and the public will tell you where they are." Sebastian tapped a commanding finger on the tabletop.

"It's hard to hide in a town, even inside a state, where you're regularly in the media because of the cases you draw as a Judge. I know."

Grayson cleared his throat. "*Be on the lookout* alerts for Judge and Detective Haddes went out to state and local units. And all public transportation has been notified."

"Haven't been missing twenty-four hours." Fredericks flipped the pages of his notepad. "Her staff described a busy motion day, her trial pled, she's off the rest of the week. He's semi-retired."

"If truly missing, maybe it is hunting season on Judges, and Judge Haddes is that next victim," Grayson said. "You didn't get along with her either, did you?"

I'm the suspect? Again? I didn't scream, but I wanted to. I spoke in calm methodical words. "Perhaps her husband killed her. You said he's missing. Isn't the spouse the first suspect?"

"Or someone wants to make it look like that," Grayson said matching my slow pace.

"Rubbish," Sebastian said. "Quit being a cobber to this Haddes."

Fredericks tapped on his notes and read: "The husband, Derrick, knew about her affair with Donnettelli. They're in counseling." Fredericks closed his notepad. "Solid information. Derrick's a retired detective, thirty-five years, and still assists with cold cases."

"We have regular contact with him." Grayson's voice lowered. "No contact this week. But not unusual."

"Are you convincing us or yourselves? Use your authority to find them." Hunter stood and pushed in his chair. "Hubby might've wanted revenge."

Mmmm. Two people/two bullets, not leading to me. I liked it. But the bank accounts were still in my name, court case assignments had been changed, money had been made. Wrong cut, color, and product. And I still needed to get that Order corrected.

CHAPTER SEVENTY

By nine that night when I returned home, Dexter had made chicken Kiev with all the fixings, during which time he'd given the boys an intensive cooking lesson mixed with a lecture on admissible evidence. He'd learned a few things from me during our years together. The menfolk not only set the table but had dinner artfully arranged in its center. They decided to brainstorm while we ate. I liked how these guys thought.

"Suppose Donnettelli was murdered because he no longer wanted to cooperate—whatever the scheme?" I said while I filled my plate.

"Possible." Josh clanked his fork against his plate.

"Suppose Jurisa," I said, "who is personally involved with Donnettelli—is approached. She doesn't want to cooperate—remember she got the asbestos cases after I left. Or, maybe Jurisa does cooperate initially, gets scared, and then decides to stop?" I met Dexter's eyes.

"Maybe they kill Peter Dune to show Jurisa Haddes what will happen to her if she doesn't cooperate," Dexter said. "Or, maybe she was in it all along, and they want to keep her, but now she knows how they treat people who misstep, and she needs a reminder of what can happen to her if she betrays them." Dexter passed me the serving platter while he spoke.

I nodded, accepted the platter, and passed it to Jake. I needed a few minutes before I thought about eating. I turned toward Dex. "Now, consider the fact that Noel got beaten and Laurel got shot. They're not dead, which translates in this scenario to more messages of how serious these thugs are about Jurisa cooperating."

"You're saying she's not running with her husband—she's dead?" Dex sounded upset. "If Jurisa is dead, goodbye to your defense. You need her alive so she can confess she killed Donnettelli."

"Damn. I do need her alive." *Never thought I'd say that.* "It only makes sense to hurt Noel and Laurel to teach Jurisa a lesson, if they're going to keep her alive."

Dexter laughed. "Lover, that's why you're the Judge. You think clearly and ask the right questions."

"I do have a question for you," I said gently. "About Hunter's man or men. Are they really there? Are they untrained floaters? Police Cadet dropouts? What's the deal with them?" I had to know how they could be so inept.

Dexter stopped laughing. He focused on the napkin on his lap and spoke slowly. "I have a confession."

Sheepish was not a good look for him. "Okay."

"I figured placing cars around you and having a few part-timers checking on you was good enough." He gulped.

I was speechless. He'd never been cheap with me or anyone else. And I felt stupid assuming there had been a human behind the dark-tinted windows. "I told you to let me pay and—"

"It wasn't about the money." He pinked. "I believed the mere presence of vehicles would scare anyone away, and if not, I'd be there for you myself."

"You—"

He looked me full in the face and spoke right at my heart. "I wanted to be the one."

Male ego and testosterone never ceased to amaze me. And appall me. I let it go, I couldn't find the words.

"Whoever is doing all of this, shooting Laurel, assaulting Noel, killing Donnettelli and Peter, sending me prank warnings to stop talking about Manville, blowing up my car, and shooting up Hunter's truck—whoever it is has a goal in mind."

Dexter drew in a deep breath and held it. I felt his arms around me despite his being seated across the table. "They want you to stop talking about Donnettelli's case-swapping so they can go on making big money. Simple as that."

"And it had to be bigger than Manville," I said. "About a million dollars bigger than Manville."

Josh asked, "What if all the asbestos companies were paying Donnettelli on the QT—"

"Then Donnettelli messed with the wrong woman," Dex said. "And she wouldn't let it go. No, I mean, she wouldn't let him off the hook."

Et tu, Dexter? But he was right. If I hadn't spoken out about Donnettelli changing my Order, he'd probably still be happily manipulating the judicial system and cheating victims out of help.

"No, I didn't let him off the hook. I tied a freaking anchor around his neck and let him sink. That's on me," I said. "Now it looks like whoever was in it with him wants to put Jurisa in his place. Or Jurisa is the one trying to tie a noose around my neck. I'll think about this after dinner."

CHAPTER SEVENTY-ONE

I was with Hunter in his Escalade when I clicked in a call from Trisha.

"The alarm company—Firefighters have been dispatched to the café. Some sort of bomb or explosion discharged in the back of the building. Margo and I are headed there to meet—" Trisha's voice was breathy.

"We're ablaze?" I ordered Hunter to drive faster. The Escalade engine hit high cruise. "We have plenty of time to catch up with Hollywood. Get to the salon."

"They're securing the premises," Trisha said.

"See you in a few." I hated to cut her off, but I needed to think. I white-knuckle-gripped the door handle.

"This is 'bout to get as entertaining as a June bride on roller-derby wheels," Carlye said.

"You mean heels," Dinkie-Do said.

"I say what I mean, Blue Streak. Ain't you never seen the Roller Derby Queen? She wears wheels, not heels. Uh-huh."

"Hey, you two are supposed to be watching what's going on, not jabbering." Annoyed, I didn't mean to take it out on them, but it was nearly three. We were working on beauty-sleep hours, and there was no hope of waking into a wrinkle-puffy-free morning. Anticipating my wilting face made me grouchy.

"Whooey. Drop us off," Carlye announced. Hunter revved the motor into outer-space drive. "My baby can't afford me getting hurt."

Hunter ignored Carlye and skidded around two more sharp-right corners. "We're close." The engine roared.

"Oh my, Honey, big bumps land smooth in this ride." Dinkie-Do's voice was rushed.

"D'you smoke something funny *and* bump your head? She ain't your Honey," Carlye moaned. "You tryin' to make me sound like Shazam, repeating myself?"

Umbrellas of color emerged above the treetops near my building. Shooting blazes highlighted the sky, and emergency sirens screamed behind us. A mob of onlookers had descended across the street and gazed toward my building and the blazing sky.

"Party's getting started," Carlye said. "I'm not dressed for this except for my lucky perfume." She took a long whiff of her wrists and closed her eyes. "Very relaxing. You ought to get you some."

I shook my head at her. Now wasn't the time to discuss perfume.

"You best reorder, Honey." Dinkie-Do pointed above at the exploding fireworks. Hunter raced to the back of my building. Windows shattered and crashed. Alarms wailed. Clouds of colored smoke billowed.

Shocked at the sight, I angled back at Carlye, who continued to talk as she pointed toward the dumpster, the ricocheting sparks, multiple explosions, and continuing fireworks. "That there sight is just beautiful."

Hunter parked at the opposite end of the parking lot, and I opened the door and jumped down. Emergency sirens were getting close. The building wasn't on fire. But the dumpster was.

"I thought my building had been bombed." I wasn't unhappy to see it erect, but I was surprised the glass was shattered.

"Explosions can shake the earth enough to shatter windows. Some of the fireworks could have backfired and acted like a bomb," Hunter said. "Look for a remote operator. Display fireworks like this don't just happen. Don't blink—be aware of your surroundings."

"Don't blink," I said. "Be aware of your surroundings," I repeated robot-like. I had visions of Laurel getting shredded with bullets. My skin felt taut, like I was a lightning rod attracting danger.

"Let's wait til law enforcement clears the area before you go all Lone Ranger on us," Hunter said.

I opened the door.

"Damn. Security cameras have been pulled down. I saw only wires. That must have triggered the building alarm." Hunter grabbed for my arm. "Stay here til I give the all clear."

"My life." I slid out.

"That's why I'm the lookout," Carlye said.

Hunter pushed onlookers back, and he checked the back doors of the salon and the café. They were both locked. And then he checked the parking lot perimeter.

Dinkie-Do hopped out of the truck, slammed the door, and skated a few paces.

I leaned in and over the front seat to face Carlye. "Keep your phone on picture, pull out your spray. If you get out, stay upwind so EMS doesn't get distracted with your scent. Stay clear of flying sparks." I slammed the door and caught up to Dinkie-Do.

He gave me a shoulder-wiggle pause. "Honey. I'll follow you anywhere, but you'll be adding extensions to this beloved head if Dinkie-Do's do gets melted." He snapped a selfie and trailed slightly behind me toward our smoky, exploding dumpster.

Smoldering garbage was ghastly, but I'd learned curiosity overcame disgust, especially when someone might be in danger. My dancing feet quickly figured that while flames were frightening, dodging fireworks sparks was a lot like playing parking-lot Zumba.

The closer we got to the dumpster, the more I felt like we were trapped in a bad thriller. Careful to stay clear of flames to avoid explosion of the aerosol in my left hand, my right-hand Taser ready, I plunged forward. Dinkie-Do coughed hoarsely, but I didn't let that distract me. I came upon a tree branch and instead of stepping over it, I stuffed my hairspray under my arm and picked up the branch. I called out to Dinkie-Do, "Aim your phone flashlight on the dumpster. Let's look for a computer around the outside."

I stopped. Three feet was as close as I was getting to explosives.

"Honey, from your berry lips to my hand." Dinkie-Do scanned with his phone flashlight. He slowly rocked it back and forth ahead of us. The fireworks were beginning to pace down.

"Do that again." I side-winded over to the right side of the dumpster, where the first fire engine had parked alongside a police car. I ignored the commotion. "Project the light onto the ground." From my pocket, I flipped him my cell. "Keep flashing. I want this documented." I didn't remember seeing the blue tarp that now lay next to the dumpster. I bent, and with the toe of my boot prodded it slightly upward, and then I flicked the tarp toward the back of the dumpster. Oddly strewn stacks of newspapers showed. I toed the edge of the top papers and watched a few slide off. Something.

I gasped.

I threw off more papers. I worked speedily.

As the papers thinned, I focused on what I thought was an animal. Hands shaking, I aimed the Taser with my right hand and plucked off the remainder of the closest stack of newspapers with the stick. I squinted. Oddly colored strands of—human hair? It played against the shooting lights. I stepped in closer. Intense heat emanated from the still-blazing fireworks. I tossed the papers further from the dumpster, and my brain fired sparklers. The top of my head was buzzing down to my ears. Was I wrong? Had the overpopulated up-north bear population made it to the city?

I bent. "Shine the light. There's something familiar about—" And there she was.

Jurisa Haddes.

I dropped the stick, slid Taser and spray inside my pockets. I checked her pulse and breath.

"Oh, Honey." Dinkie-Do snapped pictures from a few feet to within inches. "Ghastly. She looks like she's wearing ghoulish, Halloween," he paused thoughtfully then said, "Perfect makeup effects line." He sent over-emphasized arm signals to the uniforms, who'd just parked their flashing vehicles and jumped out. Hands on holsters, they ran over with the firemen.

"Step away." The serious fireman edged in from the rear and didn't offer anything besides the order.

I obeyed and cocked my head toward Dinkie-Do. With a stiff bob of his head, a twist, and a wiggle, he aimed toward the truck with me. I hadn't seen his eyes that wide since the leaky Plasti-gal incident.

We double-timed it as the fireman and his team hovered over Judge Haddes and handled her like a porcelain doll. In rhythm with the blaring crack of the fireworks, they checked her vitals, stuck an IV in her arm, slapped on a neck brace, surrounded her, picked her up, slid her onto a backboard and loaded her into the newly arrived ambulance. She was stiff enough to be dead. No sound, no movement, no signs of breath. I hadn't heard a peep. I wondered if she'd ever peep again. A lump in my throat formed.

With the shock of Jurisa's wilted body under the tarp and newspaper, I didn't immediately notice the police officers flanking my shoulders. This wasn't how perfume was supposed to capture men.

CHAPTER SEVENTY-TWO

"Hooroo, officers. I need to speak with my client unless you're hauling her away in the divvy van." Sebastian's fingertip strength jolted my right shoulder and infused me with newfound energy. His step-in-and-rescue maneuver reminded me to lose the Taser into the truck.

The officer on my left broke stride and marched across the parking lot toward the truck, where another uniformed officer stood kissing-close to Carlye, who was outside it. That officer curled his finger in the come-over command to my attached officers, and they dumped me like a cold rinse.

Sebastian blocked my view of everything that wasn't him. "Let's file out of here before they decide to give you that divvy-van ride."

Before I could answer, Carlye reached us and pointed to the fireworks. "Why'd those firemen have to go and ruin those happy pops of color?"

"They're illegal and a fire hazard. And, when they exploded, they shattered the salon windows." I studied Carlye's unscathed reaction to the whole situation, including finding Judge Haddes. It occurred to me I shouldn't be surprised.

"In my neighborhood, fireworks arise on regular occasions. Like when someone wins some scratch in the lottery."

"Four words." I held up four fingers. "Not at my salon."

Sebastian tapped his boot. "You sheilas can discuss fairy floss later."

"Who you calling a fairy?" Carlye demanded.

"Never mind him." Sebastian's Australian slang was nothing but trouble. I pointed her attention toward the truck. "Sebastian will take me home. Go with Hunter, who is where?"

"With the firemen." Sebastian pointed to the dumpster.

"Ah, dumpster dive." I wanted to stick around for it, but I was fearful officers would realize I was still available for bond condition: search-without-warrant-and-arrest bait.

"Where did Dexter disappear to?" I asked.

"Redirected to the hospital to figure out the real story of what happened to Haddes before there is any kind of lockdown on information," Sebastian said. We scooted into his vehicle.

"Going home, Judge?" Grayson's voice boomed through Sebastian's window. "Very interesting that you, our key suspect, found our person of interest."

I leaned forward. "See that's where telephone tag gets it wrong," I said. "I'm not the key suspect. I'm the wrongly accused."

"Yeah, well you found Haddes." Grayson mumbled into his radio—something I couldn't understand.

"Like the wise men," I said. "We followed the lights in the sky." I placed my hand over Sebastian's and stopped him from driving away. I chin-pointed to the scene in front of us.

An officer paraded out from behind the dumpster holding a black metal box. His hands were gloved. Fredericks ran over to meet him, pulled open a large evidence bag, scribbled something on it, and dropped the box inside. The officer sealed the bag, walked to his patrol car and locked it inside his trunk.

Fredericks, gloves removed, ambled toward us. "A remote-control box was found about ten feet behind the dumpster. Controlled the fireworks. You know anything about that?" He reached into his shirt pocket and pulled out his trusty notepad.

"I barely know how to use my phone. It's five. I'm tired. I'm free. I'm leaving."

CHAPTER SEVENTY-THREE

In the morning, the officers guarding Jurisa's hospital room didn't want to let me see her, but we compromised. I got fifteen minutes with her and not alone.

Badge 67 was on me like a clarifier and wasn't leaving til rinse time. Jurisa's husband was asleep on the lounge chair next to the bed. He opened one eye, lifted a wave, and resumed snoring. He looked more wiped out than she did.

An IV line fed into her arm, and another monitor with a bouncing thread gave the appearance of stable breathing. Okay, it verified Judge Haddes had body heat; there were times I'd wondered.

I leaned over the bed rail to study her. A few scratches on her right temple with a hint of bruising, her lips were swollen, dry, cracked, bloodstained—scabby.

"Jurisa?" Finger poke. "Jurisa? It's Nicoletta. Do you need anything?" I dragged a chair to the edge of her bed, sat, and peered at my contorted reflection in the metal bed frame.

The officer perched himself against the wall.

"Jurisa?"

This time Jurisa's eyes fluttered. Her forehead creased. She clawed the sheets.

"I have questions—if you're up to answering." I rested my arms on her bed. "I'm convinced what happened to you, Laurel, Noel, Peter Dune, and Judge Donnettelli are related."

I saw real fear in her eyes. Was she scared of me or someone else? A loud annoyed whine escaped her. It was the first time I'd seen a human emotion from her, which meant I could get to her. "I didn't kill anyone."

Jurisa jetted a cold dark glare.

I kept my voice steady. "If you're not proactive, whoever did this could try again. You have nothing to lose by helping me."

Her voice low, it cracked as she spoke. "I'm now a suspect."

"I know."

"I didn't kill him." Her voice was a pebbly whisper.

"I have ankle jewelry. You're being protected and aren't under arrest." Who was she kidding? She might as well claim she didn't use hair color.

Her hands dropped to her chest. "Water. Please, my water?"

I helped her sit up, placed the Styrofoam cup from the bed stand into her frail fingers, and waited.

She released the cup back to me.

When she lay back, I asked, "What do you recall?"

"They knew me." She shook her head. "Two men in masks. I didn't know them."

"Did they use your name?"

"Yes. They knew a lot about the court." Her eyes looked swollen.

"What did they want to know from you?" I asked.

"Insider details."

"About what?"

"New filings, case files, clerk's office. It's a blur."

"Did you get the idea they might be upset lawyers?"

"Lawyers? No. They knew the kind of detailed information trained court clerks learn."

"Our clerks?" I stiffened.

Jurisa shook her head. Her frail body almost looked like she was seizing. "Our court personnel staff wouldn't, couldn't do this."

I hoped that was true, and it was likely the first thing I'd agreed with Jurisa on in a long time. But she had motive to kill Donnettelli over a lover's spat or a scheme involving the asbestos cases.

"The men wanted me to cooperate, but I couldn't help them." Jurisa closed her eyes tightly and her balled hands shook. "They didn't believe me."

"Cooperate how?" I asked. I wasn't sure I believed her.

She opened her eyes and studied my face. I remained emotionless despite my churning innards.

"They assumed I knew everything about Warren—whatever he was into. They assumed he'd let me in, that I'd participate since I hadn't ratted anyone out. I wouldn't do something wrong." She paused. "I'm shocked I'm alive."

Her skeletal underweight face lied very well. I wanted to scream: *Cheating on your husband is wrong, and you are lying which is wrong. So, you could be involved, did know something, and if so someone has motive to get rid of you or send a serious warning to be quiet.* I didn't have time to fight and felt the pressure of Badge 67's presence. "What do you recall last?"

"They forced me down, held me, and injected me. I woke up here." An uncharacteristic tear blossomed. She didn't acknowledge it.

I wasn't sure she noticed it. I went in for the final spritz. "They didn't kill you because they're still counting on you to help." I said, "Someone thinks you know something or have something important as a result of your relationship with Donnettelli." I left it at that. She could interpret what I meant by relationship. She wasn't a dumb woman.

Slight jitters morphed into a tremble through her arms and shoulders. "Help with what?" She was so fragile she looked like a child playing hospital. "Have or know what?" She said it more like a challenge than like she didn't know the answer.

I was game to play. I smoothed her blankets over her, sat, and focused solely on her expression before I uttered a proposal. Okay, maybe it was a challenge. "Check out Donnettelli's reassignment of cases without notice, request, or cause."

Her face froze.

"Unless you knew," I added. That sparked her eyes into widening. I just couldn't decide if I'd witnessed surprise from the mere thought, or shock that I'd figured it out.

"Why don't you just go to prison?" That seemed to take all her energy, and she turned her face away, and closed her eyes. But then added, "Or, simply leave. You can afford to hide anywhere in the world."

Had she been the one sending me warnings? How would she know whether or not I could afford anything?

Badge 67 thrust a beefy wrist between Jurisa's crinkled face and mine. With a wide pointer finger, he clicked a fingernail against the face of his wristwatch.

I stood and said goodbye to Jurisa's protectors.

On my way out, my phone vibrated in my back pocket. Down the hospital a few steps outside officer view, I read a text from Trisha. "Noel in today for haircut. Stressed. It's urgent. He must speak with you."

I love it when a suspect wants to talk.

CHAPTER SEVENTY-FOUR

By the time I reached my station, Dinkie-Do and Carlye were busy combing and cutting, and Noel sat with his arms wrapped around his backpack and his feet propped up on my station counter.

Dinkie-Do pointed at me with one very mobile hip. "Honey, you're in need of a Dinkie-Do special."

"Gee, thanks." It was true, but the announcement was like an unruly white hair corking up.

"Yeah, she can't help it. Fireworks and bodies popping up in the middle of the starry night." Carlye wagged her head. "All these creepy calamities forced me to leave my Shazam at home."

As expected, Trisha marched toward me with resolve and the appointment book clasped to her chest. "Judge, Hunter posted a man outside, who is checking everyone for appointments and not letting in anyone without one. He's interfering with walk-ins, he is." Her brogue got thicker. "He comes in and inspects room-to-room about once an hour." She looked alarmed.

I shrugged and whispered that loss of walk-in business temporarily was a small concession I'd made in the name of a secure workplace. I apologized for not explaining immediately. Trisha calmed. She hugged me, and I aimed for my station.

When I gently tapped Noel's shoulder, he pulled his feet down and turned his head slightly toward me. I skipped a breath when I inspected his face. Swelling—green, blue, a little red next to some yellow along his chin and above his right cheekbone. His fingers were scratched and scabbed over.

He flicked his eyes open into a wide-eyed, silent glower.

"Need a fresh look, heavy concealer, and a hit of chloroform?" I tried to sound sympathetic and leaned against my drawers. His toddler-eyed expression read *I'll balk at the first snip*.

"Where's Renée?" He snaked his head around the room.

"Next door, helping out in the café."

His shoulders drooped. "Your merry men, Hunter and Sebastian, didn't exactly protect me from a beating for information I didn't know, didn't have access to, and didn't have any opportunity to be part of." Noel glared and winced but didn't groan.

That was a bad beginning. I grabbed my sharpest shears and snapped them a few times, so I could think. This technique was getting to be fun.

Our eyes linked, but we'd been apart on this issue from the beginning. He dropped his backpack toward me, and it landed at my feet.

I kicked it under my station and slapped a folded towel over it like a triumphant flag. "Did you recognize the goons?"

His eye rings crêped up full wrinkle. "Two men." He lifted the bottom of his hoodie and gave me a look at his battered chest. Bruising, bandages, swelling. "Round-robin beating. Two broken ribs, a few cracked.

I left the hospital against advice." He paused, gulped, and changed his snarky tone to bland with a scared-under-shiver tone. "Truthfully, I ran under cover of darkness."

I cringed at his still swelling face. "On the upside, a haircut and shave won't hurt." I forced an upturned corner of my mouth. From my vantage, the top of his head and earlobes were the only body parts they'd missed. I shouldn't have guaranteed a no-pain shave. My body sympathy-ached.

"I'm alive the same reason Judge Haddes's alive—yeah, I heard about it—courthouses and hospitals stink of rumors. That's why I hiked."

I waited.

"Okay. The works." Noel's shoulders sank.

I pointed him toward the washbasin. He waved away my arm of help while he slowly crossed the room.

When I bent to shampoo him, he whispered directly in my ear. "Slugs demanded I continue Judge Donnettelli's work."

"Did the breaks and bruises jog your memory?" I whispered back.

"I was only his court reporter. We occasionally shared a few beers. Nothing more."

I rinsed and wrapped his head in a towel, and we returned to my station. The beating had broken his spirit. I felt the break in his words. I saw it in his eyes. I hated it because I felt that way too but was lucky enough to have good people around me who kept me afloat.

Noel kept twisting the chair out of view of the waiting room.

"No one can see my station from the outside." I clipped a cape around him and handed him a fresh towel. "If that is what you're thinking."

He stilled but looked surprised.

I reached into my drawer for shears and found a pink envelope labeled *Monopoly*, and I tucked it into my back pocket. It looked like an unopened birthday card. I snipped, clipped, and shaved, and a new Noel emerged. There wasn't much I could do for the bruises.

"It's okay." I lightly patted Noel's shoulder. He'd wilted since I'd first seen him. "Are you able to drive?" I searched the work area for Margo.

"I got here," Noel said unconvincingly.

Ever-vigilant Margo appeared at my side.

"I'm finished for the day. Please help Noel follow me out." I handed Margo his backpack. "I'm driving him home."

I headed toward the rear exit.

"I got to go wit you," Carlye called after me. "My ride, my Herbini, is in your garage." She whisked her client toward Trisha.

Dinkie-Do called, "Shotgun."

I snatched my bag from my office, Carlye and Dinkie-Do trailed behind me into the heat of the afternoon across the rear parking lot. Noel and Margo caught up to us. He gasped at his Explorer.

"Four new tires, slashed." Noel's voice cracked. "They've followed me." He didn't wait for any response, he tossed up his hoodie. Margo didn't wait for any direction, she aimed him toward Dinkie-Do, Carlye, and my Audi. She was about to open the passenger door.

I thought Noel was going to cry.

The guys were still repairing the security wiring from the last incident.

Keys in hand, I ordered everyone to stand back. I clicked the remote starter. We waited. Doors unlocked; engine hummed. Carlye ran up front. Dinkie-Do slid into the back seat behind her. Margo tossed Noel's backpack into the back seat and helped him in. In the rearview mirror, I saw him close his eyes and slide downward.

Margo said she'd follow me and bring Renée home. I nodded and hit the gas with a gut full of jelly. I spun in the direction of home, despite wanting to drop Noel off at the emergency room. My gut was warning me, but about what?

The ride wasn't long enough to calm my gut or to figure out what exactly to do with Noel. Once home, Renée listened to voicemails and used one hand to help me make up a couch into a makeshift bed, while Dinkie-Do and Carlye helped a much slower-walking Noel inside.

Soon, dosed with pain meds he'd pulled from his backpack, Noel instantly fell asleep on a plump pillow. Renée brought him a bottle of water. I turned off the family-room lights, and Renée set her cell on the coffee table, gave me an almost-happy face, and went to get another light blanket. It was obvious she liked to be helpful.

But there on the coffee table, I noticed a folder in her emails titled "Donnettelli." I wondered why she hadn't mentioned or shown that to me. What else was on that phone?

Quietly, she reappeared and tossed the light blanket over Noel.

Shazam squawked upside down from my plate rack, and Dinkie-Do was busy making coffee and entertaining Carlye with his makeup. I ducked into the bathroom and opened the new pink envelope. A list of appealed cases. Some to the Court of Appeals, some appealed to the Supreme Court. All asbestos cases. If someone was trying to leave me helpful information, "So what?" seemed like an ungrateful response. But I really needed to understand why this mattered.

About fifteen minutes later, Dexter came up to the kitchen and greeted me. I explained that I had work to do. He said the boys were at the mall, and they'd texted they're bringing home Chinese and big news.

I hoped it was good big news. This was my chance to snatch Noel's backpack. It wasn't stealing. He'd intended to give it to me; he'd just run out of energy. As soon as Dex went back downstairs, I grabbed the backpack from the foot of the couch, scurried upstairs, and climbed onto my bed.

From the backpack, I pulled out a shaving kit, pill bottles, a Ziploc bag of camera SD cards, and two rubber-banded stacks of papers, which I thumbed through. It looked like he'd spent months, not days tracking asbestos cases.

I clicked on my personal copy machine. We were both revved to go.

Copies made, I shoved everything back inside. Now I had big news, too.

CHAPTER SEVENTY-FIVE

At the dinner table, the lazy Susan was heaped with open boxes of Chinese food. Dex, Hunter, Sebastian, Josh, Judd, and Jake were wielding chopsticks like champs. And near the edge of the lazy Susan sat Donnettelli's fancy metal box. I scanned the couch and realized Noel was missing and so was his backpack. I thought it odd he hadn't said goodbye. I checked both garages and the outside. All cars were accounted for. I guessed he'd Ubered it home. I'd check on him later—no—I chose safety and asked Hunter to cover that task.

Jake palmed the ex-cookie tin and said they'd gotten bored earlier in the day and played football in the family room, which led to a discovery.

I swear his eyes twinkled, and it gave me hope.

"Thing is, Mom. One of the corners flipped out of the paper footballs." Judd opened his hands like a blooming flower. "There's writing inside." He opened the box, lifted the unsealed football, and centered it in my open palm.

I placed it on the table and unfolded the remaining triangle edges. Sebastian leaned into to see. The first fold revealed the letter PETER. I flipped until the paper was fully opened. Each flip engaged me. Dates, dockets, stocks, and numbers. Neat columns and rows. Explicit detail. It was all there. Every printed detail related to 'H'. And in the lower right corner was written: Nic 3-15."

"Donnettelli's private tracking system." Sebastian whistled.

Jake laughed. "No one would think of looking inside one of those things."

I nudged Sebastian and pointed to my name in the corner.

"I'll bet that's the date Mr. PETER deposited one hundred thousand dollars," Sebastian said, his eyes studying the paper.

"We'll be able to match all the dates," I whispered. I was afraid to say it louder as if it might evaporate.

"Josh, hand me two more footballs." I gave one to Sebastian and pulled the corner out from the one I kept. I captured each one with my phone camera. Mine revealed "PETER." His: "S."

I dumped the remaining nine in front of me, and we opened them all. "H-W-M-C-S-J-E-K-N-D-J-C."

"I'll be back." I shot away from the table, up the back stairs, and directly to the bookcase. I grabbed *The Michigan Bar Journal* and raced back down to the table.

I took my spot at the table and opened *The Michigan Bar Journal* to the "Judiciary" section.

Names of all seven Michigan Supreme Court Justices glared up at me. I read their last names out loud while the guys looked for matches on the footballs. No.

I flicked through first names only. Instead of three names with four initials, it could represent one initial from twelve different names. I read the first four names:

"Jerome, Haley, Kirk, and Nicholas." My writing blurred. I focused.

"Four of the seven Supreme Court justices," Judd said, as if his team had just scored. And it had.

And from the Court of Appeals, seven first names matched Donnettelli's notes for a total of eleven initials: Carla, Charles, Daniel, Ellington, Jason, Jerome, Haley, Kirk, Maverick, Nicholas, and Savannah. Eleven names between the two higher courts. And Warren Donnettelli was the only Circuit Court Judge involved.

And it fit. I had all twelve names, and they matched Donnettelli's football notes. These were twelve powerful Judges who had made enough illegal money to have motive to plant twelve, one-hundred-thousand-dollar accounts in my name.

Sebastian laughed out loud. "Holy dooley, it's a contribution club." He explained to my sons that when a group of people conspire, sometimes they protect their scam by equally funding a bribe or—in this case—planted evidence to make me look guilty and keep eyes off them. "No wonder the bloke liked paper football."

My turn. I needed to explain Noel's backpack. "I have a story to tell you."

CHAPTER SEVENTY-SIX

Armed with supplies and the copies I'd made of my loot from Noel's backpack, I started to explain about the Manville case, but my sons wanted the big picture first, so I explained.

I showed them Noel's chart, where he'd tracked asbestos cases for a six-year period. When there was a trial, Noel noted the decision. Then that case went to the Court of Appeals.

For the Court of Appeals, Noel noted which three Judges were hearing the case and their decision. If a case went up to the Supreme Court, Noel noted the final decision. He analyzed the decisions on cases that had large settlements. He did a great job.

It amazed me that Noel got all that accomplished in such a short time. I wondered how he'd managed to hide it from his attacking thugs. Then I'd decided they were likely after something else. But what? Something else to ponder later.

I stood at the end of the table with the big pages spread out so everyone could see. Zigzagging my finger down columns and from page to page, I showed them the life of a case. "If you look at the case names, you'll see that the cases were publicly held corporations that dealt with asbestos."

"So these cases have to match the notes and initials on the footballs," Josh said.

Judd studied the papers so closely I wondered if he needed glasses. He ran a forefinger across and down. I followed the back and forth of his gaze between the flattened footballs and the court files. As a small child he'd delighted in puzzles, and he had that same aura now.

He separated one appeal file from the rest. "This case says Supreme Court." Judd read the name of the Judge and handed Sebastian a football letter that matched the name. After four names were read and footballs passed, Judd stopped.

Sebastian stacked the football letters in order of the Supreme Court justice named on the decision.

"Finish the last eight," I said. I grabbed records from the Court of Appeals and looked for matches with the remaining initials on the footballs. After I paired seven, I set the footballs on top of the matching files. Elation and concern battled for control of my mind. "Hand me all of the Court of Appeals decisions." Papers fluttered in front of me. I did the same for the rest.

"I can't believe this wasn't as apparent as split ends. I got arrested to create a diversion. I'm not supposed to live long in prison. I'm certain they're counting on somebody murdering me—a Donnettelli fan or someone I sentenced. Any related investigation is or would be dropped."

"And Jurisa could certainly be part of all this," Sebastian said. "Including framing Nic. She had to know what Donnettelli was doing."

But I was still missing a killer. Two men in a black SUV rammed us, two men in black beat Noel, two men in black ran from Renée's apartment.

Sebastian stood and announced that he and I needed a privileged chinwag, and he wrapped an arm around me. "Pack this up for her, will you guys?"

Everybody reached for paper, but Judd claimed it all. "Something's not just right. I want to take this mess up to my room and look at it. Okay, Mom?"

Quick, grateful nod.

Sebastian led me to the front stairs—a small concession to decorum—to take the long way to the bedroom.

CHAPTER SEVENTY-SEVEN

Before we left the privacy of my room the next morning, I told Sebastian what I'd seen on Renée's phone, and we discussed the need for me to have a private playdate with Renée's phone. I phoned the detectives and let them know about the folder on Renée's phone marked "Donnettelli," which she'd neglected to mention. As we'd hoped, they invited her to the station.

When Sebastian and I got down to the kitchen, the Kikkra Circus was live and loud.

Squawk. "Mr. Shakely's a slave driver."

Carlye's hair was pinned up pineapple-high with varied parrot feathers braided throughout, and her heels tap, tap, tapped on the kitchen tile. Dinkie-Do, Renée, and Noel trailed her. Jimmy Jack jumped on my lap, buried his cold nose in my bent elbow, and purred.

Dinkie-Do wiggled to his Plasti-gals and smoothed them out for their morning glow-over.

I focused my attention on Noel. "You're still here."

"I didn't think you'd mind." Renée bit the tip of her thumb. "When I got home yesterday, I didn't want to disturb you. I checked on Noel and could barely wake him. I decided he wasn't in any condition to leave and helped him to the first spare room I found. He slept in the room with your sewing machine."

I followed Noel's silent gaze to the table and the folder I'd pulled from his backpack, and I thought about his fear. "Renée, you did the right thing. You and Sebastian have an appointment with detectives. When you're finished you can pick up Noel and help him grab anything he needs from his house."

I passed Jimmy Jack from the comfort of my arms to Dinkie-Do and crossed back toward Noel. "You'll heal here over the next few days. Hunter will investigate and make sure it's safe for you to return home."

Noel blinked. "Sure, okay—thanks."

Carlye and Dinkie-Do left through the garage door. "Don't forget to turn on Cartoon Network," she hollered.

Door slammed. Tiny Renée trotted out with her arm linked through Sebastian's. He maneuvered her away from my desk and kept her from noticing she'd left her purse behind.

What a man.

CHAPTER SEVENTY-EIGHT

I waited until Noel was sleeping again and then slipped into the secret closet with Renée's purse, a notepad, and my own phone. I'd become the ever-ready eavesdropper and prying spy to find Donnettelli's killer and save myself from prison stripes.

The mission of being my own superhero called me into immediate, guiltless action. I unsnapped Renée's bag, unzipped each compartment, and then set out each section so I could easily replace the contents, after I photographed and documented it.

Examination of her cell phone had to be first. I tapped in four ones, and it opened. In email, I found the folder marked *Donnettelli.* It held slobbery love notes from Donnettelli to Renée that turned my stomach. Nauseating-Yuck. Selfies of them kissing, and one looked as if they'd just gotten out of the shower. Hitchcock-Halloween-Horror-Yuck. How many women had the courthouse Casanova duped? I hit *send,* and copies of the Donnettelli folder zipped to my phone. I forwarded a copy to Sebastian and one to the detectives. Then deleted evidence of the forward. Whew. That was a close call. My sons had shown me that move months ago when I'd gotten the latest iPhone.

A stack of Visa gift cards were next. I checked each balance. Together they totaled just under twenty-three thousand dollars. When I started to replace Renée's things, I noticed a lumpy bottom compartment and realized I'd not unleashed it. I flipped the bag over, unzipped the final zipper and freed its contents. A black clip clunked through. Folded tissue with dark smears inside. Blood? I rotated the clip with my pen tip. There were bullets inside. Damnation!

The front doorbell rang. I froze, feeling like I'd been caught snooping. I shuffled everything back inside the purse, slung it over my shoulder, and locked the secret closet. I slid down to the first floor, then found Hollywood et al. at my door, beckoning to enter. I seated them at my kitchen table and busied myself making coffee and small talk, texting Sebastian every few minutes begging him to hurry and return.

Nearly an hour passed before Sebastian returned with Renée. My text included a request to Velcro himself to her because I knew it would not be pleasant once she realized who was seated in the kitchen awaiting her.

Detectives had parked down the street to avoid detection. Just as I'd anticipated, when Renée saw her purse and phone, the clip, and tissue-covered bullets spread out on my kitchen table in front of the detectives, she wilted like a wintering desert rose.

Sebastian steadied her, and the detectives stood.

Fredericks handed Renée a search warrant and an arrest warrant and read her rights, and Grayson cuffed her. Seeing the handcuffs and hearing them click together caused sympathy aches to spawn from my brain into my wrists.

Renée opened her mouth, but Sebastian was shaking his head, and she snapped her lips tightly. I waived any conflict with Sebastian, at least for now, if any arose in representing us both. I was betting that having as much information as possible would help sort everything out, even if I wasn't yet clear on Renée's role in all this. Knowing Donnettelli was involved made her a victim of his lunacy, just like me. Tears glistened in her eyes. I wanted to make her feel better but sharing my boyfriend lawyer felt generous enough.

After the detectives took Renée from my house, the place was subdued. Sebastian and I sat on the tall counter stools with the Plasti-gals, and I hung my legs over his. He gently massaged my calves. I rested my head against the thick of his arm.

When Jimmy Jack jumped up and nestled in my lap, I finally asked the never-ending question. "Is this over?" I stretched my tethered ankle, and his fingers circled the tender skin and nerves under it.

Sebastian's silence didn't reassure me of anything; it reminded me we weren't close enough to the answers we needed.

"Okay then." I swallowed hard. "Let's continue until there's a dismissal of all charges against me." I'd lost faith in the system I'd once trusted. "We still need to know Jurisa's and Renée's roles and who put which bullet in Donnettelli."

"Given their close relationship, and the way she watched her docket, Jurisa had to know Donnettelli was moving cases," Sebastian said. "As his Judicial Assistant, Renée likely knew, as well."

"Exactly. And Jurisa might have been jealous of Renée, if she knew what was going on between them."

I thought out loud. "Or, was Renée the jealous woman, the shooter, and part of the whole conspiracy? Who gained what from setting me up?"

Sebastian rubbed his cheek against mine, and his beard infused me with comfort. I wished it could deliver the answers we needed. "Working for the County, Renée had access to all three courts, the salon, the café, and my house."

"Her access doesn't explain the two men in black." Sebastian liked to think linearly. "And she didn't have access to the house when Shadow the Snake visited."

"She could have had help," I said.

"But I don't think she's the ringleader. Her place was demolished."

"Could have paid someone to ransack it. She could be on *Team Killer*," I said. "There are any number of options—"

Judd texted me. A problem with the spreadsheets. I accidentally smacked Sebastian—my outrage leaking out. The second time my arm flew, Sebastian caught me by the wrist. He took my phone and shot Judd a text: *Take care of it.*

Then Sebastian tossed the phone, directed me upstairs, and took care of other things. He was a master at relaxation. When we finally resumed our conversation about Renée, I summed up questions that had been floating through my brain.

Had Renée been in love with Donnettelli? Had she killed him when she realized she was trapped in a love triangle? I began with the most revealing question. "Did Renée make a statement?"

"Despite your waiver of conflict, I made sure she has a court-appointed lawyer. She's pleading not guilty."

"She can have my spot in that club."

"In her interview with detectives, Renée admitted that when she found Peter Dune, she saw the gun and accidently touched the clip. When she realized it contained her fingerprints—she decided to take it."

My mind was shifting pieces of the puzzle to determine if any of them fit better. "Is that really different than what we already knew?"

"She said when she found him," Sebastian said, "she got blood on her wrist and blouse and wiped it off on the tissue."

"That means when I questioned her, she intentionally omitted those details." I huffed. "In fact, she tampered with evidence that could clear me."

"I'll have a barney with her and her lawyer and press hard for the truth. A few nights in the clink will loosen her armor."

"Her failure to disclose information that might clear me doesn't *ipso facto* make her a cold-blooded killer." Timid Renée pulling an angry trigger nagged at me like a crooked haircut.

"A broken-hearted pull of the trigger would be a manslaughter charge." Sebastian shrugged. "A charge that equally applies to Renée and Jurisa."

A cold chill tiptoed from my brain to my heart. I rolled up onto his chest and kissed him. "I'm betting Jurisa suspected Donnettelli and Renée's sexual relationship. In a jealous fit, Jurisa fired that second bullet."

CHAPTER SEVENTY-NINE

The front doorbell chimed, and Sebastian returned with the detectives in tow. Without invitation they sat at their usual kitchen-table seats. I hated that they had usual seats at my table. Sebastian and I sat on either side of them.

Fredericks pulled out his damned notepad. "We do have a confession as to the second bullet. Not for public knowledge." He clicked his pen.

Damn him. "Judge Haddes?"

Double nods. "Prosecutors and her defense counsel are meeting with her now," Grayson said. "Those videos of her and Donnettelli. She doesn't want her husband or the public to view them."

"Lovers' spat, and she shot him?"

Grayson interrupted. "Prosecutor isn't charging her for shooting a corpse. Donnettelli was dead when she shot him."

"She says." Were they being serious?

"One more thing, before we get too far," Grayson said. "We searched her residence and found a moveable floorboard."

"That revealed a nest she slept upside down in?" I couldn't keep myself in check. I was confounded that she wasn't going to be charged.

"Better." Grayson handed me a stack of photographs. "A bag she didn't dispose of. It contained your Courthouse ID, wig, boots—the whole bank DVD outfit. A Nicoletta Kikkra look-alike Halloween costume." He folded his arms and looked proud of himself, while I flipped though evidence that would help clear me. I was dumbfounded. Finally they'd done something right. I veered off that topic out of fear it wasn't real and remained hopeful for her arrest. "How did you verify Jurisa fired the second shot?"

Grayson looked exasperated, as if spelling it all out for the dimwitted woman took so much energy. "Unprompted, she admitted she shot him in the chest. Kill shot was in the left ear, through and through."

"Blimey, that tidbit wasn't in the news." Sebastian accepted the photos I passed to him.

"The bullet and those photos are not for public dissemination." Fredericks pointed at me with his pencil.

"Claims she refused to get involved, and that's why she landed beside your exploding dumpster," Grayson said.

"Refuted by the evidence she opened the twelve bank accounts," I said.

Grayson blew past me. "She blamed you. But we're smarter than you think. We believe you were all in it together. She worked closely with Donnettelli." His head jutted closer to me. "What did they do, try to cut you out?"

I ignored him. "Jurisa played along, probably enjoyed setting me up. They played hardball with her because she delayed changing a newly filed case that would have resulted in a barrel of cash payoffs. I'm betting they wanted her in Donnettelli's role. They needed a Judge in our Courthouse."

"You still need to tell us your role in Peter Dune's death," Grayson said.

"Zilch. I had no part in Peter's death."

Fredericks kept his head down, appeared to be writing, and mumbled, "There was the grand inquisition in the café."

Against my express instructions, my face heated up, close to the point of glowing red. What could I say? I had pushed Peter, and I'd been wrong. I had to keep moving forward. "What about the attacks on Laurel, and Noel, and Hunter's truck?" It came out like a whisper. I guessed my voice was too ashamed to join in.

"Scare tactics to keep you in line. You've pissed off a lot of people," Grayson said. "Warnings not to tell us what you've done."

"Guess again." Now I folded my arms.

Fredericks pointed at me. "Haddes will testify that you and Donnettelli being at odds was a great cover for your financial scheme."

"She says the fake ID—and her posing as you at the bank—was your idea, and you and Donnettelli forced her to do it." Grayson sounded bored.

Damn. Her hair color had leached in and further demented her substandard personality.

Fredericks flipped back to the beginning pages of his notepad. "You were the only Circuit Judge who financially benefited in cold, hard *tax-free*—twelve bank account—cash."

If he only knew how true that was. Picturing the cash pile in the hollow of my bed caused me a momentary hot flash.

Grayson couldn't seem to help himself. "Your co-conspirators gave you a cash muzzle."

"Jurisa—" My skin prickled.

"Jilted girlfriend—not the same." Fredericks grunted. "Forced to help you hide your payoff."

Grayson liked the double team. "Fess up to the accomplice charges? Easy enough to buy with your kind of dough."

Fredericks snapped his notebook shut.

It felt like the whole world was against me.

"Nice rack, Jack." *Squawk*. "Ranger coming."

Shazam could keep his feathers a while longer. I stroked his feathery back.

CHAPTER EIGHTY

As the front door slammed behind the ousted detectives, Dinkie-Do and Carlye plodded in.

I pulled Dinkie-Do into the far end of the family room and heard Hunter quietly enter from the garage. I took a minute to admonish Dinkie-Do for getting his blue eyeshadow on my towels and advised him to bring salon towels to use next time. He protested and denied disturbing or decorating my towels. I shrugged it off; saving my towels wasn't a high priority.

Sebastian was already busy in the kitchen. The coffeemaker sounded, and the refrigerator opened and closed a few times. Finally, he presented me with a tall cup of coffee with scoops of coffee ice cream, dollops of whipped cream, and a maraschino stemmed cherry, complete with cloth napkin, tall spoon, and wide straw. I felt fifteen.

"My Last Supper drink?" I sucked down the longest drink I could, only stopping when I needed to breathe. Sebastian led me into the kitchen.

At the far end of my table, José Alvarez sat handcuffed to Hunter.

Hunter raised their linked arms. "My man found him in your office, and he wasn't cleaning."

"José, my *friend*."

"Madam Judge. Many years you treated my wife and me very well. I pay you back, but I had to be secret."

"You left me the notes!" I pointed to the handcuffs, gave Hunter the stink-eye, and he removed them.

José rubbed his wrists and handed me an envelope from inside his jacket.

I slit it open. Fourteen one-hundred-dollar bills. "My recipe box?"

"I hoped you be scared, think someone break in. Make you more careful. I'm sorry."

I'd given the money so little thought. I'd been busy trying to exonerate myself. I finally saw some of the pieces clicking together. "You figured out what Donnettelli was up to."

"In time. *Si.*" José's face was dark, eyes and brows low.

"How?"

He sat, one hand on the table, one in his lap, and said he would tell me everything as soon as he saw a lawyer.

José said, "I need what you call immunity—"

Sebastian raised a hand to interrupt him. "Why do you think you need immunity?"

"I be clear." José wiped his brow on his sleeve. "These past half-dozen years, I been listening to Judges. I—my family, we poor. My mother, so ill—"

"Stop right there," Sebastian said. To me, he added, "José and I are going down to my office. I'd like to record this. I'm not sure it's in your best interest to hear any more."

I understood why he didn't object to Hunter's handcuffing. I needed to be able to provide clean testimony if—when—the time arrived. I held up a finger to Sebastian. "José, which of these Judges were at the meetings you listened to?" I read my list. Sebastian stared at me like Jimmy Jack, ready to pounce if I moved too far.

"All. But never all at same time."

"Did I miss anyone?"

José shook his head. "They meet after hours. I see them when I clean the Chief Judge's floors in courthouses."

"In Court of Appeals Chief Judge Maverick John Young's office? And in Chief Judge Donnettelli's office?"

He nodded. "But I don't hear who do what," José said.

"Did they ever mention my name?"

"No." José made a sour face. "If so, I don't hear it."

"Did they ever see you?" I'd slid into Judge-questioning mode. Someone had to. *Hit-slap* to wide-eyed Hunter and Sebastian.

"I work in shadows. Look at me, easy to hide. I learn as a small child." He gave me a wide grin. "I talk to no one. After you charged, I focused to help you." José sulked. "I don't do so good. Others got hurt and died." He signed the cross.

"Were any court staff inside any meeting with the Judges?" My staff were as loyal as hairspray.

José shrugged. "Law clerks stay late sometimes. They carry files. Not inside with the Judges. They play cards or tap with their phones outside chambers when meetings went late."

"Did you overhear any reason why someone would want Donnettelli out of the way?" Sebastian pushed away his chair and walked around the kitchen and set a glass of water in front of José.

"I never hear bad words about Donnettelli." José gulped half the water. "They talk about bringing different cases or moving cases, maybe that is the term. Donnettelli say *no*. Voices loud. Firm.

"Judge Donnettelli voice stern. He say they get caught. Say they should start fresh in the new year. Then two weeks later he is dead." José finished his water.

"And the next day I opened my salon." I thought back to what happened when and to all the headlines.

"I think so," José said. "*Si*—yes."

"How did that meeting where they argued end?" I felt lightheaded.

"I see door crack open; they shake hands. Like ghost, I flee down hall." José shrugged. "I think, all good."

I confirmed the obvious. "Until he's murdered."

"Until you arrested," José said.

"You left her cryptic messages—why not just tell her?" Sebastian asked.

"They killers. They'll kill me, my family, if they know I tell," José said. "Besides, Miss Judge has very good memory. I think soon she remember the birthday card I make her when she first elected." He turned toward me. "You so smart. You would figure it—find a way to ask me and keep us safe."

José and Wanda had keys. I'd forgotten to count the cleaning crew's key to the salon. Damn my math.

José looked away. "If Judge go to prison, I promise, I would have tell everything." He paused again. "I only want Miss Judge to be careful, to understand bad people want her to get blame."

"I understand." Bullied people make different decisions than they might otherwise make. My gut knew things were not right in that courthouse. "When, I mean how, did you get Judge Donnettelli's gavel?"

"I got the idea when I see Miss Renée packing his things. The night she finish, I open box and take it out. She not notice me watching which box she put it in."

"But having Donnettelli's gavel helped place Nic, Judge Kikkra, there," Hunter said.

"I figured Judge recognize it. I did not think Judge get in more trouble."

I had to ask the question that loomed. "Did you see who shot Judge Donnettelli?"

"Miss Judge," José sighed and hung his head. "I don't know who pulled the trigger. Am I under arrest for not telling what I know?"

"No." I tapped the handcuffs that lay in front of Hunter. "Whose bright idea were the cuffs?"

In unison, Dinkie-Do and Carlye pointed toward Hunter.

"I wanted to guarantee he showed up." Hunter pulled out a roll of bills and pushed them at José, leaving the bundle directly in front of him.

Sebastian cut in. "José, these blokes should've invited you without the cuffs."

"I would've freely come for my Judge." José eyed the wad of bills and pushed them into the center of the table.

"You are free to do what you want." Sebastian put his hand over the money. "It appears you've just retained me to negotiate state and federal immunity."

He pulled a one-hundred-dollar bill from the roll and handed José the rest, waiting until José accepted the money. "You've paid my retainer, and you've earned this money for lost wages this evening. This is not a bribe."

"Si. All is good." José blushed and shoved the money into his shirt pocket.

His barely five-foot-tall-stocky body seemed ten feet tall to me.

Hunter tapped in a text and then looked up at Sebastian, while he told José, "A dark-windowed vehicle is pulling into the garage. When you get in, lie down in the back seat to avoid being seen. You'll be driven to Attorney Pearce's office."

Sebastian gave a single nod.

I stood and hugged José as hard as I could, kissed his cheek, and whispered thanks. "As long as I'm free, you have lifetime haircuts and coffee on the house. Your family, too."

José laughed. "You mean for as long as I have hair, Miss Judge." He bowed his thinning hair in my direction and then followed Hunter toward the garage.

Sebastian left, too.

CHAPTER EIGHTY-ONE

The next morning while Hunter and Sebastian checked out the law clerks' finances, I visited Renée in lockup. She didn't look any better than I had in jailhouse gray stripes.

As soon as they brought her in, she blurted, "I'm sorry," and sat across the table from me.

I ignored the uniformed officers stationed around the room during the visitation hour and focused on her. "How are you?"

"Scared." She looked more frightened than that dark night she'd appeared at my door.

"Renée, I have to ask. Did you kill Donnettelli?"

Renée shook her head. "No."

"Did you kill Peter Dune?"

Renée shook her head. "No."

"Why didn't you tell me everything?" I held back any expression.

"I was too scared. I wanted to trust you." Renée blinked.

"But—?"

"I couldn't. I didn't. Not until later. I'm sorry."

"Who killed Donnettelli and Peter Dune?"

Tears fell. Renée shook her head. She remained silent.

"Do you know who hurt Judge Briggs or Noel?"

Her head rested on her left shoulder and tears flooded. She shook her head. "If they know you're here, I'll be dead."

"Who are 'they'?"

She hung her head in silence.

"Donnettelli's colorful metal tins. Do you know who gave them to him?"

Renée's forehead creased. "He walked in with them. Said they were a thank-you gift."

"No worries, Renée." I shot her my best reassuring face. We engaged in some small talk, and I promised to return. She promised to think about anything that might help. I left. Jailhouse anything made me want an immediate shower.

I arrived home just before noon intending to jump directly into my shower. I also needed alone time to consider what Renée said and what she'd refused to say. I sensed she was being framed, like me. If she didn't commit murder, who did? But before I made it to the third floor, my front doorbell rang. I trotted back down the steps to find a group of uninvited guests at my front door.

Rosa stepped inside as if she were my next roommate. Behind her stood the two disappeared suits from that first week after Donnettelli's murder.

Too tired for rap or a new-roommate fight, I plunked myself on the stairs, four steps up, and stretched my legs down. I had no interest in inviting anyone in beyond the foyer.

Rosa, in bad rap, finger snap, and foot tap began. "Serving a cup in the café to the man with a plan—"

"Get on with it," I said. The men nodded, which I took for appreciation that I'd stopped her. But they seemed to be happy about this meeting.

Rosa, with her I'll-do-as-I-damn-well-please attitude, had no Judge-fear—an attitude I'd respected until this very moment. I started to stand, but she got around me and body-blocked me from going upstairs.

"Sorry. Time to listen." She placed her hands on my shoulders and pushed down.

My anger bubbled.

"Sit."

Our roles had been reversed.

"For your own good, listen," she said. Rosa spoke so determinedly and without rap, I knew it was important.

"Fifteen minutes." I slipped my phone out of my pocket, set the timer, and glared. "Speak."

"When they didn't see you at the salon or at the café—" She paused and gestured toward each of the men. "Edward and Steven approached me."

Edward and Steven reached out and shook my hand.

"They'd read about you on the bench, flown in a few times, sat in on motion days and some notorious trials."

"What?" I wasn't following. "Are you from the SEC?"

The men looked confused.

"No, they are not. You have to listen. You were being considered for a role as a television Judge." Rosa stopped me. "After your arrest, this ain't no jest, they decided *movie.*"

"I'm confused." With the return of the rap, it was no wonder.

Edward interrupted. "Your cases tended to make national headlines. You could be more popular than Judge Judy."

"I want my quiet life back." I frowned because somehow felony charges didn't scare them.

"We know you were charged after you retired from the bench." Steven handed me his writer-producer card. "We researched, took notes, developed a script, a movie, a series—"

"Still charged with murder," I said.

Edward held up what I thought was a contract, but it was so close to my face, I saw double. "We want exclusive rights to your news story, book on your life, and any related merchandise. All rights. Movie comes out first."

I pulled the paper down without reading it and discovered a partial script underneath. "There is still no solid answer, no happy ending—"

Rosa latched onto my boots. "I knew you'd be mad." She sat next to me on the stair.

The three were going to hold a stair-in until I agreed.

Then I saw it. If the killers thought they were about to be publicly exposed, they'd be forced to do something. I could force them out into the open.

"I need my life back. I'll sign with you; I retain copyright. Damn it, I'll star in any clothed role if you agree to help me smoke out the bad actors. You follow my lead—even if you disagree with it."

Edward and Steven eyed each other, whispered, and extended their hands, and we shook.

I promised myself an anti-aging mask and a chin-wag with my Sebastian.

CHAPTER EIGHTY-TWO

The media spray was as effective as the strongest wedding-day hairspray. By early morning, leaks to every national newspaper resulted in headline news. Of course, that included Ingham County, Michigan, Sunday papers.

My phone vibrated, and I answered.

"Lover—"

My throat clearing drowned out Dex's voice and calmed my innards. "Good morning, Dexter. Despite Ingham County ignoring my innocence, Hollywood heard me, noticed me, and believes me."

"Increased notoriety isn't safe—"

"Take our sons back to Colorado. You've given me protection; you need to take them back and keep them safe. I've set a trap. Something I don't need permission to do."

"We need you safe."

Me, too. "I've got this covered."

"Baiting thugs?" Dex conveyed definite undertones of concern and anger.

"There's a key piece to this puzzle still missing—and it's the key that'll get this damn tether off my leg. These thugs don't want publicity. Hollywood researchers are all over this story. Something's got to give."

"It had better not be your life." Dexter's voice deepened. "You were always a step ahead. I just didn't always see it."

My insides felt like warm spring rains, and I softened my voice. "Take our sons home."

"We'll return to celebrate."

"Nope. The second this tether's off, I'm staying in your best Colorado suite."

"Done." Dexter clicked off.

It was barely seven when I cracked my front door open to snatch the morning newspaper. I leaned behind the closed door and unfolded it. "Hollywood to Make Movie of Accused Judge."

CHAPTER EIGHTY-THREE

Sebastian was not pleased with me. He came by the house, scooped me up, and took me off to our secret hideaway—a stately old hotel, which was big on luxury and discretion. It was just the rejuvenating treatment I needed.

The next morning at work, news cameras, *Hollywood Insider*, *Nancy Grace*, and similar vehicles surrounded my building.

I parked behind Hunter's man—or maybe Dexter's planted empty car—entered my building through the front door, acknowledged Trisha, and approached my chair. My hormone radar immediately identified Hunter's backside, and I sauntered toward his electrifying cuteness.

"Here for a crew cut, a shave, or a scolding?"

Hunter clutched my wrist. "Toots. Sebastian can't be happy with this. You compromised your case, your safety. Dexter and your sons are camped out in a hotel near Metro. They refuse to get on a plane until they know you're safe."

Hit-slap. "It's my life, Winky-Dink, I'm in control."

"Protection in the middle of media chaos is problematic." He sounded more serious than I'd ever heard him.

I crossed the room to examine Dinkie-Do and Carlye, oddly contorted and perched on step stools.

"Bull's-eye for the cameras," Dinkie-Do said, proudly staring at his station. It could have been a tribute to Liberace via Christmas lighting decked out in shoes.

Carlye stood and hip-bumped me. "Like I keep telling you. Have some fun with alla this." She thrust up her chest grenades.

I had a disco flashback and decided hot flashes might be more fun.

Dinkie-Do snapped his fingers. "Free publicity. Clients will fly in." He climbed higher to layer LED lights. I suspected Dinkie-Do's glass was always more than half full, brimming over and splashing onto the floor.

Their station decor looked as trendy as a half-shaved female spiked scalp.

All I wanted was a complete freedom rinse. "While you work, maintain your safety sense."

I turned toward my office, and Hunter followed me.

Wasting no time, Hunter closed the door behind us and produced a big envelope. He held it up and slapped it on my desk.

I opened it and thumbed through clipped papers. Circuit, Appellate, and Supreme Court Judges, with a list of bank stocks held by each. "How did you get this?"

Hunter pulled in a chair next to me and sat. "When you were in law school, did you ever learn about asking *the question too many*?"

Ah. "Sometimes a question was better left unasked." Now I knew why Donnettelli had to die.

Hunter exited. I phoned Sebastian and told him what I had, but I had to cut some hair, and then I needed real sleep and a fresh can of hairspray before we handed off the evidence to detectives. I asked Sebastian to make an appointment with detectives for ten o'clock the next morning, told him I'd be home by nine, and I hoped to see him soon thereafter.

Sebastian promised to make my night and be over as soon as possible.

CHAPTER EIGHTY-FOUR

I hadn't felt so optimistic in a long time. Still warmed from my bubble bath when the doorbell rang, I put the last clip in my fresh updo, tied my robe tight and slid downstairs. I couldn't believe I wasn't completely dressed before Sebastian arrived. I wondered why he didn't use his house key. Playing coy wasn't his style.

I checked the monitor and set my phone to 911 for quick dialing. But one glance showed me it was a delivery from Labellefleur, the florist I'd used for years. I opened the door and received a huge vase filled with red roses and baby's breath. *There must be three dozen roses here*. I properly showed my gratitude to the deliverer for making a late-evening delivery and then shut and locked the door.

The tiny white card read: *You were superb today, like every day. Love, Sebastian.* That man. I buried my face in the soft petals and breathed in the lemony rose scent. That was new. *These will go on my bedside table where both of us can enjoy them.* Imagining the evening to come, I giggled all the way up to the third floor. I placed the flowers on the highest chest of drawers I had and then finished getting dressed, put just a little bit of makeup on, and re-secured a charged Taser in my updo. Home alone, I wasn't taking any chances. I hoped I wouldn't be alone for much longer.

The phrase "grinning like a shot fox" kept running through my mind and made me long for Sebastian's arrival. It was barely six. I felt like I'd worked overtime hauling giant shampoo bottles up the beanstalk. And, there was still Renée and Noel to figure out. Damn. It never stopped.

Renée was safe for the moment in lockup. But something about Noel kept nagging at me. I yawned and headed inside my closet to choose my outfit and boots for tomorrow. I set my choices next to my oversized bag on the closet floor and then slogged to my bed for thinking time. I needed to analyze everything in logical order while I waited for Sebastian.

After a few rounds of Connect the Evidence, my tired eyes needed a short break on my cool pillow. Jimmy Jack yawned and stretched bed-center, and I was about to join him.

Sebastian would get here soon, and he'd snuggle with me, and the dots I was failing to connect would magically join up. I'd texted him but didn't get a response.

Tired, I clung to my phone certain he'd text me any minute. I yawned and pictured everything I knew about Noel on a timeline. I'd seen him at breakfast and then at the salon.

I chuckled, and it sounded deep and funny to me, like it was coming from a raw place buried deep inside me. I was so tired. I pictured the day of the skunk perfume. I yawned. Noel had laughed so hard.

My eyes felt like soggy sponges. He'd said we were fun. He'd said Donnettelli—his exact words were—*Donnettelli wouldn't listen.* He'd said that was why he was shot . . . in . . . the . . . ear.

Damn.

It was Noel.

The killer was Noel.

CHAPTER EIGHTY-FIVE

Suddenly awake. Why? Pain under my eye. The room was dark. I must have slept for hours.

Cold metal dug into my cheekbone. I didn't hear anything. I stiffened and blinked. A gun barrel.

I stayed stone still and gripped the phone, still beside me under the sheet. I flicked it to silent, tried to hit resend, then slipped it into my front jean pocket.

Just when I wondered if I'd actually connected to Sebastian, a man ripped the sheet away.

I could see his silhouette, and he breathed like old fireplace bellows with the flu.

"Who else is here?" a gruff voice demanded. He was the one with the gun, and he jammed the end of the barrel harder into my face.

Up from my core, into my arms and face, fury surged. I wanted to rip away the gun and the bastard's hand that held it.

"I asked you a question, Judge, Your Honor, Ma'am." His tone was mocking, but his voice was muffled, as if he were speaking through a too-tight surgeon's mask.

It was someone who resented my position. Someone I'd sentenced? This kind liked to be feared, so I trembled. "Everyone will be home soon." My voice sounded terrified, too. That would please them. "It's me you want. Right?"

In the bit of moonlight that filtered through the sheers, I made out that the one with the gruff voice had his head covered in a nylon stocking. I couldn't identify him or the guy across the room he motioned to. I squinted—another stocking head.

"You're about to violate tether." The stocking heads sinister-laughed, like Cartoon Network dropouts. "You're about to abscond and become as famous as Hoffa."

Thank God for my tether. Someone would see me leave my house without permission. My eyes, now accustomed to the darkness, I searched the room. No electricity. They'd bypassed Hunter's system. "How'd you get around the alarm?"

In the shadows of my room the two stocking heads grunted. Stocking Head One shook his head. "Too easy," he said. "I ducked under the garage door when you drove in, and I stayed behind your other car. When you went inside your house, I got up into the attic. When the garage door went up again, I limboed out. You think you're so smart. A twelve-year-old could have done it."

Pinpoints his maturity level.

Stocking Head Two clicked the inside of his cheek. "We beat your alarm, your cameras, and your high-priced, inept babysitters."

My shoulder jerked as if it weren't attached to my body, and a wave of grief rose from my gut, and up behind my eyes like thick, sickening fog—mind fog to keep me from focusing on impending death. I needed to sit up to get air, but I was afraid to move. I had to buy time. "But how'd you beat my alarm?"

Stocking Head One answered but was late in remembering his deeper voice. "We stuck our own high-tech mini-cam on your keypad and punched the code in, same as you. Thanks for sharing."

The criminal mind always wanted to tell how smart it was.

"And a little help from your friend didn't hurt—"

"Shut up." Stocking head two didn't like that.

I grunted. "Honor among thieves and killers, best joke in prison stripes."

Stocking Head Two cocked his gun just so I could hear it, I hoped. "Dead judges don't talk."

"Except to coroners." I had to keep them talking. Where the hell was Sebastian? Had they done something to him?

"We got time." Stocking Head One's voice sounded deep and wicked. "We knocked out the electrical in your neighborhood." He pushed out an abysmal evil laugh. "That'll slow up your friends."

I slightly turned my head and strained to locate a third accomplice. No third person—what friend were they talking about?

"Disabled your generator, too." Sounded proud of himself.

Renée was safe in lockup. That high-pitched edge to his voice had to be Keldon McKean. Laurel's description, "techno-savvy," also fit. Jurisa's arrest meant things were closing in. They needed me convicted—at least in public opinion—to stop further investigation.

The one with the gun went down on one knee and was struggling to fix something, but he kept the gun pointed in my general direction.

Noel. Noel had access. Damn. Noel was either dead or working with them—who else could plant the camera to learn the code and knew that much about me, about my house? "When did you do all this?"

"Shut up," the second gruff voice ordered. "Get up."

Stocking Head One clunked the cold barrel against the side of my skull. Yellow light flashed deep in my skull, and searing pain stabbed through my eyes and reverberated through the bones around them.

"Move it," the voice commanded and hit me again.

"I. Need. A. Minute. Can't stand."

I got my legs around and sat on the edge of the bed but made my posture slack and tried to sound more exhausted than I was. "No one will believe I left without my boots and my bag." I mirrored gun-guy's breathing.

The stocking heads aimed their faces at each other. "We've got no problem splattering your blood. Get your things. We're watching," Stocking Head One said.

Stocking Head Two stood closet-side.

I stood, and my shirt hung loosely over my pants, covering the pockets. Slowly, seeing in the dark between the floating dots of light created by the clunks to my head, I glided to my closet.

The bully one jabbed the barrel against my back.

I envisioned chips of vertebrae perilously close to my nerves and skated forward. "Hey, it's dark. I need a second to grab my things from my closet. You want this to look like I left on my own, not like I was kidnapped, right?" I got past Stocking Head Two and slid my feet into my boots.

I could barely see my own hands. I relied on my fingers being quicker than stocking-smushed eyes. Jimmy Jack screeched louder, and his door-pawing intensified. Under my arms and down my back, my shirt was drenched. I'd never felt so out of control.

I wondered where Dinkie-Do was and if Sebastian had clicked into the conversation. And, if Hunter's man had been alerted.

I risked another second, set my silenced phone to record, and then returned it to my jeans pocket. I hoped it could be on speaker and record at the same time. Damn me for not understanding technology. Had all Dexter's security failed? Were any of the house speakerphones or backup cameras on? Damn.

"Take any longer, and I'll dress you myself." Stocking Head Two flashed a penlight on me. I firmly stepped forward and swung my bag over my shoulder.

"Ready."

He pulled at my bag and zigzagged his light inside.

I pulled it back. "Like I said, if it's not with me, there's no absconding. Might as well shoot me here."

"Tempted." He yanked at the strap. We were at a standstill.

"Credit cards. A little cash. Lipstick, backcomb, hairspray, blush, eyeshadow—"

"Shut the eff up." With each syllable the bully banged the barrel into my spine. A scream broke loose. Hearing my fear scared me more. I was losing it. To brace myself from collapsing, I grabbed the closet doorframe, and I missed a breath.

"Move."

I gasped, got a few steps forward and stopped to get air. "When you're in prison, I hope your payout was worth it."

"Shut your frickin' mouth. You're not all that smart with a gun cracking your back." He banged the butt of the gun into my shoulder and shoved me forward. The sensation of falling headlong confused me. For a second, I thought, *Okay, I don't want this to be happening.* Like I could turn it off like bad TV. The thought of going crazy scared me more. I had to fight back. "Smart plan—maneuvering cases and investing on sure things. Until you killed Donnettelli."

The pair grunted, and one of the Stocking Heads interjected, "Donnettelli and Dune were dead weight. You are sheer sport."

"Donnettelli was a jerk, but he was your ace." I tried to get them mad so their voices would carry into the phone recorder and into Dinkie-Do's room in case he was home.

Stocking Heads laughed. "He and his prissy girlfriend wanted out—"

"He's married." *Come on, guys, keep talking.*

Stocking Head Two pushed at my back. "That idiot-nympho convinced him to quit—"

Stocking Head One interrupted his partner in abduction. "Shut up. She's wasting our time."

I pulled open the bedroom door. Jimmy Jack felt the bad aura and zipped downstairs. "Promise. Don't hurt anyone. It's me you want." I wanted to ask why Jurisa wanted Donnettelli to quit but held back.

"Then get moving." Another welt to my back.

I latched onto the staircase, descended slowly, gun barrel punched in my back, the other Stocking Head flanking my left shoulder. I wasn't sure whether it was my imagination or wishful thinking, but I thought I saw a shadow along the foyer wall. Jimmy Jack had completely disappeared. Shazam was unusually quiet. I could learn to love that bird if even a wing rattled. I hoped they were hiding and stayed hidden. I called out to Jimmy Jack to stay away, and the men grunted.

At the bottom of the staircase, the gun barrel shoved me in the direction of the front door. I almost tripped but caught myself. Why didn't Hunter's man run in to save me? Where was my curious cat? I had a sick feeling.

Stocking Head Two opened the door, and we headed out. "Shut the door; I don't want my cat to get out."

"He'll need to catch a mouse to eat." They laughed again. It was an evil sound.

"Ranger coming! Balls to the walls."

Keep talking, I thought, but all was suddenly quiet.

"Let's get the hell outta here," Stocking Head One said. "Who is that?" Another welt on my shoulder.

I didn't respond; instead, I stepped back and slammed the door shut. Stocking Head Two squeezed my arm, so hard I was certain it was going to snap. Number One cocked the gun next to my ear. "Blood-and-brain pavers would clash with your neighborhood. Don't step out of line again."

"It's not the first time you've done this." I squinted across the street to the security vehicle.

"He'll be asleep for a long time," Stocking Head One said.

Number Two laughed. "Yeah."

A column of chill crisped deep inside me, and all around it, nausea roiled. Damn. Discreetly reaching for either Taser would be tricky. "My car? I wouldn't abscond without it, would I?"

"That's part of the whole disappearance mystery," Number One said. He pushed me forward.

I stumbled. My back throbbed. The neighborhood was quiet, not a minivan, bicycle, or frog. We neared the black, muscle vehicle parked behind the security car.

"Get in." Stocking Head Two opened the back door and waited.

Legs unstable, I clambered in and got myself onto the seat.

He popped in next to me, shoving me aside. Stocking Head One skipped around to the driver's side and turned the engine on, no lights. As he backed away from the security vehicle, the tires gave an odd screech.

Stocking Head Two left the motor running, jumped out, ran around the car, kicked the tires.

"What the hell—?" He sprinted ahead and checked the security vehicle. "All slashed."

Stocking Head Two opened the door and jerked me out of the vehicle, and I landed hard on the road. I didn't hear a snap, but it felt like my wrist was broken.

"She's got cars."

I slipped a hand inside my bag and pulled out the keys. "Here." I stretched out my arm, and he pulled me to my feet and snatched the keys from me.

Tossed them to his twin. "Rev any engine she's got, that's our ride. Before you leave, hand me that duct tape and a couple of those handkerchiefs. I need to tie her hands." He grunted. "And, I'm gonna stuff her loud mouth."

I grabbed my hair-buried Taser.

Stocking Head One laughed and tossed Stocking Head Two a white cloth. One of Laurel's handkerchiefs.

I forced myself to breathe and waited while Stocking Head One lumbered away and his footsteps grew faint.

Stocking Head Two turned toward me with the handkerchief ready—

I planted my feet, aimed, and fired. Repeatedly.

Stocking Head Two dropped. I opened the other door and fled into the shadows. Hooves clomped toward me, and I spun.

"Honey-girl, climb up on this wild beast before I forget I don't have a license to drive him."

I scrambled toward a horse-scented shadow and Dinkie-Do's whisper. "No driver's license, no violation of the law. Just a little Mr. Ed magic."

Before I could think how impossible it was, I climbed up behind Dinkie-Do, bareback. My bruises blazed, and I pulled a few ligaments, but gut fear made me more ready to ride than an Olympic jumper. I re-secured the Taser into my hair, wrapped my arms around him, and we trotted forward.

Dinkie-Do felt like he'd packed for battle. I heard my garage door winding up. Without electricity, the creep was lifting it by hand. We had mere seconds before he came slamming down my driveway.

"Stealing the neighbor's horse?"

"Borrowing, Honey. No different than lending a hairclip. Mr. Ed can be cleaned and returned." He patted my clasped hands, and I felt the horse's reins. "The whole block is outta lights. I heard those thugs and twirled out the same way they slunk in."

"Kick him into gallop; we're about to be run over." I wanted to clench my Taser, but it wouldn't do much good against a hit-and-run vehicle, so I left it hidden in my updo.

"Miss Judge, I bet he knows your roads. Two more houses, and we're making a sharp turn. Hang on, Honey-girl."

I corked my head back and clung onto Dinkie-Do with both hands. I felt like a soda can ready to explode. Mr. Ed bounced along the pavement masterfully, and my rear pounded painfully on his back.

"Slow up, just a little. Time to bedazzle," I shouted. Sirens in the distance. Too distant. The Audi engine roared crazy loud. Audi lights appeared. Aimed at us. I stuck a hand into my bag. My heart flounced into my throat, but my adrenaline crashed into my chest and kept me moving.

A cascade of gunshots cracked around us. Bullets whirred around us like leaves in a fierce wind, shooting shivers through my body.

"Honey-girl, I'll zig so you zag. We ain't turning into no mounted sieve." Dinkie-Do pulled up on the reins.

"Hold your breath and stay the course." I reached into my bag, clasped the treasure, and pulled it out. With a quick twist I tossed away the cap of the canister. With as much reverse thrust as I could command, I unleashed the canister of Dinkie-Do's explosive blue glitter shadow behind us. With a flash and a bang, the stench of burned Kaopectate permeated the area behind us. I heard the Audi's tires squeal and yelled. "Go!"

"We're going, Honey-girl." Dinkie-Do shifted Mr. Ed into overdrive. Mr. Ed hung a hard left, and before I knew it, the Audi engine revved in the electric-blue distance.

I heard a familiar yowl and patted around. Dinkie-Do had strapped a backpack to his chest, and it held a howling Jimmy Jack. "You saved Jimmy Jack—"

"Honey, no one messes with Pussy JJ. Hang on; we're about to Baja through your fancy neighbors' yards."

A shower of bullets was suddenly spraying way too close behind us.

The noise caused Mr. Ed to whinny and jerk. Dinkie-Do used the reins to control him, and he whinnied with the horse and pulled up on the reins. Mr. Ed smoothly jumped us over a fence. I held my breath, and we landed upright, not a hair out of place. We must have sprouted wings.

CHAPTER EIGHTY-SIX

Falling off a horse was better than falling from a bullet, so I hung on. Mr. Ed jumped and galloped through dark yards toward a still-lighted part of the neighborhood, away from bullets, thugs, and maniac law clerks. A very smart horse.

When the horse finally stopped in a quiet, well-lit corner lot, I wanted to jump down, but my legs were weak, and my gallop-pounded rear objected. Okay, sitting is good.

"Where'd you learn to ride?" My voice still reverberated.

"Lessons as a boy," Dinkie-Do said over his shoulder. "Animals and I have an understanding."

"Way to keep your head, horse-man," I said. "Thank you." In the direction of my house, the night sky was ablaze with police lights. The haze grew, more sirens sounded, and my homing instinct kicked in. "Talk Mr. Ed into a slow trot home?"

With each hoof-fall toward home, I calmed.

When our final trot landed us next us to an ambulance, Dinkie-Do hit pause. EMS was about to transfer a body from the surveillance car onto a stretcher; Hunter's guy—his mouth and nose were covered by an oxygen mask. Not a sheet. Sudden relief.

I didn't recognize him, but Hunter had wanted it that way. I spotted Hunter speaking with an officer standing amid the emergency vehicles that now clogged the road at odd angles.

Behind Sebastian's car in my driveway, a cruiser held nasty-mouthed Stocking Head Two. Keldon McKean's face was tinged with cop-car-blue light. My bet: Wade Mazour had carjacked my Audi.

Before I could dismount, Hunter jetted toward us, and Sebastian shot over from where he stood with Fredericks and Grayson. They followed but didn't look as eager to see me.

"Holy dooley. How'd the pair of you find a brumby?"

I slid down into Sebastian's arms, and he held me close. Then he gripped my shoulders and inspected me at arm's length—hairspray to boot toe.

Hunter circled the horse like he was checking out a new car.

"Dinkie-Do and Jimmy Jack borrowed him."

"Dogs balls." Sebastian paused until Hunter stopped next to us. "It was the law clerks."

"And I know who the shooter is."

Sebastian laid an index finger across his mouth, and I saw Hunter saw it, too. Alrighty, then. Evidently we weren't ready to share with Hollywood. Sebastian stepped aside and let the detectives approach the horse. Grayson grabbed ahold of Mr. Ed's mane.

"McKean's raw from where you tazed him and is whining for his lawyer," Fredericks said. "We have a BOL—for Wade Mazour and your Audi."

"Mind if Dinkie-Do and I put Jimmy Jack in his room before we talk?" I needed to stretch before I replayed my neighborhood steeplechase.

Dinkie-Do dismounted and handed Mr. Ed's rein to Grayson, and, side by side, we eventually got into the house. Dinkie-Do took the lead up the staircase rubbing noses with Jimmy Jack, while I clung to the railing and struggled with each step.

The lights had returned, and I wasn't sure if the generator had been turned on or the electric company had made repairs. I didn't care. I was grateful to be out of the darkness.

When we reached the second floor, Dinkie-Do turned to go to his room, but a shadow from underneath the door to my left caught the corner of my eye and landed in my throat. I tiptoed to Dinkie-Do with a *shhh* finger pressed to my lips.

I again plucked my Taser from my updo.

Dinkie-Do's eyes widened. He lay Jimmy Jack bed-center, closed the door, and followed me to the sewing room.

I pushed the door open slowly. In fire stance, I aimed at the dark figure. "Noel, drop your backpack and put your hands up."

"How—?"

"On the count of two, I'll fire," I said.

Dinkie-Do flicked on the lights. "Mr. Noel, why are you here?"

"I lost something when I stayed here. Don't point that at me." Noel dropped the backpack at his feet.

His face didn't show a single contusion. He'd faked it. I brain cataloged what I'd seen in his backpack when I pulled the papers. Damn. "Dinkie-Do, grab the backpack, and get Sebastian and the detectives. Tell them to stop looking for Noel; he's up here. Now."

I stepped away from the door to let Dinkie-Do out and placed myself in front of it.

"Why the hell would detectives be looking for me?"

"Keldon and Wade are telling tales—fast and furious—like how much you enjoyed shooting Donnettelli in the ear—big on metaphors as you are."

He didn't say anything, but he paled a bit.

"You knew I'd seen the SD cards. You were here to kill me—if the absconding didn't work."

"You've never been shy about sharing what you think," Noel said. "Whether it was pure truth or shit. Shovel away."

I made my voice sincere. "The poker-party alibi was brilliant. I can't figure how you guys pulled it off."

"You can barely figure out how to pull your ridiculous boots off."

The little fucker could insult *me* all day long—but *my boots?*

I'd try again. "I know Keldon had you all well trained, so there was no chance—"

Now Noel *had* to set me straight. "We used the same lemon-scented compound on Donnettelli that we'd put on your roses. You're so arrogant you'd believe some dude sent you three dozen roses when it wasn't even a holiday." His tone suggested I ranked up there with mold on way-too-old limburger.

"It wasn't the first time," I said smugly. "It's the boots that get them."

He ignored me. "One nose-full of the compound, Donnettelli was subdued. Peter, Keldon, and Wade wrestled the whale onto the floor; I warned him he should've listened to me, and then I shot him."

"He didn't listen about—"

"The moron had been skimming money using confidential information to move his profits in the stock market. He got very wealthy and very greedy." An evil hoot filled the room. "He was going to leave the country with Judge Haddes."

"How'd you know it was her he was leaving with?" I wanted to keep him talking.

"She had moon-eyes every time they were together. He called her his courthouse gal, thinking no one could figure that out." A deeper, more evil, guffaw.

"How'd you manage to be at the poker party and shoot Donnettelli in the courthouse at the same time?"

Noel shook his head. He'd obviously lost all respect for me. "I shot him at eight p.m. We had garbage bags full of another new compound with powerful cooling capability. We cooled his body for almost three hours, knowing the ME would, at least initially, place the time of death around four in the morning."

"And you instigated the fight on the front lawn—"

"And called the news teams to document our alibis." Noel radiated self-congratulations and almost purred at the end of every sentenced. He was clearly aching to tell someone how cleverly he'd set all this up.

"Well played." The pieces were falling into place. "That cooling compound, it turns into a gas?"

Noel looked offended. "How'd you know that?"

"The exploding garbage behind Peter's house," I said. "You guys threw the garbage bags full of the coolant into the dumpster, right?"

"Untraceable." The surliness I'd seen that day at the café—it was back—and I suspected this was the real Noel.

This nasty man had also tricked me into blaming Dinkie-Do for leaving makeup on my good towels. Damnnation. I owed him an apology. It was actors' makeup.

"What about Renée—"

Fredericks and a uniformed officer burst in and clobbered me with the door. A minor apology, and then they were all over Noel, read him his rights, and handcuffed him. The officers escorted him out without any extra gentleness.

"We got background checks on all your inmates," Grayson said.

Finally Grayson did something right.

He added, "Noel Lemmon has a lengthy juvenile record, but no adult convictions since he worked for Donnettelli."

I heard another vehicle arrive in front, and I ran to the window and saw a dark sedan pull up. The real Hollywood suits had arrived with notepads and cameras.

Grayson saw it, and I thought his face would explode. "No dice," he yelled and bounded down the stairs and out the door. "No access."

Dinkie-Do and I followed at a much tamer pace. Only my bruises shouted. But we could hear Grayson on the front lawn before we reached the door.

"Remain behind the yellow tape," Grayson bellowed, "or we'll arrest you for interfering with a police investigation."

Finally, Grayson had taken charge. It gave me hope.

The suits stepped toward Mr. Ed and worked their way to the house. They made notes about how the evidence markers were placed and snapped a gazillion pictures. Dinkie-Do posed on the horse and aimed Jimmy Jack's face toward the camera. News crews parked behind the Hollywood crew.

"Behind the yellow tape," Grayson repeated until everyone was several feet back. At times, the flashes seemed to paralyze him as he spoke.

I put my hands over my face. "I'm outta here."

"I'll secure the house," Hunter said.

"Hunter, I'm sorry about your man." Without warning, my tears flowed.

"Bulletproof vest. Looks worse than it is. Goons'll pay."

"If he smells like lemon, check for a new compound Noel made," I said. "Dispersed like dust or mist."

Hunter thanked me and spoke to Dinkie-Do. "Trucks are everywhere fixing the electric. Got Nic's street up fairly quickly. Neighborhood will be up soon. You staying here or—"

Dinkie-Do said, "Pussy JJ and I will stay. I'll return Mr. Ed after a few carrots and apples."

I was afraid Dinkie-Do had decided to keep Mr. Ed, since he'd named him and was rewarding him in treats. I was too stressed to highlight *return* meant to the neighbor, not to my garage.

Hunter pointed to the empty security car. "I'll double-check security."

I tossed Grayson my phone. "Charge it. Listen to this evening's recording." Without waiting, I took shelter in Sebastian's truck.

We pulled out, Sebastian lent me his phone, and I dialed 4-1-1. The polite robot system found me the number of the Marriott near Metro Airport and connected me, and within minutes I was talking with my sons.

Twenty minutes later—after I'd refused to go to the hospital—I swallowed pain medication, stretched out on Sebastian's California king with extra pillows under my head and knees and ice packs under my back.

Sebastian curled around me.

I stroked his hair and cheek, and my hand dropped. "So tired."

CHAPTER EIGHTY-SEVEN

I awoke to the smell of rich coffee, Sebastian's musk, and a newspaper announcing my night's adventure and imminent court hearing. He announced Dinkie-Do was in the kitchen and had brought me a pantsuit, matching bag, shoes, and his best makeup. He reassured me it wasn't the exploding kind, and we all laughed. Sore, I needed Sebastian's assistance to don his bathrobe. When I padded into the kitchen, Dinkie-Do's face brightened.

"Honey, you're a hot topic."

"We're due in court soon as you can get dressed," Sebastian said.

Dressed and in pain, Sebastian promised to drive like he was on nitroglycerin transport. I squeezed his right hand while he drove with his left, thankful his muscles shielded him from feeling the shrieking pain I was sharing.

Minutes later, we arrived at the courthouse, and Sebastian parked in the handicap slot, leaving a note in the window. I hoped that worked, because that was a monster-ticket and expensive towing. He said I was worth it and offered to carry me inside. I declined and instead leaned against him with each step. When the case was called, I stood in solid form on the outside, but a gelatin jiggle flowed throughout my insides. I was comforted with Sebastian nearly touching me as we stood in front of Judge Evans in a courtroom filled with media. The prosecutor rose and asked that the entire case against me be dismissed. After all we'd been through, it didn't seem real.

The Judge ordered immediate removal of my tether, and, as a courtesy, the tether people were in the courtroom to follow that order.

Ever since I'd traded my gavel for clippers, I'd struggled to be free of Donnettelli. Now, I was so overwhelmed, I'd hardly noticed my staff in the filled courtroom. I wondered if they'd tucked Jimmy Jack, Shazam, and Mr. Ed somewhere amid the onlookers. I secretly scoured the room for backpacks.

When we finally escaped the courthouse, a flurry of reporters flanked, filmed, and flashed. Hunter and Sebastian tried to shield me, but I stopped to address the media.

"I've always maintained my innocence. I'm not the story." I decided to make the most of it. "I have one meeting with federal agents and local law enforcement, and then I'm returning normalcy to my life and my business; *Ratification Hair Salon, Spa & Café.*" I strode forward. "I'm in need of a triple espresso." The media chuckled. We promenaded through them blinded by Fourth-of-July-worthy flashing bulbs.

CHAPTER EIGHTY-EIGHT

We zipped across town and straight into an interrogation room, where Grayson and Fredericks sat at the long table. Two strangers stood facing me and Hunter, and Sebastian came around and stood next to me. The strangers trained *just the facts ma'am* eyes on me.

I big-eyed the detectives. "Guests?"

"Feds," Grayson said. "Agents McClure and Diamond." He looked as if he was already dreaming about the promotion he was about to get.

Sebastian spoke quietly. "Reaction to your one-woman media act—Federal blokes have questions."

I wanted a reaction—not necessarily from the Feds.

As if they'd practiced their timing, Hunter and Sebastian looked at me, tilted their heads, crossed their arms, and zapped me their macho-man I-told-you-so looks. *Not my favorite.*

But I *had* asked for it, so I stepped up, introduced myself, and shook hands with the Feds. "I am so glad you're here." A muscle in Sebastian's jaw tensed, but otherwise, he managed to look as if this were his plan, too.

Grayson's phone rang.

Right on time.

Grayson looked pissed. He mumbled something and banged the phone down. "Your Highness, I'm told your sons have arrived, and they're toting information you've ordered them to deliver to my interrogation room. You don't mind if law enforcement sits in on whatever wack-a-doo thing you've planned this time."

I spoke unblinking and without missing a beat, "Your Ineptness." I bowed. Two could play the name-calling game. Sebastian touched my arm, but that didn't stop me. "Let's be clear from the beginning. Agent McClure and Agent Diamond, is it your intention to cover up this mess here and be back in DC in time for last hot-donut call, or do you want to find the truth?"

They assured me they wanted nothing but the truth.

We took a short intermission because just then two of my handsome sons carried in boxes of case files, transcriptions, notes, and a pretty tin box made in Germany. The boys emptied the boxes on the table as previously instructed and left without a word.

Hunter and Sebastian not only relaxed but were grinning.

"What is all this?" Grayson barked. On that side of the table, he had his own personal black cloud.

Fredericks gave the slightest listen-and-learn gesture, and Grayson leaned back, making it obvious he was only tolerating me and "all this."

Good.

McClure and Diamond pulled up chairs and looked entirely interested.

"Detective Grayson," I said respectfully, "this is going to take a while and some careers could be lost here this morning. Maybe you want to have some coffee and water brought in."

Grayson didn't budge.

McClure said, "Donuts would be good." And I swear I saw a glint of smile in his eyes.

Grayson jerked himself out of his chair and left the room, and while he was gone, I filled the Feds in on the background Grayson had already heard multiple times, detailing the Chief Judge bullying some, favoring others, and up to the day he threatened me in the elevator.

When I got to the part about Donnettelli accusing Laurel of insider trading, it was clear I'd pushed the investigators' buttons—they both whipped out notebooks and started scribbling.

Detective Grayson entered balancing a loaded tray, but the Feds were no longer interested in deep-fat-fried carbs. McClure gave me the go-on nod.

"Twelve Michigan Judges were leeching money from big corporations. Big-money court cases that should have been randomly assigned—these Donnettelli manipulated. He did whatever it took to get the decision the big corporation wanted, and he pushed all the asbestos cases onto my docket, so at least one of them would look as if it were my bad decision."

Without a word, Sebastian went to the table, found the chart that showed how cases were transferred over and over again.

He had eight copies, just in case. He passed out a copy to everyone in the room and put the others back on the table. Hunter was already there, locating the next exhibit.

"You say cases are assigned to Judges randomly by computer?" said McClure.

"Correct," I said. "The Chief Judge has authority to transfer a case when there's a real need."

"But this kind of manipulation is outrageous," Diamond said. "Why would they do that?"

"At least two reasons," I said. "First, Judge Donnettelli was getting payoffs from the asbestos corporations or their insurance companies."

"Both," said Sebastian.

"Secondly, they moved the cases so judges who were part of their group would hear the big-money cases and decide the way the ringleader needed them to decide."

"They'd never get away with it," Diamond said. "The scam would become apparent immediately."

"Not exactly immediately. In their 'scam,' we have three levels of judges: Circuit Court, where I worked, Court of Appeals, and Supreme Court. We have wealthy corporate defendants versus traumatized victims. If a side loses at trial, they can appeal the decision."

"It's a long process without enough checks and balances on the Chief Judge and case transfers. Attorneys wouldn't catch on for a long time, if at all," Sebastian chimed in.

"The scammers could control the outcomes in lots of ways, and that made it very hard to track," I said.

"Until they pissed off our girl," Hunter said.

Agent McClure asked if I could prove it, and I nodded toward Hunter.

He handed a packet to each participant. "This shows the decisions of those transferred cases, where they were appealed, and those outcomes," Hunter said. "Note that in every case, no matter what happened in Nic's court, by the time all the appeals were done, defendant *Big Bucks, Inc.* prevailed."

"Thank you, Hunter." I asked the investigators to look at the chart on the last page. "Here you see the date the decision of the final appeal was made public. It matches the date of a deposit in Judge Donnettelli's bank account. No single deposit is less than $400,000." I sipped some water and gave them time to read the chart.

One of them muttered, "Buy-a-verdict."

When they looked up again, I pointed to a stack of similar packets on the table. "We've identified eleven other Judges with big-money cases that were transferred to begin with, always decided in favor of defendant corporation, and always correspond to large deposits in Donnettelli's bank accounts."

Grayson and Fredericks had drifted from red-faced into the pale zone, and Fredericks was mangling a donut and downing coffee faster than any caffeine moment I've ever had. The Federal investigators had lots of questions, including how the participating judges knew their verdicts wouldn't get overturned in appeal.

"Here's where they got creative," I said. "Judge Donnettelli was working with four Judges from the Court of Appeals and seven out of nine from the Michigan Supreme Court. That's how he made sure he'd keep the decision he wanted."

Grayson blurted, "This is so far-fetched—" but McClure sliced off his sentence with a look.

"In the Court of Appeals, two out of three votes are needed, so there's no worry if one judge decides differently. And if one of the judges disagreed, you'll find it was appealed to the Supreme Court."

"The dunny rats formed a court cartel to profit at the expense of litigants," Sebastian said.

"Right," I said. "They rationalized big business would see it as the cost of doing business, and the little guy was too broke or intimidated or uninformed about the legal process to figure it out."

"Enough motive for multiple murders and blackmail," Sebastian said. "A truly under-the-radar scheme."

"We checked into this when you first started whining about it." Grayson sounded disgusted.

McClure turned pointedly to Grayson. "Exactly when did Judge Kikkra notify you of illegal activity in the courthouse?"

Grayson blustered and tried to form a cogent sentence, but Fredericks took over. "We'll leave all of that to Judge Kikkra. This is her showtime to present what she's uncovered."

I wanted to hurl at the Hollywood detectives, but then I felt an unusual calm pour through me when the Agent sat back and refocused on me. The Agent's demeanor told me he'd be pressing the detectives for an answer soon enough.

Sebastian explained what everyone knew: "People aren't allowed to trade stock based on information that's not public."

"If they did, they'd make a killing on the stock market using that information. It's not fair," Agent McClure said. "Insider trading."

Sebastian added, "And so damned illegal, they set Nic up to take the fall if anything was ever discovered."

I nodded.

The corners of Hunter's eyes crinkled. "Sometimes judges don't enter the Orders until weeks after they know how they'll rule. The judges traded based on their decisions still being private and just kept reinvesting, with all the proceeds going into their retirement accounts."

"You have proof," Agent Diamond asked, "that sitting judges profited from stock-market changes directly impacted by their decisions?"

"We do," I whispered.

Sebastian had a tall stack of portfolios sorted by judge, and he passed one to each of the four investigators.

"Open folder one to page one, please," I said. And page by page, we worked through six years of trades and twelve Judges who collectively benefited in excess of sixty-five million tax-free dollars as best as we can figure. Every time they won a decision and invested, their stock went up; they reinvested, so their retirement portfolios are on the fast track to the billion-dollar mark."

It took two hours and twenty-seven minutes to walk through the dirty dealings of all twelve Judges.

"I'm sure the Feds here appreciate you doing their homework for them," Grayson said.

I opened my mouth (to keep cartoon steam from escaping through my ears), but Sebastian dropped his hand on my shoulder.

Grayson yawned loudly.

The Federal investigators were not amused. They wanted to know where and how I got my information, and I showed them the football triangles and listed the avenues of research we'd pursued. They did acknowledge that certain bank deposits and transfers matched with stock trades and cases on Donnettelli's docket. "Matching it up was the hard part," I said. "All the information was there, though some of it had been heavily encoded."

"We leaned on a bloke to track the life of cases through the various courts through all appeals until a decision was reached," Sebastian said. "Trouble is, he turned out to be the mastermind of the scheme and scrambled the information on the spreadsheets he'd provided."

"Noel Lemmon," McClure said.

"Fortunately, my sons were able to decode it, and they spent hours creating accurate reports for each case." I tried not to brag on my boys too much. "You have those corrected reports in the folders you've received."

"You say," Grayson bawled. "All you've got is a paper trail you created yourself. You haven't got one witness—"

I showed him a palm. Grayson stopped speaking mid-sentence, and Hunter and Sebastian stepped back. *I've still got it.* "One moment, please." I plucked out my phone and hit the speed dial.

In twenty seconds, someone knocked on the door, and Hunter opened it.

CHAPTER EIGHTY-NINE

My oldest son, Jake, entered and introduced José Alvarez. José didn't step up and shake hands, but he did nod politely to everyone in the room. I smiled my gratitude to Jake, and he left us.

"José, you know what the agents need to hear. Go ahead," I said.

"Hello. My family business is a cleaning service," José said. "The Ingham County contract to clean the courthouses—this is mine."

I nodded when I heard him pause, he nodded back at me then continued with more confidence.

"You see, I am a little person, and important people like judges and law clerks—they don't notice me. And while I clean, I hear things. I see meetings. Many, many meetings. Judges from different courts meeting long times."

Agent McClure interrupted. "You mean like Supreme Court justices meeting privately with a Circuit Court Judge?"

"*Si.* With the Circuit Court Chief Judge and the Court of Appeals Chief Judge, but Judge Donnettelli die, and then they meet in Chief Judge chambers, but he's not there."

"Tell how you learned about the insider trading," I said gently.

Sebastian interrupted. "Let's take a little a break here. We've been at this for hours, and I'd like a private word with Agent McClure."

I handed José a glass of water and watched Sebastian and Agent McClure leave the room. I slid the plate of food in front of José and made small talk with him while I watched him eat. Within fifteen minutes, just as José finished the last donut, Sebastian and Agent McClure returned to their seats. Sebastian dipped his head half an inch to indicate that José was protected. "Tell us what you did, José. The whole thing," I said.

"I pull documents from garbage, recycle bin; one by one. Judges be sloppy. It add up."

José named the judges, who were at the meetings he'd listened to.

"Did you overhear any reason why someone would want to kill Judge Donnettelli?" Sebastian asked.

"They talk about bringing in different cases," José said. "Judge Donnettelli wanted to stay with only bank and asbestos cases. Judge Donnettelli voice stern. He say they get caught. Say they should stop everything, start fresh in the new year. They all chuckle. Two weeks later he is dead." José gulped his water and laid the empty bottle on his plate.

"Great, you've got a felon for a witness," Grayson said.

"José and his family have immunity and are in protective custody," Agent McClure said. He stood, crossed the small room, signaled someone in the hall, and told José to go with the Agent. As soon as McClure took his seat again, he asked Agent Diamond to present.

"And we have a little bit to comingle into the evidence pot," Agent Diamond said.

He lifted what I guessed was a report. "Nicoletta Kikkra didn't regularly trade in the stock market. Her advisors handled everything for her and kept her informed."

Agent Diamond held up a pen. "Your hundred-thousand-dollar accounts don't match up directly to any insider-trading suspect. Nor did we find them associated with any of your withdrawals."

I assumed that must have included Laurel. Yay! I wanted to do a *yippee* dance and end it by popping dunce caps on the detectives' heads that flashed neon *told you so*.

Fredericks flipped a page in his notebook. "They are near dates of trades—"

Agent Diamond took off his reading glasses and pointed them at Fredericks and Grayson. "Wrong stocks, wrong amounts, wrong dates." He pushed a stack over to the Hollywood team. "Read much?"

"They rely on their vintage fashion sense." A tad of unchecked resentment lingered in my voice.

"Judge Donnettelli was involved with multiple women," Agent Diamond said. "One of them has admitted shooting him."

Agent McClure tapped the stack of bank documents on the corner of the table. "The twelve accounts in your name clearly indicate a contribution scheme designed to make you look guilty in the event their operation was discovered. Without connection, even circumstantially, we can't tie it directly to anyone other than Donnettelli."

"But what about the murders of Donnettelli and Dune and the masked men who shot Judge Briggs and Peter and beat Noel?" I asked.

"I understand Noel beat himself with a cue ball in a tube sock. The rest is under investigation because of the ties to insider trading. We'll be working with local law enforcement and keep you updated." McClure's attention focused between Grayson and Fredericks instead of me. "Just to be clear, we'll be thoroughly investigating every aspect of this ordeal, and we expect your cooperation."

I enjoyed this so much that I had to turn away from the red-faced Hollywood Twins.

"I'd like copies of whatever you can release," McClure said.

Sebastian pointed to two stacks on the floor next to his briefcase.

I took Hunter's car keys from him and scooped up one stack from beside Sebastian, thanked the Agents, and jingled the keys. "Me disappearing." I finally felt in control.

"Hunter, your truck'll be parked outside my home." I strode down the hallway. Just before I got to the door, I saw Jurisa—cuffed and surrounded by officers. Damn, too close, I needed an immediate bubble bath.

Uniformed officers were chain-locked to her. Her husband and a man I assumed was her attorney followed intently behind. When she passed by, her defiant face bolted onto me. I smiled. I snapped a picture with my phone and forwarded it to Sebastian.

Before I exited into the lot, Jurisa hollered back at me, "Bitch, you killed him. I hope you burn in hell."

"No worries, hell isn't big enough for me and Donnettelli. But, I hear he saved a special heated corner for you." I inflected my voice ending in a naughty sensual tone. Sweet honey ran through my veins, watching her seething expression. I was suddenly struck with the realization of why Donnettelli had her court ID. It was time to clear my name.

CHAPTER NINETY

Almost everything had been explained, but I had to know all of it, and I had some explaining to do about the bank accounts. After all, my life had been held hostage, and everyone I loved had been put in danger. My best friend had been shot.

Sebastian stayed in close contact with the Hollywood Twins, and eventually I had answers.

The Feds put Keldon McKean—who I'd Tased—in protective custody. He was talking up a chartreuse streak. Police found my Audi at the airport and Wade Mazour aboard a flight to Montego Bay. I couldn't imagine Wade on a beach in Jamaica trying to blend in.

I provided Jurisa's court ID with an explanation of how I found it and my theory she'd dressed up as me and made her film bank debut to further Donnettelli's scheme and framing of me. Her retirement comment when I visited her in the hospital finally made sense to me. A few more key questions to her by the Feds revealed she had in fact deposited the money but never understood why she was directed to do so. She also claimed no knowledge of the actual source of the money, other than being directed it was to be gifted without question. Jurisa had received a cut of each deposit she made in my name.

Noel turned out to be the brains of the scheme. Once he and Donnettelli tested a few stocks, they were hooked. It was easy to snag underpaid, over-egoed judges, who hadn't gotten raises in over a decade.

The scheme quickly snowballed.

Then when I'd found out about the case swapping, I denounced him for changing my Order, and he was getting too much attention. Donnettelli wanted out.

He had decided to take the $1.5 million he'd hidden in his chair and abscond with Jurisa. I was certain there was a lot more money abroad and tucked away elsewhere but had no proof. Their plan included Jurisa dressing up again and withdrawing most of the money in my name, but she'd been afraid to go near the bank after Donnettelli was killed. No wonder she didn't get upset about giving me such a large sum of money. She planned to retrieve it and, whether she said it or not, figured Donnettelli would frame me with it. She was no dummy, except to think she was above the law and to get involved with a dishonorable bully.

When Noel figured out Donnettelli was bailing, Noel threatened him with exposure. The trip was off, and Jurisa was pissed.

Then Peter, Noel, Keldon, and Wade conspired to kill Donnettelli. Keldon confirmed that it was eight p.m. Thursday when they'd drugged Donnettelli, and Noel shot him in the ear to ensure instant death.

Sometime that evening, Jurisa came in, found him asleep in his chair in the dark. No question she was beyond angry at him and didn't take the time to try to wake him up. Had she done that, she would've discovered he'd already been shot. Nobody jilts Jurisa without her getting the last word. Her last word to him was pulling a trigger.

Of course, José found Donnettelli in the early morning when he came in to clean.

Various plea deals resulted in Noel, Keldon, and Wade being charged with two counts of open murder, attempted murder, and conspiracy to commit murder. The Feds took over their cases and planned on adding SEC violations.

Because of his expected testimony, Keldon got a life sentence with a possibility of parole after thirty-five years.

Wade pulled the trigger and killed Peter. Keldon was the video mastermind and saved and destroyed video files as his skills were called for. That included getting into the underground parking and removing evidence of their truck.

"Anyone look at Noel's SD cards?"

"He was documenting everything for blackmail of his own."

"Keldon edited out the relevant parts."

I needed to know. "Renée—she's—"

"Guilty of bad choices in blokes."

"This was never primarily about asbestos cases." I raised my chin at Sebastian. "It was always about illegal insider trading?"

"Abso-bloody-lutely." Sebastian picked me up and gently kissed my lips and every inch of my face he could reach.

There was an open investigation into the Court of Appeals and Supreme Court justices. But not one had been removed from office, censured, or sanctioned.

Federal appeals were being filed on hundreds of cases that were cited as having been tainted. All of that would take time. Talk would eventually die down. How many careers would be assassinated remained questionable.

While I was soured on the Judiciary and legal bureaucracy I'd worked within, I still believed in our legal system. The legal system I'd been trained to trust wasn't as reliable as everyday-is-wedding-day hair-spray—but that was no real surprise.

CHAPTER NINETY-ONE

Two days after my name was cleared, I returned early to the salon tether-free, plane ticket to Colorado in my hand. I planned to keep my promise and return when my bruised body was flesh-tone and my mind was fully rejuvenated.

Trisha penciled my four-week vacation into the appointment book and typed it in bold red letters on the computer schedule.

I explained my rationale for leaving for so long. "My sons deserve my undivided attention." I handed her an envelope.

She flipped it open. "Highly unusual." She opened it wider. "And extraordinary."

Seeing spilling tears, I ignored her.

Dinkie-Do and Renée, who was cleared of all charges, approached me.

"Honey, we need to chat." Dinkie-Do pointed toward Renée and himself.

"Chat at me." My heart swelled. These people had become my family.

"Honey, now that you, my Judge, are free, and I have my makeup line and a portfolio of red-carpet-worthy Dinkie-Dos to show Marie Clare, I'll be treading back to New York." Dinkie-Do's eyes lowered. "No worries." Blink. "I'm still here for you and Pussy JJ. Just click in my number or sky-write me a message, Honey-girl."

I hugged Dinkie-Do. "You saved me. Your room will be waiting for you."

"Renée's joining me as my assistant." An excited wave ran up Dinkie-Do. His blue hair streak seemed suddenly puffier. "With your permission, I mean."

I hugged Renée. "I'm sorry about Noel," I whispered. I felt stupid for having trusted him.

"Fresh start." Renée looked excited, and a little scared. "New York is going to be a wonderful adventure. Dinkie-Do and I are sharing a place, at least for now."

"You're a gem. Dinkie-Do's beyond wise taking you."

"I'm so sorry I lied to you."

I held up my trusty STOP hand. "My investment in you." I handed them each an envelope. Cashier's checks in the amount of one hundred thousand dollars each.

When they opened the envelopes, they gasped.

"They let me keep the twelve accounts," I said. "State and Feds say as far as anyone can prove, it's my money. And Jurisa verified it was mine from legal sources. No one could prove otherwise. I enjoyed thinking about all the ways me keeping the money would upset her. Law enforcement can't, or maybe doesn't want to claim the funds under forfeiture. So, I decided we all earned it."

I turned away from their open mouths, walked around the salon, and continued to pass out envelopes.

When Carlye opened her envelope she stuffed it into her bra and hugged me so hard I thought I might not have a chance to spend my share. "You the world's best john, I mean legal-like."

"What did you just call my Honey-girl?" Dinkie-Do asked.

I laughed. "I think that means we are all very good friends," I said.

"Best friends," Dinkie-Do and Carlye said in chorus. Finally, agreement.

I kept two hundred thousand dollars tucked away for good measure, and with my secret cool million and change under my bed and the Visa cards, I planned on doing a lot of magnificent things helping people in the world.

It was the first time the salon was silent with all of us there, except for Shazam demanding "pic-a-nic baskets."

I figured sometimes the gray areas of the law needed to work for the little people instead of collecting gray dust in an evidence room. This was my tiny way of tilting the legal spray bottle upright; making light in the dark.

"Sebastian," I grabbed his hand and led him into my office closing the door behind us. "Would you please sit, next to me."

Sebastian tilted his face like he did when he woke up and radiated his maleness at me in the morning, and I wanted to crawl under the sheets with him, but I had a matter of priority. Instead of sitting, he pulled me to my feet and placed his hands around my waist like we were about to waltz. I grabbed his wrist and my right foot lightly stepped on his left boot.

"No wonder Hunter still calls you Toots." Sebastian released a deep laugh.

I'd have to work on operation get-rid-of-old-nicknames another day. "Don't go there," I said and hung a salon bag on his wrist.

"A gift? Being free has brought out the naughty, mischievous girl inside you."

"Open it," I said, and crossed my arms denying him further access to me.

Sebastian lifted the green tissue paper off the contents and locked his focus on the contents. Methodically he pulled out bills, sat them on my desk, and counted the stacks he'd made. He scanned the door, and then me. "Am I going to have to deal with Hollywood and Company again?"

"Really?" I tried to look upset, but I knew he saw through me. "Is that what you think of me?"

"I'd grown rather fond of your bedazzled ankle."

"Two hundred thousand dollars. You represented me, and you didn't ask to be paid." I paused. "Don't tell me if Dex paid you." I felt a sick feeling rise at that thought, and the only word I could think of to describe it was "ick" at the thought of my ex-husband and my lover getting along that well, so I talked through it. "I know you'll use it where you need it—expenses, a vacation, to help those who can't afford to pay you—like the ones Donnettelli harmed by changing Orders, whatever."

Sebastian lowered a brow and lifted the corners of his mouth.

"Please don't refuse because it's from me. That money is business." I unfolded my arms and kissed him deeply. "From now on it is pleasure. Promise."

When Sebastian and I returned to the workroom and rejoined my staff, my phone rang. I clicked in. It was Dex.

"Lover—"

"Time to stop that. Airport awaits."

"I know." Dex laughed.

"Still having me followed?"

"Not exactly." Dexter paused. "I arranged a ride for you to the airport. Walk out the front door. Merry early Christmas from the three of us." He clicked off. I tossed the phone into my shoulder bag. I wondered if he'd misspoken and meant to say: "the four of us."

I did an about-face toward the front door and wondered where Sebastian had disappeared to. My staff followed me. I had a feeling they already knew what I was about to see.

I stepped out onto the sidewalk. My mouth opened without words.

Hunter and Sebastian stood shoulder-to-shoulder in front of a midnight-blue, vintage Lincoln Continental that could have been a sibling to my Elvis. The engine was running, and the car was pointed toward the airport.

I ran toward Sebastian, grabbed the keys, dashed around. "She's stunning." Then it struck me. She was from the three—Dexter, Hunter, and Sebastian. "I'm going to name her Priscilla. My Elvis would have liked that."

"Sure thing, Toots." Hunter winked with a thumb up.

Sebastian laughed. "Abso-bloody-lutely, Babe."

"Thank you," I called back. "Priscilla and I are going for a freedom spin." I slid into the front seat, stepped on the brake, shifted into drive, and latched onto a bedazzled, pink-fur steering wheel cover. I glanced into the rearview mirror and watched them all waving goodbye. I wanted to wrap them all up and take them with me.

That's when it hit me like a boot kick: I'd forgotten to pack the other most important thing in my arsenal of living: Hairspray.

Damn.

I drove around the block and pulled up in front of the salon. "Aussie, grab a can of hairspray. You're with me."

Made in the USA
Middletown, DE
27 December 2021

57142109R00291